Unconditional Commitment

by Kathleen Willett

Chapter 1

Rebecca had a little less than three years left on her sentence. Well, that's what Mitch called it. Rebecca still referred to it as her "term in office as Governor of Colorado." Mitch and Rebecca had met, began a precipitous affair and managed to, through thick and thin, stay together for one year. Mitch's not-so-close friends had given them three months. Some state residents hoped for three weeks. Rebecca's staff had prayed for three minutes. It took them, Mitch and Rebecca, a while to decide which event they would celebrate as their anniversary. Several options were available. The first kiss? The first date? The first press conference? They hadn't as yet had a public statement of vows as such. Rebecca had been in a disastrous heterosexual marriage once. And that seemed like once enough for now. Speaking of now, here they were, together for a year from their first close encounter, beating the odds and toasting their one-year-old, loving, supportive, lesbian relationship.

Not without problems, of course. "Unwelcome mats" were out all over the state of Colorado for this turncoat Republican governor. Some of her supporters had gotten used to, if not become all warm and fuzzy over her lesbian status. A few of her enemies spewed hatred. Still. That had to be a record. Who could possibly be nasty for months on end? Oh yeah, remembered Mitch. This wasn't just any group, it was the fanatical right wing. Oh well, at least they had torched the Governor's mansion *only* once. Mitch always tried to say something nice. This was the only thing that popped into her mind at this moment.

"What are you thinking?" Rebecca asked, looking over the edge of her fluted champagne glass.

"Uh nothing."

"You had the strangest look on your face."

"It's been an interesting year."

"Taking a mental stroll down memory lane?"

"More of a quick jog. Gee, I'm tired. Let's go to bed."

"Anyone would think you're in a hurry to get me between the sheets!"

"Anyone would be correct!"

"Oh, that pesky anyone. Always with the good ideas!" Rebecca smiled.

Mitch went weak in the knees.

Which was pretty much how their entire relationship had started. Rebecca showed up one day at the bar where Mitch was pretending to work, and Mitch went weak in the knees. Very weak. Way weak. Down-the-road-and-never-to-return weak. A weakness that many thought seeped clear into her brain when she began to pursue the prospect of actually getting romantically involved with the honorable governor herself. But with nothing better to do, and only pretending to work since she was incredibly wealthy after winning the state lottery, she began to dabble in politics starting right at the very top. Rebecca didn't resist the dabbling very long, due to the abrupt demise of her aforementioned bad marriage and a gay nature to nurture. If the truth were known, Rebecca was the pursuer, and Mitch only half-heartedly tried to run. In fact, it was Trish who gave Mitch the necessary prodding.

Ah, Trish. Trish was one very busy lady right now. In the summer, she had discovered that not only was she adopted, but that she was Jewish. Her then-current love interest, Judy, had guessed correctly that Trish was Jewish, and, being a bit of an idiot and a prejudiced one at that, held her at arms' length. The adoption part was just another twist of events that made Trish do some detective work of her own. Her grandmother had survived the concentration camps of the holocaust, only to have her daughter be so ashamed of being Jewish that when she gave Trish up for adoption, it was stipulated that she never know about her heritage unless she asked about it. So Trish had gone from being Trish Sullivan, Irish as green beer on St. Patrick Day to Trish Weingarten, granddaughter of German Jews. She had never even eaten a matzo ball, let alone cooked one.

But that was changing. She had a few photographs of her ancestors, and enough cash set aside to do a little freelance research. The first week, she sold her BMW. Mitch didn't quite know why until Trish explained that BMW used Jewish slave labor during the war.

Mitch remembered the discussion like it was yesterday.
"Trish, that was years ago."
"I know."
"It's a whole different country. A whole new ballgame."
"I'm selling the BMW."
"Okay, but I think you should remember one thing."
"Just one?"
"Some of the industries helped to keep the Jewish people alive. It may not have been the best thing to do, but some of the Jewish factory workers fared a little better than the camp labor workers."
"It was still complicity."

3

"Of course it was. That's the key word here, *was*. This happened years ago."

"And it could happen again tomorrow."

Mitch couldn't argue further. Trish had her mind made up about several things. Any more debate about a car would have been fruitless. Besides, Trish had a point. Not only could intolerance flourish again, it did flourish in far too many countries.

When Trish had decided to write a book about gay survivors of the concentration camps, Mitch had encouraged her. She even let her use her new, super-fast, wonder-dunder computer when she came to hang out at Mitch's Ranch. That was a helpful step in the process, but the library had become Trish's second home away from home as well for researching the subject. For a while, Mitch had worried about Trish. She had become so absorbed in the subject that at least twice a week, she would visit her home on the acre only to discover Trish sitting alone in the dark on the porch. Not even Doozie, Mitch's beagle pup, could stir Trish from her meditations. Writing had its bright and dark moments. These were dark times for Trish.

"Hey you," Rebecca prodded Mitch back to the moment.

"Sorry, I was just thinking."

"You were practically in a coma."

"Trish has been on my mind."

"She's been very diligent, hasn't she?"

"What would you do if you found out that you were Jewish?"

"I don't know?"

4

"Me neither. That's why I'm not too terribly worried about Trish, because I figure that what she's going through is perfectly normal behavior."

"What do you think would be abnormal behavior?"

"I guess if I saw any signs of self-abuse, I'd be worried."

"And how would you find out about that?"

"I guess I'd just keep a close eye on her, like any friend would do under the circumstances."

"That's what I love most about you, your deep abiding sense of friendship."

"Yeah, that and my incredible sexual prowess."

"Yeah, right."

Mitch laughed. They had become so compatible in every way, shape and form this past year that they could kid around about any subject with the greatest of ease. Just like those guys on that trapeze.

"I guess I'll just have to show you!"

"I've been waiting."

Mitch kissed Rebecca like she had the thousand other times before. And for the thousand and first time, she was reborn.

Since the ownership of Mitch's bar, The Lucky U, was still in legal limbo, she had a lot of free time on her hands. Rebecca was happy most days about this situation. Running the bar had worn Mitch down and frankly, bothered her arm. One of the first causalities of Mitch and Rebecca's relationship was Mitch's left elbow. It had been shot by a nut case and healed rather awkwardly. Some doctor that looked three years younger than Doogie Howser had fixed it as best he could, but Mitch would never swing from the chandelier again. Which worked out well because the staff at the mansion frankly looked upon the activity with disdain. For a while, the staff looked at just about everything Mitch said or did with disdain, but that was gradually changing. Since she was hanging around a lot more, no pun intended, they were tolerating her presence. Barely.

Doozie was another matter. Everybody adored Doozie. Even before Mitch and Rebecca began talking about starting a family, a brave new subject for Mitch, Rebecca had bought a beagle puppy for her. They shared equally in the upkeep of the dog, and even let her run free at the mansion. Tonight, Doozie was safe and snuggled up in her doggie bed at the foot of Mitch and Rebecca's bed at the mansion.

"That was some kiss," Rebecca remarked dreamily.
"You taught me well."
"I don't think so."
"Well, I do."

It was a good thing that when Rebecca kissed Mitch for the first time in their relationship, Mitch had been lying down at the time. Otherwise, she might have collapsed from the sheer ecstasy of the moment. Of course, she was naked at the time, but that didn't seem to matter. What mattered was that from that moment on, Rebecca was a goner. Which is why they had such a time figuring out what day to celebrate. First, Mitch kissed Rebecca in a hospital bed. Then, Rebecca kissed Mitch in a bed at the mansion. Things really got going a few days later when they were on the parlor sofa after one fateful dinner. Suffice it to say that one thing led to another, and that's the day they chose to celebrate.

"What are you doing tomorrow night?" Mitch asked.
"Spending it with you."
"And the night after that?"
"Spending it with you."
"And the next?"
"Spending it with you."
"Aren't you ever going to get tired of me?"
"Tired, yes, of you, no."

Mitch smiled back. She had the tired part right. If Mitch was anything in bed, she was ponderous. She took her time, did things right the first time, and usually lulled Rebecca into a deep sleep soon after. It was her specialty. Rebecca, for her part, was usually more of a "type a" personality, in every respect. It is said, but probably only with a grain of salt and a little tongue in cheek, that heterosexuals are goal oriented in bed. Get it on, get it done, get it over and watch the Late Show. Apparently, Rebecca had gotten used to this over the years, and considered it the norm. When Mitch had slowed things down – considerably – it had thrown Rebecca for a bit of a loop. Little had she known that Mitch was the biggest tease on the planet. If she had known, they would have probably had sex even sooner!

What went unsaid most days was that Mitch had had a good teacher. Her first love, the larcenous Lisa, was gone from Mitch's life, but not forgotten. Lisa had stolen money from Mitch twice. Not once. Twice. Actually, technically, three times if you count the two million double. Not to imply that she ended up with four million. She just took the same two million twice. And Mitch didn't consider the second, or third time to be theft. In fact, Mitch had encouraged Lisa to take the money and run. What she hadn't counted on was, because of this running, Mitch had ended up in jail long enough to pee her pants and get on the wrong side of the justice system. Soon after, her bar, the Lucky U, was under investigation for a series of trumped-up charges. Which leads us back to where we were, Mitch having a lot of time on her hands to meddle in everyone else's lives.

Right this minute, she was enamored with meddling with Rebecca. Until there was a knock at the door.

"We are not alone in the universe," Mitch announced with sotto tones.
"Who is it?" Rebecca inquired loudly, and with an edge to her voice.
"It's me."
Ah, Mary. "Me" translated into Mary, Rebecca's daughter. Rebecca's grown up gorgeous lesbian daughter. Like mother, like daughter.
Rebecca looked at Mitch, who nodded assent. They were both covered up, just snuggled together.
"Come in."
"Hi, you guys, uh, whoops!"
"It's okay, come on in."
"What are you two doing in bed? Wait, don't answer that. I'll talk to you later."
"It's okay, really. Come on in. We're celebrating our first anniversary."
"Of what?"
"It took us a while to come up with that answer, ourselves," Mitch answered with a grin.

"You two have been together a whole year?"

"Pretty amazing, huh?" Rebecca half asked, half stated.

"I just don't believe how quickly time passes when you're having fun."

Mary's idea of having fun was throwing herself into her work. Her work itself was heartbreaking, she helped coordinate a domestic violence safe house. Her first affair was with a woman named Hilary. Things went south very quickly when Mary found out firsthand the hard way that Hilary had an abusive streak. Hilary was now long gone, studying pre-med at the University of Maryland, a solution cobbled together by Mitch in order to get the woman out of the state. Still, from time to time, Hilary tried to keep in touch with Mary, mostly with letters. Sometimes Mary read them, sometimes she threw them out. Once in a great while, she showed them to her mother, which explained this particular interruption.

"What's up?" Rebecca asked.

"I just got another letter from Hilary. She wants to come for a visit."

"What? Medical school isn't keeping her busy enough?"

"Spring break is coming up soon."

"I heard California is nice this time of year."

"California is nice all year round. She just wants to stop by and see me on her way through."

"An airport visit?"

"I don't think she plans to drive."

Rebecca was agitated. She hid it well from Mary, but Mitch was under the covers and could feel the tension arc its way through Rebecca's body.

"Whatever you think is best, Mary. If you want to see her, and you need our help, just let us know. We'd be more than happy to go with you to the airport, wouldn't we, Mitch."

"Oh, yeah, sure," Mitch agreed absentmindedly. She was thinking about one of her last encounters with Hilary. It involved a shotgun and a bottle of booze. Well, at least they didn't allow you to bring guns on board airplanes. Thank you, Jesus and the FAA.

"Well, I'll let you get back to your anniversary celebration. By the way, what do you give lesbians on their first anniversary?" Mary asked on her way out the door.

"A gift certificate for matching tattoos," Mitch piped up. Even Rebecca had to laugh at this one, which helped ease the tension. Where this tension had vacated, Mitch replaced with another, more exciting tension. A year's worth of practice was coming in very handy. Soon, Rebecca forgot about everything but Mitch's gentle hands on her willing body. Who said the magic was gone after a year? In this area, Mitch was a master at legerdemain, and Rebecca was her able assistant. All they needed now was a cape, a hat and a rabbit. Abracadabra!

Mary's announcement about Hilary's visit was just one surprise that was in store this evening for Mitch. It must have been the night for announcements.

"I want to talk to you about something," Rebecca began their post-sex discussion.

"Hmmmm," replied Mitch, almost asleep and not showing any signs of waking up.

"Are you awake?"

"Hmmm, yeah," Mitch opened her eyes. Usually when Rebecca wanted to talk about "something", she had sex on her mind. Always the curious one, Rebecca had developed a wonderful sense of openness when talking about sex. Mitch wondered what was on tonight's agenda.

"And I want you to know that this is just preliminary," Rebecca continued on, in her best hedging manner.

"Okay, preliminary. Got it."

"And you can really, truly tell me exactly what you think."

"Don't I always?" Mitch countered, becoming more and more interested by the moment.

"Right. Well, I'm thinking about running for office."

Mitch looked over. Maybe she had transported to an alternate universe or something. Maybe this was a different Rebecca, just like in all those science fiction shows. Or maybe Mitch and Rebecca had traded bodies or something. Maybe Mitch was Rebecca and Rebecca was Mitch.

"I'm not sure I understand. Didn't you already do that?"

"Oh, sure, I know. But I mean *really* run for office. Like, 'Senate run for office.'"

"Oh, I see," Mitch said with a modicum of relief. At least she was still in her own little universe. "You mean like United States Senate?"

"Right."

"Wow. That's a big step. Good thing you gave yourself three years to think it over."

Rebecca looked over at Mitch. Mitch looked back.

"What?" Mitch asked. Densely.

It was a fact of life that Mitch didn't pay much attention to politics. When Mitch had first met Rebecca's daughter Mary, Mary had said something about how politics gets in your blood. Once it starts, it can never be controlled. So, Mitch had assiduously kept out of the political arena for this purpose. One politically-addicted person per family, please. Sure, she listened to Rebecca's stories about who said what and who did what and who voted for what, but that was about it. She listened. In her heart, Mitch felt that Rebecca would never again be elected to any office, and so

11

she hadn't been exactly taking notes. Rebecca's announcement changed all that in a heartbeat, but what had she said about preliminary?

"The election for Senate is this coming year."

"It is?"

"Right. If I don't run this year, then when my term of governor is up in three years, there won't be a Senate election that year. The timing is all screwed up."

"Aren't you going to run for governor again?"

"That's the decision I'm trying to make."

"I see."

"What do you think?"

"I think that if you're ever going to run for anything again, the first thing you need to do is change your political affiliation. You're never going to get another Republican nomination for anything. Ever."

"So you think I should become a Democrat."

"It would be a good first step."

"A part of me feels like I would be deserting my supporters."

"You mean that group who torched the mansion? If becoming a Democrat helps at all in the process of distancing us from those people, I'll arrange the press conference myself!"

"So. You would support this decision?"

Mitch shifted around to face Rebecca.

"Haven't you always felt supported?"

"Well, yes."

"That's never going to change. Ever."

"Strong words from the significant other of a potential Senate candidate."

"How hard is it going to be to get the Democratic nomination? I mean, haven't they already decided on who's running?"

"I'll start on that first thing in the morning."

"Not first thing!" Mitch corrected her.

"Not first thing?" Rebecca teased back, knowing full well what Mitch was talking about.

"Maybe not even second or third thing!"

"Three, huh?"

"Just say 'hocus pocus' and leave the rest to me!"

"I bet you say that to all the governors."

"Just the ones I sleep with!"

Two days later, Rebecca held a news conference to announce her change of party affiliation. She hadn't planned to mention the run for the senate but you just can't slide these kind of pesky omissions past some of the sharpest reporters in town.

"Does that mean, Governor Fairbanks, that you have your eye on the Democratic Senate seat?"

It had been common knowledge that the man now in that seat, the honorable Dennis Fitzpatrick, had all but announced his intention to retire from the Senate after twenty-four years. For weeks, speculation had run high on who would run for the seat.

"My change in party affiliation has everything to do with my reassessment of my political beliefs."

"What does that mean?"

"It means that I've discovered that the Democratic Party is more open to ideas. In the political arena, it's always good to keep an open mind to new ideas, new ways of thinking, new approaches."

13

Mitch, sitting in the back and beaming as usual, was asked in whispered tones by the reporter next to her, "Did you put her up to this?"

"As if," Mitch replied.

Everyone who heard the exchange chuckled.

The next morning, the man in charge of the Democratic Party in Colorado called on the governor. Things were moving quickly. Becoming a Democrat had been easy. One down, about a thousand other things to go. She didn't want to change her sex, that's for sure. Far too few women had ever been elected to the United States Senate. Far fewer gay people. It was much easier to find gay and lesbian representatives in the United States House of Representatives. "Didn't Rebecca want to start there and work her way up?" was the logical first question.

"No."

"I see," Jake McManus replied.

God, he was handsome, Mitch silently noted from the sidelines. Rebecca had begged pleaded and cajoled Mitch to be present at the meeting. So far, the conversation was barely keeping her awake. The view was another story.

"How can we know for certain that you won't change your party affiliation back after you're elected?"

Fair question, Mitch nodded. It does happen. Once in a while.

"I'll see to it that she doesn't," Mitch volunteered.

They had been introduced hurriedly when the meeting had begun, and now, only now, did Mr. McManus look at Mitch. If it was meant to be a withering stare, it had no effect on her.

"I don't think you understand the serious nature of the situation you are in," he turned his attention back to

Rebecca. "There are people who have had their eye on this candidacy for a long time. People who have paid their dues to the party for years. People who have demonstrated loyalty above all."

"And for the most part, people who have little, if any, true electability," Rebecca summarized his sentence. Not the way he would have, but he didn't argue.

"I'll discuss your request with the committee, but it would take a miracle."

He rose and left without further comment.

"I don't think I like him," Mitch said once he was out of earshot.

"What? You! Not like a fellow Democrat?"

"He just seemed a little rude."

"He told us the unvarnished truth. I appreciate his candor." Mitch had appreciated more than that, but only in an aesthetic look-but-don't-touch kind of way. Maybe he had had the same or more effect on Rebecca? Nah!

"What are you thinking about? You have that look on your face again."

Mitch wondered what this look looked like. One day, she swore she was going to study her face in a mirror. Should she articulate further her views on the incredible hunk of man that had just made quite the impression on Rebecca?

"I was just thinking that, although it's great that you want to try and run for Senate, it probably puts our plans for having a family on hold. Probably?"

Rebecca leaned back in her chair. Damn. She really hadn't thought much more about this after they had had a discussion way back in the summer. Now, it was the waning weeks of winter. They were still well within the time frame that they had discussed in June. Having a family for them had been narrowed down to adoption, since

15

neither one could sustain a pregnancy. Rebecca was a little old for that sort of thing and Mitch was physically unsuited. "I don't see why?" Rebecca said boldly. "I'm thinking about running for Senate, not relocating to Mars."
"You're sure about this?"
"You hadn't mentioned it in quite a while. I didn't know how you still felt."
"I think I should think about it for a while longer."
"Okay. Whatever you decide. Just don't worry about me. I'll support your decision."
Mitch hated conversations that ended this way. It was so ambivalent. Actually, Mitch knew she was hiding behind this excuse, and self-scrutiny was always difficult. Mitch had wanted a child about the same time that her first lover, Lisa, had formed a close bond with another woman and her child. It was a little like wanting to buy a dog after watching old Lassie reruns or wanting a bunny at Easter. It sounded like such a good idea at the time. Kids and dogs and bunnies and houses with white picket fences. Toss in a run for Senate and see what happens. And that was just it. Rebecca would take anything in stride. Anything. It was one of her best qualities.

It didn't take the committee long to decide that although it wouldn't actively fight Rebecca's bid for the nomination, they weren't going to go overboard to entice her to do as much. The road was long and guaranteed bumpy. Little did they know that this was just the kind of challenge Rebecca enjoyed. And if she lost, she still had the governorship to come back to.

16

Chapter 2

Trish, on the other hand, was finding her path nearly
impossible. Researching the Holocaust would never be
compared to anything enjoyable. Not even in the same
realm. How many accounts of torture, beatings and
starvation could one person read before becoming
emotionally drained, depressed at the evil in the world, and
unsure as to the hope of changing anything in the world so
that this tragedy would never be repeated? Sure, Trish had
heard about the Holocaust in school. And from her
adoptive parents. And from movies and newspaper articles
and such. But when she listened those times, it was as an
uninvolved bystander. A mere witness to history and
nothing more. Now, she heard things in a different way.
She didn't understand how something could be so much
more painful now that she felt personally involved. But it
was.

If asked one year ago, Trish, like so many other Americans,
wouldn't have been able to name more than one or two of
the concentration camps. Auschwitz and Dachau might
jump to memory, and perhaps even Treblinka and Bergen-
Belsen. Maybe Americans only talked about the camps that
they could pronounce easily? What other reason would
there be for omitting places like Majdanek or
Sachsenhausen? Besides, we didn't need a good reason to
avoid talking about the Holocaust, Trish discovered as her
research progressed. The survivors knew this truth already.
Not very many people wanted to talk about the Holocaust
in 1945. Even the survivors. Years of time didn't change
that trend. Only when the survivors began to grow old did
many of them realize that their stories would be lost forever

if they didn't commit something to the record. They themselves noted that if they died, the Holocaust would die, and then the revisionists would have their way and the camps would no longer be believed.

So, many survivors who had already experienced enough pain for countless lifetimes began to share their experiences with churches and schools and community groups. Many had outlived their tormentors. That irony that did not bother them at all. What bothered them was their survivor guilt where other prisoner victims were concerned.

Undaunted, Trish continued to delve into the records. What she was looking for was perhaps gone forever. In all the writing of survivors and historians, little was written about the oppression of gay people by the Third Reich. If the word homosexual was used, it was usually in reference to the homosexual acts that the sadistic capos committed against the young boys in the camps. These same capos committed all sorts of acts against anyone who suffered the misfortune of being in the wrong place at the wrong time. It would indeed be an uphill battle for Trish to refute the claims by the right wing that the Nazis were all a bunch of homosexuals just waiting to torture the Jews, as she had read in various right-wing sponsored publications. But try she would.

It was this that she was contemplating, and jumped about a mile when Mitch tapped her on the shoulder.
"Oh my God, don't sneak up on me like that!"
"Sorry," Mitch said, "I knocked twice."
"I didn't hear anything."
"I noticed."

Mitch had brought out a couple of beers to the enclosed porch area where Trish had camped out. This addition had been hastily built after Lisa had left town in order to make things a little more roomy, for company and such. Between Mitch's computer and her art work, the spare bedroom was full. The porch was chilly, but bright most days.

"You seem to be kind of jumpy lately," Mitch remarked.

"You don't need to worry about me."

"So, who said I was worried."

"Just your face."

Mitch could never keep her emotions a secret. She wore her emotions on her face and her heart on her sleeve. Politics would never be her forte.

"Okay, I admit, I'm watching you carefully. You've had quite the difficult month or two."

"Have you ever read much about the Holocaust?"

Mitch mulled the question over in her mind. It wasn't an easy subject.

"What little I've read, I couldn't stomach."

"Because of the horror of it all?"

"Right."

"So, you never doubted what you read?"

"No."

"Why?"

"I don't know. I just feel that there's enough evidence to support the claims that the Holocaust actually existed."

"But you've never talked to a survivor."

"I never had to."

"But I do."

"To convince yourself that it actually happened?" Mitch was getting more confused.

"No. I just need to hear it with my own ears."

"If that's what you need to do, then do it."

19

They drank in silence for a while. Winter began to chill the room, and Mitch offered to go in and light the fire.

"No, don't!" Trish stopped her cold.

"Why not?"

"Just, don't. Okay?"

"Sure."

"Aren't you expected at the mansion for dinner?"

"Yeah, but before you kick me out of my own house, are you going to be okay? Really?"

"Really. Really, really."

Mitch drank up and was on the road home before rush hour. She forced herself to keep her mind on the road, which was easier than fretting about Trish. By the time she got home, dinner was on the table. That's what happened when you were two minutes late.

"Just in time," Rebecca greeted Mitch. She was glowing.

"You look beautiful tonight...and every night."

"With a line like that, you could run for office."

"One in the family is enough, don't you think?"

"Probably more than enough."

Through dinner, they chatted about all those pesky political issues that Rebecca enjoyed so much. Some of the reports were fun. Like, for instance, the homeless dinner that they had put on over the holidays. Mitch savored the absolute panic on the faces of the staff when they were informed about this situation. Since Mitch had lost ownership of the Lucky U, where she had promised early on to serve a Thanksgiving dinner for the homeless, Mitch and Rebecca had decided to open up the mansion to the event. It could have been a logistical nightmare. Dozens of people were expected to show up, the staff whined, and there just wasn't room to handle all of them.

"Well, we're going to make room," Rebecca had put her foot down.

And so they had. Mitch went out and bought extra tables and chairs just for the occasion. Those millionaires can do that, you know. The next big fight had been over the serving arrangement. The staff had assumed that there would be a food line. Mitch absolutely went ballistic over this suggestion.

"There will be no waiting in line for food!" she had made it clear. "Even if I have to serve it myself!"

From there on, compromises were forged. People would be seated and served, but there had to be more help hired for the day. No problem. Millionaires can do *that*, too! And she had.

Those who couldn't get to the mansion easily were transported by cab. This was a gift given by the cab companies of the city, much like their free service on New Year's Eve. Reminiscent of the wake held for Marge weeks prior, Mitch worked side by side with the staff: preparing food, setting tables, arranging centerpieces and filling water glasses. It all came back to her pretty quickly. At noon, the doors were opened to the first arrivals. They were given a tour of the mansion, a place to sit and a piping hot turkey dinner served in front of them by wait staff. Mitch and Rebecca sat with as many people as they could through the course of the day, and were completely exhausted by nightfall. They had gone to bed right after the last guest had left, and celebrated by falling asleep. Instantly. Christmas was a grand repeat. Only this time, they not only had a dinner, but a gift for everyone. Particularly the children. Much of the gift collection had been coordinated by the Advocates for the Homeless in Colorado, but little did they know what Mitch could do with an afternoon in a toy store as well.

"I'm only buying a few spare things, just in case we need them."

"Yeah, right," Rebecca nodded as Mitch fingered the soft clay that came in sets of five colors and smells.

"Does this smell like raspberry to you?"

"Smells more like strawberry. Are you sure you have the right one?"

"No, but then again, I'm not three years old."

"Prove it!" Rebecca teased quickly.

The young college student at the checkout lane didn't even bat an eyelash when Mitch and Rebecca pulled up to the front of the line with four shopping carts full of various toys. It was beginning to look a lot like Christmas, and about one month early to boot.

When their guests had gone home, or homeless as the case was, it had left both Mitch and Rebecca with mixed emotions. Trish had remarked to them earlier that being homeless in America was a little bit like being Jewish during Hitler's rise to power. No one could or would believe that terrible things were going to happen to them. Until they did. Which was worse? Starving to death slowly in terrible living conditions in Poland, or starving to death slowly in terrible living conditions in Colorado? In fact, Trish had thought through a lot of comparisons between many modern day issues and the plight of the Jews in Germany and points surrounding in 1939. So much so that she had more or less become consumed by the passion to know more, about all things Jewish.

"Have you talked to Trish lately?" Rebecca asked over dessert.

Dessert was one of the wonderful things in Mitch and Rebecca's life. So many truly important things were discussed over this treat. And sometimes, dessert was used in other ways, for other purposes. Rebecca's way with a chocolate cake was one of their first and most precious encounters. And sweetest.

"She said she was tracking down a Holocaust survivor for an interview."

"She said it in those words?"

"No, I don't think so. Why?"

"Well, I just wouldn't put the words 'tracking down' and 'Holocaust survivor' in the same sentence."

"Why?"

"Because so many Jewish people were literally tracked down, with dogs and such."

"Am I that insensitive when it comes to the Holocaust?"

"I wouldn't put it that way. I'd just watch what I said around Trish for a while. That's all."

"I never had to before."

"And that's what you're angry about," Rebecca surmised.

"I'm not angry."

"Sure you are."

"I'm not angry, I'm just concerned. I've been watching her sink deeper and deeper into this melancholy and I can't snap her out of it."

"But part of you is ticked off because she isn't the friend you once had. You feel deserted by her."

"Are you running for Senate or Mother Superior?"

"I'm just keeping an eye on you just like you're keeping an eye on Trish."

"And I appreciate it."

23

"Just do what you always do," Rebecca advised.

"Buy my way out of it?"

"No, silly. Just be the best friend you can be and try to understand what she's going through."

"I hope I can get through to her."

"Hey, you got through to me, didn't you?"

"And look how that turned out!"

Trish stood on the porch of an older brick home in Northeast Denver. Even in winter she could tell that the lawn and garden were immaculate. There wasn't a crack in the sidewalk, porch or front steps. Obviously, someone took great pains to keep the cement in top condition. That was definitely a sign of a conscientious home owner. The front door was oak, the trellises in huge flower pots on either side would soon be enticing miniature roses to climb up from the dirt and take their rightful place in the world. Trish, taking all this in, knew in her heart she was stalling. It had taken her two weeks to summon the courage to call these people, and now, she was here. Three times she raised her hand to ring the doorbell. Three times her hand had fallen back down to her side. As she contemplated a fourth attempt, the door silently swung open.

"Is that doorbell broken again? Max! Max Goldstein! Come out here now. Your doorbell is broken again!"

"So, how come when it's broken, it suddenly becomes my doorbell!" Max bellowed from the not-so-deep recesses of the house.

In the meantime, the woman of the house beckoned Trish to enter.

"Come in, come in!"

"How did you know I was here if I didn't ring the bell?"

24

"See," Max pleaded his case, still arguing his case from the other room, "It's not broken. I suppose it's your doorbell now!"

"Max, get on your feet and come out here. We have a guest!"

Trish stepped further into the room. It was an old fashioned parlor, complete with two upright chairs that looked serviceable but not exactly comfortable. If this was where the interview was to take place, it would be a long afternoon. By now, Max had appeared. Trish was taken aback at his upright, sturdy appearance. For a man going on seventy-two, he looked like the picture of health. Vitamin companies would have paid to have him endorse their products. He stretched out his hand and shook Trish's hand with a firm, dry grasp.

"So, you're the girl who's here to talk to us."

"I'm Trish Weingarten."

"I thought you said Sullivan over the phone?" the woman asked.

"It's a long story."

"Of course it is, my dear. Come into the family room. We'll have tea, or unless you prefer, coffee?"

"Maybe she wants something stronger, Rose. Like a good brandy? Or sherry?"

"I'll have what you're having."

"He's having carrot juice, on orders from his doctor."

"Between my doctor and his staff, they're trying to finish what the Nazis started! They'd starve a man to death and ask for payment to do so!"

Rose more or less herded them both into the family room. Now, here was a place with comfy chairs. Trish could tell at once where the "daddy" and "mommy" chairs were. One overstuffed recliner had a glass of thick orange liquid in it. The bent wood rocker had a teacup on the table right beside it. Trish knew not to sit in either of these chairs and was eying her remaining choices when Rose steered her to the love seat. It was roomy, and faced both of them. In the meantime, Max had found a bottle of wine that he must have purchased for this special occasion. He poured three glasses. Two, however, were woefully short on contents. A polite drink. Trish's glass was the correct one-half full. This was done so that the person drinking the wine could get the full aroma of the wine. You could always tell a greenhorn wine drinker. They filled the glass practically to the brim and held the glass by the bowl rather than by the stem.

"I appreciate your taking the time to see me," Trish said after taking a modest sip of this outstanding wine and putting the glass down on the nearest table.
"So, is it Weingarten or Sullivan?" Max asked.
Trish liked his directness.
"It's both, actually."
"Is that one of those married names?"
"Like a hyphenated name?" Trish clarified.
"Like if Rose had kept her maiden name, she would be Rose Mayer-Goldstein."
"It isn't really a married name, because I'm not married."
"Is that so?" Rose said.
Maybe it was just Trish's imagination, but she thought she detected a match-maker tone in the interrogatory. She expected the next sentence to be about a fine young man that Rose knew. Maybe a son?
"The name Sullivan is my adopted name. Weingarten is my real name. I was adopted by Irish descendants."
"But you're Jewish?"

"That's correct. I've only recently discovered it."

"You didn't know you were Jewish?" Max said with a little more incredulity than seemed proper for Rose.

"Max!"

"Well, all she had to do was look in a mirror!" he explained the truth according to Goldstein.

To Rose's relief, Trish laughed.

"You're absolutely right, Max. I should have known just by looking at my nose."

"It isn't just your nose that looks Jewish! Your whole face looks Jewish!"

"He means you look beautiful."

"I mean she looks Jewish! She sure as hell doesn't look Irish!"

Trish chuckled again. This guy was precious.

"I was always told I was Black Irish."

"You gotta watch those Moors every minute, I always said!" Max wagged a finger.

At least he knew his history. When the Moors set forth to conquer the world, and Ireland was in the way, let's just say that many Irish descendants were no longer "pure" Irish, but a combination of Irish and Moor blood lines. Many modern day Irish people have dark hair and brown eyes, much in contrast to their more fair skinned, red-haired counterparts.

"Well, you're beautiful!" Max said to Trish. "As beautiful a Jewish woman as I've ever seen, except of course for my own flower, the lovely Rose!"

"And your daughter!"

"And my daughter, of course!"

This was going to be some interesting interview. She took another drink of wine and then pulled out a spiral-bound notebook and three black pens.

27

"So, I understand that you do public speaking about your Holocaust experiences?"

"Yes, I do," Max nodded.

"And could you tell me a little about what you say to the audience?"

"It's a long speech. I'd prefer that you just ask me questions and we can build a story from there."

"Okay, well, in which concentration camp were you placed?"

"Before I ever went to a concentration camp, I was in school. Except, of course, it was in secret."

"Why?" Trish was catching on to his style in a hurry. He would tell the story his way and about the only questions she would need to ask were the usual 'reporter type' questions: who, what, when, where and why.

"Why was I in school?" he looked stunned at the question.

"No, I'm sorry. Why was it a secret?"

"You don't know anything about this, do you?"

"I've read books."

"Books smooks!"

"Max! You be nice to the lady!"

"This is nice! I'm being nice!"

"You're being annoying!"

"Okay, okay. The school was a secret because Jews weren't allowed to learn."

"About their own faith?"

"That's right, but other things as well. You don't try to teach a pig to read, do you?"

"Excuse me?"

"The Nazis considered us to be pigs! Why would a pig want to read?"

"I see."

"My mother and father didn't believe that the Nazis would be so powerful. They stayed. We stayed."

"How many were in your family?"

"Not enough," he replied with a tremor in his voice. The strong man who had bellowed about door bells a moment ago had vanished. This man who replaced him was sad and shaken. Rose picked up her yarn and started to work. Almost furiously. It must have been her protective device against the story of pain that she had heard over and over.

"I was one of the lucky ones," Max nodded, as his eyes drifted away from direct contact and his voice held a certain story-telling tone, almost as if he was now just talking to himself. "Me, and a few others were saved. Lucky us. Lucky, lucky us."

And then, he began to sob.

Trish gave him a moment to regroup. Then another.

"You might as well keep asking questions, Ms. Weingarten. The crying rarely stops all the way once it starts," Rose assured her.

"After seventy-two years, you think it would stop," Max added, through his tears. His voice carried a shameful retribution of himself.

"It's okay. You can cry as much as you need to," Trish reassured him.

"I never cry in front of audiences anymore. Why is that?"

Trish shook her head. "I don't know."

"You should see these teenagers who come up to me before the speech and think my tattoo is...what's it they say, Rose? Wow cool?"

"Probably 'way cool,'" Trish guessed.

"That's it! Way cool! And then they hear my story and then they get it, except for the Nazis in the audience."

"The Nazis in the audience?"

"Sure, you bet. Lotsa those young kids are already Nazis. Shaved heads and skull T-shirts. What their parents are thinking, I have no idea!"

"If at all," added Rose.

Trish nodded. She saw the same kind of young people on the streets in downtown Denver. Complete with swastikas, billy clubs and chains. What a world.

"Anyway, the mud was red."

"What mud?"

"The mud in the camp, but, I'm getting ahead of the story," Max looked a little embarrassed at losing his place.

"He always gets ahead. It's his *thing*," Rose stated, proud to know one hip saying.

"I studied and then pretty soon, they started rounding us up like cattle."

"Your family?"

"My family, your family, anyone who was anything but pure Aryan. Those crazy Nazis thought that being pure-blooded would be their salvation. At least that's what they told everybody. In truth, they were jealous of the success the Jews were having. They lied about us, told people we *stole* from them. So, they turn around and steal from us. Every stick of furniture my parents had was taken by Nazis."

"How did they know who to round up?"

"Well, I've skipped several steps, I guess. Didn't you know that Jews had to wear special things?"

"Like a star on their clothes," Trish noted.

"Right. And there were all sorts of anti-Jew laws. We couldn't work at certain jobs anymore, we had to walk in the street instead of on the sidewalk, and there were curfews."

"So, the Nazis knew who was Jewish?"

"And if they didn't, there was plenty of people to point us out!" Rose said with such a sudden vehemence that Trish turned to face her.

"Everywhere there was a Judas!"

Trish waited for more. It didn't come. Instead, Rose went to check on lunch. When Trish had called to set up an appointment, Rose had insisted that she come for a meal. Good thing they hadn't known she was single. There would have probably been an eligible bachelor in attendance as well.

"My Rose is the best cook this side of Warsaw!"

"She seems like a sweet lady."

"She's the best, to put up with me."

"Do you think you'll ever get over the Holocaust?"

"I hope not."

"Why?"

"Don't you know? If we forget, then it could happen again!"

Rose called them to the table. It was a meal fit for a king, a queen, and single Jewish lady.

"Do you know how many calories we got in the camps?" Max quizzed.

"One thousand?" Trish answered, figuring that the guess was about minimal subsistence.

"Try about two hundred."

"No one can live on two hundred calories!"

"Well, I did."

"For how long?"

"Too long."

Trish nodded her head. Maybe the real answer would come later.

"I was lucky because I had some fat stored up when I went in."

"To the camp?"

"No, to the war. Very few people had any fat stored up after living in the ghettos, you know, Lodz and Kovno. The invasion of Poland on September 19, 1939, marked the beginning of the war for us, but the camps came later. I know you've studied a little about history, haven't you, Ms. Weingarten?"

"I actually know a little more about the Pacific Theater."

"Funny name for such a tragic event," Rose gave her opinion.

"I agree," Trish nodded again.

"Why was that?" Max asked.

"My interest in the war with Japan? Because that's where my family fought. I heard all about the Bataan death march at family reunions."

"That was a terrible thing!" Rose stated firmly.

"It was just a drop in the bucket to the death marches that went on in Germany and Poland!" Max remarked with fervor.

"But, Max, if it was her family's bucket, then it was an important drop!" Rose scolded. Softly.

Max shrugged his shoulders. "I guess you're right. We fall into this trap of wanting our experiences to be the worst."

"I know," Trish pretended to understand the concept of bragging rights where death marches were concerned.

They chatted about other things while they ate. Trish breathed a quiet prayer for this. She knew she wouldn't be able to eat and discuss human atrocities at the same time. Because of this, however, she knew that she would ask to visit again. She hoped it wouldn't look like she was begging another meal. This meal was worth begging for. The Goldsteins believed in the theory that the noon meal should be the largest of the day. They were truly a "breakfast, dinner, supper" type family. But chicken and dumplings and biscuits as well? She would be fattening up if she didn't watch herself.

After the meal, they talked a bit more about the camps. Max had started out in 1939 with every advantage afforded to a Jewish person. It took a moment for Trish to realize that he wasn't in Germany when the war broke out.

"You lived in Norway?"

"My parents moved there in the early 30s. We had lived in Germany, but they felt the pressure to move. I just wish they had felt more pressured! Moved farther away! So many people who died in the camps could have escaped if other countries had opened their borders quickly enough. But there were so many who couldn't believe that Hitler could get away with this. No one wanted the Jews."

"But you got into Norway."

"My father was a builder. He knew about construction, cement, things like that. I learned a little bit of that before the war broke out. It saved my life."

"How?"

"Because I had a trade! I was useful to the Nazis. I could build. But I didn't need to do that for quite a while. You must know that although there were work camps from the onset of the war, they were mostly just that. Work camps. Prisoners of war were brought to camps to work as part of their punishment. Since I was in Norway, it was a while before I was deported."

"And Norway allowed that?"

"They didn't have a choice! And even if they did, isn't it always easier to send one minority group to the gallows to save your own neck?"

"So, it was a case of 'Hand over your Jews and you'll be okay'?"

"That's right. And don't you for one minute believe that crap about Jews going without a fight!"

"Max!" Rose admonished. She apparently ruled the roost where language was concerned.

"Okay, okay, so don't believe that 'hooey.' How about 'hooey'? Can I say 'hooey' in my own house?"

Trish stifled a smile.

"And as long as we're talking about … hooey…," Max checked in again with Rose, "I know you hate the idea that Jews helped the Nazis kill other Jews."

"It's a disturbing historical fact."

"But did you know that there were Jews from other countries that came to Europe to help relatives and ended up in the camps themselves? And do you know that there were many Jewish uprisings! You've heard about the French resistance, but there were so many other pockets of resistance that no one should believe that Jews went willingly like sheep to their death."

"Why is that believed so readily?"

"Because Auschwitz was a big damn secret."

Rose didn't admonish this time. Obviously, damn was okay, crap wasn't. Max fell silent. As Trish studied his countenance, she could tell that he had had enough for one day. Frankly, so had she, even though she didn't entirely understand his final comment.

"Would you mind if I cut our meeting a little short?" Trish asked.

"You have to go so soon?" Rose asked, genuinely disappointed.

"I promised a friend I would stop by to see them as well, today."

34

"But you will come and see us again?" Rose affirmed.

"I would love to. I need to hear more."

"Let's get together next week. You come for supper!"

"That would be wonderful. Can I ask you one more thing before I go?"

"Of course."

"You mentioned that you have a daughter."

"Yes, we do."

"But you don't have a picture out. Why is that?"

"Rose is still in hiding." Max explained.

"In hiding?"

"When the Nazis came into our homes, they took family photos. They looked at the pictures and knew who lived there and what they looked like, so we hid pictures. Some we mailed away to relatives. It didn't do much good, but we did what we could."

"So, get out the pictures of our sweet Roberta, already," Max exhorted with the enthusiasm of a proud papa.

Rose went to a bureau and opened one of the drawers. She pulled out two framed photographs, the first showing a teenager receiving what appeared to be a high school diploma and the other a more mature young lady in cap and gown.

"Does she live here?" Trish asked, admiring the pictures.

"No, she works in Sun City, Arizona. We go to visit her when we can. But not a lot in summer when it's too hot."

"What does she do?"

"She works in geriatrics."

"That's a noble profession."

"When we get old and dotty, she can take care of us!" Max assured Trish.

Trish smiled. They were about as far from old and dotty as any other two people Trish had ever met.

"You're a close family, I can tell."
"We keep in touch. We call and write, but she wants us to email her and we don't"
"You don't email?" Trish asked.
"We don't have a computer."
"Oh, I see." Trish understood.
"Do you have a computer?"
"Yes, I do. And I have email." It sounded for some strange reason like Trish was bragging.
"What do you do for a living?" Rose asked.
It felt to Trish like she was taking notes for a matchmaker.
"I sell real estate, but I'm taking a sabbatical, of sorts. To write."
"About us?"
"I think your story is important," Trish hedged. It wasn't yes. It wasn't no. Not yet.

Trish left after making an appointment for their next visit. At this rate, she would need to begin visiting the health club at regular intervals to work off the gravy calories. She stopped off at The Ranch, but Mitch was apparently at the mansion. She called there, and was put through immediately.
"Hey, stranger!" Mitch said.
"Can I come over?"
"Sure. Are you okay, is anything the matter, how was your visit?"
"Yes, no, fine."
"Okay," Mitch chuckled over the phone, "I deserve that. Come over for dinner."
Trish audibly groaned. It was either feast or famine.
"Before I do, can I use your e-mail?"

"Sure, as long as you make it clear to whoever is getting the e-mail that it's you and not me."

"Maybe I should set up an account here?"

"Great, whatever works. But use mine in the meantime if it helps."

"Thanks. I'll be over in a little while."

Trish fired up the e-mail program on Mitch's computer and then found herself staring at the screen for so long that the screen saver came on. Maybe she wasn't ready for this. It could be so hard to strike up a conversation with a total stranger! Before Trish had left Max and Rose's, they had written down Roberta's e-mail number wrong. Twice. Between the three of them, they had finally managed to get all the @s and .coms down in the correct place. Now, Trish had entered the address in the "to" space and was ready to compose.

Dear Roberta,

My name is Trish Weingarten and I've just had a nice visit with your parents, Max and Rose.

Trish studied this opening sentence. It sounded so awkward. After all, Roberta would know her parent's names! But at least it added credibility. She continued.

I'm sending this e-mail to you because I promised your parents I would.

This was getting worse by the minute. Why in the world did Trish think she could ever write a book when she couldn't even get two sentences right!

I'm doing some research on the Holocaust because I've just discovered I'm Jewish. (It's a long story).
Anyway, I'm borrowing a friend's e-mail account, just so you know that I'm Trish, and not Mitch.
Reply to this letter if you want to.
Trish

Trish read it through twice. It sounded hopelessly naive. Her finger hovered over the left mouse button for a moment and then without further delay, hit the send feature. It was on its way now, no turning back. She changed her clothes, having gotten into the terrible habit of keeping a small but usable wardrobe at The Ranch. It was beginning to feel like she had moved in. Mitch, being too kind and considerate, hadn't said a word. Trish was at the mansion in plenty of time for a before-dinner glass of wine. Mitch had decanted a good red for the occasion.

"How do you always know when I'm in the mood for red wine?" Trish asked as they settled into comfy chairs in the den.
"You're always in the mood for red wine."
Trish didn't reply. She was still caught up in her earlier meeting.
"So, how was your day?" Mitch asked, after studying Trish's quiet mood.
"I met these really nice people, Max and Rose."
"And what did you eat?"
Trish finally smiled.
"Chicken and dumplings."
"Can I go next time?"
"How do you know there will be a next time?"

"I'm just kidding around, Trish. You do remember what that's like?"

"What's that supposed to mean?" Trish came back quickly. "It means that ever since you started on this quest, you've been pretty serious."

"And being serious is a crime?"

"No, it just isn't like you."

"So, our friendship is based solely on my ability to be a cornball?"

"I didn't say that, either."

"Well, what exactly are you saying? Let's get it on the record!"

"I'm just worried about you."

"Let me get this right. I refuse to be a chucklehead where the Holocaust is concerned and you're worried about me."

"You know, Trish, you're the one who called and wanted to come down here."

"And I'm beginning to wonder why."

"Frankly, so am I."

"Fine, I'll go."

Trish stood to leave. Several phrases popped into Mitch's mind, all at once, and stumbled over each other trying to be the first to be vocalized. By the time Mitch had it all sorted out, Trish was out the door. Rebecca came in a few minutes later to find Mitch still sitting in the parlor. Still drinking red wine. Still shaking her head.

"Hi there."

"Hi," Mitch said back, distractedly.

"What's wrong?"

"I don't know."

"Is it something I did?"

"No," Mitch stood up and pulled Rebecca into an embrace.

"Then, what?"

"Trish and I are having a fight."

"About what?"

"I don't know."

"It's about her book again, isn't it?"

"It must be, if you say so."

"How about another glass of wine?"

"I've probably had enough."

"Well, pour me one and let's talk. How did the argument get started?"

"I told her I was worried about her."

"And that started an argument?"

Mitch thought back to the conversation as she poured two more glasses of wine.

"No, it started when she accused me of thinking of her only as a chucklehead or cornball, or words to that effect."

"You called her those things?"

"No, those were her words. I just said that she had been so serious lately that I was worried about her."

"I understand."

"You do?"

"Sure."

"Well, could you please explain it to me because I'm confused."

"Okay," Rebecca pulled Mitch over to the parlor couch and sat down next to her. "What if it were true that only gay people had been persecuted by the Nazis?"

"Gay people were persecuted by the Nazis."

"Right. And so were other groups, like gypsies and trade unionists and such."

"Right. So, what's your point?"

"My point is that personal accounts of the Holocaust show beyond reasonable doubt that while Hitler persecuted only the homosexuals in Germany, he went outside of the bounds of Germany to hunt down and exterminate every Jew. He didn't do that with gay people. Only with the Jews."

"You've been doing some research?"

"I've studied the Holocaust off and on for quite some time."

"You and Trish should get together. You would have a lot to talk about."

"You and Trish have to get together and iron out your problems."

"I know. I just can't seem to say anything right."

"So, do what you always do."

"Buy my way out of it?"

Rebecca laughed. This was becoming Mitch's canned response to difficult situations.

"You need to be a little more sensitive than just *not* watching reruns of Hogan's Heroes. Do some research at the library. You have the time, and it wouldn't hurt."

"Promise that it won't hurt."

"I take that back. It will hurt. Some hurts you just can't avoid."

"Should I call Trish and see if she'll come back down for dinner?"

"If you think it would help."

Rebecca went upstairs to change out of her work clothes. Mitch drank her wine while she considered her options. After fifteen minutes of rehearsal, Mitch dialed the phone.

Trish had driven back to the Ranch with every intention of packing. She didn't want to impose further on Mitch. As she walked into the bedroom, she remembered the e-mail that she had sent scant minutes before. Curiosity overcame her anger, and she parked herself in front of the computer.

She had mail! One thing she liked about e-mail. You didn't risk getting a paper cut opening it. The message read:

Dear Trish, not Mitch,

Trish chuckled. At least her new correspondent had a sense of the ridiculous.

I was glad to get your e-mail. Surprised, but glad. As luck would have it, I checked my e-mail between shifts. Today, I need to go in and cover for someone who called in sick, and just stopped off at home for a quick bite. That's the problem with living so close to work. You're the first one they call when there's a problem! But, enough about me. You mentioned that you stopped in to see my mom and dad. How are they doing? I haven't seen them since their last trip to Vegas. I wish they would learn to e-mail. It's a lot of fun and I think they would enjoy it. Well, got to get back to work. Keep in touch.
Robbie

Trish reread the letter. Once for facts and the second for any stray nuances. She hit the reply button and then stared at the blinking cursor. For some reason, it was harder to reply than it had been to send the original e-mail. She wondered why for about two minutes, and then canceled the reply for now. This would take some thought. She disconnected the line and about two minutes later, the phone rang. It was Mitch. Trish could tell by the caller I. D.

"Hello?" Trish said.

"Hi. I finally got through. The line was busy."

"I was using the e-mail."

"Oh, good. Did it work okay?"

"It worked fine."

"Good. I'm glad."

"Did you want something?"

"I wanted you to come back for dinner. Rebecca does, too."

"She knows we're fighting?"

"She only has to look at me to know. I could live with a paper bag over my head and she'd still know."

"You are pretty transparent."

"My middle name is Saran Wrap."

"Okay, I'll come back down for dinner, but then, I'm going to move out of the Ranch and go back to my place and upgrade my computer."

"Can I go shopping with you when you do?"

"Sure."

"Okay, see you for dinner?"

"Sure."

Dinner for three at the mansion was no big deal. After the famous Thanksgiving celebration, dinner for three hundred was no big deal. But those three-hundred people weren't all entangled in an argument. Trish pulled up to the front in a Ford truck. She would never have admitted to the fact that she had gotten hooked on truck driving after the big Texas adventure that Mitch had gotten her involved in. When Trish had met Judy, there was one complication. She was living with Mitch's ex-girlfriend, Lisa. They had all ended up in Texas, pulling a scam on Lisa. Unfortunately, the wool they had tried to pull over Lisa's eyes had been about seventy percent polyester and Lisa had seen right through it. Somewhere in the shuffle, there had been plenty of exposure to trucks. Trish had fallen in love and consummated the passion by trading in her BMW earlier in the month for a Ford truck. It was blue, just in case that mattered.

After the initial awkwardness, Trish and Mitch chatted through dinner. Rebecca had stayed through the entrée, and then was conveniently called away on business. Too convenient to be believed, but Mitch appreciated the consideration.

"We didn't get much of a chance to talk about your meeting today," Mitch stated, and then added, "If I volunteer to take the blame for our argument, will you talk to me about your interview."

"You don't need to take sole responsibility for our fight. I was there, too."

"So, what happened today during your visit?"

"I met Max and Rose Goldstein. Max is a concentration camp survivor."

"It must have been awful."

"They are really quite funny people. You should hear them talk to each other. It's just like in the movies."

"Describe it."

"They banter back and forth about broken doorbells. Max can't say bad words without Rose giving him the business. He cried."

"He cried?"

"Sobbed was more like it. Think about it, it's been over fifty years and he still cries about it."

"What was it like?"

"His crying?"

"No, his life in the camps."

"He didn't say much. That's why I need to go back."

"Another wonderful dinner?"

"Supper. They call it supper and it is wonderful."

"Maybe I could go with you sometime?"

"Maybe. I can always ask."

"But you seem hesitant."

"I haven't told them that I'm lesbian."

"Oh, okay. And you don't want them to catch on by bringing a date, as such."

"I want them to talk to me without prejudice."

"They probably want the same thing."

"What's your point?" Trish asked, trying to understand without starting another argument.

"I'm just wondering if too many people over the years have looked at Max as an oddity rather than as a person. I know you don't do that, of course. But the Goldsteins are probably so used to it that they respond as such."

Trish thought for a moment. "You mean like people think of him as Max Goldstein – Holocaust survivor first and foremost and never get beyond that."

"Right. If you can break through that barrier, you will have a best seller on your hands."

"I don't want a bestseller."

"What do you want?"

"When I find out, I'll let you know."

"Fair enough. Shall we entice Rebecca back for dessert, or do you want me all to yourself for a little while longer?"

"Gee, let me think about it. Go and find Rebecca!"

Whenever dessert was involved, Rebecca was easy to find. In fact, she had been hanging out in the kitchen. Right this minute, she was sitting at the kitchen table, drinking coffee and reading reports. The table was full to overflowing with files.

45

"Guarding dessert?" Mitch asked with a hug from behind. "You two okay out there?"

"We're suffering from sugar deprivation," Mitch said, holding on to Rebecca and showing no sign of letting go anytime soon.

"Oh, I don't know, you're already sweet enough for me."

"You say the nicest things!" Mitch replied.

"Nice things are easy to say to you."

This wasn't their usual mode of conversation lately. After a year, they had pretty much gotten over some of the sickly sentimental things that newlyweds say to each other. But since there was staff present, they put on quite a show. No one would ever make a fortune in the state of Colorado and beyond by blabbing to the press about how there were arguments and fights every day. Unless, of course, they lied.

Rebecca held on to Mitch's arms just to make sure that the staff didn't see too much. It wasn't as though Mitch would have done something on purpose just to further annoy the staff, but it was what Mitch would have done from habit that would get them noticed.

"So, bring on the cheesecake, or whatever it is that we're having," Mitch said.

"The whatever is warming in the oven. I'll be out in a minute. Grab a cup or two of coffee if you and Trish want some."

Mitch had forgotten to ask Trish about this, but took two cups anyway. Better safe than sorry. Trish was grateful. The wine they had for dinner seemed to be building cobwebs in her brain. Nothing like a good, strong cup of coffee to sweep things clean.

"Her honorable will be here in a minute with dessert."

"I'll have to go home and write today in my diary."

"Why?"

"It's the first time I've been served dinner in the governor's mansion."

Mitch scanned her memory. She was right. In all the time that Mitch and Rebecca had been together, they had never had Trish to dinner. Oh, sure, she helped serve dinner to the homeless on two different occasions and shared a plate of food with Mitch in the kitchen when time allowed. A moment here, a moment there. But she was correct, she had never been the guest of honor. Mitch felt the sting of embarrassment. How easy it was to take good friends for granted. It would never happen again. Mitch would see to it that Trish had a monthly, no make that weekly invitation to dinner. She would talk it over with Rebecca in bed. No sooner had Mitch made the vow than Rebecca was standing in the room, ready to share brownie pie. This was one of their favorites, brownies topped with coffee flavored ice cream. It was only about ten trillion calories per serving. Thank goodness Mitch had brought the coffee! Rebecca took care of refills and after chatting about inconsequential things for a few minutes after dessert, Trish took off.

"You two seem okay," Rebecca commented.

"It's the first time she's been to dinner here. I feel so ashamed."

"You've been busy."

"I should never be too busy for friends."

"She's practically living at your other house. You see each other all the time."

"I want her to come to dinner more often."

"She can come every day as far as I'm concerned."
Mitch looked at Rebecca. She was always so willing to agree to Mitch's requests.
"You're in an agreeable mood tonight," Mitch said with a tease in her voice.
"You say that like it's a special event!"
"It could be!"
They went upstairs in their now usual calm, quiet fashion. There was never any chasing around the couch for these two. They preferred to save their energy for other activities. In one year's time, Rebecca had slowed down a little, Mitch had speeded up just a bit and they were now captured in each other's embrace. In bed. Sans clothes. Big smiles.
"So, how's that Senate campaign going?" Mitch asked as she kissed Rebecca's shoulder.
"Slowly."
"I'm kissing slowly."
"The campaign, silly!"
"Kiss the campaign?"
"I'll kiss your campaign in a minute."
"I can hardly wait!"
"You won't have to!"
With that pronouncement, Rebecca took charge of things. It was her specialty.
Afterwards, Mitch tried again for campaign talk.
"How is your run for Senate going?"
"Slowly," Rebecca teased again.
"How slowly?" Mitch asked, always confused by politics.
"These things take time."
"I don't understand."
"Running for office involves more than just intent. It takes a lot of time and consensus building and meetings."

"That's a lot to add to your already busy schedule."

"Is that *concern* I detect in your voice?"

"No, just the facts. Have you hired a campaign manager, I guess you already did?" Mitch asked and answered in one sentence.

"Yes, you're right."

"So, whom did you hire?"

The struggle to remain nonchalant was not well masked.

"I thought you knew. I hired Jake McManus."

"I thought he was head of the Democratic committee already? Can he do both?"

"He quit his other position."

"Just to be your campaign manager."

"He's very committed to my success."

"He seemed less than thrilled that you were running at all only a short few days ago."

"I guess he knows a winner when he sees one."

"Uh huh," Mitch muttered.

"And it's such a relief to have him running things. I can relax and leave all the scheduling up to him. He's a cross between a bodyguard and a chaperon."

"All rolled into one."

"That's right."

"And he's going to have you scheduled up the wazoo with a million functions."

"I thought you understood what it takes to get elected," Rebecca raised up on one elbow to make eye contact with Mitch.

"I guess it looks easy from the outside."

"Well, you're not on the outside anymore."

"Yeah, I guess not."

"If you had any reservations about this, you should have told me sooner."

49

"I don't have any substantial reservations," Mitch skated around the truth.

"So this big black cloud hanging over us all of a sudden is my imagination."

"Oh that. That's just my political naivete coming home to roost."

"Every politician has handlers."

"He handles you once and I'll break his arm."

"You are truly upset about this, aren't you."

"You ask me to tell you the truth about what I'm feeling and then you make me feel like somehow I'm wrong about it. I know what's going on here. I'm surprised that, with all your political astuteness, you don't see it."

"Jake has my political best interests at heart. Period."

"Right. And I'm the Easter bunny."

"Well, you do have cute, floppy ears."

"Don't start with my ears!"

"If you're concerned about anything, you can come to every single solitary function. In fact, I want you with me all the time. Now that you don't have the Lucky U to worry about, you would be a wonderful asset to the campaign effort."

"You better run that by Mr. McManus first. He may think that the last thing you need is for your lesbian lover to go trailing around after you everywhere you go."

"I don't need to run this by anyone! If you want to be with me, consider it a done deal."

"I'll bet you a hundred dollars that Mr. McManus blows his cork when you tell him about this."

"Let's make it interesting. How about a thousand dollars?"

"You're on, Ms. Money Bags."

"Now, about those ears...."

50

Chapter 3

"No, she's not!" Jake was emphatic. For the third time.
"Yes, she is!" Rebecca repeated for the third time.
It was a standoff at which to marvel. Here they were, the
two most beautiful people in the state of Colorado standing
practically nose to nose, arms crossed, eyes flashing.
There's just nothing quite like your first fight as
campaigner and campaign manager.
"If you weren't serious about winning, you should have
never hired me!"
"I wouldn't have hired you if I wasn't serious about
winning."
"And you aren't going to win this election if *she* trails
along behind."
"You don't need to refer to her like she's vermin! She has a
name!"
God, Rebecca thought to herself. This was beginning to
sound like a "Doozie" argument.
"She will screw over any chance you have at being a
Senator."
"Well, we will just have to take our chances, won't we."
Jake fell silent. He was only two or three inches away from
Rebecca. The heat radiated, and not just from the
argument. Mitch waltzed in about this time, and quickly
surveyed the situation. It looked like an easy thousand
dollars from where she stood.

Then, as if transformed by magic, Mr. McManus thrust his
hand out, grabbed a hold of Mitch's hand and shook it like
she was some long lost rich relative.

"Welcome aboard the campaign! Governor Fairbanks has just given me the terrific news that you want to join the campaign effort!"

Mitch's arm might need a long soak in Epsom salt after this pumping.

"And you think that's going to be okay?" Mitch asked, eyebrows arched.

"It is the next best thing to happen to this campaign!"

"What was the first best thing?" Mitch followed up, wondering how long it would take him to mention his own appointment.

"Why, Governor Fairbanks's decision to run! Of course!"

"Makes sense to me," Mitch nodded, still rather unaffected by all this false enthusiasm. Silently, she was pissed off because she knew damn well that the thousand was due and payable, and she was getting screwed over by McManus. Jake checked a couple more details with Rebecca and then took his leave. Mitch stood for about half a second and then said, "Hold out your hand."

"You don't have a ruler, do you?" Rebecca feigned concern.

"Why would I need a ruler when I have a governor? Hold out your hand, you chicken."

Rebecca held out her right hand while Mitch extracted a bundle of hundred dollars from her back jean pocket. She began to count them out slowly, one after another, into Rebecca's waiting palm. When she got to one thousand, she locked eyes with Rebecca.

"Don't spend it all in one place."

"How about lunch? I'm buying."

"I should hope so!"

Lunch today meant sandwiches at the desk. That was okay by Mitch. Any time she spent with Rebecca these days seemed special just being in her company. Mitch had not done well with nothing to do. Now that she was officially "not vermin" in the eyes of the campaign manager, things might pick up.

"I know that Mr. McManus isn't crazy about this idea. That acting job wouldn't have gotten him a role as a ham in the third grade nutrition play."

"I suppose you want your thousand back?"

"No. There's plenty more where that came from."

"I'll buy dinner, too."

"I'm sure I'll be in the mood for something expensive."

"I hope you're in the mood for something late. I'm not free and clear until…" Rebecca was leafing through her daytimer, "About nine?"

"Nine works for me."

"Okay."

"Okay."

"And if I don't get back to work, it will be even later."

"I know. I'll go and keep busy somewhere else."

"Why don't you track down Jake at the new headquarters and see if he wants to coordinate schedules with you," Rebecca suggested rather too breezily as she answered the phone.

"I'd rather get a root canal," Mitch muttered under her breath as she left Rebecca to her duties.

"Hello, Jake."

Mitch found him in a half-moved-in office. He looked up, flashing way too many teeth her direction.

"Good to see you again so soon!"

"You don't need to smile. Rebecca isn't right behind me."

His toothy grin tarnished just a smidgen.

"I don't quite understand."

"I think you do. I don't like you and you don't like me."
He didn't reply, but his smirk began to slip.
"But we both really like candidate Fairbanks," Mitch
added. "I fact, I'm very much in love with candidate
Fairbanks. What about you?"
"She's a nice employer."
"And you'd do just about anything to sleep with her."
He remained silent. Gee, thanks, Miranda. Mitch
continued, "I will cooperate with your campaign strategy to
the best of my ability. However, I will not downplay my
relationship with Rebecca under any circumstances. Is that
clear?"
"Crystal."
"Rebecca suggested we coordinate our calendars."
"I'll prepare a computerized printout for you and then I will
input your data."
"That won't take long. I'm free and clear for the rest of my
life."
"Well, then you sound like the perfect person to coordinate
the volunteers."
"Fine. If that's what you need, that's what I'll do."
"Of course, we will need to get some volunteers first."
"Sounds like a good place to start. Do you have a phone
list?"
"I have a core group and a lot of possibilities."
"Oh good, I thought I'd have to start at 'A' in the phone
book."
"That might be step two."
Begrudgingly, Mitch smiled. He could be decent when he
tried. Now, if he would just turn down the charm when
Rebecca was around, like maybe to only dazzling.
"I will help set you up with a team of volunteers to gather
in more volunteers. How does that sound for starters?"

54

"Sounds fine."

Within thirty minutes, he had a printout of a data base with names, addresses, and phone numbers of the pillars of the party. It was impressive, the Who's Who of the Democratic movers and shakers of Colorado. It made Mitch feel a little better to have such resources available. Without a moment's hesitation, Mitch pulled up a chair and picked up the phone to make the first call. Jake stopped her before she got past the first three digits.

"What are you doing?"

"I'm calling these people."

"You don't have a script."

"I'm not trying out for Broadway."

"You need a set spiel."

"Maybe you do, but I don't. You do your work and I'll do mine."

"I'll set you up in another office."

"Oh, no, you don't need to do that. We're going to share an office through this campaign. Mind you, it will be the *only* thing we share."

"I'm not sure office sharing is wise."

"Of course it is. How else will I learn what I need to know? Being with you every day, watching and learning from you. It's an experience I can hardly wait to, well, you know, share."

Jake rubbed his forehead like he was trying to push his skin clean off his skull.

"We'll sort all this out tomorrow. I have a meeting. Start addressing these envelopes and put stamps on them."

"I'll do that after making phone calls, without a script."

He looked like he was about to argue the point again, and then raised his hands in mock defeat. After he was gone for about five minutes, Mitch sat down and scribbled out a few notes. Who needed talking points when you could speak from your heart. Fifty phone calls later, she had 37 yes, 5 maybe, 4 think about it, 3 out of town and 1 drop dead. Not literally, of course. It's just that even some Democrats can't seem to find their path clear to help a gay person get elected. All in all, not a bad percentage for a rookie with no script.

Rebecca wandered in about 8:45, catching Mitch with tongue to envelope. They needed better tasting glue on these if Mitch was going to last much longer.
"Where's Jake?"
"Beats me," Mitch replied as she took a swig of water to unstick her tongue from the roof of her mouth.
"You don't know?"
"He left right after lunch."
"And you've been here all by yourself . . .?"
"Making phone calls. I'm in charge of the volunteers."
"That's a big responsibility."
"I'm sure he gave it to me so that I would screw up big time and then you would fire me."
"I see. How are you doing so far?"
"Thirty-seven out of fifty. Do I get to keep my job?"
"Keep it, hell. You can work overtime! Except that I'm hungry, and I bet you're starved."

Over dinner, they avoided discussing Jake. It was quite the accomplishment. In fact, Rebecca seemed to want to avoid talking about everything political in general. Mitch noticed, but didn't comment outright until dessert.
"You've been unusually reticent about all things political tonight."
"Even I get tired of it some days."

"Is that a good thing to happen when you're about to embark on a run for the Senate?"

"Am I doing the right thing?"

"Of course."

"You're just saying that."

"What's troubling you?"

"Did you stop to consider that those thirty-seven people who volunteered to help out are doing so just to get me out of the state?"

"No, I didn't."

"I did."

"You think that if you were running for emperor of the moon, I would have gotten all fifty to help get you elected?"

"I wonder sometimes if this is the right move. I'll be foregoing the hands-on work I love here in Colorado in exchange for deciding issues that seem mundane by comparison."

"If those issues are important to Colorado, then they'll be anything but mundane!"

"I guess that I know, deep in my heart, that the farther up the ladder I go, the farther away I get from the grass roots work that I enjoy."

"I promise to keep your feet on the ground, except for later tonight, of course."

Rebecca gave Mitch that now famous look. It was all Mitch could do to make her hands behave themselves, at least until they got home. After that, all bets were off. As were Rebecca's clothes. And Mitch's clothes. They stretched out next to each other, languidly touching here and there; starting slowly, and enjoying the snail's pace. Mitch blamed the mellow atmosphere on chocolate overdose, but wondered if Rebecca's distraction was more than just political in nature.

"I'm going to have a talk with Jake tomorrow."

"About what?" Mitch asked, squeezing jealousy out of her voice at the last possible moment.

"I think your involvement in the campaign should be more than licking envelopes and stamps, although you do show quite an aptitude for that sort of thing…."

"It is one of my fortes, isn't it," Mitch was agreeable.

"Most definitely."

Mitch situated herself closer to Rebecca, who still seemed lost in thought. After one or two kisses, Mitch lost count, Rebecca pushed her away. Not forcibly, but with the kind of strength that Mitch understood immediately. For once, Rebecca wanted to talk now and make love later. Mitch pulled back and rearranged her body so that while she still cuddled Rebecca, it was a comfortable arrangement for them both.

"What are you thinking?" Mitch invited dialogue.

"I'm thinking about your future role in the campaign."

"And?"

"I want you to make speeches."

"You must be joking!"

"I'm serious. You have a way with the public and the press."

Mitch looked over one shoulder first, and then the other. "What *are* you doing?"

"I'm looking to see who you're talking to! You can't possibly be speaking to me."

"Why not?" Rebecca asked as she casually began to run her fingers up and down Mitch's thighs. It was distracting at worst, and anything but casual to Mitch, who ached for more than this touch.

58

"Because," Mitch struggled to think logically, "I'm not good in front of an audience."

"You're very good in front of me."

"That's because you're an audience of one," Mitch grinned, trying to ignore Rebecca's hands. Silly bantering wasn't working.

"A lot of politician's wives make speeches."

"That's because they are considered an asset to the candidate."

"You're my asset," Rebecca reassured as she moved her fingers to even more strategically bothersome areas.

"If I didn't know better, I'd think you were trying to take advantage of me."

Mitch leaned over for another kiss. This time, she was held closely instead of being pushed away. Still, Mitch could sense a lack of closure in their conversation. Rebecca was ready to hear "yes" from her, but Mitch's commitment remained as elusive as Rebecca's touch.

"I won't give a canned speech. I'll need to have some sort of input so I'll sound natural."

"Okay. That can be arranged."

"And I won't lie about anything. Ever."

"I think that's wise."

"So if one of the press corps asks me how hot you are in bed, I'll just have to answer as truthfully as possible."

"How hot am I in bed?" Rebecca asked, running Mitch through a test.

"About as hot as the internal temperature of the sun."

"And you should know, you're getting warmer yourself," Rebecca stated as she touched Mitch exactly where she had hoped for all day.

"Oh, yes...," Mitch exhaled slowly.

"Yes?"

"Yes! I'll do it. I'll give speeches, I'll kiss babies, I'll do anything you want."

"Anything?"

"But if the press ever asks me if you are good at manipulation…."

"You wouldn't!"

"I'll only mention your index finger," Mitch nodded wisely. "And the wonderful way in which you crook it."

Chapter 4

Trish had taken Mitch up on her offer to shop for her new computer. She had everything set up and ready to go and was studying her email draft to Robbie. She had *only* rewritten the e-mail message about nineteen times.

Dear Robbie,
It was nice to hear back from you, and so quickly. Your parents mentioned that you work in geriatrics, so that explains the "shifts" you mentioned in your e-mail.
I'm confident that the reason you are called in so quickly to work is due more to your expertise than your proximity to the hospital.

Anyway, I'm once again going to your parents' house for dinner. Is there any message that you would have me convey?
BTW, I now have my very own e-mail address, as you have already noticed.
Sincerely,
Trish

Trish had sent this a day prior to her next appointment with Max and Rose, and worried that Robbie wouldn't pick it up in time to make a reply. Besides, Trish chided herself mercilessly, Roberta didn't need an intermediary to talk to her own parents. Now that Trish was rereading the e-mail in her out box, she felt moronic. She was all ready to shut down the e-mail connection when the message popped into her in box. Trish inhaled twice before reading the response.

Dear Trish,

You are *so* thoughtful to volunteer to carry a message to my folks! I could be humorous and simply have you reassure them that "I'm eating enough!" But that would truly be an oversimplification. Tell them, instead, that I love them and that I'm not working too hard (although I have been doing my share of double shifts, but don't tell them that) and that the weather is beautiful down here and they should come for a visit. Soon!

One day, when I'm not working too hard and you have a moment, you must tell me your "long story" about your recent self-discovery about being Jewish. It sounds fascinating.

I did notice that you are no longer "Mitch" but "Trish" on your e-mail. Good for you! Now, if you could just get my parents to get on the e-mail bandwagon, it would make it even handier to keep in touch with them. Having an email and using it are two different things with my parents' generation.

Keep in touch,

Robbie

Trish couldn't stop smiling. Why, she didn't know. Well, actually, she did know. Robbie made her smile. The woman's gracious manner and obvious good nature came through in her messages.

Armed with good wishes and up-to-the-minute news, Trish headed to the Goldstein's home for dinner. It was about eleven when she tested the doorbell. It rang. Rose answered the door, all smiles and greetings. What nice people! Max, carrot juice in hand, welcomed Trish.

"Hello again, Ms. Weingarten. So, how are you?"
"For goodness sake, Max, let the woman get through the front door first," Rose said.
"Don't mistake my curiosity for impoliteness."
Trish smiled and answered, "I'm wonderful, Max! How are you?"
"I'm drinking my carrot juice. How do you think I am?"
"Probably sick of carrot juice," Trish teased back.
"Do you *know* how many carrots it takes to make this much juice!"
"Five?" Trish guessed, enjoying the banter.
"Try ten!"
"And I end up making carrot bread by the dozen loaves with the pulp!" Rose added, guiding Trish to the love seat.
"Sit, sit, sit," Rose instructed.
Trish complied, feeling comfortable in the somewhat familiar surroundings. A glass of wine was placed in front of her without so much as a inquiry as to her thirst. A "yes" last visit meant a "yes" this visit.
"So, how are you?" Max asked again. Either he had forgotten the answer in all the hubbub or he wanted more information. Trish gave him the benefit of the doubt where memory was concerned and answered in more detail.
"I have been feeling great, Max, if somewhat affected by spring fever."
"Do you have allergies?" Rose inquired.
"No, I've just been lazy, I guess."
"You! Lazy? Never," Max argued the point kindly.

"Well, I've worked pretty hard for many years, and when I decided to take a break, as such, I found myself catching up on all the rest that I had been missing. So, I've been a little extra sleepy lately."

"I know what you mean. The same exact thing happened to me after the liberation."

"I imagine so," Trish nodded, wanting above all for Max to steer all the conversations about the Holocaust without prompting.

"Max was exhausted!" Rose picked up on the topic. "He needed weeks of recuperation and medical care before he was even able to function."

"Is that so?" Trish watched Max for further clues.

"It took a while, but I was back on my feet before long. You can't keep a Jew down forever!"

"What sort of medical attention did you need?" Trish probed, now that the subject was on the table.

"Well, I needed to get, uh, what do they call it nowadays?"

"Get rehydrogenated?" Rose ventured.

"Rehydrated?" Trish took a guess.

"I needed water!" Max explained in plain English. "I was dehydrated."

"That's extremely serious."

"It was worse than the starvation. People can live for weeks without much food, but you don't live very long without water. At the end of the war, clean water, along with everything else, was in short supply, and they sure didn't give any to us Jews!"

"So how did you survive?"

"Sometimes, we ate snow. Talk about manna from heaven. We were freezing, but we ate snow. Some prisoners ate grass, right out in the field."

"And some prisoners stole things. They hanged children who stole food to eat, you know," Max elucidated.

"I had heard that."

"Well, I saw it!" Rose stated fiercely, and then, as if taken aback by her sudden disclosure, excused herself to check on dinner.

"Rose doesn't feel comfortable talking about her wartime experiences, does she?" Trish asked Max.

"She doesn't talk much at all, and never right afterwards."

"After the liberation?"

"She didn't say anything for *years*!"

"Do you think that was healthy?" Trish wondered more to herself than Max.

"Healthy, I don't know? It was Rose's way of dealing with it."

"And you dealt with it by talking about it."

"Not really a lot at first. First thing was to get back on your feet, second thing was to start life over, third thing was to have a family."

"So, that's what you did."

"Number three took a while."

"I see," Trish hedged, not wanting to pry into such intimate details so close to dinner. The procreation of Robbie wasn't her idea of an appetizing discussion. Rose came to the rescue, calling them to the table. It was loaded with goodies, and this reminded Trish to report about Robbie.

"I e-mailed Roberta after our last visit."

"Aren't you clever!" Rose beamed. "We called her last weekend."

"I assumed as much," Trish said. The call would certainly trump any message Robbie had given her.

"So, what did she say?" Max wanted to hear anyway.

"She said she wasn't working too hard."

"That's not true. She works very hard."

"And she said the weather's fine."

"And we should go for a visit!"

"Right, and she said she loves you."

"She's a good daughter. Now, if she could find herself a good husband, all of our worries would be over."

Trish nodded, hoping that this simple gesture would allay any quizzes about her own search for true love. It seemed even more important at this juncture, but she didn't quite know why. Perhaps, it was the possibility of matchmaker Rose to the rescue.

"So, you're not married?" Rose asked.

So much for the effectiveness of nodding.

"Not yet," Trish said nonchalantly.

"Still waiting for the perfect man?"

"Still waiting," Trish nodded.

"Take your time," Max entered the fray with his own advice. "Don't rush into things. We didn't rush right into having a family, and that turned out okay, right, Rose?"

"Right, Max," Rose agreed, and then fell silent again.

Sensing a lull, Trish ventured into the subject of e-mail.

"Roberta says that she has talked to you about emailing more."

"That's more of a young person's way, isn't it?" Max said. This sounded more like a case of lack of confidence. Trish ought to know, she had suffered from it a few years ago herself and would have used the excuse of age, had she been seventy.

"E-mail is a powerful tool. It helps people communicate, almost instantly."

"It would have come in handy during the war, maybe?" Rose said.

"How so?" Trish asked, always interested in Rose's opinion.

"Well, it's like Max said last time, Auschwitz was a big secret. You remember that?"

"I remember you mentioning that," Trish looked at Max.

"It was! People criticized Jews for years after the war for marching readily and without question to their death. But in reality, Auschwitz was one of the best kept secrets of the Nazis. People thought they were going to a work camp, and when they got off the train, they were almost immediately put to death. It was so efficient, it was sickening. Woman with child, over here. Straight to the gas chamber! Men who were old or frail, to the ovens! A pimple on your skin! Immediate gassing!"

"Maybe if we could have communicated faster, fewer people would have been killed."

"But who was to send the message, Rose? The dead can't e-mail."

"I guess not. But if even one person could have sent word. Somehow."

"People did sneak out photographs and such, but they weren't believed. You think an e-mail would have convinced them?"

"Maybe not," Rose stood her ground, "But a thousand, or a hundred thousand might have."

Max conceded the point, "Enough about the war! Let's have dessert."

Suffice it to say, dessert wasn't carrot bread or carrot cake or carrot anything. Instead, Rose had baked a cherry pie. God was in her heaven, thought Trish as Max produced ice cream for a topping. And not just any ice cream, butter pecan. The next best, closest thing to an orgasm for Trish.

She kept the moaning to herself. Who needed a husband when you could have this.

"It's okay?" Rose asked, perhaps seeing the restraint in Trish's expression.

"It's heavenly! Do you bake often?"

"Oh, just once a day or so."

"Once a day! Wow! I don't bake once a year."

"Neither does Roberta. You modern women don't have time."

"I'll make you a deal," Trish brightened suddenly.

"What?" Rose asked.

"You teach me how to bake a cherry pie, and I'll teach you how to surf the net."

Rose looked at Max, not necessarily for approval as much as out of habit. He shrugged his shoulders.

"I'll do it!" Rose agreed eagerly.

"Me, too. But I can't teach you anything about baking?" Max confessed.

"That's okay. You're already teaching me enough with your life story."

"So, when do we start?" Rose asked.

"With the pie or the net?"

"Oh, let's do the net first! We can do pie any old time!"

"That's easy for you to say!" Trish kidded, knowing full well how difficult it was to make decent pie crust from scratch.

"So, how do we get started?" Max looked askance at Trish.

"Why don't you practice on my computer first. You can come over to my house for dinner and spend time on the computer. Then, if you really like it, I have a friend who can help us shop."

"A boyfriend?"

"No, actually, just a good friend."

"What's his name?"

"Mitch, and he's a she."

"A girl named Mitch?" Max weighed in on this latest development.

"Short for Michelle, I guess?" Trish tried to remain composed. She had done what she least expected, open the door for the truth about herself. It wouldn't take these people long to put two and two together and realize that they had seen Mitch on the news. Hopefully, it wouldn't be an issue. Maybe Mitch could go by just her first name for a while?

"So, what day is good for you?"

"Any day is good for us! We're retired, remember!"

"Okay, well, how about next Monday? Come about noon, stay for dinner, play on the computer." Trish was penciling this in her daytimer.

"Monday is perfect!" Rose beamed. "Wait 'til Gerta hears about this! Rose and Max on the net!"

"Gerta?"

"Gerta the 'Know-it-all' in my bridge club! Not even she's been out on the net!"

Chapter 5

"This doesn't sound like me!" Mitch stated firmly.
"Which part?" Jake sounded absolutely exasperated.
"Just all of it!"
"I'm not having the entire speech rewritten."
"Yes, you are."
"No, I'm not."
"Fine. I'll rewrite it myself."
"Yeah, right."
"And what exactly do you mean by that?"
"I mean that you couldn't write your way out of a wet
paper bag with a sharp pencil."
"Oh yeah!"
"Yeah!"
Mitch was ready to storm out of headquarters when
Rebecca blocked the door, just by coming through.
"What's up? You look upset."
"I'm beyond upset. Upset is a really polite word for what I
am," Mitch was holding it together for the sake of the
discussion.
"You and Jake are fighting again, I take it."
"That's right. I told you that I wouldn't give a fake speech.
I assumed you told *him* that," Mitch indicated his general
direction as Jake brought all six foot two luscious him into
closer proximity. Being that handsome should be against
the law, Mitch thought as he pulled a humble, little-boy-
picked-on moue. Rebecca just smiled sweetly, and just as
sensual. Mitch felt like an ugly worn out tennis shoe at the
prom.
"I did give her full say in the speech department, Jake."
"It's just a rough draft. I thought she knew."
Mitch had enough of being "her" and "she."

"I thought I was going to write the speech, without a paper bag, and then you, Rebecca, not *him*, would edit it."

"Sounds fair to me, how about you, Jake?"

"An admirable suggestion," he smiled broadly and then returned to his duties.

"An admirable suggestion," Mitch intoned through her nasal passages and then with normal, disgusted tones, "What a kiss up!"

"I just have one question?"

"Sure, what?"

"Why were you going to write the speech on a paper bag? Were you shooting for something Lincolnesque?"

"I was, but we were out of envelopes."

"Oh yeah, you must have licked them all."

"It's my job," Mitch couldn't resist a chuckle.

"Lucky envelopes."

"The stamps are green with envy."

Rebecca ignored the pun and turned serious.

"What will it take for you and Jake to get along?"

"He'll need to take an ugly pill twice a day."

"An ugly pill?"

"He's just too darn cute for his own good. Did you see the sludge he called a speech?"

"No, but I'm sure the problem didn't rise to the level of declaring World War III."

"I'm doing my best."

"You don't need to be jealous."

"Who said I was jealous."

"It's more than clear that you feel about Jake exactly like how I feel about Lisa."

"I'll admit that I don't like the way he looks at you."

"I'll make you a deal. You can begin to worry if you ever see us kissing, okay?"

Mitch thought it over. Quickly. How patient Rebecca had been through all the turmoil surrounding Lisa. Not one kiss, but two. Not one hug, but several. Dinner invitations. Overnighters. Mitch realized how one sided the double standard was that she held Rebecca to.

"I've been really out of line, haven't I?" Mitch admitted.

"Not out of line."

"Out of line."

"A little. You don't need to worry."

"Okay, you've convinced me. Just make me a promise."

"What kind of promise?"

"If I ever get angry and ask to be left alone, don't do it. Don't leave me alone. I may say it, but I don't mean it."

"You got yourself a deal. And if you ever do want to get away from it all, you-and-me wise, kidnap me and take me down to Santa Fe for a little R & R."

"You just snap your fingers, and I'll be here with the RV!"

"Deal. Now, go and write a speech! You have speaking engagements in two days."

Mitch did as she was told. The writing attempt was pretty terrible, even Rebecca grimaced as she read through it. As per their prior agreement, Rebecca made liberal use of a red pen to edit. Mitch took the criticism well, even if it looked like someone had bled on the paper. Profusely. Like, from a head wound. By the ninth rewrite, it was in field-test form, which, coincidentally, took two full days to accomplish. The greatest achievement was that Mitch and Rebecca were still speaking. The bad news was that it didn't allow any slack time for memorization. Mitch thought that was good, that it would give the speech a more spontaneous feel. Jake worried that Mitch would flub it up by losing her place on the page. Rebecca had faith in

Mitch's flair, and was relieved that Jake and Mitch had stopped sniping at each other long enough to do a run through.

By the time Mitch reached the lectern for her debut in politics, all the moisture that was normally in her mouth had seeped down to her palms. It is widely believed that there is only one thing people fear worse than giving a speech in front of strangers. It isn't death, but rather giving a speech in front of friends. Thank God there were no personal friends in the audience, jokingly referred to as a "critter club" by the pundits because so many of these organizations were named after wildlife, you know: elk, moose. There were, however, lukewarm supporters who needed convincing that Rebecca Fairbanks would be the best senator Colorado ever elected. Mitch conveyed the message well, and found the words flowing out. Rebecca could keep her job as editor!

What hadn't gone according to plan were the questions that came from the floor after Mitch wrapped up the speech. Although most were honest attempts to clarify issues, a couple were clearly "plants" whose sole purpose was to unnerve Mitch. It was the usual rigmarole about living in sin, being morally disgusting, and spiritually bankrupt. Mitch listened closely to the questions, and answered with honesty and forthrightness. She admitted to living in sin, only because the law didn't allow her to do otherwise at this point in time. However, she disagreed with the moral and spiritual points. Mitch professed her true moral commitment to Rebecca and even confessed that they were still attending church. And donating money. So the spiritual bankruptcy charge really didn't stick on either count. For not having a pre-written, edited answer to every question, an impossibility, Mitch was doing pretty well. She thought.

Then, things got a little more complex. Someone who had obviously researched the whole Lisa/Mitch/Rebecca situation asked Mitch whether or not she had broken the law by helping a woman flee the jurisdiction of the court system. The "Pam Case." Mitch had, after all, ended up in jail. Mitch remarked something to the effect of the wisdom of going to the bathroom every chance you got, which drew a mixed response of twittering laughter and strange looks from the audience. Then questioner got down to the heart of the matter, accusing Mitch of obstruction of justice, aiding and abetting a kidnapping, harboring a fugitive and covering up the governor's complicity. Glancing at Jake only long enough to see him frantically signaling her to wrap things up, Mitch instead freely discussed the situation, noting for the record that Rebecca cooperated fully with the authorities in the matter and summarized her answer by reminding the audience of two things: number one, she had spent a total of about two hours in jail, and number two, it was Rebecca, not Mitch, who was running for senate.

After shaking a few more hands and extracting promises to help the campaign, Mitch was feeling pretty good about the evening, and remarked as much to Jake. He disagreed, and lit into her after they were in the car on the way home. "Don't ever field questions again!"
"Don't tell me what I can and can't do. I will answer questions if I so choose. Rebecca knows and gave her consent."
"Your answers stunk."

74

"The questions stunk. The answers were perfect."

"The press is going to crucify you over this."

"Better people than I have been crucified over telling the truth."

"This campaign isn't about you. It's about getting Rebecca elected."

"Rebecca and I are a package deal. The sooner you get that through your Cro-Magnon skull, the better it will be for all parties concerned."

They both lapsed into an uneasy silence. If Jake had plotted to discourage Mitch from further campaigning so that he could have Rebecca all to himself, he was doing a good job. Jake dropped Mitch off at the sidewalk outside the mansion. Debriefing would happen in the morning at headquarters, since, for legal reasons, the mansion and capitol were off limits for campaign strategy meetings. Mitch walked in to discover that the welcoming committee consisted solely of Doozie. It was after nine, and Rebecca was still at work. Too tired to either cook or raid the pantry, Mitch went upstairs and played catch with Doozie until she flopped down, ready for a nap. Doozie, not Mitch. The staff didn't exactly approve of playing the game indoors, up and down the hallowed hallways, but Mitch was uneasy about being outside in the dark. Too many previous events had made her gun shy. Quite literally.

Just as Doozie and Mitch stretched out on the bed, Rebecca appeared in the doorway.

"Back already?" Rebecca quizzed.

"It's after nine."

"So it is," Rebecca nodded. She seemed as distracted as Mitch.

"What's up?" Mitch remarked, not ready to disclose her most recent fight with Mr. Perfect Teeth.

"It's Mary. She's agreed to see Hilary during spring break."

"Right. I remember."

"Well, it isn't going to be just an airport visit. Hilary is staying a few days."

"Here?" Mitch pointed to indicate the mansion.

"Over my dead body."

"Why don't you change clothes and I'll find something to eat."

"I'm not hungry."

"Are you thirsty? I'll get you some wine or something?"

"I think I just need you. And a hug. And some good old fashioned support."

"All three, right over here," Mitch whispered a command to Doozie, who for once cooperated by jumping down and sacking out in her doggy bed. Then, Mitch fluffed a pillow and beckoned Rebecca to the spot beside her. Skirt, pantyhose, high heels and all, Rebecca snuggled up next to Mitch. They held each other closely for a few moments, a breather before the debriefing.

"I'm not putting up with this," Rebecca picked up where she left off.

"Okay, so let's come up with a suitable plan. We can arrange for Hilary to stay at a hotel."

"And that's it. One simple answer." Rebecca snapped back.

"Well, just one so far. Give me a minute and I'll come up with a few more."

"Ah yes, the lady with all the answers and money to back them up."

76

With that terse assessment, Rebecca disentangled herself from Mitch's embrace and stood to leave.

"Where are you going?"

"To work."

"It's after nine."

"Thank you, Big Ben," was Rebecca's parting comment. Mitch waited a couple of minutes before going after her. It seemed like a good idea to give her a head start. No use chasing down the hallway, giving the staff a good show. When Mitch went to find Rebecca, it was probably just good luck that made her detour through the kitchen. Rebecca was digging into a quart of ice cream.

"I thought you were going to work."

"I'm working on this ice cream, aren't I."

"Can I pull up a spoon and join you?"

"Better get a couple of bowls."

"Good idea. And some chocolate syrup, maybe. What flavor ice cream?"

"Rocky Road."

"How apropos."

Rebecca squinted a look at Mitch. It was either another flash of anger or a last-second attempt to thwart a smile. Didn't much matter, Mitch rambled on.

"Are we going through one of those Jupiter-Pluto things?"

"You mean Mars-Venus, don't you?"

"Never was very good at astronomy," Mitch hedged.

"Tell me what you're talking about, and I'll tell you if we're going through it."

By now, they both had a bowl full of gooey ice cream in front of them, and had a chance to make eye contact.

"There's a theory that when you tell a man your problems, he gives you an answer; but when you tell a woman your problems, she gives you support."

"I see."

"And so, I was giving you answers when you needed support. I was even too dense to comprehend that when the exact words about needing support came out of your mouth."

"You weren't dense."

"But I wasn't very smart."

"Let me tell you about my typical day," Rebecca offered as she poured more syrup in her bowl. "I go to the office, and my chief of staff has all the answers to everything. Then, as I meet with legislators, they have all the answers. Community leaders have all the answers, advocacy groups have all the answers, and everybody else for good measure has all the answers!"

"So, it doesn't help when you come home and I have all the answers."

"I don't mind that you have all the answers, I just want you to be able to discern when I want to hear answers and when I don't."

Mitch nodded agreeably. "Makes sense to me. I'll just listen for the key word, 'support.'"

"Look, I really didn't mean to jump down your throat...."

"Let me guess, you've already had words with Mary over this?"

"I told her I'd talk to her later, but I was pretty abrupt."

"I understand."

"I don't."

"You don't?"

"I don't know why I let this get to me."

"Maybe because your daughter has been hurt once already? Gee, there I go with the answers again. I guess it's just gut instinct."

"But you're correct."

"I don't want to be correct. I want to be supportive. How do I go about that?"

"Do we have anything besides chocolate syrup?"

"There's butterscotch."

"Why don't you get me some of that."

"Sure, whatever," Mitch nodded, willing to help in whatever way she could.

"Don't stop giving me answers. That's really not why I'm upset. I just wanted to pick a fight with someone who wouldn't hold a grudge for centuries."

"Who holds a grudge for centuries?"

"You really don't know much about politics, do you?"

"I try my best to be ignorant."

"Politicians can hold grudges for dog years."

"Dog years?"

"Yeah, like a grudge that you might hold for a year, a politician can hold for seven."

"Too bad Doozie isn't here. She'd know all about this."

"Let's take this discussion back upstairs. Along with the butterscotch syrup."

"You're taking butterscotch syrup to bed?" Mitch raised her eyebrows.

Rebecca met Mitch's gaze. "Does that excite you?"

"I'm right behind you with the chocolate!"

"And the rest of the ice cream."

"Yes, Ma'am."

As they finished dessert in bed, still clothed, Rebecca confessed her trepidation about Hilary's impending visit.

"I'm worried that Mary will get back together with Hilary."

Mitch nodded and waited.

"I think that's a terrible idea."

"Did Mary give you any hint that she would?"

"I didn't give her much of a chance."

Mitch waited to hear more. This was harder than it looked.

"I should call her. She's probably still at the Center."

"What are you going to say?"

"I haven't figured that out yet. Got any good ideas?"

"I never had kids. I wouldn't know what to say. What did you always say when you were worried about her?"

"I used to tell her that I loved her."

"Sounds like a good start to me."

"I wish you would've come up with that answer sooner," Rebecca watched to see if the teasing was appreciated.

"Me, too!" Mitch nodded animatedly.

"And then what? What comes after 'I love you'?"

"How about 'I'm worried about you getting back together with Hilary'?"

"You think that's a good idea?"

"It sure beats her wondering what's bothering you, which she will know already since you're calling her."

"Okay, I'll do it."

"Good. You make the call while I do the dishes."

Mitch took the empty bowls and sticky spoons down to the kitchen and washed them out by hand. It took a few extra minutes, but she wanted to give Rebecca all the time she needed. Breathing room is generally a good idea where family issues are concerned, and once in a while, absolutely essential. By the time Mitch had done the dishes, and eradicated any trace of her presence in the kitchen, Rebecca was off the phone.

"How did it go?" Mitch asked when she arrived back upstairs.

"Things are fine. Hilary is staying in a hotel."

Mitch nodded, "Sounds like a good plan."

"And I'm not supposed to worry."

"Okay."

"So now, the child has become the mother and the mother, the child."

"This is more confusing than that planet stuff."

Rebecca smiled, beckoning Mitch closer.

"You haven't told me how your evening went."

"Damn," Mitch thought to herself. She had hoped to glide right on by this discussion.

"That's quite a face!" Rebecca caught the expression before Mitch knew it had even escaped.

"Do you really want to know?"

"Sure I do. It is my campaign."

"Then why does it seem like Jake's campaign."

"Are you two fighting again?"

"Let's just put it this way, he's not very happy with my performance."

"The speech?"

"No, I think it was the question and answer portion of the evening."

"You answered questions!"

"I thought it would be rude not to."

"Did Jake provide you with a typed talking points sheet?"

"A what?"

"I guess not."

"All I had was my speech. I did pretty good on that."

"But the questions were tough?"

"Some of them were vicious. All about my brief but soggy visit to jail and impeding justice and living in sin. You know, that stuff."

"They really put you through the wringer."

"Jake said they are going to crucify me and you in the press."

"So what's new. That's a daily occurrence."

"So, you're not totally angry at me."

"I'm super pissed off at Jake for not giving you everything you needed."

"I think that was by design."

"His 'not having a job' is going to be by design if that's the case."

"Oh, for goodness sake, don't fire the boy. He's too much fun to vex."

"You! You don't want me to fire him?"

"No."

"Why?"

"Because then he would be a martyr."

"And that would ruin the campaign?"

"Something like that," Mitch agreed, even though that wasn't her one bright shining concern. She just didn't want Jake to play the part of the martyr to Rebecca. However, if she won the election, he would be the hero. Damn politics anyway!

"It's a long way until August."

Mitch nodded. Her neck was beginning to get sore from all this agreement. The August primary season couldn't be ignored. And neither it seemed, could Mr. Perfect Teeth.

The phone rang.

"Hello," Rebecca answered. "Yes, Jake. What's up?"

Mitch could only cringe at this choice of words, but kept silent in order to eavesdrop further.

"I see."

Pause.

"Uh huh."

Another pause.

"I understand."

A longer pause.

"We'll talk tomorrow."

Hardly any pause at all.

"Thank you."

Rebecca hung up the phone. Mitch had kept count on her fingers. Sixteen words. Unless you counted the contractions as two. Then the total was....

"What are you doing?" Rebecca asked.

"I was just counting."

"To ten?"

"Almost to twenty."

"He didn't seem too upset."

"Like, he's going to yell at you?"

"He yelled at you?"

"He talked loudly, but I guess that's to be expected from a guy with a big mouth."

"We're going to have a get-together tomorrow. All three of us."

"Oh goody. I'll bring the noisemakers and party hats. What are you going to bring?"

"Maybe the butterscotch syrup?"

"Oh, no you don't! I have plans for that!"

"Good plans?"

"Great plans!"

"You've got gum on your shoe."

Mitch looked around her feet at Rebecca, who was sitting in Jake's chair. They had arrived at campaign headquarters early, which led Jake to scramble around for coffee. He was brewing, Rebecca was in his chair, and Mitch had her feet propped up on the edge of the desk.

"I do?" Mitch said and then checked first one and then the other.

"Made you look," Rebecca announced impishly.

Mitch pretended to scowl. It was a transparent effort at best. "You certainly are in a feisty mood after last night."

"Hey, I'm not the one who decided to play thirty-one flavors."

Any further cleverness on Mitch's part would have to be postponed. Mr. Coffee was back.

"Here we are. One hazelnut for Mitch, one vanilla for the Governor, and one Folgers."

He wasn't a frilly coffee kinda guy, and had cheated by simply adding flavored creamer to the other two cups. After filling the orders, he sat in one of the visitor's chairs and waited for Rebecca to begin the conversation.

"You wanted to debrief me about last night," Reb stated.

Mitch held her face still. With great effort.

"I think that the newspaper coverage will tell the story much more succinctly." He held up the paper so everyone could once again read the headline, "Gay Governor's Lover Details Illegal Acts."

"Sounds about right for that newspaper," Rebecca stated.

"I think it's kind of catchy," Mitch nodded.

"It's exactly this sort of coverage that will drive this campaign straight into the ground."

"I don't think so," Rebecca countered. "Everyone knows what kind of rag that newspaper is."

"But they read it with glee anyway," Jake shot back.

"What sort of coverage did we get on TV?"

"None."

"Why not?"

"They weren't there," Jake answered, looking from Rebecca to Mitch and then back.

"Why not?" Rebecca asked again with a calm, cool, collected demeanor, but everyone knew the truth. She was smoldering underneath. At least Mitch knew it. If Jake didn't, he wouldn't last long in this business.

"They were contacted. I guess they didn't think it important enough to show up."

"After this headline, they will. And when they do, I suggest you have talking points prepared for Mitch or anyone else who speaks on my behalf."

"Yes, Ma'am."

"Do you need anything from me? Information? Money? Photos?"

"I'll make a list."

Mitch fought the urge to say, "And check it twice." It was, after all a little early for Christmas carols.

"Okay. I expect Mitch to have at least one speaking engagement a week right now and more as we get closer to August."

"Yes, Ma'am."

"And I want to see your strategy for commercials by next week."

"Sure thing."

"And one more thing."

"Yes?"

"Get some decent coffee in here. This stuff sucks."

"Will do."

"It's better if you put something in it," Mitch piped up.

"Like what?" Jake asked.

"Butterscotch is the flavor of the month."

"Maybe for you," he replied with loathing.

"You just said a mouthful," Mitch answered back.

Rebecca couldn't respond. She was doing her best to suppress a throaty chuckle as it was. "You'll be home for dinner?" was the only question she could think to ask Mitch.

"Just as soon as I get the gum off of my shoe."

Jake appeared absolutely mystified. Which made him even more handsome. Damn.

Rebecca left. Mitch stayed. Jake glowered.

"I guess I'll work the phones for a while," Mitch offered.

"Don't bother. I have someone coming at eight to do that."

"Well, then I guess I'll work on some envelopes."

"I have someone coming in at nine to do that."

"So, what do you want me to do."

"You heard the governor. Go find some decent coffee," he snapped, now that it was safe to do so.

"Good idea," Mitch picked up on her punishment like it was a plum assignment. Actually, she had a plan in mind. She walked five blocks to a coffee shop where Mitch and Rebecca had had one of their first encounters. Aptly named the Millster, it was an adequate coffee house two blocks away from the capitol. She ordered a cup and sat down to soak up the ambiance of the café. Being on the front page of the morning newspaper didn't allow for much quiet soaking.

"Long time, no see," the cashier intoned as she pulled up a chair and sat down. She was fearless.

"I've been a little busy."

"I know. We've been watching with interest."

"You have?"

"Ever since you brought the governor here for coffee, you've been an icon."

"Icon?" Mitch repeated the word, uneasy at its weighty nature. The Artist Formerly Known As Prince was an icon. Mitch preferred to think of herself as a thorn in the rosebush of society.

"Still having your usual, I see."

"I like this butter pecan flavor. Say, could I ask you a favor?"

"Depends."

"I want to have your coffee at the governor's campaign headquarters. Can we set that up?"

"Are you buying or expecting a donation?"

"I'm buying."

"We'll donate. For a mention."

"You mean, like, the Millster is the official coffee supplier of the Fairbanks for Senate campaign?"

"We support you, despite what we read in the paper."

Mitch smiled. Strong words coming from a small business. They stood to lose it all in the treacherous waters of political endorsements. Lately, in politics, you made half the people angry at you no matter which side you chose.

"You'd be taking a risk."

"Bad publicity is still publicity. As long as they spell your name right!"

Mitch thought to herself, "Gee, why couldn't you be the campaign manager?"

Out loud she said, "I'll expect the first shipment of freshly brewed coffee to campaign headquarters tomorrow morning."

"Why not today?"

"Right now?"

"Sure. Are there people to drink it?"

Mitch remembered the crew coming in to do envelopes and phone calls.

"Yes."

"I'll send something over right after break."

"Hey, thanks."

Mitch returned to headquarters much the conquering hero. Two urns of hot coffee were en route and delivered before she had a chance to get into another fight with Jake. He objected, of course, balking at the promise of publicity. Mitch ignored him and introduced herself to the volunteers who had arrived for work. They were efficient and genial. A nice combination for a change.

At lunchtime, Mitch ordered in enough pizza to ensure that everyone would have both lunch and dinner. Not that she expected people to work past dinnertime, but rather so that they could take some home to their families as well. Mr. Delmonico's Pizza was thrilled to be a part of the process, and to be paid as well. Very few Americans realize the important contributions made by small businesses to community and political efforts. Mitch insisted on paying again, less it look untoward.

"You'll need to report everything you spend as part of the strict accounting that accompanies political campaign law," Jake warned as he stuffed another bite of pepperoni pizza into his mouth.
"I'll pay by check and keep track of the receipts."
"No, I'll keep track of the receipts."
"Are you the treasurer as well?"
"No, but I'll see that she gets them."
"So, we have a treasurer?"
"Of course we do!"
"What's her name."
"Susan Lockhart."
"Never heard of her."
"That's because you haven't been paying attention."
"And I plan to do more of that."
"Really. Well, then I guess we'll just have to call you by your nickname."

"Which is?"

"Gumshoe."

Jake had finally gotten the joke. Took him long enough...

Chapter 6

If the computer could talk, it would have squawked "You have mail!" like a parrot on steroids. But it didn't. Talk, that is. Trish saw the tiny, itty, bitty letter pop up on her desktop and checked her mail. It was from Robbie. She was thrilled.

Dear Trish,

Can't believe you've talked my parents into being more computer savvy! When do the lessons begin? And, more importantly, when does the spending begin? I know they will be so involved that they will want a computer of their very own. What should they get? Would you please help them with the purchase? I know you are good at it, buying computers, that is. God, listen to me babble on and on about this. How are you? Things are busy here. Work, work, work. Nothing else new. So, e-mail me the minute you get this so I'll know what's going on up there.

Robbie

Trish took a moment to catch her breath. Gosh, what exuberance. If Robbie could get this worked up over computer e-mail, imagine what she could be like in a relationship. Trish shook her head. Don't even go down that road, she chided herself silently. The woman's in Sun City, Arizona, for goodness sake. And probably straight as a stick to boot.

Dear Robbie,

I think the only people/persons more excited than you about the prospect of exchanging more e-mails are your folks! I can understand that. It's a subtle cross between a phone call and a letter. It doesn't "ring" in the night, and is faster that a speeding mail truck ;-). And let's not even get into the plethora of smiley face combinations!

The first lesson happens tomorrow. Monday. I think by one in the afternoon here we will be sending more greetings and missives. You'll probably be at work. Unless you can get a long lunch hour??? But with your busy schedule, that might be tough. Let me know.

Trish

Trish popped the send button and went out to fetch herself a fresh glass of iced tea. It was getting to be iced-tea season already, unseasonably warm and dry. That's what living in the prairie will get you. By the time the sugar had been stirred to a state of dissolve, Robbie was back in the box.

Dear Trish,
I will be here tomorrow! At about one. I will, not have, but absolutely will arrange a long lunch hour so we can chat as live as we know how. I don't know a thing about chat rooms, do you?
R

Trish took a long drink from her glass before answering.

R,

I haven't gotten into chat rooms myself. Besides, we don't want a bunch of strangers interfering with our conversations, do we?

T

Another draw. Lemon and sugar competed for Trish's attention.

T,

You're absolutely right. Didn't even think about it. But tomorrow will be fun. And if things bog down for any reason, have my folks call from your place. I'll pay the charges.

R

Trish realized that she didn't have the phone number. Robbie was a cautious soul. It was a good idea this day and age. People who send their phone numbers around unsecured e-mails get what they deserve.

R,
I probably should have your folks call you anyway, and then they can give you my number here as well, so it can be handy for you.
T

Trish inhaled and sent the e-mail. Handy for what, she hoped Robbie wouldn't question too deeply.

T,

This has been fun. More fun in store tomorrow. Talk to you then.

R

Trish closed down her e-mail program and went to bed. Just how much fun would tomorrow be? The question didn't keep her awake past midnight.

Chapter 7

"Hey sleepy head! Wake up already!" Rebecca shook
Mitch from a fabulous dream. She was on a deserted island
with all the cappuccino she could drink. Maybe it was a
good thing the governor had awakened her. She needed to
use the bathroom right now.
"Back in a minute!" Mitch announced as she scampered out
of bed.
"I might not be here when you get back!"
"You better be!"
Mitch took a lazy five minutes in the master bathroom.
Sure, it was the governor's mansion, and the bathroom was
nice enough. But dripping luxury it wasn't. Sometimes it
was more a case of dripping faucet. She wandered back
out, refreshed and ready for anything.
"You still here?" she teased Rebecca, who was looking
snug and lovely as ever, lounging away the early morning.
"You still there?" she teased back.
"Always, for you."
Mitch slid back under the sheet, and into Rebecca's arms.
"So, what are you up to today?" Rebecca asked. Normally,
the question sounded tossed off. Today was different.
Mitch had the feeling that Rebecca was on a fishing
expedition and Mitch was the catch of the day.
"Oh, I thought I'd cause more trouble down at campaign
headquarters. You know, like usual."
Rebecca looked at Mitch. "How do you always know what
I'm really asking?"
"Has Jake been reporting my sins hourly or minute by
minute?"

"He mentioned something about pizza and coffee and gifts in kind and product endorsements and all that other stuff that we all need to be concerned about in this business."

"He told me to get decent coffee. I obliged. It was your idea, anyway."

"All you had to do was buy a decent coffee maker and some good coffee."

"Did I do something illegal?"

"No."

"Well, then get off my case."

Mitch got up and started to dress for the day's activities, which didn't even include going to campaign headquarters. The changing of the clothes took about one minute.

"Where are you going?"

"I don't know yet."

"Santa Fe?"

The tone wasn't quite snotty enough to warrant an acerbic come back, but it was damn close.

"I think I'll go see what Trish is up to."

"That will be nice. Tell her I said 'hello.'"

"Sure."

Mitch was out the door before further instructions or fighting could take place. They had learned, rather quickly, that it was best to analyze their fights later, after a cooling off period. Why Mitch was flying off the handle over any discussion about the campaign would require a calm, quiet atmosphere. Maybe it was just the morning's effect. Or maybe just not enough good coffee.

She buzzed around town for a few minutes until she found a non-partisan coffee shop. There were only about three per block to choose from, but the driving helped. By the time she had sucked down half of a mortal sin class and type mocha, she dialed Rebecca on her cell phone. Always in the office, what a predictable gal she was.

"Hi, again, so soon," her honorable chirped.

"Hi. I took off in a huff, didn't I."

"A huff and a puff, it seemed. Are you okay?"

"I don't know. I just felt cranky this morning."

"Maybe you need a medical checkup?"

"I just had one."

"You just had some ob-gyn work. Maybe it's time for something a little more thorough."

"Or maybe I just needed a triple mocha."

"So, that's what you're doing!"

"Yeah, guilty on all counts."

"Maybe I just need to lay off any comments about the splendid work you're doing for the campaign."

"You know, I don't understand all the rules about this stuff. If what I did wasn't illegal, then what was the problem?"

"Anytime someone goes out and gets contributions, it's just a good idea to make sure everything is, well, above board and legal and ethical and moral and all that other stuff. You were fine, but Jake needs to know what you do before you do it."

"So, I need to ask Jake for permission?"

"I wouldn't call it permission…."

"What would you call it?"

Mitch waited a few seconds while Rebecca thought it over.

"How about 'agreement'?"

"How about you and I have a long talk tonight about finding my replacement for the campaign?"

"I don't want you to quit."

"Don't think of it as quitting."

"What would you call it?"

"Taking a twenty-two year leave of absence."

"Let's talk tonight. Okay? Please. And I'm sorry about the Santa Fe remark."

"Okay. Accepted. I am still going to drop in on Trish. I'll tell her 'hello' from you."

"Thanks. I love you."

"I love you more."

"Not possible."

"Possible."

"Bye."

Mitch drained her mocha and then went on an early morning shopping spree for Doozie. Since the only store open at this ghastly early hour of the morning was Target, she puttered around there for over an hour, buying dog toys and other assorted stuff that would be pleasing to her favorite pet. She thought, if only for a second, about a gift for Rebecca. Now, what on earth would a millionaire buy at Target for the governor of the state of Colorado? Nothing jumped out at her, so she went through the checkout lane with doggie toys. Doozie would be ecstatic. By now, the malls were open as well, so Mitch stopped by Victoria's Secret to find something more fitting, in every sense of the word, for Rebecca. She was either going to be in big trouble tonight, or in heaven. Only the governor could decide for sure.

By eleven-thirty, she pulled up in front of Trish's place, noticing only with a cursory glance the other vehicle parked close by. Maybe she should have called? She knocked on the door, and after a long moment, was greeted by Trish.

"Well! Hello there!" Trish seemed just a little out of breath.

"You've been exercising?"

"No, I just had to hurry out here. Come in. We're getting ready for dinner and e-mail."

"Dinner and e-mail?"

"Come and meet my company."

"Are you sure? I didn't mean to barge in."

"Not a problem. Come on."

Mitch followed Trish through the house and into the kitchen. There, up to her elbows in flour, was a plump, beautiful woman. She seemed right at home.

"Rose, I'd like you to meet a dear friend, Mitch."

Rose wiped her hands as flour free as she could in two seconds and shook Mitch's hand.

"And this is Max, who's staying clear of the kitchen."

"That's a long name," he chuckled as he held out his hand as well.

"You wear it well!" Mitch joked back. She recognized their names from the prior conversation with Trish. Mitch remembered to try and act straight. At least until Trish gave further notice.

"So, what are you guys up to?"

"We're making a pie," Trish answered for the trio.

"I see."

"Actually, Rose is making the pie and we're watching," Max explained.

"And taking notes," added Trish.

"And then, while it's baking we're going to learn more computer stuff."

"Sounds like a busy afternoon for all of you."

"And then maybe some preliminary computer shopping."

"Really!" Mitch sounded more interested by the minute.

"After dinner."

"That's pretty late."

"Not if dinner is lunch and supper is dinner it isn't."
Oh yeah, Mitch had forgotten. They were going by "old world" meal monikers. Meanwhile, pie school resumed as Rose regaled everyone of the benefits of keeping everything that touched the raw pie dough cold and handling the dough as little as possible with your hands, lest the warmth from your hands soften the fat used to make the crust flaky. Nobody wanted a tough crust. They didn't even need that vote to be by secret ballot. With a flip of the wrist, Rose had the dough in the pie pan and poked it for pre-baking. This woman had a process as close to real science as atom splitting. She thickened the pie filling as the crust pre baked and then filled the crust, latticed the remaining pie dough across the top of the pie and placed the masterpiece in the oven. To avoid overt drooling, they went into Trish's computer room to begin the e-mail fun. First, they called Roberta, as promised. She was there, waiting. Then, with a few strokes of the keyboard, they began sending messages back and forth. Trish gave control of the computer over to Rose and Max so they could have a relative amount of privacy and pulled Mitch into the dining room and put her to work. That was her excuse. Her real motive was the third degree.
"So, what really brings you here?"
"Oh, I just thought I'd drop by, say 'Hi.'"
"Are you and the governor fighting?"
Damn, the psychic Trish!
"Not much," hedged Mitch.
"How does 'not much' work?"
"Oh, you know how it is, living with a Senatorial campaigner…."
"Oh right. I remember now. My last ten girlfriends ran for public office."

99

"It's hell, ain't it," Mitch chuckled, losing at least half of her tension all at once.

"What, specifically, are you and the campaigner fighting about?"

"The campaign."

"The entire thing?"

"Jake and I don't get along very well."

"Who is Jake?"

"The campaign manager."

"I see."

"I'm quitting the campaign."

"Were you ever on it?"

Had it really been that long since Mitch and Trish had talked? Mitch felt a twinge of guilt.

"I made a speech, got coffee, generally made a nuisance of myself. You know, the usual."

"I'm sure you did more than that."

"It just isn't my forte."

For a moment, it seemed that Trish was going to toss off an erudite remark, and then stopped herself. No doubt, a remark about the lack of forthrightness in politics and how everyone should hope that wasn't one of their fortes. But since Rebecca had never done a dishonest deed in her life that Trish knew about, Trish labored to rein in her knee-jerk opinions. Especially around Mitch. Instead, she said, "Not everyone is cut out for politics."

"There's a lot more to it than you see on TV."

"Isn't that true of anything?" Trish mused out loud.

Mitch didn't answer, and instead used the point to pirouette to another topic.

"Tell me about the e-mail-a-thon going on in the other room."

"It's a not-so-veiled attempt to convince Max and Rose to buy a computer."

"So you mentioned."

"And I'm learning to bake."

"A fair trade."

"So, what are *you* going to do with your time now that you're not blazing the campaign trail?"

"Shop, I guess?"

"Shop?"

"Afraid I'll encroach on your territory?"

"I'll go buy a pair of boots so I can shake in them."

"I'll help."

"Okay."

It was more than obvious that Trish's mind had wandered. To where, was the only remaining mystery. Mitch mulled the possibilities. Could it be the computer shopping that seemed inevitable? Why would that distract Trish? By now, everything but the color of her underwear was known to the sales staff at the computer store she patronized. Maybe it was the complexities of cherry-pie baking? That wouldn't be it. Rose seemed to be a patient mentor. Perhaps the "straightening" of the house was a preoccupation. How critical was it to Trish that her sexual orientation be unknown to Rose and Max? Many times the elderly were much more understanding about these things than some self-righteous yet naïve middle agers.

"What's on your mind?" Trish broke through the reverie.

"I was about to ask the same thing."

"You were going to ask me what's on your mind?"

"You seem preoccupied as well."

"So do you."

"Seems we're a pair to draw to."

Further insights, or confusions, depending on how you looked at it, were suspended by Rose calling for help from the computer room.

"I typed the message but can't figure out how to send it." Trish nodded. A couple of mouse clicks later, the message was on its way. Max and Rose eyed the monitor like they expected it to either self-destruct in five seconds or give them a standing ovation for their courage. Its only reaction was the display of a tiny letter icon in the lower right corner.

"Is that from Roberta?" Rose asked anxiously.

"Won't know until we open up the in-box," Trish explained kindly and then showed them how.

Robbie must have been composing off line, so lengthy was her response. Once again, Trish and Mitch left to afford them some privacy.

"You'll go shopping with us?" Trish asked.

"Do you really need me?"

"You, instead, need to maybe get back and sort things out with the governor?"

"I'm going to try."

"Let me know how it goes."

"Okay."

Mitch took her leave politely, saying a prolonged farewell to Rose and Max, who took turns typing as they said good-bye. The drive home felt like jogging forwards on a conveyor belt. Mitch was there before she had thoroughly practiced her resignation speech. She gathered up her purchases and meandered up to the bedroom to freshen up. It didn't take long and after running out of things to do, she stretched out on the bed and pondered Trish. What was going on? Really? Had Trish latched on to Rose and Max as surrogate parents, trying to bind herself more closely to her heritage? That was a good possibility. Another thought held itself just off the edge on Mitch's mental borders and she dozed off trying to fence it in.

Mitch felt the bed shift and opened her eyes.

"Hiya, sleepyhead," Rebecca greeted softly.

"That's where we started this morning."

"You okay?"

"I bought you a present."

"You did, huh?"

"It's in a bag over there."

Rebecca rummaged around in the Target sack and remarked, "Gee, a ball and a rawhide bone."

"Those are for Doozie."

"I should hope so."

"Your present is in the other bag."

"I see. So, you went shopping today?" Rebecca quizzed, not ready to check out her gift.

"Just a little. Then I stopped by Trish's. Open your gift."

Rebecca noted the source of the gift and furrowed her brow.

"Victoria's Secret?"

"Yeah," Mitch acknowledged mono-syllabically, feeling suddenly like this wasn't going to go the way she had planned.

Rebecca peered in the box. "It's a bit on the scanty side, don't you think."

Mitch stomached her tension subconsciously. Rebecca was not pleased. After a year, Mitch had become expert at picking up on this. Of course, she usually saw the reaction towards other people, and cringed at the sight then. Having it flow in her direction was almost unbearable.

"I thought it was the shade of green that you like."

103

"Well, they didn't need to use much green dye, did they."
"You don't like it," Mitch ventured a safe guess as her stomach burned.
"I just don't want you to buy a provocative gift every time we have a fight."
"Fine. I'll take it back. Now."
"Now?"
"Yes, now," Mitch gathered things up quickly to keep one step ahead of her anger. Twice in one day she was leaving on bad terms. Whatever comment Rebecca made was to Mitch's back as she left the room.

The great American institution of the mall was open late. True to her word, Mitch returned the gift. Graciously. It wasn't the clerk's fault that the governor was hard to please, although she would never know that.
"My mother didn't like the color," Mitch used as explanation.
"Of course. I understand." The clerk refrained from laughing. That was good enough for Mitch.
Then, Mitch wandered around the mall until it closed at ten. It wasn't planned that way, the time simply vaporized as Mitch's brooding mood lingered. It was times like this that she really missed the Lucky U. It would have afforded her a comfortable place to hide out. Of course, Rebecca would have shown up, like in the old days, and talked things out. Then, there was always the "Ranch." Mitch's other home. But Rebecca would be calling there. So, as Mitch drove aimlessly, she remembered that Trish had wanted to hear how things turned out. How welcome would a ten-thirty phone call be? Trish answered on the first ring. Cautiously.
"Hello?"

"It's just me."

"What's wrong?"

"You can tell?"

"I'm your friend. Sounds like the fight has gone to round two."

"I think we're between round two and three."

"Sounds serious. Want to come over?"

"It isn't too late?"

"Come on over."

Mitch was at her door in an embarrassingly short period of time, as if she had already plotted the drive.

"Come on in," Trish swung open the door.

"Hi."

"How about coffee and pie!"

"That would be marvelous."

Trish served up fresh coffee and pie as she chatted about the afternoon buying spree by Max and Rose. It was one thing to buy a computer. Setting it all up was another matter. Trish had volunteered herself for that adventure first thing in the morning. The patter dwindled to a stop. Trish had hoped to ease Mitch into conversation and then simply settled for the direct approach.

"Does she know you're here?"

"No."

"You should call her."

"I should, I guess."

"So she won't worry," Trish kept the pressure on.

Mitch dialed the bedroom number and connected with Rebecca on the second ring.

"Hello?"

"I'm at Trish's."

"I wondered where you went."

"I just got here."

"I see."

"And we're having some coffee."

"I see."

"And so I'm not lying dead in a gutter somewhere."

"I see."

Mitch paused. So far, she was three "I sees" into a frustrating monologue masquerading as a conversation. Having run out of relevant information, her pause stretched to a moment of silence.

"It there anything else you want to tell me?" Rebecca asked.

Since the question was more loaded than guns at a duck shoot, Mitch considered her options in "land-mine mode." One false step and kaboom!

"Why don't you take tomorrow off."

Now, it was Mitch's turn to wait out the pause at the other end of the line and the governor pondered the deeper meaning of the suggestion.

"It would require some schedule changes."

"Well, don't you think our relationship is worth scribbling up your daytimer, just a little bit?"

A year ago, the answer would have been obvious. Now, with the bloom off the rose, so to speak, things were thorny.

"It would require quite a bit of scribbling."

"Well, you were the one who just asked if there was anything else I wanted to tell you."

"And?"

"I figured it would take about a day to do that."

"I see."

Oh great! Back to the vast ocean of "I sees." Mitch dove in anyway.

"But it it's too much trouble?"

"When are you coming home?" Rebecca interrupted.

106

"In about fifteen minutes."

"I'll be here."

"You always are."

"That's me, 'old reliable.'"

"You're not old."

"Shut up—hang up—come home."

Mitch obeyed. She vowed to spend time with Trish at a more decent hour of the day.

"I'd invite you along for the 'great plugging in of the computer' tomorrow, but it sounds like you might be busy?"

"I can only hope."

"Remember, she has the entire state to run. If I were governor, I would have probably legalized beheading by now, just to deal with my detractors!"

Mitch laughed, but fully understood the implication of Trish's remark. Entire systems of government hinged on the good judgment and full concentration of Rebecca Fairbanks. The amount of stress created by that alone would send most mere mortals clear off the edge. So, Rebecca was cranky once in a while. She was entitled. This reasoning went through Mitch's mind like a recorder stuck on replay as she drove home. She parked in her usual spot and walked quietly up the staircase. The bedroom door was open and Rebecca was propped up, reading paperwork.

"Hiya," she said, glancing up from the file she held open.

"Hiya," Mitch echoed.

"I'm about done with this."

"Take your time."

Kicking off her shoes, Mitch reclined on the bed. Rebecca made a few more notes and then snapped the file shut.

"I wanted to finish this up because I'm going to be sick tomorrow," Rebecca explained.

"Oh really!" Mitch exclaimed. "I hope it's not one of those nasty flu bugs that requires a week or two of bed rest."

"You don't?" Rebecca arched her eyebrow.

"I realized, after a long talk with myself this evening, that I'm the one who is having a strange case of 'Erupt-itis.'"

"Erupt- itis?"

"It's a reactionary disease that creates a low threshold of patience and understanding."

"I think you're being a little hard on yourself."

"Trish helped with the diagnosis, reminding me that your have one of the toughest jobs around."

"Did you tell her about the negligee?"

"No."

"Thank you."

"You're welcome."

Mitch counted to three and then asked. "Why was that such a big mistake?"

"If you buy me a gift every time we fight, I'm going to need to rent one of those storage units."

"You expect us to fight that much?"

Rebecca ignored the question and continued, "Gifts keep us from confronting the issues that we fight about."

"Okay, I want to quit the campaign." Mitch caught on fast. It was a lot easier than she had imagined.

"I know you do, but you are such a natural at it. Campaigning, not quitting. You exude honesty, forthrightness, humor and family values. Maybe *you* should run for office instead of me."

The laugh that jolted out of Mitch nearly cramped her lower back, so sudden and powerful was it.

"What's so funny?"

"Me! In an elected office! That's a hoot! It's one thing to get elected. It's quite another to be *good* at it. I see how hard you work, how smart you are, how much you read and study and listen. I'd last ten minutes *maximum*!"

"Are we still fighting? This doesn't seem like fighting?"

"No, it doesn't."

Rebecca smiled at Mitch and then winced. Barely, as if she were hiding something.

"What's wrong?"

"I have a headache."

"I'm not surprised. It's late and you're exhausted. Let's just turn off the lights and get some sleep. We can 'fight' more tomorrow."

"I look forward to it."

Mitch changed for bed in double time and cuddled up in the dark only as snuggly as one dares when headaches hit. The next thing she knew, it was six in the morning and Rebecca's voice floated through the last of Mitch's dreams.

"I'm sick."

"I remember," Mitch mumbled. "You planned to pretend to be sick."

"I don't need to pretend."

Mitch woke up more and raised up on one elbow. She felt Rebecca's forehead.

"My God, you're feverish."

"Uh huh," Rebecca said through a jaw that sounded like it was locked.

"Are you having chills?"

Rebecca only nodded as she shook.

"Did you take anything yet?"

Rebecca shook her head.

Mitch got up, walked over to Rebecca's side of the bed and started to make a phone call.

"Who?" Rebecca chattered the question.

"I'm calling the doctor."

"It's early."

"I don't care if it's two a.m. You're the governor, for goodness sake!"

Mitch spoke to the answering service for a brief moment and while waiting for a call back from the physician, wrestled open a bottle of Tylenol. She handed two tablets to a very shaky Rebecca and then helped her get a drink of water to wash them down. Mitch had just guided Rebecca's head back to the pillow when the phone rang. Apparently, doctors of governors called back quickly. He also made mansion calls. By the time Mitch had alerted the staff of the situation and prepared cool wet washcloths for Rebecca's forehead, the doctor was on the premises.

He shooed Mitch out of the room just long enough to perform the most necessary aspects of a physical exam, and then he didn't need to go far to locate Mitch. She had pulled up a chair and camped just outside the bedroom, ready to hear the health report.

"She has the flu."

This much Mitch knew, but hearing the diagnosis from a trained professional seemed to allay her fears.

"What should I do?"

"Exactly what you've been doing! And then be ready to contract the stuff yourself in a couple of days."

"It's that contagious?"

"Worst I've seen in a decade."

"Thank you for coming over on such short notice," Mitch said out loud. To herself, she said "Oh, great!"

Left to her own devices, Mitch went back in to check on
Rebecca. She looked pale but a little more relaxed. The
chills had subsided.

"Go away," she demanded in her best "I'm the governor
and you're not" tone of voice.

"Why?" Mitch countered with her "Who are you trying to
fool" voice.

"So you don't get this flu."

"Oh, I think it's a little late for that."

"Do you feel like crap?"

"No."

"Get away while you still can!"

As usual, Mitch ignored direct orders, and once again
began to sponge Rebecca with cool cloths. Already, the
touch of her skin was cooler, and the medication was
making her sleepy.

"I feel better already." she breathed as she remained
otherwise motionless.

"Go to sleep."

"Check in on me?" was the new directive.

"Every ten minutes."

"You're too good to me."

"Well, you know the old saying, 'In sickness and in
health.'"

"Love you."

"You more."

"Not."

"Too."

With that final say, Mitch darkened the room, but left the
door ajar so she could look in noiselessly. Every ten
minutes. Thankfully. Otherwise, Mitch would have
nothing better to do. Except, of course, irritate the staff.

She wandered down to the kitchen and checked out breakfast. Of course, nothing was prepared. Apparently, the staff was on some sort of flu schedule themselves. At least chicken was being stewed for soup. Mitch grabbed a carton of yogurt, a spoon and a cup of coffee. She was back upstairs with her feast with eight minutes to spare. The ladder-back chair just wouldn't do for a vigil. After peeking in on Rebecca, Mitch decided by hook or by crook, to have a recliner brought to her post. It took neither hooks nor crooks, but rather a four-person conference to achieve the miracle of the rearranged furniture. Not only was a chair delivered quietly, but also a table, a lamp, a pillow and a stack of books. If Mitch was the suspicious type, she might have mused that the staff was more than happy to relocate Mitch out in the hallway. Today the hallway, tomorrow the porch. She checked once again on Rebecca and then dozed off herself in the hallway.

Chapter 8

Trish arrived at Max and Rose's promptly at nine a.m. to
facilitate the computer networking. Computer
manufacturers and retailers had finally gotten it through
their heads that not everyone who wanted to buy a
computer had a degree in systems analysis. If you could
plug it in and turn it on, billions were there for taking. Max
and Rose had one advantage. They had a new friend in
Trish, who had done this a time or two before. By lunch
time, or dinner time by old world clock time, they were on
the net and almost convinced to get another phone line.
Rose had taken the first turn so she could prepare lunch,
and was more than happy to turn things over to Max until
she realized she was out of basil. She didn't even have
time to reach for her purse, so gallant was Max. Not even
Trish could volunteer. He was the man of the house and the
designated runner of errands. He bounded out, a happy
husband on a mission.
"You are a very lucky woman," Trish declared to Rose.
"Yes, I am," Rose nodded quickly, even though she seemed
distracted.
"Yesterday was fun," Trish ventured this line of
conversation to check the depths of Rose's distraction.
"Yes, it was."
"Robbie seemed pleased to be in touch with you
electronically."
"Roberta is a good daughter."
"The best," Trish agreed amiably, noting for future
reference Rose's use of Roberta instead of Robbie. Robbie
must have acquired that nickname or bestowed it upon
herself after moving out of the house.
"How long has Roberta worked at the nursing home?"

113

"Not very long. That's why she gets all those night shifts and long hours."

"She lacks seniority, but so does everyone else who hasn't worked there for a while."

Trish mulled this over as she set the table. Couched in the obvious language about seniority was something that nagged at her. Of course, everyone who hadn't worked long at a place didn't have seniority, but some places took longer to establish seniority than others. At most fast food places nowadays, a week or two might net you the assistant manager position. What bothered Trish was the fact that people as far into their retirement years as Max and Rose usually didn't have children just starting out in any field. Unless it was her second or third vocation. Trish decided to just ask for the truth that she really wanted to know.

"How old is Roberta anyway?" Trish asked bluntly. It did seem more polite than asking Rose for her age. Besides, she could already take a good guess at Rose's age, what with the War to End All Wars dating her. Rose had to be in her seventies, give or take. Which meant that even if Roberta was forty, that would mean that Max and Rose would have been in their thirties before the blessed event.

"You should probably ask her yourself. If you dare. You know how women are about their age."

Trish would have dropped the subject then and there, but something about the evasiveness of the normally straightforward Rose made Trish all the more curious. She tried a different tack.

"I'm thirty-five myself. I wonder when it will bother me to tell my age?"

"Everyone is different."

"Not everyone is thirty-five."

Rose just nodded. Silently. Thank the stars, Max arrived with the basil. The express lane must have been empty.

Max carried the bulk of the conversation through lunch as he asked more questions about computers. Once he got the hang of it, he was as enthusiastic as any pre-pubescent male would have been. Trish tried to help Rose with the dishes, but she was shooed out of the kitchen by a firm, unyielding Rose. So, Max and Trish went on another internet excursion before Trish took off.

She flirted with the idea of going home and immediately inquiring about Robbie's age from Robbie herself, but her thoughts meandered until she found herself in front of the governor's mansion. The archway covered in green leaves was beautiful this time of year. She should have called ahead, like Mitch did, albeit at ten thirty in the night. So what if no one was home or they were busy *making up*. The footman or security guard would send her away. The staff was happy to see her, which should have been a clue right there. Apparently, unknown to Trish, they were all but under a court-ordered quarantine and bored to death. Trish's arrival served to alleviate the boredom.

"I'll inform Ms. Tanner that you've arrived."
Mitch bounded down the stairs two minutes later.
"Hiya," Mitch said, including a hug in the greeting.
"Hi back. What's up?"
"Reb's got the flu. The machinery of the state government has ground to a halt around here."
"No one noticed out there."
"Yeah, well things are pretty quiet around here. Have you had lunch? I'll rustle up something."

"No, no thanks. Don't do that! I've already eaten."

"That's right, you were over at Max and Rose's."

"You remembered."

"You told me yesterday."

"I figured you had other things on your mind."

"There's no shortage of things to keep my mind on around here, and here comes one of the more major things."

Trish had a puzzled look on her face, which slowly but completely transformed to slack-jaw admiration at the most gorgeous man she had ever laid eyes on. Greek gods would have been jealous.

"Hello, Jake," Mitch intoned with as much warmth as she could muster.

"Good afternoon."

"Have you met Ms. Sullivan-Weingarten?"

"I haven't yet had that good fortune."

Trish stayed rooted to her spot but simultaneously closed her mouth and extended her hand. He all but kissed it and Mitch experienced what felt like sympathy pains for Rebecca's flu. At least, she hoped that's what they were.

"Is the governor up for a quick meeting?" he asked brazenly.

"She *does* have the flu."

"I don't remember asking for a diagnosis."

"Upstairs. First door on the left."

Jake watched for more signs of disapproval as Mitch pointed in the general direction. He walked off, only looking over his shoulder once, and then he was just checking to see if Trish was still gawking.

"I thought being that handsome was against the law," Trish said in awe when he was out of earshot.

"Whatever."

"You don't agree?" Trish turned back to Mitch.

"Jake's okay, if you go for that kind," Mitch said in a pointed way.

"And even if you don't!"

Mitch didn't reply. At all. For moments on end. Trish finally came to, sort of.

"Oh, dear," Trish finally stated.

"Oh, dear, what?"

"I'm beginning to understand."

"You've achieved enlightenment?"

"Jake has that 'I can cause more trouble than you can' look about him. He's a scoundrel and you're worried that Rebecca is falling for him."

"I am not," Mitch tried to sound aghast at the very notion. It didn't sound as aghast as she had hoped.

"Of course you are. I, myself, would be terrified."

"It's a business arrangement."

"Why are you quitting the campaign? If I were you, I'd stick around just to keep my eye on him."

"Because the only thing I've been able to keep my eye on is envelopes and stamps and telephones and coffee. Besides, I trust Rebecca one-thousand percent and Jake and I are making each other miserable and that's counterproductive."

"And I'll bet he is just finding out that you're quitting?"

"Beats me. I neither called the meeting nor peeked at the agenda."

Just as she said that, Jake came downstairs looking absolutely tickled pink. He didn't bother to say goodbye, but simply walked out the front door. Trish looked only slightly crushed.

"You want to go up and get exposed to the flu?"

"I'll walk up with you, but no kissing."

"Fine," Mitch rolled her eyes in mock exaggeration. "Be that way!"

They walked upstairs and Mitch peered into the room.

"Come on in," Reb said.

"Trish is here," Mitch announced by way of warning.

"I'm decent."

"Couldn't make that claim myself," Trish replied.

Reb smiled. Barely.

"Are you sure you're up for visitors?" Trish asked.

"Come in, just not too close."

"Sure thing."

Trish settled into the straight-back chair as Mitch restocked Rebecca's nightstand with essentials. Water, tissue, medication. Rebecca's briefcase was too open and too handy for Mitch's liking.

"How are you feeling, Sweetie?"

"Better."

"Good! You look better, but I still want you to take it easy."

"Jake was my only appointment."

"And he did keep it brief. That was nice."

"He wishes you would reconsider quitting the campaign."

"Funny, he didn't say a word downstairs."

"I told him I'd lobby you."

"Won't do any good."

"You're so stubborn."

Mitch deflected further conversation with a kiss on Rebecca's forehead.

"You are cooler," she pronounced with optimism.

Rebecca just smiled and then looked at Trish.

"What's new with you?"

"Not much."

"You're writing a book. I'd say that's a lot."

"I'm not to the writing stage yet. I'm still doing research."

"And how is that going?"

"Slowly. Very slowly."
"What's the hang up?"
"How old are you?" Trish asked Rebecca suddenly, right out of the blue.
"Old enough to be governor."
"And you, Mitch, how old are you?"
"I'm old enough to know better than to be governor."
Even Reb got a chuckle out of that one.
"Why do you ask?" Mitch followed up, now very curious.
"I'm testing a theory about women and their ages."
"And let me guess the rest, their reluctance to reveal exact details?"
"Right."
"Why is that important to your research?"
"Rose won't tell me Roberta's age."
"Who's Roberta?" Reb asked as she closed her eyes to rest.
"Rose's daughter."
"I see."
Mitch began to wonder out loud as well, "Maybe Rose thinks that you're trying to back calculate her age."
"I don't think so," Trish stated. "Rose's age is easy to figure out. An entire world war dates her. Why would she be secretive about her daughter's age?"
"Maybe she's not her real daughter?" Mitch guessed.
"That's not it. I've seen pictures. The family resemblance is stunning."
"Maybe it's just old fashioned privacy. People never used to discuss religion, politics or age in polite company."
"There could be another more compelling reason," Reb said as she kept her eyes closed.
"What's your theory?" Trish asked Reb.
"Rose has met Mitch, right."
"Right."

"And so maybe she recognized her from TV. You know, the most famous lesbian in Colorado."

"Okay."

"And so maybe Rose figures that you are gay as well."

"Uh huh."

"And so maybe Rose thinks that your interest in Roberta is more than casual."

Even with the flu, Reb had the knack of getting down to the heart of the matter, quite literally in this case. The silence was palpable. Even Mitch got a clue of the situation and managed to refrain from blurting out a blunt question or two, at least until Trish had time to make a comment. However, Trish seemed to be observing a moment of silence, and quite spontaneously the other two joined in.

Rebecca broke the quietude with the simple yet effective pronouncement, "I'm going to throw up. Anyone who wishes to not witness the event, should leave now!"

Never in her life was Trish so happy to hear words to this effect. It allowed her to retreat quickly and without further comment other that a hasty, "Bye. No need to see me out. Stay here both of you...."

After Trish was safely out of the room, Reb relaxed back into her pillow.

"What?" Mitch was now thoroughly puzzled.

"Just a false alarm," Rebecca explained. Innocently.

"God, you're sneaky," Mitch marveled.

"It's one of my better qualities."

"I can name a couple more."

"Save it for the weekend. I'll be well by then."

Mitch laid down next to Rebecca and before she could think of any more clever remarks, she fell sound asleep.

Trish wound her way through clogged streets. It gave her time to contemplate her next strategy. So far, it consisted of asking Robbie outright about her age. The only decision left was whether to do this through e-mail or phone. Now that she had Robbie's number, she could just give her a friendly, casual call. And then inquire as to her age. And then take her lumps from there. She spent two minutes staring down the phone. It wasn't exactly staring back, but it did have an ominous look about it.

"Oh, for pity's sake, it's a simple, friendly call. Good grief!" she chastised herself. She punched the number in and while the phone rang on the other end, she felt her stomach tighten. One twist for every ring. After three tortuous jangles, Roberta answered. Her "Hello?" sounded halfway between cautious and annoyed.

"Hi, Roberta, it's Trish."

"Oh! Hi!" Robbie's voice brightened immediately. "I'm so glad you called!"

"Are you in the middle of anything?"

"This is a perfect time. I just thought for a minute that you were the people at work calling with another glorious opportunity to work a weekend shift. Again."

"Well, I'm sorry to disappoint," Trish said with an unmistakable tease in her voice. Robbie had the good grace to chuckle.

"I love your sense of humor! What are you up to this evening?"

"I'm being nosy," Trish admitted readily. She was disarmed by Robbie's enthusiasm.

"Oh, really! About what?"

"I was wondering how old you are."

"Thirty-two."

The quick answer sort of threw Trish. She said, "You certainly answered readily."

"No reason not to. And how about you? How old are you?"

"I'm thirty-five."

"You don't look a day over twenty-two!"

"But, you can't see me!"

"Details," Robbie laughed again.

"But, absolutely correct, of course," Trish giggled back.

"So, why are you doing an age check this evening?"

"I was just curious."

"It's because my parents are well into their seventies, right?"

"I just had you pegged in your forties."

"I was a late child."

"That's okay. I'm a late adult. Late for the bus, late for dinner...."

Robbie's infectious laughter struck again and carried them through a few more minutes of fun but aimless chatter. Then, somewhat reluctantly, Trish closed the conversation and hung up. She then considered following up the phone call with an e-mail, but as she sat in her easy chair trying of something else to talk about, she fell asleep.

Chapter 9

Rebecca awoke to the sound of retching, and it wasn't hers for a change. She reached over sleepily to awaken Mitch, and realized she was the one doing the retching. Without delay, she called the doctor, who balked at making a house call for someone other than the governor. A terse, pointed conversation helped change his mind. Something to the effect of, "Get over here or you're fired." Flu bugs tended to make the ruling class cranky.

Next, Reb informed the kitchen staff of the need for double doses of hot tea, cherry Jell-O, and chicken soup. Yes, in that order! They were almost overjoyed. Almost. By this time, Mitch had eased her way to the bathroom doorway and leaned against the frame for support. Rebecca mustered up all her strength and walked over to help Mitch back to bed. Even with help, it was a struggle.

"Come on. The doctor will be here soon."
"I'll bet he's thrilled."
"He's employed. We'll work on thrilled later."
Mitch's fevered brain took none of this in as she collapsed on her side of the bed. Reb tucked her in and then snuggled in herself. It didn't matter now. Germs had been exchanged all too successfully. They must have both dozed off. The reluctant physician was there before Mitch could throw up again. He administered the same type of miracle drug that Rebecca had been taking, and then checked Reb's progress as long as he had been called out. Five minutes and three-hundred and eighty-nine dollars later, he was gone.

"I should call Trish," Mitch muttered, "and warn her about this stuff."

"You think she's been exposed?"

"I'm sure of it. Just look at me."

"Except you had a lot more exposure."

"You should see me in a hospital gown."

"I already have."

"Oh yeah," Mitch nodded as she observed the phone in her hand. She struggled to remember what she had planned to do.

"Call Trish," Reb said.

"Why?"

"To see if she has the flu!"

"Oh yeah," Mitch blinked a couple of times. "What's her number?"

"I don't know."

"I'm too weak to look it up."

"Call information."

"What's their number?"

"Holy God, just give me the phone!"

Mitch complied, groaned, stood back up and stumbled to the bathroom. So much for miracle cure. Upon her return to bed, which must have easily been a week or two since she left it, she remembered Reb saying something about Trish sounding "okay so far" before Mitch passed out entirely.

So went the morning and most of the rest of the day. By evening, Mitch's temperature had returned from the upper stratosphere and moderated around 101 degrees. Barely bearable. If comfort was to be had, it stemmed from Reb's steady recovery. She was downright perky, which in any other situation would have been irritating as hell. In this

124

case, Mitch welcomed it. After all, she was now the beneficiary of coddling as only Reb could coddle.

"Tell me something," Reb asked as she fluffed Mitch's pillows.

"Sure."

"How do you manage to remain so alluring in the throes of influenza?"

"Oh please, I'm not within flying distance of alluring."

"Oh, yes you are."

"Must be the helplessness. I know that really turns you on."

"Really?"

"Yeah."

"I didn't know that!"

"Well, now you know. What's for dinner?"

"You're hungry?"

"Finally."

"I'll get you something."

"Where's the staff?"

"In hiding."

"What's new?"

"Now, now, you know you've been getting better treatment."

"I still don't quite feel the red carpet squishing between my toes."

"These things take time."

"Let's just call for a pizza."

"Oh, I don't *think* so!" Reb tutted back, still pushing a liquid diet.

"Please, please, please!" Mitch begged.

"You're carrying the helpless act a little too far, don't you think!"

"Is it working?"

"All too well. Are you sure you feel up to pizza?"

"Anything but anchovies."

"Chicken."

"Chicken pizza?"

"Never mind!"

Reb placed the call and then alerted the staff to keep watch. Not for one pizza, mind you, but for one of every kind. She figured the staff needed a break as well. And there might even be leftovers.

Mitch and Reb spent the time they had together like silver coins, cherishing a quiet dinner together. So it wasn't candle light and roses. At least they could hold off on the Tylenol and Pepto-Bismol for an hour. Mitch finally remembered to inquire about campaign managers.

"How's Jake? Have you talked to him?"

"He's sick as a dog."

Knowing better, Mitch made no outward demonstration. On the inside, she was dancing. Reb would have been mildly disappointed in Mitch had she seen the delight, so Mitch masked it well.

"I hope he gets better soon."

"Gets well," corrected Reb.

"What?"

"Get well is the correct phrase."

"Uh huh," Mitch mumbled. Heaven forbid he would get *better*.

"And Trish is okay so far."

"Well, she didn't have much contact with you."

"Neither did Jake!" Reb made the point clear.

"I didn't mean to imply otherwise. It must just be in the genes."

"Right."

Five more minutes of golden silence was either going to be punctuated by more talk about who had been more exposed to whom, or snoring on the part of Mitch. The latter won out as Mitch slipped into garlic-laden dreams.

One good solid night's sleep did wonders for them and Reb was back at work. Mitch chose to lounge around, a promise made to Reb who in return for Mitch's good behavior in bed today might just portend better behavior in bed later on. It was an easy promise to keep and Mitch slept through the day. Not so with Trish

Maybe it was just her curious nature hard at work that led her once again to the door of Rose Goldstein. By pure chance, Max was gone. Between getting new tires, an oil change, and a headlight repaired, his day was booked. Maybe it was just Trish's imagination, but Rose seemed hesitant to invite Trish in.
"Did I catch you at a bad time?" she asked politely.
"Oh, no…not really. Come in. Max isn't here to talk to you."
"That's okay. You and I usually find things to talk about. Like, cherry pie recipes and such."
"Of course," Rose led the way to the kitchen. When Max was present, discussions occurred in more formal rooms. Now that it was just Rose and Trish, the kitchen table would do. Rose poured coffee for Trish and warmed up her own before settling in her seat.
"I talked to Roberta," Trish dove right in, hoping to get somewhere this time.
"Did you want some pie?" Rose stood to serve without waiting for an affirmative answer.

"Sure, sounds great. Anyway, Roberta certainly is a charming person, a lot like you and Max."

"We did our best."

"And it shows. Even for a young woman, she is poised and mature."

"She's not *that* young."

"Thirty-two. She told me."

"You asked?"

"Well, you know me. Nosy Trish."

Rose didn't utter a syllable.

"Then, Roberta referred to herself as a 'late child.'"

Rose trembled as she raised her coffee cup to her lips. Of course, it could just be the effect of seventy-plus years of wear and tear on shoulder and elbow joints.

"Which just means that you and Max waited a while before you had children."

"Child," Rose corrected quickly.

"Child," Trish nodded agreement. "And that's interesting because in all the reading I've done about the years immediately following the Holocaust, it was prevalent that many former Jewish survivors married quickly and started families. For a while, the birthrate of the area far surpassed the birthrate of everywhere else in the world. The common age of that generation is at least fifteen to twenty years older than Roberta."

"Not everyone follows a set pattern," Rose clipped her answer. Clearly, she was agitated with the topic of conversation, but clearly not so agitated as to ask Trish to leave. Yet.

Trish forged ahead. "Tell me about your pattern."

"We had a child when God decided we should have a child."

"Sure took God a long time to decide, didn't it?"

"I had some…problems," Rose explained, and then lapsed into what seemed to be frightened silence.

Without hesitation, Trish asked, "What kind of problems?"

"The usual kind of problems! It's rather personal and I'll thank you not to pry."

"Female problems?" Trish ignored the request.

Rose snorted angrily, but Trish knew instinctively it wasn't her questioning that brought the reaction. The only thing left was the wording. Choice of two: female, problems. Since Rose herself had discussed "problems", that left "female" as the only remaining choice.

"You had problems, but not female problems?"

"I had problems."

Trish occasionally had a bright idea. Two or three per hour in case anyone was keeping track. Although a few minutes past due, this idea tumbled from her brain to her lips at the speed of sound.

"Sounds to me like you had 'male' problems."

Rose sat in stunned silence, a cross between anger and fear played across her countenance.

"You don't know what you're talking about!"

"I *know* I don't know what I'm talking about!" Trish agreed. "That's why I need to keep guessing or asking."

"I don't want to talk about this anymore."

Trish studied the woman across the table. If ever she had met anyone who wanted to unburden their soul, this was that person.

"Tell me what happened, Rose." Trish asked gently.

"It was difficult."

"What was difficult?"

"The pregnancy."

"Robbie's pregnancy?"

129

"And the others."

"The others?" Trish knew they were right on the very precipice. Just keep the questions slow and steady.

"The other pregnancies."

"I understand now."

"No, you don't *understand*!"

"You had a miscarriage?"

Tears began to well up in Rose's eyes and spill down her beautiful face. Trish had seen Max cry, almost from the instant they had met. But never Rose. Strong, resolute Rose. It had to be agonizing for her.

"I worked during the war," Rose wiped her eyes, but the stubborn tears taunted her by reappearing. Now that the tear ducts had opened, as many tear drops as possible were escaping.

"What kind of work did you do?" Trish probed. It was quite the leap from the topic of pregnancy, but it might be the logical course for Rose.

"Worked isn't the right word," Rose was looking back through the shrouded mist of memories.

"What word is the right word?"

"Slaved. I was forced slave labor during the war."

"I've read about that."

"I lived it!" Rose punctuated each word with a sharp rap on the table. Even the coffee cup was rattled. Trish, however much she was surprised by Rose's vehemence, kept her voice steady. So far, the tactic had worked.

"Tell me about living through it."

Rose glanced around the room as if someone would be listening or watching. A habit from the war years.

"No one believed Hitler would do what he did. No one."

"Not even your family?"

"Especially my family. I was an only child, just like Roberta, but for different reasons, of course!"
Trish nodded. One person at the table knew these "different reasons". Soon, maybe both would know.
"My Mama had a limp. Very slight. Her left leg was a little shorter than her right leg. She didn't last long at all. One flick of the wrist and she was in a different line."
"What about your father?"
"My father was *brave*. Too brave for his own good."
Rose's voice trailed off, leaving Trish to worry that the story was over before it had gotten a good start.
"He was shot. By a guard."
"Why?"
"He was bending over helping another prisoner who had stumbled."
"That doesn't sound like bravery-"
"What do you know about bravery!" Rose cut through Trish's comment.
"I sorry. I didn't mean that the way it came out. I'm sure your father was a brave man. I guess I just expected something more along the lines of rescuing a child or leading a charge or planning an escape."
"Any act to challenge the Nazis was brave!"
"I see now."
"I hope so!"
"So, you witnessed the death of both parents?"
"No. I told you. I was working. We were separated early in the war."
"So, how did you find out."
"I asked questions."
Trish nodded. Fair enough.
"Did Max see any of his family die?"
"Yes."

"But you didn't."

"That's right."

"When you and Max talk about that?"

"We don't talk about that."

Trish didn't quite understand this concept.

"You mean Max doesn't know your parents were killed in the war?"

"Of course he does!" Rose snapped back. "We just don't talk about it."

"What else does Max know about your wartime experiences?"

"All he needs to know."

"You mentioned that you did slave labor. What kind of work did you do?"

"Hard work."

"Like digging ditches?"

"No."

"Well, then, maybe carrying rocks?"

"No."

Exasperated, Trish tried one more time. "What kind of hard work, exactly?"

"I made bullets."

It took a moment for the fact to settle in Trish's mind. What an irony. Making bullets for the enemy.

"Did you feel guilty about that?"

"Of course not! I fixed the bullets."

"Fixed?"

"What's the word I'm looking for?"

Trish thought a second or two and then came up with the word "Sabotaged?"

"That's the word!"

"You can do that?"

"You learn how very quickly. The guns would misfire if you did it right."

What a clever woman, Trish thought to herself. So clever, in fact, that she was deftly steering the conversation away from whatever secrets she wanted to remain buried.

"Was there something about munitions work that caused problems with your reproductive system?" Trish cut to the chase.

"The Kapo in charge caused problems," Rose blurted out and then, realizing what she had said, simply stopped talking. Trish waited for tears to reappear, but they didn't. Just stone-faced silence. It was as if Rose was watching the movie of her life spin off an imaginary reel. Except that is wasn't a talkie. Knowing that both of them probably needed a break from the inquisition, Trish made an announcement.

"I have a good idea!"

"Um."

"Let's go have lunch!"

"I can cook you something if you're hungry."

"Of course you could, but let's go out instead. Let's have a 'girls' day out'!"

"Should we wait and invite Max?"

"Is he a girl?" Trish said with the hint of a smile.

"Not the last time I looked," Rose countered back, showing just a tiny flash of humor.

"Then, he's on his own."

"I should leave him a note."

"That's a good idea."

As Rose composed the brief message, Trish marveled at how they had made the leap from resistance to camaraderie. Maybe the only thing Rose needed was a persistent questioner. Rose freshened up and then climbed into the passenger side of Trish's truck. She had never ridden in something quite this big before, except for the Army transport that she had been placed in right after the war. She didn't mention that to Trish, she was having too much fun showing off. They drove to a nearby restaurant that was famous for its buffet. All the delectable food you could eat for $10.95 plus tax and tip. As they approached the door, Trish felt Rose's iron grip on her arm.

"What's wrong?" Trish asked.

"Do they have a menu here as well?"

"Yes, they do."

"Oh, good."

Rose's grip relaxed. A little. Thanks to the early hour, they were seated immediately and Rose studied the limited menu like it was midterms.

"The buffet is great, but I guess you are trying to keep an eye on your cholesterol, or something?"

"I think I'll just have some chicken."

"And pass up all those goodies over there?"

"I'm just not a buffet person."

"Afraid you'll eat too much?" Trish couldn't help but ask questions.

"I just don't like to stand in line for food."

Trish turned this phrase over in her mind and then figured out the situation.

"It reminds you, doesn't it."

Rose simply nodded.

"I have an idea."

"An idea?"

"Let's both order a buffet and then I'll serve you."

"I couldn't let you do that."

"I do it all the time. You tell me what you want and I'll get it for you."

"You do this often?"

"I help serve dinners to homeless people during holidays. It's one of my specialties, but I need to practice all the time."

"Are you sure?"

"It would be my pleasure."

And so it was. Rose savored the company more than the food, but both were satisfying. Over dessert, Trish noted, "We had a rough morning, didn't we?"

Rose nodded. Trish worried that tears would resurface, but Rose stayed tough.

"And I know that we should talk more."

"But not right now."

"No, not right now. In the meantime, I have another good idea!"

"You have many good ideas today."

"Let's go make a call on a sick friend."

"Who?"

"Mitch."

"The Mitch we met at your house is sick today?"

"One in the same."

"Will she mind us just dropping in?"

"It's *her* specialty."

"I see," Rose said, although she didn't.

Once again, they climbed into Trish's truck and revved across town.

The Governor's Mansion was quiet this afternoon and Trish banged on the front door. Security gave them a pass after searching Rose's purse. She didn't prove to be a security risk, unless they were afraid of being attacked by an honest-to-goodness lace hankie and three tubes of pale pink lipstick.

135

Someone went to inform Mitch that company had arrived and before anyone bothered to take drink requests, Mitch bounded downstairs.

"Well, hello you two!" Mitch greeted breezily. For a person who had been sick with the flu for two days, she sounded all better.

"We just stopped in to see how you're doing," Trish explained. "Hope you don't mind?"

"Of course I don't mind! It's so nice to see you again, Mrs. Goldstein."

"Please, call me Rose."

"A rose by any other name…what's the rest of that quote?"

"Smells as sweet?" Trish guessed.

"Isn't as thorny?" Rose offered.

"I never was much of a thespian," Mitch admitted as she ushered the guests into the Palm Room. It was the ivory and white room with the white leather furniture. When Mitch had first seen it, it reminded her of pictures of Elvis Presley's living room at Graceland. Usually, Mitch didn't entertain guests here, preferring the parlor or kitchen. But the arrival of someone as special as Rose Goldstein demanded the best. For all the formal trappings, the best word that came to mind to describe Mitch right now would be 'cozy'. She was garbed in flannel jammies, fuzzy slippers and a thick, sparkling white robe with the name of the hotel from which she 'borrowed' it monogrammed on the pocket. Of course the charge had appeared on her bill many months ago, but she still considered herself a thief the likes of Cary Grant in Monaco.

"So, what have the two of you been up to?"

"Trish and I had lunch. She took me to a special place."

"Trish is good at that sort of thing," Mitch nodded and then winked at Trish when Rose wasn't looking.

"We went to Carpelli's," Trish elaborated.

"Oh yeah." Mitch mustered as much enthusiasm over a buffet report as one can after having the stomach flu for a day and a half.

"And it was wonderful, and Trish was wonderful," beamed Rose.

"Sounds…wonderful," Mitch agreed, hoping that they wouldn't go into much more detail.

"If I had known that Trish was bringing me here, I would have dressed up more!"

"You look just fine," Mitch assured her. This coming from a woman in fuzzy slippers! It seemed to do the trick.

"So, where's Reb?" Trish asked about the governor. "Reb" was slowly finding its way into casual conversation as a nickname for Rebecca. It suited her well, making her sound like the rebel that she was.

"Probably in a meeting."

"Reb?" Rose asked.

"Rebecca."

"Oh, the governor honorable. Or the honorable governor. Which is it?"

"Just call her Reb."

"You call the Honorable governor 'Reb'?"

"Among other things," Mitch now winked Rose's direction. From the hallway they heard, "Honey, I'm home…."

"Speak of the devil! Here she is now."

"Her honor, the Governor?" Rose was flustered.

"Just Rebecca," Mitch tried to ease her guest. Then she called out, "We're in Graceland!"

Rebecca strode in, resplendent in a sapphire blue dress. As always, Mitch's heart jumped. Rose must have heard the

137

beat. She stood up, almost at attention. Trish stood as well
and handled the introductions.

"Rose Goldstein, this is Rebecca, Rebecca, this is my
friend, Rose."

"It's so nice to meet you," Rebecca turned on that smooth
charm reserved for heads of state, fellow governors and
radio talk show hosts.

"Thank you, your honor. It's a pleasure to meet you and to
visit this glorious house."

"Did you get the full tour yet?"

"No."

"Well, let me show you around as soon as I check on my
favorite patient here."

Rebecca studied Mitch for a moment, particularly the
stolen slippers. Ohhh, that Cary Grant was sneaky!

"Well, don't you look spiffy!" Reb said as she leaned down
to kiss Mitch. She figured that they had already exchanged
all the flu germs that they could. Then, she announced,
"I'm going upstairs to change. Come with me, Rose, and
keep me company. Is Doozie upstairs?" Reb asked over
her shoulder.

"Asleep in bed."

"Come up and meet Doozie," Reb escorted Rose to the
stairway.

"Doozie?" Rose asked with just a hint of wariness.

"The watchdog of the house."

"Is it mean?" Rose queried suddenly.

"She's a beagle pup. You scratch her tummy and you'll be
her friend for life."

After they were out of earshot, Mitch admitted, "A lot like
the governor and me, wouldn't you say?"

"I'm sure the secret is out now," Trish stated flatly.

"Were we still keeping secrets?" Mitch asked with concern.

138

"I haven't come out to Rose and Max, if that's what you mean."

"So, you're only guilty by association so far."

"Sounds like Nazi Germany."

"Something she knows about."

"All too well."

What an adorable puppy!" Rose confirmed and she petted the Beagle.

"I got her for Mitch as a surprise present. The surprise was that I had to buy about ten new pairs of slippers. Including Mitch's fuzzy ones that are really mine."

"I imagine so."

Rebecca took a scant two minutes to change, all the while carrying on a friendly conversation with Rose through the bathroom door. They talked about puppies, flower gardens, and Trish's big truck as Rose took a much needed powder-room break and Rebecca took a rest from panty hose and dresses. Then, after Rose came out of the bathroom, she tried to clarify things for the governor.

"I read the papers about you and Mitch."

"We do get our share of news coverage."

"I don't approve of the bad things people do to you."

"Well, we have to take the bad with the good in this business."

"And I can't say I entirely understand these…things."

Rebecca took Rose by the hand and motioned for her to sit on the bed. Then, Rebecca sat next to her. Doozie jumped up and snuggled between them.

"You mean, about Mitch and me?"

"I don't want to put you on the spot, so you can just tell an old woman to mind her own business if it suits you."

"I'd never do that. In fact, I had the same reaction, at first."

"You did?"

"I'm not sure I entirely understand things myself. All I know is that Mitch has made my life special in ways I couldn't have imagined two years ago."

"There's more to life than feeling special."

"Tell me what you mean?" Rebecca asked kindly.

"There's children."

"I have a daughter."

"You do!"

"Yes. She's had her share of press coverage as well."

"But you had her before...."

"Yes, I did. But Mitch and I have discussed having children."

"You have!"

"Mitch is waiting until the right time."

"She'd better hurry!"

"I agree."

Rose seemed to be weighing another question.

"What else would you like to know?" Reb prompted.

"It's a silly question."

"Try me."

"Which one of you is, you know, the man?"

Reb had to think about this one for a second or two.

"Don't worry. I don't need to know," Rose hurriedly admitted, feeling ill-at-ease.

"Of course you do," Reb said, and then followed up, "I just want to make sure I understand the question. You're asking which one of us is more aggressive? Like sexually?"

Rose only nodded, now thoroughly embarrassed.

"It's okay. I understand your curiosity. I'd have to say that as far as being the man is concerned, I think we take turns."

"You can do that?"

"It sort of balances out. In the long run."

140

Now, even Rebecca was all out of things to talk about.
"Let's go downstairs and have a drink."
Together, they descended the stairway, only to find that
Mitch, as usual, was one good idea ahead of them. Coffee,
tea, and sherry were ready and waiting. Trish chose coffee
since she was driving, which allowed Rose to indulge in
half a glass of sherry. Mitch stuck to tea for medicinal
purposes, and Rebecca followed Rose's lead with the hard
stuff.
"Just you wait until I tell Mr. Goldstein that I had cocktails
at the Governor's Mansion!" Rose declared by way of a
toast.
"Tell Mr. Goldstein that he has a standing invitation,"
Rebecca assured as she sipped her wine.

They talked like they were taking tea with the queen and
then Trish prodded Rose when it was time to depart. The
early departure was based on two things. First was the
declining state of Mitch. Despite her assurances, Mitch
was fading fast. Not even Super Mitch could vanquish the
flu in record time. Second was Trish's gnawing curiosity
about the next chapter of Rose's story.

As they left the mansion, Mitch asked Rebecca whatever
took them so long upstairs.
"She wanted to know who the man was," Reb explained.
"And what did you tell her?"
"The truth. I told her I'm the man!"
"So, go fix a car!"
"Shut up!" Reb giggled.
"I have a better idea. Take me to bed."
"I'll take you to bed, but that's all you get."
"Now, that's my man!"

141

After helping Rose into the truck, Trish drove through westbound traffic.

"I wanted to show you a couple more things, as long as we're out for the day."

"Will we run late?"

"I hope so. Why?"

"I don't want Max to worry."

"You can call him," Trish handed her the cell phone. Rose appeared to think it over.

"You don't like cell phones?"

"Don't they cause brain damage?"

Trish mused to herself. A Holocaust survivor leery of a phone.

"I can call him," she offered.

"Not while you're driving!"

"We'll be parking in a few minutes."

Five minutes later, Trish pulled up and parked in a beautiful tree-lined neighborhood.

"See that house over there," Trish pointed.

"That great big house?"

"Right. Mitch bought that house."

"But, doesn't she live at the mansion. Or does she?"

"Well, yes and no. But she doesn't live here. She gave this house away. I'll show you the other house."

As they drove off, Rose asked, "Who lives there?"

"A family who had been homeless. Hey, we forgot to call Max!"

"That's okay. We left him a note. He will know that I'm safe."

Trish had one more stop to make with Rose, and was frankly beginning to feel like the Ghost of Christmas Past when she pulled into the dirt driveway of Mitch's ranch house. They called it that name because it was rather rural in appearance, but that was the extent of its resemblance to a real ranch. The house was small and cramped, but the area surrounding the place was pure prairie. Weeds, dirt, and a splintery gazebo rounded out the landscaping so far. Mitch just hadn't had time to do much with it. Being "first lady" of Colorado took up more time than she had ever expected.

"She lives here?"
"Only on occasion."
"Occasion?"
"Oh, you know, like *argument* occasions, *barbecue* occasions…one time, Mitch's old girlfriend lived here."
"And, you're like Mitch," Rose tentatively ventured.
"Well, if you mean I've had an old girlfriend, you'd be right. I've had a few old girlfriends."
"You don't have one now?"
"Not currently," Trish felt a slight twinge over Judy. Such a beautiful woman to have such ugly prejudices. What a waste. But what a pleasant surprise to come out to Rose and find her so easy to talk to.
"I've even hung out here once or twice," Trish admitted.
"Let's go in for a while. There's always a beer in the fridge or coffee on the shelf."
"I wouldn't care for a beer, but I could avail myself of the powder room. If it has one?"
"Modern plumbing, I promise."
"It's okay with Mitch?"
"Can you imagine how much trouble I'd be in with Mitch if I *didn't* let you use the bathroom!"

The house was a little musty, which was a good sign. No recent arguments, or old girlfriends. As Rose used the bathroom, Trish started a pot of coffee. She pulled the carafe out early to get the strongest cup and then allowed the rest to brew undisturbed. The first cup needed a few spoons of dry creamer and lumpy sugar to make it drinkable. Trish was sitting on the couch when Rose reappeared.

"Have some coffee!"

"Maybe just half a cup to wash down the sherry."

"Cups are in the cabinet right over the coffee maker."

"Okay."

Rose knew her way around a kitchen and soon settled in an overstuffed chair with her sherry chaser.

"Tell me the rest of the story," Trish asked directly.

"I can't."

"You've never told anyone, have you?"

"It isn't something people discuss."

"I understand why you didn't want to talk right after the war. Many people didn't. But why didn't you talk later?"

"I've tried to put it out of my mind. It did no good to relive things over and over. What's done is done."

"Sometimes telling helps. Didn't you tell anyone?"

"I answered the questions of my doctor. A little."

"But not all."

"He knew without discussion. He was a smart man."

"I want you to tell me."

"If I tell you, it will be just like it's happening all over again."

"I'll stay right here with you."

"Max might worry."

"I'll call him so he won't worry."

"No," Rose stated resolutely. "I will call him."

144

She talked to Max in a light-hearted way that belied her emotional state. No, she wouldn't be so late that he would need to take cooking lessons!

"Drink your carrot juice," was substituted for "good-bye."

"You and Max have a good marriage."

"We work on it."

"So, you had a miscarriage, or several?"

"I was lucky to have Roberta."

"Was it the brutal prisons? Or the starvation? Or the vitamin deficiency?"

"Did you, in all your studies about the Holocaust, ever hear about the sabotage of the crematoria at Auschwitz-Birkenau?"

Trish shook her head, trying to recall such a precise detail in all the fuzzy multitudes of historical data.

"People were hanged for that."

"In front of the other prisoners?"

"Did the Nazis do it any differently?"

"Not that I know of," Trish gave the point to Rose.

"They hanged them in shifts."

"Shifts? Like clothing?"

"No. They hanged two in front of one group and then two in front of another group."

"And you saw this?"

"No, I heard about it."

"How was that possible?"

"Connections."

"People talked? Wasn't that punishable, often by death?"

"Being Jewish was punishable by death."

"But, what's all this got to do with you and your miscarriages?"

"More than four girls were involved in the sabotage."

"And you were one of them!" Trish was beginning to understand. "You talked earlier about the bullets."

"When you don't fill bullets with powder, you substitute dirt. The gun misfires, later, but the powder is collected, hidden, gathered after the end of a work shift. When you worked, you had a little leeway. Not much."

"Leeway?"

"Some days, your working clothes had a pocket. They were forbidden, but people were clever. Other times, you had the powder stuck to your clothes, scalp, and skin. Eventually, they had enough to attempt to blow up the crematoria."

"The women?"

"Men did part of it. We supplied the explosive powder. They made the device. They were hanged as well."

"My God! What a brave thing to do. How did you avoid being caught?"

"Oh, I was caught," Rose admitted readily enough.

"Obviously you weren't hanged."

"No."

"Why not?" Trish pushed for an answer.

"I guess I was just lucky."

"And the other girls weren't?"

"I paid a different price. Not willingly. Not *ever* willingly!"

"What did you have to do?"

"The Kapo. I was pretty, I guess. Now, don't think I'm being big headed. You know, some of the Nazis even passed laws about ugly people. They took pictures of what they called *ugly* people and then killed them, holding the pictures as justification for the execution."

Anytime Rose went into a long explanation, Trish knew they were getting to the heart of the story. She kept on track.

"And so you were pretty?"

"The Kapo did…things." Rose slowed to a stop.

"Like, sexual things?"

Rose only nodded.

"You were raped."

"Again and again."

"And that damaged you for future childbearing?"

"In a way."

"In what way?"

"I was one of those girls who continued to have my normal functions. You know."

"Your period?"

"Many girls lost theirs right at the beginning. The shock. The work. The starvation diet. But not reliable Rose. I could have mine in Hell. In a way, I did. And then, it stopped, and I didn't think anything about it."

"You were pregnant."

"Yes."

"And then what happened?"

"He was frightened out of his wits. A strange predicament for a brutal man. He had done the unthinkable, fathering a half-Jewish child. Out of his fear, he solved his problem."

"He didn't kill you?"

"He killed a part of me. It hurt. I bled for two days."

Trish watched as Rose grew pale, almost as if she was still bleeding. In a way, she was. Her grieving heart was full of wounds still festering after fifty years of quarantine.

"He aborted the pregnancy."

"Against my will. I have scars to prove that as well."

"You don't need to prove anything to me, Rose."

147

"I know."

She began to sniff tears back. What a brave woman she had been, both now, and back through the years. She was a war hero who would never wear a medal.

"You can imagine that I had some internal damage."

"Yes, I can."

"And that's the story of why Roberta was a late child."

"You were lucky to have her at all. And you've never told this story to anyone?"

"No."

"Why?"

"Have you researched yet what went on after the war?"

Trish shook her head, "No."

"You have read about people tracking down Nazi war criminals, haven't you?"

"Oh, yes, I have, now that you mention it. Those are interesting stories."

"So, you don't think the opposite is true as well?"

"I'm not following?"

"Many of the Jews who were liberated from the war camps were killed. Some by angry civilians who still, after all that time, blamed Jews for their problems. But as I tried to keep guard and protect myself, I saw a trend. Four girls had been hanged in the camps. More than four girls were involved. One by one, they began to disappear, the instigators, you know. One was killed in Sweden, one in Kielce, one in Bialystok, one here, one there."

"You thought it was an organized effort?"

"I know it was an organized effort."

"This is an amazing story."

"You are not going to write about me. *I won't allow it*! Not after all these years of hiding, protecting my family. No one can know. That's why I don't talk!"

148

"I would never write about someone without gaining permission first, Rose. You can trust me with your story. Besides, I'm trying to write a story about the experiences of gay people during the Holocaust."

This news put Rose's mind at ease. That, and the fact that after all these years, Rose had unburdened herself. In her mind, she had been a hunted fugitive for years. Hiding out in America from the terror of the Nazi grip that, to her way of thinking had extended past 1945, had been her obsession. The stigma of the abortion was also understandable. Years ago, women would be to blame no matter who did what. In many places today, that still held true.

Rose drank her coffee and then stood up. She was ready to leave. Trish switched off the coffee pot, emptied the coffee and grounds and then ushered her out to the truck. When they arrived at the Goldstein house, Max was there, obediently drinking his carrot juice.

"You've been to see the Governor!" he exclaimed upon hearing the censored version of the day's events.

"And you are invited over someday as well."

"That day, *someday*, isn't on any calendar that I've ever seen."

"It will be, right, Trish?"

"I'll see to it!"

"Now, let me alone and I'll cook supper."

"I've had my appetizer." Max pointed to his empty carrot juice glass. "Take your time. You're staying for a meal, aren't you, Trish?"

"As wonderful as that sounds, I have something else I must do."

Reluctantly, Max ushered Trish to the door. They parted with a spontaneous hug.

"You have a great wife," Trish informed him.

"I know," he agreed readily, if somewhat confused as to what brought on the unsolicited comment.

Trish drove around town for a time before she phoned Mitch.

"How are you feeling?"

"The governor made me go to bed."

"Alone?"

"Yeah, darn it. She's in a meeting."

"Are you going to be up for company again tomorrow?"

"Sure, you coming over?"

"Whatever is best for you."

"How about lunch out. I'm going stir crazy around here."

"Sounds great. When and where?"

"Pasternack's at one."

"Okay."

Rebecca heard the tail end of the conversation as she entered the bedroom.

"You think you'll be well by tomorrow?"

"I'm well now. Come over here and I'll prove it."

"What are you going to do, pretend I'm a theorem and you're a mathematician?"

"Just call me the Trig Master!"

"Trig Master?"

"Hey, you want good jokes, watch Letterman. You want some tender loving, come over here."

"Let's see…Letterman or the Trig Master. Hummmm. Tough choice," Rebecca smiled as she settled next to

Mitch. To no one's surprise, they were sound asleep before the monologue even began.

Chapter 10

Lunch at Pasternack's was interesting. Years of friendship had created a link between Mitch and Trish that was difficult to explain, but nevertheless ubiquitous.

"What's wrong?" Mitch started in soon after they were seated.

"Nothing's wrong."

"You look a little washed out. Are you getting this flu bug?"

"No, I just couldn't get to sleep last night."

"What's on your mind?"

"I need to ask a favor."

"Of me? Sure, anything. Name it."

"Actually, I need two or three favors. And not all from you."

"Okay, so let's go one at a time. What do you need and from whom?"

"Max is green with envy at Rose's tea party at the mansion."

"I'll have Rebecca arrange a dinner. Next week, maybe?"

"Whenever. I know her schedule is nuts."

"I'll work on it. What else?"

"I need tickets to the Holocaust Museum in Washington."

"I thought you could just call?"

"There's a long waiting line, it would take a while to get in."

"And you want Rebecca to exert some influence?"

"I didn't know if it was possible."

"With Governors, all things are possible."

"It won't get her into trouble?"

"Here's my philosophy. What good is a position of power if you can't abuse it once in a while, especially for a good cause."

"So, you'll ask her?"

"Sure. Now, what else do you need?"

"You're a great friend."

"Yeah?"

"My best friend."

"Uh huh?"

"I want you to go with me."

"To the Holocaust Museum?"

"Right. I would really want you to be there with me."

"Why me?"

"Because I rely on your strength."

Mitch thought it over for a moment. "I'll go with you."

"You don't mind. Just like that?"

"I'll run the idea by Rebecca."

"That's a smart idea. Always run these things by the significant other. That's my motto."

"Okay. Dinner with Max, tickets to museum, field trip permission slips. Got it."

Even with all of this settled, Mitch still picked up on an uneasiness. Something else was bothering Trish, but she was unwilling to delve any deeper. Three things on the list was enough for now.

Dinner for Rose and Max was a snap. Rebecca had a free evening on Wednesday. It hadn't started out as free, but it ended up free. Max and Rose were just that important. Tickets to the Unites States Holocaust Museum and Memorial were a little more difficult to secure. Difficult, but not mission impossible. Darn, they didn't have to call

Tom Cruise. The field trip took a little more explanation, which Mitch made up as she went along.

"Trish has been through a lot."

"She has."

"And I haven't been as good a friend as I could have been. Even you have helped me see that."

"I have?"

"And I know that the Holocaust Museum is a traumatic experience for anyone, and it must be really difficult for someone who is Jewish. Trish has asked for some support. I want to go and provide that support."

"And so you shall."

"So, it's okay?"

"Absolutely."

"Trish made me ask," Mitch lied.

"Trish is a wise woman."

"Yes, she is."

"And how will you steel yourself so that you can provide that support?"

"I don't know. I haven't thought that far ahead."

Trish avoided e-mailing Robbie until after the Goldsteins had been honored guests of the governor. She would have put it off even longer, since she felt ill-at-ease with Rose's secrets, but somehow, it seemed rude. Besides, Robbie had been in touch right after the dinner, so a reply was necessary. In reference to Trish's age question, Robbie began her e-mail humorously.

Dear Curious One,

I've heard so many wonderful stories about the now-famous dinner at the mansion, that I'm really grateful that my parents have met you. They were wowed beyond belief by the state dining room, those walnut chairs and table must be something to see. And the chandeliers! My Mom went on and on about those. (A little like what I seem to be doing right now, I guess.) Well, I just really wanted to thank you again for how nice you've been to my folks. I'd better get some sleep. I feel a double shift lurking somewhere this weekend.

Later,
Robbie

Trish found her eyes reading over the note again and again as if it held some psychic meaning for her. She asked herself bluntly if she was using her friendship with Mitch and ultimately, Rebecca, to impress Robbie in this round-about manner. "Using" was such a strong word. Maybe "relying on" was more like it. Trish had counted on Mitch to make the evening special, and she had delivered a home run. And Rebecca! What a total and complete charmer she had been, regaling the Goldsteins with a half a dozen humorous anecdotes about politics in Colorado. Trish recalled the evening with a twinge of envy. Mitch and Rebecca were the luckiest two people on the planet and the fact that they were gay didn't seem to faze the Goldsteins one little bit. Trish surfaced from her reverie to reply.

Dear Robbie,

It was my pleasure to be able to share the evening with your folks. Mitch and the Governor really outdid themselves. You probably heard about the Beef Wellington and chocolate pie. Only about ten-thousand calories per serving. And even though I know that your parents felt every bit the honored guests, truly, Robbie, it was Mitch and Rebecca and I who were honored by their presence. Two Holocaust survivors at the same table. What strong stuff your parents are made of. There I go again, ending a sentence with a preposition. Not good for an aspiring writer. Try to enjoy your weekend, in spite of those double shifts.

Ever curiously,

Trish

A few things said, a hundred or so omitted. The impending trip to the Holocaust Museum for instance. Rebecca had produced the reserved tickets like a magician. And so there was no backing out now. Why would she want to? Mitch would be there. The ever-faithful friend, Mitch

"So, what *are* you going to do while I'm gone?" Mitch asked matter-of-factly.

"The same thing I do every day," Rebecca answered blandly. "Run the state during the day and then campaign like crazy at night."

"Sounds like you won't even miss me."

Rebecca stopped helping Mitch pack and then further hampered the process by embracing her from behind.

"I miss you every minute of the day when you're not this close to me."

156

Mitch stopped packing as well. She really didn't have much choice since Rebecca had by now gently taken the items of clothing from her hands and turned her around."
"I miss you already," Reb confirmed and she pulled her close.
"Me, too," answered Mitch.
"But, I do want you to go, because I know Trish is counting on you and friendships should never go by the wayside."
"I'll only be gone a few days."
"Three days, four hours, twenty-seven minutes."
Mitch could have checked her airline ticket to verify the figures, but instead came up with a better idea. A much better idea. She began to unbutton Rebecca's blouse, but was working too slowly for Rebecca. Reb had Mitch stripped to the waist and on the bed before Mitch had gotten to Rebecca's third button. Oh, those Type A political personalities. Then, to throw Mitch off, she slowed down considerably, taking her sweet time with kisses and tender finger strokes. It was all Mitch could do to concentrate on her unbuttoning mission and drew out the process so as not to disrupt Rebecca Of The Magic Fingers. It didn't matter. Reb slowed down. Almost to a stop. Which was her way of saying, "I want to talk."
Mitch picked up on the unspoken signal.
"What are you thinking?"
"I was wondering what all was on your schedule. The Holocaust Museum is only one day. What about the other time?"
"The other two days, four hours, twenty-seven minutes?"
"Yeah, that," Rebecca nodded as she began to explore due south of Mitch's belly button.
"I suppose we'll go to the Smithsonian, maybe," Mitch said as she closed her eyes and took a deep breath. As she did

157

so, Reb's hand traveled back north. Mitch could swear she was reenacting Civil War skirmishes. North, South, North, South. Her Mason-Dixon Line had fingerprints all over.

"You're not going to sleep, are you?"

"Not a chance. I'm just enjoying the attention."

Reb traced Mitch's lips with her index finger.

"What are you thinking?" It was Reb's turn to ask.

Mitch pondered mentioning the Civil War, but was afraid it would distract and confuse.

"I was thinking that this trip feels a little like a scouting mission."

"Scouting mission?"

"Yeah, like I'm checking out the town so that when you get elected, I'll know my way around a little."

"That's a lot to expect for a three-day trip."

"Well, you know me. I set high goals for myself."

"That's always been apparent in at least *one* area," Reb teased, and then followed up with a scouting mission of her own. Mitch stirred and stretched under her touch, willing to be on the receiving end of such expert technique. She wanted to hold steady for a few minutes, but found herself doing what she always did, namely, making sure and certain that all of her most sensitive areas followed the direction of Rebecca's tongue. Mostly like a little lost puppy. Begging for attention, hoping for non-stop contact, rising to touch and eventually whimpering softly.

Eventually, she relaxed to the point of absolute stillness. Her arms and legs had mysteriously become leaden, and she was helpless to even lift her head. After a few moments, Rebecca's face hovered over hers.

"You okay?"

"Never better, but you have sapped my strength," Mitch said. Rebecca stroked her arms as energy flowed back to them. Mitch held her in a strong embrace.

"I have two hours until my flight, and I'm bound and determined to cut it very, very close."

"Promises, promises," Reb laughed. Mitch only smiled and then made good on her word. Glaciers moved faster than Mitch for this moment in time. Mitch set forth to taste every square inch of Rebecca's skin. Of course, some perimeters needed a second, third, and in one case, numerous encores, which Mitch provided with gentle, if terribly prolonged, mercy.

It was a scamper to the airport, as promised. During the hasty limousine ride, Rebecca held Mitch close, as if to soak up every last ounce of ambiance.

"Don't campaign too hard," was Mitch's parting comment. "You're going to need all your strength when I get back."

"I promise to be fully rested."

With that, Trish pulled Mitch into the walkway that led to the airplane. Only after they had settled into their pre-assigned seats, did Trish mention, "You certainly didn't come early!"

"You've just said a mouthful," Mitch nodded and smiled. Trish glanced over, rolled her eyes, and prepared for takeoff.

Mitch slept through most of the flight. No surprise there. Trish stayed occupied with her reading material, a book about the Holocaust. When that became too overpowering, she studied tour books about the D. C. area. She was determined to ride the Metro whenever possible and walk the rest of the time.

"You brought comfortable shoes, didn't you?" she asked when Mitch finally came to.

"I brought comfortable everything. I'm wearing ten-year-old underwear as we speak."

"That's more than I want to know."

"Then don't ask."

"I didn't ask about your ten-year-old underwear," Trish stated loudly enough to be the recipient of several curious looks. It struck Mitch as funny and she remarked, "I packed a pair of socks that I wore in high school."

The curious looked elsewhere for further amusement. Trish lapsed into silence clear through the cab ride to the hotel. Check-in was tense, yet efficient, and they were assigned rooms. Luggage in hand, they rode up the elevators and inspected their rooms. They were small, clean and each outfitted with a beautiful basket of goodies, compliments of Rebecca. Wine, fruit, chocolate. She had thought of everything. God, what a woman! What a classy thing to do! Mitch called home to gush, but, of course, Reb was in a meeting. Mitch left a message that she received the gifts and had arrived safely and would be home in three days. Knowing that both would be busy, they had agreed to keep the phoning to a minimum. No use irking the staff. However, Mitch did call and arrange to have a dozen, no make it three dozen, roses sent to the Governor. Then, she turned to face the challenge of the taciturn Trish.

"You're mad at me, aren't you."

"Ten-year-old underwear?"

"Hey, my parents were raised at the tail end of the Great Depression. We'd give stuff to the poor, and they'd give it

160

back because they thought we must need it more than they did."

"And socks from high school."

"They're my lucky socks. I won the school's tennis tournament in them."

"You brought your lucky socks."

"The laundry service at the mansion was behind schedule."

"Next time, I hope Rebecca helps you pack."

"Me, too," Mitch agreed enthusiastically, but for different reasons.

"It was nice of Reb to send us those goodies. Do you know how lucky you are?"

"I thank God every day for bringing her into my life."

"Everyone should be so lucky."

Mitch looked at Trish and her mind flashed back to the conversation they had during the not-so-great flu epidemic.

"You will find someone," Mitch stated firmly.

Trish remained silent. Miranda would have been proud.

"Unless, maybe, you already have?"

Trish looked away and then met Mitch's gaze.

"You have, haven't you!"

"No, not really. I mean, it really isn't possible."

"What isn't possible?" Mitch had to know.

"You just don't fall in love with someone you've never met."

"You're in love with a complete stranger?"

"Not complete, exactly."

"This is Rose and Max's daughter we're talking about, isn't it!"

"Robbie. Or rather, Roberta Goldstein."

As soon as Trish spoke the name, Mitch grinned.

"What?" Trish demanded, fighting back a blush and failing.

"It's obvious. You say her name like you've loved her for a thousand years."

"I do not."

"Yes, you do."

"I do?"

"Absolutely."

"Remind me not to say her name around her parents."

"Do they object?"

"I don't know."

"They seemed okay at the mansion, didn't they?"

"It's one thing to attend a dinner party given by gay people but it's a whole different universe when you think your own daughter might be gay."

"I suppose so," Mitch agreed and then asked, "But how does Robbie feel?"

"She doesn't know."

"Oh, I see."

"Yeah, it's a real mess. I'm in love with a woman who lives hundreds of miles away and I don't even know if she would ever be able to love me in return."

"You could just ask her."

"It's not that simple."

"Why not?"

"It just isn't."

Mitch had two choices. She could argue herself into another fight with Trish or suggest dinner at a classy restaurant. Okay, so it wasn't the toughest decision on the planet. They chose a seafood restaurant in the gay section of town and then turned in early.

Chapter 11

Jake was impatient. He had set the schedule to include no more than fifteen minutes of questions after Rebecca's stump speech before the Antelope Lodge civic group. The audience, virtually all male, was grilling Rebecca on everything from preschool to prescription drugs for the elderly and she was taking her own sweet time satisfying their inquiries. She barely noticed Jake pacing back and forth in the back on the hall. The appearance had been a close call from the beginning. The Antelope Lodge, situated in the mountains just west of Denver had been devilish to locate. By the time Jake had deciphered the directions, they were behind schedule and he couldn't drive fast enough to make up the time due to the treachery of the mountain roads. One slip and they would be stranded.

So, it was only fair that Rebecca spend the extra time afterwards, talking to people individually. They had formed a line, much like at a wedding. Except that there was no groom. However, there was Jake, nervous as a groom, and for reasons that only he would know. He had plans. So, as soon as was politely possible, he escorted Rebecca from the premises and into the passenger side of his Corvette. He slid into the driver's seat and roared off. "You were wonderful tonight," he assured her as they began the journey home through the pitch black night.
"I was okay. I hate to be late."
"You were on time and magnificent."
"Whatever."
After they had driven a mile or two, Jake struck up a different conversation.

"Have I ever told you how sexy you are, especially in front of male audiences."

Immediately, Rebecca felt the hair prickle on the back of her neck.

"It's not my intention to be sexy on the campaign trail!"

"Well, I know it's not your *intention*, but it sure is an automatic response."

"Let's not dissect this evening's performance. Just drive."

"I can drive and dissect at the same time. In fact, I can drive a do a lot of things at the same time," he explained in a sickening, braggadocio sort of way. With that pronouncement, he reached over and patted Rebecca's thigh. She pushed his hand away immediately.

"Knock it off," she demanded.

"You know," Jake bragged on, "I can do anything and everything Mitch can do, as well as a few things she can't. Check out things just below my belt buckle."

"I said stop it and I mean it. Stop the car."

"You want to park?" he asked with a leer. "So soon?"

"No!"

"Okay," he grinned and then put his foot on the accelerator. As they picked up speed, he grabbed Rebecca's left wrist and guided her hand closer to his legs.

"I'll let you touch it now, but only that. Pretty soon, you'll be begging to do all sorts of other things. I imagine your licking abilities are in great shape. After all, you've had all that practice on Mitch."

Revolted, Rebecca struggled to pull her hand back, but his grip was like a cruel vise. The closer he moved her hand, the harder he stepped on the gas. He glanced over at her and in that split second, a car came at them the other direction. Blinded by the light and his lust, he over corrected the car. They pitched off the steep embankment and rolled over and over through the underbrush. Rebecca was jarred into unconsciousness and when she awoke, the staring dead eyes of Jake McManus were still on her. She finally pulled free from his dead grasp and then succumbed once again into blackness.

Searchlights and screaming sirens were the next thing Rebecca remembered. Thunder rolling in the distance soon metamorphosed into instructions hollered in her direction. A screeching, nausea-inducing sound was bearing down on her, with hot breath and crackles. Emergency paramedics cracked the Corvette open as easily as an egg. It was either still nighttime or Rebecca was blind. She forced her eyes into what must have been the open position, and discovered that the rescue crew had used a shield of some sort to protect her eyes. She worked her mouth to ask for help, and then remained helpless as people administered to her. She stole one last glance at Jake. He was still and forever dead.

Chapter 12

Mitch almost managed to oversleep, but not quite. Trish
was at her door early and they grabbed a quick bite at a
hole-in-the-wall bagel and coffee shop just outside the
doors of the hotel. Then, they arrived at the United States
Holocaust Museum and Memorial in time to get a place in
line fairly close to the front. Still, after all the months,
there was a line clear down the block. Mitch was content
to stand, but Trish was restless. She paced around as Mitch
held their place. When the doors opened, they filed in
respectfully, as if treading on holy ground. In a way, for
Trish, it was. When visitors come to the Museum, they are
given an I. D. card of someone who was in the Holocaust.
Mitch's card had the name Jacob. When Trish checked her
card, she went pale.
"What is it?" Mitch asked.
"Look!"
The card had the name Roberta.
"Do you want a different card? Mitch offered to trade.
"No…It's okay. It will be okay."

As they entered the Hall of Witness, Mitch strained to read
the inscription on the wall, "You are my witnesses" Isaiah
43:10.
It evoked an immediate emotional response from Trish,
who looped her arm through Mitch's. Mitch understood,
and said softly, "I'm right here for you. All day."
Trish only nodded.

The gray and brick structures on the Hall of Witness cast a
somber mood for the tour group. As people began to
ascend the stairway, Mitch felt Trish's grip tighten. It was a

166

signal she would become accustomed to as this day progressed.

"What is it?"

"The arch up there."

"The brick one?"

"It's a replica of the one at Auschwitz-Birkenau."

"Tell me something."

"Sure."

"Why is it that you say Auschwitz-Birkenau instead of just Auschwitz?"

"Well, I guess because I associate them as one place because they were so close. Some people write that there were as many as thirty-nine sub-camps at Auschwitz. It was a big place. A lot of work was done by a lot of people who are no longer with us."

Mitch took in the long answer with a nod. If it helped Trish to explain at length, then it was good for Mitch to listen at length. When the tour began in earnest, Trish's hand slid down Mitch's arm and sought her hand. They linked fingers as they walked from display to display. One picture of female prisoners deeply affected Trish. Hand squeezing conveyed the anguish.

"What are you thinking now?" Mitch asked.

"Any one of these women could have been Robbie."

"Or you."

"Or me. Or anyone else who stood up to the Nazis."

Side by side, they took in the other disturbing exhibits. There was a mountain of shoes from Majdanek, thousands upon thousands that had been confiscated by the Nazis. They had been looking for a way to reuse the leather and other materials for war efforts. The prisoners received wooden shoes in their place, so that they could not sneak up

167

on a guard or run to a successful escape. Of course, they were still expected to run in the camps. They were to run when they worked and run for what the Nazis called "sport" and run to their place in line for food. Except for when they were expected to crawl on their knees for the food. Or crawl on the ground to pick weeds and grass with their teeth when the guards were sadistic enough to forbid the use of hands.

Trish looked for a long time at the photos of prisoners and their numbers. Photos of tattooed forearms were also of interest to Trish. The elaborate numbering system was developed after a time, but very few of the earlier numbers were left at the end of the war. Some prisoners had even had their blood typed and that was part of their prisoner information and Jews were marked with a triangle.

It had been about three minutes, and Trish was still standing at a blow up of a photograph of charred bodies on a pyre. Mitch took her away gradually and steered her to one of the lounge areas for a break, holding her close as they sat together.
"I needed a break," Mitch admitted.
"Okay," Trish said as an involuntary shiver passed through her body.
"Are you cold?"
"No."
"Are you okay?"
"No."
"Me, neither."
Another shiver and then a long sigh. Mitch pulled her closer, as if to protect her from events long since recorded in history books. And, unfortunately, from several current

disapproving stares. All at once, Mitch felt an ephemeral connection to the Jews of 1939. Is this the same kind of looks they received? People still didn't get it. In nervous conversation on the way over to the museum, Trish had mentioned that some Jewish group had threatened to boycott the museum to protest the inclusion of material concerning the persecution of homosexuals. When are we ever going to learn?

"Uh, hello?" Trish said pointedly.

Mitch came back to the moment. "Sorry. Did you say something?"

"You were very lost in thought."

"This place gives one a lot to think about."

"We'd better get going if we want to see the rest."

"Are you sure you're ready?"

"Come on," Trish rose and pulled Mitch to her feet.

They took in more displays, walked through a railroad car similar to the type used to deport thousands of Jews, lit candles in the Hall of Remembrance and listened to recordings of Holocaust survivors. By early afternoon, they were emotionally spent. They hailed a cab and went to a fashionable steak place. It was famous for its oak wood lounge, which had a distinctly clubby atmosphere. At least, that's what the travel book said. Mitch selected an obscenely expensive wine, muttered all along about being able to get this at wholesale in another lifetime back at the Lucky U.

"Pretend you don't remember that."

"Fine."

At least the place was quiet. No blaring TV sets tuned to three or four sporting events that nobody gave a damn about. Just tables and chairs and cloth napkins and crystal glassware.

"You held up well today," Mitch commented.

"It was a struggle."

"Your strength never ceases to amaze me."

"What would you have done if you had been in one of those concentration camps?"

"I haven't really given it much thought. I don't think I'd be as brave or resourceful as some of the people I read about today."

"I think you would have surprised yourself."

Mitch thought about the question. Usually, when Trish asked a question, she had already worked out her answer. Mitch resisted asking the question back to her. If Trish wanted to talk about it, she would need to do it on her own volition.

Three glasses of wine went down real smooth. If Mitch considered the price of the wine to be high, the entrées on the menu were stunning.

"Are we getting a steak or a whole cow!" Mitch muttered.

"Order half a herd. I'm buying."

"No, you're not."

"Yes, I am," Trish wasn't budging.

"Not."

"Yep."

"Fine, be stubborn."

Trish laughed. It was a welcome sound after the grueling day. Once their dinners arrived, they found that they were hungry. More so than expected. As they ate, they went over plans for tomorrow's excursion. It would be an easier day, a trip to the Smithsonian. After dessert, they cabbed it back to the hotel and wandered silently to Trish's room. Trish tugged at Mitch's sleeve.

"I want to tell you something."

"Okay."

"And I want to hold you while I do."

"That's fine."

Trish gathered Mitch in an embrace.

"First, I want to thank you for everything today. You gave me so much support that I truly know how much our friendship means to you."

"I'm glad."

"And I also want to tell you that back when we were fighting…remember?"

"I remember."

"I wasn't angry at you. I was angry at me."

"Why?"

"I was angry at myself because I didn't take the Holocaust very seriously until I found out that I was Jewish. And at the first opportunity, I took my anger out on you and I'm sorry."

"It's okay. Really. I should have been a lot more supportive."

"You've been great."

"You're pretty terrific yourself. I hope Robbie gets a chance to find that out."

"Me, too!"

"I ordered breakfast," Mitch announced in the morning. She knocked on the adjoining door again. Trish had wanted to get up at a reasonable early hour but answered the door groggily.

"Mornin."

"Little too much red wine last night?" Mitch inquired.

"Too much red meat, I think."

"That will do it, too. Well, maybe the hotel coffee will wake you up."

"If that doesn't do it, nothing will."

"Do I have time for a shower?"

"Of course you do," Mitch smiled. "We have a nice, relaxed schedule today."

Trish went over and switched on the TV set. They caught the tail end of a report on a fatal accident involving the Governor of Colorado. "We'll have more of that breaking news story out of Colorado right after this...."

Mitch's stomach went cold and she looked at Trish for confirmation.

"Did you hear that?" Mitch asked in a voice she didn't recognize.

"I did. Oh, my God. Let me see if we have a paper."

Trish hurried over to check the hallway just outside the door. No complimentary copy was out there. Meanwhile, Mitch had pulled the phone within reach as she sat on the edge of the bed. She shook involuntarily as she tried to dial the mansion and subsequently got two wrong numbers.

"Jake was supposed to be taking care of her. I'm gonna kill him!"

She managed, on the third try, to get the number to the mansion dialed in correctly, but all she reached was a recorded message.

"Damn it!" she hurled the phone as far across the room as it would travel. It gave a pathetic ding as it hit the wall, then the floor.

"Calm down, Mitch. The news is back on."

"I'm changing my flight," Mitch said as she retrieved the phone. It buzzed and hummed and then finally produced another dial tone. This time, Mitch dialed the hotel's front desk, who patched her through to the concierge. She gave rapid instructions and then waited on hold. "I'm gonna strangle Jake. With my bare hands."

"Not any more," Trish said quietly.

"What? What are you talking about?"

"Jake is dead. He's the fatality."

Mitch began to watch the news coverage in earnest. They confirmed the report. Jake McManus, campaign manager for Rebecca Fairbanks was pronounced dead at the scene. The Governor was still in critical condition, but had stabilized. No drugs or alcohol had been found at the scene of the accident.

"Hello? Are you still there?" a tiny voice traveled through the phone that Mitch was holding in her lap. Trish gently took the receiver and followed up on Mitch's earlier request to change flights. Except that she changed both flights. Meanwhile, Mitch gazed at the TV screen. They had put up a picture of Rebecca, one of her campaign poster photos. So calm, so intelligent, so photogenic.

"And now for more on the top story of the hour," intoned the news anchor, "Rebecca Fairbanks, governor of Colorado and United States Senate candidate, was seriously injured sometime late yesterday in an automobile accident. The Corvette that she was riding in apparently went off the road after a campaign stop. The driver of the vehicle, Mr. Jake McManus, was pronounced dead at the scene."

Trish went over and shut off the TV. Mitch stared up at her with a puzzled look.

"Come on and get dressed."

"I am dressed."

"Go downstairs. A car is waiting. I'll be there in two minutes."

"You can't pack everything in two minutes."

"I'm not going to pack everything in two minutes. Now, stop arguing and go downstairs and find the car that's taking us to the airport. The flight's been changed."

"I'll wait for you for two minutes."

"Why?"

"Because if I stand up now, I'm going to fall over."

"Put your head between your knees. I'll be right back."

It only took her one minute and thirty-five seconds to throw on her clothes. In that time, Mitch was feeling a little less dizzy. Amazing what a minute and thirty-five seconds with your head between your knees can do. They hurried down the hall and caught an elevator going their way. The concierge practically dragged them through the lobby and into a waiting limousine. A newspaper was on one of the seats of the vehicle but it was sketchy compared to the TV report. Trish tried to carry on a conversation to ease Mitch's distress.

"I'm surprised you didn't get a call."

"I'm not."

"What about Mary?"

"She probably didn't know where we were. She's been so preoccupied with work, I haven't even spoken to her in a week. Besides, I'm sure she's in shock as well."

"What about the staff?"

"Like I said, I'm not surprised."

"But isn't there some sort of emergency calling tree or something?"

"Not that I know of. If there is, I'm at the bottom of the list."

"What's in the paper?"

"Nothing we haven't already heard."

"Does it say that her condition is serious or critical?"

"It said serious."

"That's good news."

Mitch only nodded. She was nervous as a cat, so Trish gave up on talking and instead just held her hand. She squeezed a couple of times and then held on through the duration of the ride. The flight back was just as tense. Although there were phones, Mitch kept running into bureaucratic brick walls. No answer at the mansion, the Center or the office. Even the hospital had taken a vow of silence and would not release any information.

Although they gained time flying westward, the minutes crawled by. Neither felt like having an airline meal and drinking was out of the question. Finally Mitch became curious about one thing.

"What about all our stuff back at the hotel?"

"I'll take care of it."

"How?"

"I'll go back on another flight and pack stuff up and then check out."

"You're going to fly all the way back?"

"Sure."

"And then back here again?"

"Why not? People do it everyday."

"That's a lot of trouble I'm putting you through."

"Don't think another thing about it."

From Denver International Airport, they went directly to the hospital where Mitch first kissed Rebecca. A photo of the event, planned as blackmail by an unscrupulous politically-minded lout, was now framed and hung over the

175

mantle at Mitch's house. Trish followed Mitch to the ICU area, as directed by the Pink Lady Volunteer corp. It was worse than she thought. Rebecca wasn't in her usual "Governor's Suite."

As Mitch approached the area, a formidable woman blocked the way. On purpose. She wasn't in a nurse's uniform and didn't have a nametag like hospital administrators, but she still gave off that unmistakable air of someone who belonged there.

"Are you Ms. Tanner?" she asked with cold authority. Mitch's heart sank to her knees. This sounded too official. Much too official.

"Yes, I am," Mitch answered. A trembling feeling was working its way up through her legs and was plotting an overthrow of her upper body as she stood rooted to her spot.

"I have just one thing to say to you."

"Okay."

"I hate your perverted guts for what you've done to my sister!"

Before Mitch could think this through, the woman brought her right hand up and slapped Mitch completely off balance. Stumbling sideways and backwards, she hit her lower back on a chair and landed awkwardly on the floor. Had Trish and security not intervened, the woman would have kicked her as well. Within five seconds, the woman was subdued and handcuffed. Too bad they couldn't gag her as well.

"You're the kind of filth I've always warned people about. *You make me sick!* You're not getting in to see Rebecca. I've seen to that! You're *never* going to see her again. You hear me! Never!"

Over the constant invectives, the security guard asked, "You wanna press charges, lady?"

"Sure," Mitch replied as Trish helped her to her feet. "Anything to shut her up."

"Don't think this is the end of this!" she shrieked as she was escorted down the hallway. Once the disturbance was quelled, Dr. Doogie appeared in the waiting room. Okay, so he really wasn't *the* Dr. Doogie. But he was about young enough to be. Over the course of the summer, it appeared that he had "lightened" his hair. Now, he looked like a surfer. Mitch resisted the urge to call him Dr. Surfer Boy.

"What's going on out here?" he asked.

"Beats me, Doc. I just got here myself. How's Rebecca?" A strange expression crossed his face.

"I'm under orders to not give out information to anyone outside the family."

"Who ordered that?"

"I think you've already met. At least, your face has. Want me to take a look at that for you? In my *private* office?" It was the way he said "private" that prompted Mitch to agree. Whatever he wanted to say, he would do so without prying ears. She and Trish followed him to his cubbyhole office. He indicated a chair for Mitch and Trish and then perched on one of those stools with wheels so he could roll around the office while he examined Mitch's lip. He touched the corner of her mouth with a gloved hand, and it stung like crazy. Mitch had to admit, she was a real wimp where pain was concerned.

"Ouch!"

The doctor had a bit of blood on his thumb. Apparently there was a bit more damage than Mitch had known. But not much.

"I could try to put a stitch or two there."

"Is it absolutely necessary?"

"Not absolutely. Maybe just take it easy for a while. If it doesn't heal, I could maybe try to cauterize it?"

"I'll take it real easy. Don't worry about it. I'm a fast healer. Tell me about Rebecca."

He hesitated for a second and then there was a knock on the door. It was Mary. A very panicked, very pale Mary.

"Oh, Mitch. Thank God you're here. I just got here. What is going on down the hall? The police are everywhere. Where's my mother? Is she going to be okay?"

Mitch took hold of Mary in order to, first of all, stop her talking long enough for everyone else to get a word in edgewise and second, to just calm her down.

"Your mother is in serious condition," the doctor began.

"How is she, Mitch?" Mary looked to her for a more personal report.

"I just got here myself."

"You haven't seen her yet?"

"There was a bit of a problem."

"What's the problem?"

"There was a directive from a family member to restrict visitors."

"Who the hell did that?"

"Your mother's sister."

"Aunt BeBe? You mean Aunt BeBe is here? Oh my God."

"Aunt Beebee?" Mitch repeated.

"So, that's what happened to your face," Mary sighed knowingly.

"Don't worry about me. You'd better go in and see your Mom."

"Can I?" she asked the doctor.

"You can see her for about five minutes."

"And then Mitch?"

"A family member would need to lift the restriction."

"Consider it lifted," Mary said as she stood up.

"Tell her I love her and I'll be there in a little while."

"Sure thing."

Mary and the doctor left the office. Mitch sat quietly. Knowing that Mary was in charge of things made her relax.

"We still don't know much," Trish muttered.

"I'll find out more after Mary visits. I wonder why she just got here and how Aunt Howitzer beat us all to the hospital?"

"The aunt's name is probably on some emergency notification card."

"Mary's must be, also."

"I'm sorry I took you so far away. I feel this is my fault."

Mitch took Trish's hand. "Don't even think that way. It was just bad luck. I'm here now."

"I need to get going to fly back to D.C."

"Maybe the hotel would just ship everything back?"

"I don't want to leave it to chance. I'll be back tonight if I have to charter a jet."

"Okay. Have a good flight."

"Say 'Hi' to the Governor for me."

Mitch escorted Trish to the cab stand just outside the valet parking entrance and made sure she had a ride to the airport. Then, she walked back to the waiting area. Two police officers were waiting for her.

"We understand you want to press charges against one, Beatrice Knight?"

Mitch thought it over. "I've changed my mind."

The police exchanged exasperated glances.

"I'm sorry if it was a bother. I didn't know at the time that I was dealing with a family member."

179

The officer in charge snapped his notebook shut and led the other officer out of the area. Any minute now, Aunt BeBe would be on the loose again. Mary was nowhere in sight, but the doctor reappeared and sat next to Mitch to continue their conversation.

"As I said, the Governor is in serious condition, but she's stabilized quite a bit since we admitted her late last night."

"So, she's going to make it?"

"Barring unforeseen and highly unlikely circumstances, yes."

"So, what aren't you telling me?"

"The Governor has sustained a life-altering injury."

"A life-altering injury? What's that?"

"There's been some damage to her spinal cord."

"I see," Mitch absorbed the news with all the courage she could muster.

"Is it like Christopher Reeves' injury?"

"No. He had a broken neck. The Governor's injuries aren't that complicated."

"Will she ever recover?"

"We're waiting for some of the swelling to go down before we make a determination."

"Give me your best guess and please, no medical jargon."

"My guess, no medical jargon, is that she will be paralyzed from the waist down."

"It could have been worse."

"She's lucky to be alive, but she will need a lot of rehabilitation."

This news was just beginning to sink in when Mary reappeared. She looked understandably distraught. Mitch stood up and gave her a hug.

"I'm so scared," she admitted.

"Of course you are," Mitch calmly patted her on the back. "We're going to get through this together."

"She's asking for you," Mary said to Mitch.

Mitch looked at the doctor.

"Whatever the Governor wants," he nodded. Wise man.

"Tell me about it," Mitch practiced sounding casual.

She walked with feet that wanted to run into the restricted area. Rebecca was lying flat on her back. Motionless. When they said stabilized, they meant stabilized. Mitch leaned over until she could make eye contact. Rebecca's eyes were shut, so Mitch touched her arm gently. Slowly, she opened her eyes.

"Hi, there," Mitch said in a quiet voice.

"Don't tell me that I'm lucky to be alive! If one more person, and I mean one more person tells me that I'm lucky to be alive, I'm gonna punch 'em right in the nose."

"Okay," Mitch nodded. "No 'lucky to be alive' speeches out of me."

"And where in the hell have you been?"

"I was in Washington D. C., remember?" Mitch explained, wondering if there was some temporary amnesia at work here.

"What, and they don't have TV sets there!?" Reb asked with just a hint of sarcasm. It was a bit more than Mitch had expected.

"Yep, they do," Mitch replied, fighting off the urge to be sarcastic in return. She chalked up the attitude to Rebecca's knowledge about her injuries. How cranky would Mitch be if she knew she'd probably never walk again. Pretty damn cranky.

"Look, Sweetie, I know that you're really scared because you're probably never going to walk again. But lots of

people live very productive lives in wheelchairs. Gosh, even a President was in one! I'm right here for you."
Mitch suddenly stopped talking. Something wasn't right. She saw the utter and absolute look of fear creep into Rebecca's eyes. Oh shit! Mitch said to herself. The doctors hadn't mentioned this tidbit of news to her yet. Oh damn!
"Uh…" Mitch said, almost by habit.
"Don't 'Uh' me Goddammit! What are you talking about! What is going on around here?"
"You have a spinal cord injury."
"I know that."
"And chances are, it will be a permanent injury."
"They told me they were waiting for the swelling to go down."
"That's right, but you might still have extensive damage."
All at once, tears and invectives poured out.
"You go get that Goddam doctor in here and you get him in here *now*!"
So much for tender reunions. Mitch walked out on feet that would have preferred to stay rooted to the spot. It didn't help that Aunt BeBe was now present and trying to re-exert control of the situation.
"Can I speak to you for a moment, doctor?" Mitch asked him.
"You're not speaking to anyone, anymore, Ms. Tanner!" Aunt BeBe started in on her immediately.
"Yes, she is, Aunt BeBe," replied Mary.
"Mary, let me handle this-"
"NO! No, Aunt BeBe. Let me handle this. Mitch has my permission to stay and visit and confer with the doctors."
"She was my little sister before she ever even thought about being your mother!"

182

"Aunt BeBe, I'm calling the shots now! Don't make me have security escort you out of the building."

Mitch practically glowed with pride, seeing this wonderfully assertive side of Mary. Aunt BeBe thought it over and then backed down. Mitch was relieved. Not enough to forget about the problem she had come out to discuss with the doctor.

"You wanted to discuss something?" he asked.

"Come on, she wants to see you."

They walked a few feet, hopefully out of earshot of the big sister, before Mitch confessed, "I did something stupid."

"You told her about the injuries?"

"Yeah. I thought she knew."

"Well, she had to know sooner or later. Her sister didn't want her to know until it was absolutely necessary."

"I understand," Mitch said, although she didn't. So, there they were, the doctor on one side and Mitch on the other, answering all of Rebecca's questions. Mitch had never wanted to be so wrong in her entire life.

"How soon will we know?" Reb squeezed Mitch's hand. It was her way of making sure Mitch knew she was 50% of the partnership.

"Tomorrow or the next day."

Then, he went to the foot of the bed and uncovered the Governor's feet. He ran something up the bottom of her foot.

"Feel anything?"

"No."

"I'll check in again later."

Quietly, like a specter, he drifted away, leaving Reb back in Mitch's sole custody.

"Come here. I want to tell you something."

"I'm right here."

183

"Closer."

Mitch bent over to better make eye contact.

"I'm sorry if I snapped earlier."

"It's okay."

"It's just been an ordeal."

"It was a bad accident. I saw coverage on the news."

"You're one ahead of me."

Reb raised her left hand to try and reach for Mitch and then let it drop back down. It wasn't until then that Mitch noticed the purpling bruises. She made a mental note, but nothing more.

"So, what can I do for you?"

"Could you get rid of my sister?"

"Ohhhh, that might be tough. What do you suggest?"

"Send her on a bus back to Kansas."

"You've never told me much about your family."

"Maybe now you can see why!"

"She sure dropped everything to come out here. She beat me here."

"And Mary as well. Where was she?"

"I don't know."

"She didn't say?"

"I didn't ask."

"I see."

"Reb?"

"What?"

"I'm really sorry about Jake. I know that he and I didn't get along, but I know that he was important to you as a friend and confident."

"I really don't want to talk about him right now."

"I understand. But when you do, I'll be here for you."

"I need some sleep," Reb announced and then closed her eyes. Mitch left her to rest. Now, to see about Aunt BeBe.

The waiting room had filled up considerably since Mitch had been in with Rebecca. Mary and Aunt BeBe were joined by Mary's dad, Jeff, and several staff for the Governor's office. Apparently, the authority of the Governor had been temporarily shifted to the Lieutenant Governor. It was not the best kept secret on the block that the office of Lieutenant Governor was little more than window dressing. Now, a man named John Burns was in charge. Mitch considered, only to herself, his longevity. After being in with Reb, Mitch figured that Mr. Burns wouldn't have time to warm up the Governor's chair. Forget about living in the mansion!

Speaking of which, how were they going to manage that in a wheelchair? For years, the first floor of the mansion had been open to the public for tours. There was no way they could change that, but it would be time consuming to install an elevator. Not to mention the red tape involved in altering a landmark. They could always stay out at Mitch's ranch until things could be altered. After all, they had done it quite successfully before. Of course, no one had been in a wheelchair, either.

Mitch took the time to talk to Jeff. He had been Rebecca's husband for many years, but they had called it quits about the same time Mitch came on the scene. There had been no animosity between them through the transition, so it was no surprise to anyone, except Aunt BeBe, when they hugged for a long time.
"I just heard," Jeff explained through his tears. "I was in Hawaii."
"It's okay, I was out of town, too."

185

"I want to see her."

"She's asleep right now, but I'll put you at the front of the line the minute she wakes up."

"In front of Aunt BeBe?" he whispered in mock surprise. Mitch gave him her famous "Be quiet, you naughty boy!" look. Out loud, she muttered, "Why didn't somebody warn me about the in-laws?"

"Why should you be any different!"

"You didn't know?"

"She showed up at our wedding and scared the hell out of me."

"I can imagine."

"Can I tell you something?" Jeff grew serious.

"Sure. Let's go have a cup of coffee."

They ordered coffee and donuts at the little snack shop down the hall. It was far enough away from the crowd so that, for once, Mitch felt like there was air to breath. Yet, it was close enough for emergencies.

"You wanted to say something?" Mitch followed up after they were seated.

"I just wanted to say thanks for being so good to Rebecca." Mitch tried to think of a response that sounded neither glib nor offhand. It took a moment.

"I've just been myself, but thanks all the same."

"And by being yourself, you've made it possible for Rebecca to be herself. That's something that she could never be when married to me."

"It sounds like you've come to very comfortable terms with all of this."

"I've worked on it. I just wish that this could've all happened sooner. We were pretty miserable those last couple of years."

Mitch resisted the urge to say, "Try five," and instead asked, "Are you seeing someone new?"

"Does it show?"

"Just a little, around the edges."

"We're going really slow."

"Nothing wrong with that."

"*And*, she's not a politician."

"Whew!" Mitch pretended to wipe sweat off her forehead.

"I heard that Rebecca was running for U.S. Senate."

"Still is, as far as I can tell."

"You can't be serious!"

"Why not?"

"A paraplegic lesbian in the United States Senate? When was the last time *that* happened!"

"There's a first for everything."

"And this would, indeed, be a first."

"So, we can count on your support?"

"Well, sure, I guess."

"Good! Now, we had the endorsement of the ex-husband! Rebecca will be pleased. Let's go see if she's awake so you can talk to her."

Not only was she awake, but she was taking back the duties of Governor and requesting transfer to the Governor's Suite so she would have access to phone, fax, and e-mail. The request was being processed. Slowly, on purpose, by the doctor. Which resulted in still more crankiness.

"Look who's here!" Mitch pulled Jeff into the ICU.

"Well, well, don't you look tan."

"I was in Hawaii."

"Lounging under the pineapple trees?"

"Taking a much deserved vacation."

"I suppose so," Reb sounded unimpressed.

187

"Say, Rebecca, Jeff said he whole-heartedly supports your candidacy," Mitch wandered head-first into the conversation.

"Anything to get me out of the state?"

"I hope you win. The Senate needs good leaders like you." With that pronouncement, Jeff left the room.

"You were pretty rough on him," Mitch remarked.

"It's a habit that's hard to break."

"I think he deserves an apology."

Rebecca didn't answer. She was busy reading some sort of paperwork. Mitch wasn't about to let go of this.

"I said I think he deserves an apology."

"I heard you the first time."

"Well?"

"He's the one who asked for the divorce. I don't want to renew old ties with ex-husbands."

"You're still that bitter about it?"

"The more men I can keep at arm's length, the happier I'll be. Now, go see what's taking so long with my room transfer."

"No."

'No?"

"I'm your life partner, not your slave."

Mitch walked out, leaving her to think things over. Maybe another dose or two of Aunt BeBe would help her appreciate Mitch and Jeff.

"She's all yours," Mitch informed the self-appointed matriarch as she went for a drive. Actually, it was less of a drive and more of a restocking trip. Mitch drove to the mansion and packed two suitcases with everything Reb would be allowed once she settled into her usual hospital room. Regular jammies, cushy robes and all her routine toiletry items. Hairbrush, toothbrush, shampoo and hand cream were just a few of the many items that Reb would be asking for in about ten minutes. Instead of hurrying to return to the hospital, however, Mitch took a few minutes for herself as well. She showered and then dawdled over her wardrobe until something crisp and clean suited her. Apparently the laundry had caught up while she was out of town. Mitch was rejuvenated and ready to go back to face the uncertain future.

As she suspected, Reb had been moved by the time Mitch had arrived. Probably not so much because she was ready, but the circus was beginning to get on the nerves of everyone else in the ICU area. The crowd had thinned considerably. Most of the staff had been given assignments and sent on their way. Particularly John Burns. Mary was absent. It was rumored that Aunt BeBe was in the cafeteria. Geez, it was actually quiet for a change. Mitch padded into the room and set the suitcases down noiselessly.
"Moving in?"
Apparently, not noiselessly enough.
"I brought you some things from home."
"Thank you."
"How are you feeling?"
"Rotten."
"Are you in pain?"
"No. I just know that I'm being cranky and I'm really sorry."
"You're forgiven, although I am glad to see you so feisty."
"Would you please help me call Jeff?"
"Sure. What's his number?"
"Did you bring my personal address book from the house?"
"It was at the top of the list."

"He's in there."

"Under X?"

"Ha. Ha."

Mitch dialed the number and chatted for a moment before she put Reb on the line. Things were patched up in a few minutes and then Reb relaxed into her pillow.

"Now, we have to talk," Reb said.

"Okay." Mitch drew out the word. When Reb said, "talk" it could mean a variety of things. Most days it meant "listen."

"You start," Mitch requested.

"Two things are on my mind."

"What's number one?"

"These bruises on my left wrist."

"I saw those earlier. You don't have a lot of bruises from the accident. That's a strange place to bruise, don't you think?" Mitch found herself babbling. Why, she didn't quite know. Perhaps it was the look on Reb's face?

"Jake did this."

"What? Was he trying to break your fall? Or hold you back?"

"He was man-handling me."

Mitch turned the words over in her mind. "Man-handling?"

"That's what I said. Are you going to repeat everything I say?"

"You mean, sexual assault?" Mitch asked for a distinct clarification.

"The beginnings of sexual assault. The trip over the cliff put an end to it."

"So, it wasn't an accident, as such."

"We were struggling."

"God, Rebecca. I'm sorry."

"He was a lecher and a brute. You were right all along about him."

Mitch had heard enough about Mr. McManus. For now. "What's the second thing you wanted to talk about?"

"I'm withdrawing from the campaign."

"No, you're not," Mitch stated calmly, but firmly. Like she had final authority in the matter. Rebecca looked surprised at her attitude.

"Yes, I am!" she said, trying to re-exert her authority.

"No, you're not," Mitch just repeated herself. Steadily.

"I want to."

"No, you don't."

"Why are you arguing with me about this?"

"Because you're making the wrong decision."

"Why?"

"What are you going to do with your life if you don't run for office?"

"Go through rehab."

"That won't keep you satisfied!"

"You think I can still run for office?"

"Run, Hell! I know you can win. I just got home from Washington. I like the place. I can hardly wait to live there."

"And you think I can still be a good Senator."

"Honey, you can be a better Senator in a wheelchair than most of those guys can be standing up."

"Do you think I can go through rehab that quickly?"

"Has the doctor talked to you about that, yet?" Mitch hedged.

"Learning that lesson a little late, aren't we?" Reb picked up on Mitch's caution.

Mitch laughed. "You got me there!"

"They've mentioned a thing or two. I'm wheelchair bound, I can tell already."

"And so, if that's how it turns out, we'll adjust."

"I'll never be the same again," Reb's words focused the conversation.

"You want to talk about that?"

"I just want to say one more thing."

"Okay."

"I would understand completely if you walked out that door and never came back."

Mitch pondered the statement long enough to form a cogent response.

"You might understand, but I sure as hell wouldn't. Why would I ever walk out on the woman I love?"

"Because I'm not the woman you fell in love with anymore."

Call her dense, but everything was pretty much the same as before the accident as far as Mitch was concerned. "I'm here. With two suitcases. To stay. If I brought any more stuff, we'd get charged double occupancy rates. Does that pretty much settle it for you?"

Rebecca might have, in any other instance, cried. But she didn't. She was still on duty as Governor.

"So, don't just stand there. Unpack."

"Yes, Ma'am."

Mitch stayed busy with this chore for a long time, all the while chatting about what she had packed and why. Reb would still need permission from Doctor Surfer Boy to wear "civilian" pajamas and frankly, Mitch had yet to be baptized in the practice of working with a paralyzed person.

Halfway through the second suitcase, a young woman appeared at the doorway with a briefcase and a yellow tablet.

"I'm sorry," Mitch said succinctly, "The Governor isn't granting any more interviews to the press today."

"I'm not from the press. I'm the case manager, Chris Shephard."

"Oh, sorry. Hello. I'm Mitch Tanner and this is Governor Fairbanks."

Chris walked over to the bed and gently shook Reb's hand. "It's nice to meet you, Governor."

"Please call me Rebecca."

"Right. I was assigned to your case upon your admission to the hospital," Chris explained. It was obvious to Mitch that the woman was a tad on the nervous side of the universe.

"Really? That's mighty efficient."

"Happens all the time. Normally, I have a busy caseload, but when you were assigned to me, my other cases were redistributed."

"So, I'm your only patient?"

"For a few weeks. Then, we'll reevaluate."

"A few weeks!" Rebecca intoned. Mitch recognized the nature of her voice pitch. It wasn't good.

"Right now, you have been immobilized. Correct?"

"They told me I had special rods attached to the bone."

"Correct. Which means that your doctors have selected a very aggressive course of treatment. You could be up and ready for rehab in a few days."

"Which suits me just fine!"

"Good," Chris brightened. "It suits me as well."

"Do I begin tomorrow?"

"No. You begin in four or five days, barring further complications. In the meantime, you need to rest, gather your strength, and prepare yourself for rehab."

"Are you going to be tough?"

"I'm going to make sure they work you clear down to your nubs. I'll see you again tomorrow. If you have questions, make a list."

"Will do."

Chris marched out. Mitch practically saluted.

"What do you think?" Reb asked Mitch when the coast was clear.

"For a thirteen-year-old, she sure packs a wallop."

Rebecca laughed. "They are all getting younger, aren't they."

"I think I already have one question."

"Better write it down," Reb shook her finger at her.

"Okay," Mitch pretended to pull out a note pad and pen. She scribbled in the air and she said out loud, "What are nubs?"

"I suppose you'll want to watch as well?"

"I wonder what I will be doing, actually?"

"Now, that's a question worth asking."

"I think that should be your decision."

"I think that's their decision. In the meantime, could you please find a nurse or someone. I'm feeling a bit nauseous."

Mitch could tell that this was not a false alarm. She went out the door into the hallway, looking like a person who needed some assistance. Immediately, three nurses came up to her.

"The Governor needs help."

They went past her like the proverbial dirty shirt and went in to administer to her honor. Meanwhile, Mitch, not

194

exactly wanting to know about this latest development, went to the cafeteria. She was starving. Aunt BeBe was just finishing up dessert.

"Hello," Mitch went up to the table.

There was no reply. Not even a glance upward.

"How's the food?"

Nothing.

"I'm going to have dinner. Could you keep an eye on Rebecca for a while?"

Aunt BeBe stood up and walked away. Imagine an aversion so strong that it would make you leave half a piece of lemon meringue pie uneaten. Mitch shrugged her shoulders and went through the cafeteria line. They were five minutes from shutting down for the night and the food looked like rejects from a cheap Las Vegas buffet. Bad food and not much assortment. Mitch fought the urge to try and reclaim that half-eaten slice of pie and instead opted for the vestiges of a salad and a bowl of Texas-style chili. Between these two items, she would be awake with heartburn until at least midnight. Which brought her to another interesting question. Where was she going to spend the night? And the night after that? And the next?

"Looks like they would need to dig up just to bury you."

Mitch glanced up into the kind eyes of Trish.

"How'd you get back so soon."

"Very cooperative airlines. Besides, it's not that soon."

"Thanks for taking care of things."

"You've had a horrible day. What can I do to help?"

"The day has been bearable. I'm just contemplating the night."

"Where are you staying?"

"Here. I guess."

"They won't let you sleep in the cafeteria. Something about State Health Board regulations, I'm pretty sure. Come stay with me."

"I can't do that."

"You'd be a phone call away in case they needed you. Why don't you ask Reb?"

"My worry is that it leaves her here alone with Aunt BeBe."

"Here's a thought. I'll stay here with you. Keep you company."

"I can't ask you to do that. You must be exhausted yourself."

"I slept on the plane. Twice."

"Well, it's okay with me if it's okay with the other three-hundred and eighty-seven people around here who seem to need to be consulted about everything."

"I'll stay until they throw me out."

Contrary to Mitch's assumptions, they were all welcome to stay. Aunt BeBe was directed to a couch in a spare room. Mitch and Trish had to settle for recliners which turned out to be deliciously comfortable and in closer proximity to Reb. Mitch was sound asleep two minutes after she said goodnight to Rebecca. Trish and Rebecca talked quietly until the Governor dozed off. Trish closed her eyes and surprised herself by dropping off to sleep as well.

Hospitals aren't always the best places to get a good night's sleep, but when you are as exhausted as Mitch, anything is possible. She awoke feeling rested if a bit bent out of shape. Literally. Trish was absent. Aunt BeBe was watching over her.

"Good morning," Mitch greeted quietly.

Aunt BeBe just put her finger to her lips like a sour puss librarian. Slowly, Mitch stood up and tried to get her legs to respond after the different sleeping position. They were stubborn and reluctant. Mitch resembled a newborn calf. She walked carefully down the hall and used the visitor's bathroom. Whoever was staring back at her in the mirror could have easily passed for the "before" picture in any advertisement of your choice. She splashed water on her face and then trudged back down the hall. Trish came up beside her and shoved a cup of gourmet coffee in her hand.

"Four sugars?" Mitch checked.

"And real cream!"

"My arteries are clogging up just thinking about it."

"You sure slept soundly last night."

"How could you tell?"

"My ears!" Trish explained as she stifled a yawn, and then clarified, "You snored."

"Loudly?" Mitch grimaced.

"The morgue complained that you were waking up people down there."

"Oh, shut up!" Mitch replied with more than a touch of humor.

"It's fine. At least you slept."

"Tonight, just to give you a break, I'll sleep with Aunt BeBe."

"Now, *this*, I gotta see!"

"And I'm sleeping in a bed. I don't care where it is or whose it is. I'm sleeping in a comfy, womfy bed."

"Maybe you can move one in."

"I'll run it by the case manager."

"What's that?"

"It's a who. She's pimply and prepubescent and has a frightening amount of what would seem to be self-appointed importance."

"Sounds like my first girlfriend."

"Looks like her, too."

They arrived back at the room in time to nearly collide with some doctor. It wasn't the surfer boy, and he didn't bother to introduce himself. He was coming out and they were going in and that's all that seemed to matter to him. Perhaps he had already had his fill of Aunt BeBe?

Reb was awake and sitting in a more upright position with the aid of three people and six pillows.
"Well, look at you!" Mitch smiled broadly.
"Don't look too hard. I might tip over."
"Why would that happen?"
Chris, case manager extraordinaire, jumped into an explanation.
"She's learning about her new center of balance."
"Really!" Mitch exclaimed. "For a long time, she leaned way to the right."
Reb gave Mitch one of those famous governor looks. Trish smothered a giggle. Aunt BeBe appeared very confused.
"Took a whole year to tip her a little to the left," Mitch finished the thought.
The unsuccessfully stifled giggle now escaped Trish's custody and she went clear out of the room by herself before she would need the escort of Warden BeBe. Mitch stood her ground and even advanced to the front line, holding Reb's hand and kissing her lightly on the forehead. As they made eye contact, it was as if no one else was in the room. At least, for Mitch. When she finally looked around, indeed, Aunt BeBe was gone.
"How long do you get to sit up?" Mitch asked Reb.
"Until she gets tired," Chris answered for her.

"If I wanted to see a ventriloquist act, I'd go to an amateur talent show."

"I get to sit up until I'm tired," Reb answered as she squeezed Mitch's hand. The squeeze meant, "Don't give the nice lady any trouble." Mitch looked down at the bruises on Reb's wrist.

"I should've stayed in town."

"Don't blame yourself. Jake was Jake. Sooner or later, he would have tried something."

"His funeral is tomorrow."

"I'm busy."

"Me, too."

"What's up with Trish?"

"Jet lag is making her giddy. She's been to DC and back twice in two days."

"Why?"

"We left the hotel so quickly that we didn't take time to pack."

"I didn't even ask you about your trip."

"You've been a bit preoccupied."

"How was your trip?"

"Emotional and tiring."

"I understand."

"Have you had enough sitting up?" Chris interrupted.

"I think so, for now."

"We'll get you up later in the day."

"I'll look forward to it."

Slowly, they lowered her back down, but not all the way. "We want to try and avoid pneumonia and skin ulcers," Chris explained to Mitch.

"Good," was all that Mitch could think to say.

Minutes later, it was just Rebecca, Mitch, Aunt BeBe and Chris in the room. Trish had gone home to catch up on her chores, after promising to stop by for dinner.

"I believe, Mitch, you had a question for Chris," Reb reminded by way of starting the conversation. Mitch thought back to the jumble that comprised yesterday's events.

"I think I just wanted to know a little more about rehab."

"That's a good question, and I'll go over it in a few minutes, but first, I want to know who is going to be the primary support person for the Governor?"

Gosh, and it seemed to be such an innocent question!

"I am," Mitch and Aunt BeBe answered in unison and then looked absolutely stunned that the other one had the nerve to open her mouth.

"So, there are going to be two primary support people?" Chris was waiting with poised pen.

"No!" came another answer in duet.

Chris cast a look of utter confusion Rebecca's way.

"Apparently, Governor, you should probably discuss this further with these two ladies. I'll come back this afternoon."

So, after starting the fight, Chris walked away. "Fine," thought Mitch. "Be that way."

Mitch watched Reb for a clue, picked up on it after having been around Rebecca for the better part of a year, and then excused herself from Round One as well. Sisters needed some quality time to sort things out.

After walking for two blocks, Mitch came to the diner on the west side of the hospital grounds. The last time she was here, Marge was dying. After ordering a full breakfast, Mitch read the paper to keep her mind off current events.

Unfortunately, the paper offered little reprieve. Rebecca was the main story, with articles on pages one through five and twelve. Jake and his obituary were relegated to page seven. Were it not for incessant hunger, his photo would have ruined Mitch's appetite. She closed the paper and tore into breakfast. It was ten times better than the hospital cafeteria. After four cups of coffee, and a trip to the restroom, she walked back to the hospital. Reb was asleep, so Mitch walked around scanning the halls for a familiar face. None was to be found, even in the room where Aunt BeBe had slept. She crept silently into Reb's room and sat in the chair she had earlier cursed. There were several hospital pamphlets on the table, so Mitch began reading through them. She closed her eyes for a moment, which was all it took to send her back to sleep.

Chapter 13

Trish had caught up on her chores quickly. That was one advantage to living alone. About the only one she could think up right this minute. Then, she had taken time to check her e-mail and found another letter from Robbie.

Trish,
I've been reading, and listening to news about the Governor. And I also called my folks. They are extremely concerned. Is there any way you could get in touch with them? Calm them down, especially Mama? If she was Catholic, she'd be saying a novena! Thanks.
Robbie

Trish was happy to be of service.

Robbie,
I'm dialing your folks with one hand while I'm typing this reply with the other. I'll let you know what happened.
Trish

As promised, Trish connected with Max at the same time she hit the send button.

"Hi, Max."
"Hello, Trish. So, how is the honorable Governor and how, by the way, are you, as well?"
Even though he sounded agitated, he couldn't forget his manners.
"The Governor is doing well. I'll make a couple of phone calls, and see if I can get the two of you in to see her."

"We wouldn't want to be a bother," Rose answered. Trish had heard the click on the line before she spoke, and wasn't surprised to hear her voice.

"It isn't that it would be a bother. I just need to check the rules."

"Well, we don't want to get in the way," Max confirmed their old-world politeness.

"Let me check and I'll get back to you this afternoon."

"Only if it's no trouble," Rose stipulated.

"Is it true what they say in the papers?" Max asked.

"Which part?"

"That she will be in a wheelchair?"

"I don't know what all the doctors are saying. In a way, I'm sort of staying out of the way myself. But I will call you back."

After Trish hung up, she checked the time. Taking the gamble that Robbie had come home for lunch, she dialed her number. This was getting easier and easier, she thought to herself as she punched in the last digit.

"Hello."

"It's Trish."

"I know. How are you holding up?"

Trish considered the question honestly for the first time in two days and said, "I'm feeling vulnerable."

"I understand."

Somehow, Trish knew she did.

"I just talked to your folks. I'm going to see if I can get them in to see Rebecca."

"That would really put their mind at ease."

"And it would do wonders for the governor, as well."

"I'm so happy you and my folks have become friends."

"They are very special people."

Trish and Robbie chatted about other things for a moment, and the simple exchange of words between them calmed and soothed Trish's frazzled nerves. It was a balm to her spirit and soul. Then, Robbie asked out of the blue, "Is it true that you are a writer?"

"Well, yes and no," Trish felt a warmth begin to spread through her face. "I would like to be a writer and I am trying to be, but I haven't been published."

"Yet!" Robbie offered encouragement.

"Yet," echoed Trish.

"Are you writing about my parents?"

"No, I'm afraid not," Trish admitted as she began to worry about more pointed interrogation.

"What are you writing about?"

"I wanted to write about gay survivors of the Holocaust."

"Well, my parents certainly don't fall into that category."

"No, they don't. I was just interviewing them to get a sense of the era. A foundation."

"So, who are you going to interview next?"

"I don't know. I've done some research and am becoming more discouraged every day. Some sources I've read indicate that it is difficult to find gay survivors of the war. Most were tortured to death. Those who survived stayed in the closet, understandably."

"Understandably," Robbie agreed.

"So, I don't know what to do."

"Keep your hopes up. Someone will turn up."

"In the meantime, I'm going to arrange for your parents to see Rebecca and then I've promised to help out however I can at the hospital."

"You are one very special person, Trish. I work in an institution where far too many people are abandoned by everyone. I commend your loyalty."

Trish felt that burn start up again.

"Now, don't go on like that! I won't be able to fit my head through the door."

Robbie laughed her standard kind-hearted laugh.

"Thanks for the call. I need to get into work."

"Anytime. I'll keep in touch."

Chapter 14

"Do you want a tray as well?"
Mitch opened her eyes. She had fallen asleep with the pamphlets in her lap. Rebecca was asking her about lunch. A food-service worker was patiently waiting for an answer.
"What kind of tray?"
"Chicken, beef or vegetarian?"
"All three."
"Excuse me?" the aide asked.
"Well, we're going to need one for me and one for Aunt BeBe and probably one for Mary."
"Aunt BeBe went home," Rebecca said.
"To the mansion?" Mitch asked, still groggy from her nap.
"No, to Kansas."
"I'm sorry to hear that. We were just beginning to make headway."
"You weren't even speaking!"
"No, but she had gotten past the slapping-me-around stage."
"The what?"
"Never mind. Mary should be here soon. She'll want lunch."
"Mary was here and I sent her home as well."
"Sounds like you've found something you're good at."
"I don't want to talk about it. Do you want lunch or don't you?"
"What are you having?"
"Chicken."
"I'll have chicken as well."
"Two chickens," the server confirmed and then left the room.

Mitch only smiled. At last, they were alone. It was awfully quiet.

"How was Mary?"

"She and I had a fight."

"And I slept through it? Must have been a very quiet fight."

"Do you know where she was when I had my accident?"

"No," Mitch answered honestly.

Reb studied the look of absolute innocence. It was genuine.

"She was with Hilary!"

"Really!" Mitch registered shock at this revelation.

"I don't mean *with* her. She was just visiting."

"And the two of you are fighting about that?"

"You know how Hilary treats her."

"Did anything bad happen this time?"

"Mary didn't say."

"Did she get the chance or did you just send her to her room?"

"I don't need my parental skills critiqued by you right this minute!"

"Fine. Next time, I'll schedule an appointment."

"I'll be available for criticism between midnight and one, three weeks from today."

"I hope you and Mary patch things up before then. If for no other reason than the list of people available to help around here is dwindling rapidly."

Rebecca didn't have an instant reply for this and lapsed into silence. The word "pouting" came to mind. Mitch didn't feel like having an extended time out. She walked over to the bed and perched gently on the edge. Reb ignored her.

"I'll make you a deal," Mitch said and then waited for Reb to acknowledge her.

"What kind of deal?" Reb asked, always willing to respond to something that smacked of politics.

"You sort out things with Mary and I'll figure out a way to smuggle some decent food in for dinner."

"Mary's situation is serious."

"I agree with you! But how are you going to help if the two of you aren't even speaking?"

The Governor thought it over for a moment. Why did Mitch always make so much sense? She grudgingly agreed to terms.

"I'll call Mary. This dinner had better be fabulous."

"Nothin but the best!"

Lunch arrived right after Reb hung up the phone. It had been touch and go for a minute, but in the end, Mary agreed to attend the dinner party. A party of four, just in case anyone was keeping track. Which, of course, Mitch was. After the fabulous chicken lunch, Mitch was even more determined to order something good. It was only just plain luck that Trish got through on the line before the all-call to catering restaurants went out.

"How are things going?" Trish asked.

"Busy."

"Oh okay"

"Oh, okay what?" Mitch could tell a pregnant "Oh, okay" when she heard it.

"I was just wondering if there was any way that Max and Rose could see Rebecca soon. They are worried beyond belief."

"Let me check."

Mitch ran the idea by Reb.

"Of course. The more the merrier. Did you see those beautiful roses delivered yesterday?"

Mitch shook her head.

"Max and Rose," nodded Rebecca.

"The Governor says of course bring them over. For dinner. We're doing a catered affair."

"You aren't?"

"I'm calling all the Governor's favorite restaurants just as soon as you hang up!"

"I'm hanging up."

"Bye."

A party of six, just in case anyone was keeping track.

Mitch almost got to the phone book before Chris dropped by.

"How are things this afternoon?" she asked, bright and cheery.

"Quieter."

"I see you are sitting up. Does it feel good?"

"It feels great."

"Have you given anymore thought to your personal support system?"

"Mitch will be the primary support person and the liaison with the family."

"And, okay, so, Mitch, you are Rebecca's sister?"

"No, that was the other one."

"I see. What is your relationship to the Governor?"

"I'm her significant other."

"I see." It took Chris a moment to write all that on a very short line.

"And you are willing to coordinate all family and friend support and contact?"

"I'll do my best," Mitch nodded. Suddenly, this was feeling closer to taking marriage vows than anything Mitch had ever experienced before. Love, honor, deal with the in-laws. Yup, that's what she was promising to do.

"The reason I ask is because during rehab, we want to be able to spend as much time as possible concentrating on Governor Fairbanks. If we find ourselves spending time communicating repetitious information to countless individuals, it detracts from our ability to--"

"Work Rebecca clear down to her nubs?"

"Exactly!"

"Okay. Consider it done."

"You will also need to learn how to be helpful to the Governor in other areas."

"Such as?"

"Physical inspections."

"Sounds like something I'd be good at," Mitch nodded, but kept a very straight face.

"Skin ulcers, and other pressure sores can become deadly. They are something we take very seriously."

"I'm listening."

"We will demonstrate for you and the Governor how to do the inspections and gradually you will be responsible for these. One bed sore could delay the Governor's progress for weeks."

"Do we start today?

"In a few minutes. I just had a couple more things on my list. Have you planned for expenses not covered by insurance?"

"I'm assuming all financial responsibility," Mitch responded quickly.

"You won't need to do much for a while. The Governor's insurance plan is excellent. But it may not cover many things that you might want to consider."

"Such as?"

"Extensive private residence remodeling. Specially equipped transportation vehicles. Things like that."

"Those aren't covered?"

"It depends on how much work is necessary versus how much work you want to do on your house."

"I'm confused?" Mitch admitted.

"Okay, I'll give you an example, but don't hold me to it. Let's say you want to remodel your home. Certain things may be covered, like railings in the bathroom. Other things might not be covered, say, for instance, a swimming pool for aqua therapy."

"I understand. She is probably covered for things deemed essential."

"That's a good way to think about it. If something isn't essential, then consider it not covered until you do the research. Don't jump right in to a project and then find out later that your assumptions were incorrect."

"Either way, I don't think we will need much financial assistance."

"That may be true, but keep in mind that there are foundations out there who may be willing to help. I can keep an eye out for them, if you like."

"Only if you get bored."

"Okay. Now, to the subject of rehab itself."

"That's covered in the policy, isn't it?" Rebecca asked.

"Mostly, yes, but I was going to discuss more along the lines of Mitch's role in rehab."

"Okay."

"Mitch, there will be times when you will be asked to attend and learn. Other times, we strongly encourage just Rebecca's attendance."

"You want me to stay out of the way most days."

"We find that it works best if you are here for support at the end of the day. For a while, the rehab team is going to seem like we're the bad guys. You, Rebecca, will want to

211

spend time with Mitch to relax, to rest, to make the afternoons and evenings a time to enjoy away from the work. The worst thing that could happen is for the rehab experience to drive a wedge between the two of you. I know it sounds like we are relegating Mitch to a second-hand position, but if you align her with the rehab experience, you will resent her after a while."

"Makes perfect sense to me."

"Good, now let's learn a little about bed sores."

Ten minutes of lecture and photos was making Mitch's head swim. Pressure sores were repugnant. Mitch made a vow to never, ever, ever have Rebecca develop one. The key signs of early bed sores included hot areas of the skin and/or redness. After the classroom lecture was over, it was time for the lab. Three nurses specially trained in rehab appeared at the doorway. Together with Mitch, they inspected every part of Rebecca's body for possible problems. Perhaps the exam was a bit on the clinical side, but they were doing it more as an exercise in instruction than actual work. Then, Mitch heard an "Uh oh," out of one of the nurses. So did Reb.

"What!" Rebecca asked, alarmed after the lecture.

"Please go and get the shift supervisor," one of the nurses instructed Chris.

"Right."

"What? What is it?" Mitch was now curious but afraid to look.

"There's no need for alarm," the nurse assured them. "We just need the supervisor in here to witness."

It sounded too close to court proceedings for Mitch. Before she could turn around, the supervisor was in the room. The three nurses and the supervisor and Chris were now huddled around Rebecca's derriere. Good thing Mitch

wasn't the jealous type. She hadn't seen anyone's ass
inspected that carefully since Tom Jones opened in Vegas.
They conferred, made notes and then broke up the
conference as quickly as they had called it. Everyone was
gone, except Chris.

"Now, can I know?" Rebecca asked, becoming just a tad
irritable after being the subject of such scrutiny.

"Let's just suffice to say that there will be more attention to
your hygiene by the nurses in the future."

Before Chris had a chance to elaborate, which Mitch wasn't
sure was completely necessary anyway, the shift supervisor
reappeared with two different nurses, and they set about to
give Rebecca another thorough sponge bath.

"I'll wait outside," Mitch told Reb.

"Come back soon," she made her promise.

Chris excused herself as well and walked down the hall
with Mitch.

"Do you have any other questions so far?"

"Just one. We're having a dinner here later. Would you
care to join us?"

"How many people are attending?" Chris asked. God, she
was the ever-curious one.

"Just a couple of friends. I'm catering the meal."

"Remember two things. One, that bed sores can be kept at
bay with a good diet. Not a lot of fats and things like that.
The healthier the diet, the faster the Governor will heal."

"What's number two?"

"Don't tire her out. She needs rest."

"I'll have a quiet, healthy dinner party. How's that? And
you are invited to come and supervise and enjoy."

"I might stop in, just to keep you from swinging on the
chandeliers!"

"I only do that at the mansion!"

"What else is on your mind?"

"What was going on back there just now?"

"The Governor's nurses need to keep her skin sparkling clean. That's being taken care of as we speak."

"Maybe I can help there, as well?"

"You want to give her daily sponge baths?"

"Is that allowed?"

"You might be doing that sort of thing as time goes by. You'll want to learn eventually."

"How about tomorrow, eventually?"

"When they told me the Governor was a Type-A personality, they didn't mention that it was a two-for-one sale."

Mitch had to laugh.

"I just want to be helpful."

"Then, here's what you do. You take care of the things that we can't do for the Governor. Let us take care of the few things we can do for her. At least for a little while. You need some coddling too, although you don't know it yet. Plan those special dinners, coordinate visitors, make the Governor rest and sleep and laugh, hopefully at all the appropriate times, and generally keep her spirits up. That's what you do best. It's going to be a long four months, but you can make it seem doable."

"Rebecca is going to go stir crazy during four months of rehab."

"Crazy, perhaps. Stir crazy, never. We will fill eight to ten hours per day with her therapy program. She will not be bored."

"Particularly if she also needs to do her official duties and run for Senate."

"The primary election is the first week in August, right?"

"Right."

"So, she's still running for the office?"

"It's too late to change the ballots."

"What do you think will happen?"

"Whatever the people decide."

"I think we can go back in now."

Chris fought the urge to lead, and instead walked side by side with Mitch. Rebecca looked refreshed, if somewhat tired around the eyes.

"If you don't have any other questions, I'll leave you to rest, Governor."

"Please, call me Rebecca."

"Thank you. Do you need something before I leave?"

"You are coming back for dinner, right?" Mitch asked.

"I will try to stop by."

"Good. Party of seven," Mitch was going to need to take her shoes off in a minute if she didn't stop inviting people. Chris finally took her leave.

"Okay, now that we're alone," Reb said, "can you *please* tell me what the big deal was all about!"

"What? You've never had five women gazing at your butt before?"

"Only once or twice a month!"

"Well, good, then you'll be used to it. It's probably going to happen a whole lot more!"

"I needed a bath?" Reb guessed.

"You needed some special care. You heard the lecture from Chris."

"I just don't know if I want a bunch of strangers staring at my naked butt every day."

"Boy, you governor types can be so hard to please."

"Tell me something else before I take my nap."

"Sure, anything."

"How long am I going to be in here?"

"I think that depends on how fast you recover."

"How long?" Reb rejected the platitude.

Mitch went close and held both of Rebecca's hands in hers. Maybe it was just a precaution in case she took after her older sister in moments of true crisis. That was a lie Mitch was telling herself. She just wanted a good excuse to hold Reb's hand.

"A few months."

"Months?"

"Three, maybe four."

"MONTHS!"

"I'll be here for you."

"What about the campaign?"

"I have a good idea about that. Want to hear it?"

"Sounds like you're going to spring something big on me."

"It might work, it might not."

"Let's hear it."

"Why don't you ask Jeff to be your campaign manager?"

Rebecca's eyes narrowed, which meant that she was either giving the suggestion serious thought or she was preparing to sneeze.

"Do you want a tissue?"

"No. Why?"

"Just wondering."

"Why would you suggest Jeff?"

"Well, I can't do it and Mary doesn't have time and Aunt BeBe's back in Kansas. You have a better idea?"

"Let me think about it."

"Speaking of campaign managers, I noticed your quote in the paper about Jake. It was nice."

"Politics as usual. No use upsetting the family."

"When did you have time to talk to the press?"

216

"While you were getting my jammies, which I still don't get to wear!"

"Soon, my dear. Now, take your nap before you have dinner company."

With the help of two nurses, Rebecca was lying down flat again in no time. She slept like the proverbial baby for three hours.

In the interim, Mitch went around the hospital and counted up the number of nurses, doctors, and other personnel assigned to this particular wing of the hospital. And she didn't really need to go shoeless! Then, she began to call restaurants and arrange for food for fifty. Ten meals from each of five establishments. There would be a lavish assortment for everyone. Trish and the Goldsteins showed up at five-thirty and Mitch scrounged up enough ice for drinks. No cocktails, but a nice quenching pitcher of lemonade was ready. Mary arrived at six. Punctual as ever.

"I would have parked closer, but there are five catering trucks in the parking loop."

"My fault," Mitch raised her hand.

"Five trucks?"

"I was hungry."

"You and the entire floor?"

"I had five different restaurants deliver their best stuff."

"It all smells wonderful. How are you doing, Mom?"

"I'm feeling much better."

"You look rested."

"Mitch made me take a nap."

"Good for Mitch."

"Mitch helps me do a lot of things that turn out well."

A few minutes later, Chris dropped in, as promised.

"Checking on my favorite patient!"

"I'm your only patient," Rebecca reminded her.

"Don't push it," Chris kidded back.

Meanwhile, the various representatives of each restaurant checked in with Mitch. She carefully weighed their attitude over the sudden notice of the delivery. Consider it an audition for future occasions. Four made the grade. One flunked. She paid them all with a personal check and then announced "Dinner is served" to all within earshot. Grateful hospital employees were pleased with the break from routine hospital fare. Before the grazing commenced, Mitch fixed something healthy for Reb and got the Goldsteins settled as well. Mary, Trish and Chris were on their own. After everyone had their fill, the leftovers were sent home with hospital personnel who had families to feed.

It took Mitch a few minutes to catch Trish up on the latest news, but she figured she could use the practice, now that she was the chief of communications for the family. Besides, Mary and Rebecca needed some time alone together. The more, the better. So, Mitch was regaling the events of the day to Max, Rose, and Trish.

"We had all these people in the room, doing an inspection."

"An inspection? You mean, they were checking the floor? Or the bed?" Trish asked.

"No, we were inspecting the Governor?"

"Reb needed an inspection?" Trish asked.

Perhaps she was puzzled, but Rose and Max weren't. At the mere mention of the word, "inspection," they stiffened.

"It was, 'Learn about bed sore day.' We had to inspect Reb's skin for red spots. Like little blemishes-"

218

As Rose paled, Trish signaled for Mitch to halt the narrative.

"Are you okay, Rose?"

"I'm fine," she assured with a shaky voice. "Max, we should go. We don't want to overstay our welcome and you have the yard work to do tomorrow."

When she stood up, everyone stood up. Max escorted her to the elevator.

"Is she going to be okay?" Mitch asked.

"It's been sixty years. You tell me."

"So, this has something to do with the Holocaust?" Mitch needed more clarification.

"Prisoners in the various concentration camps had to go through what were called 'selections.' They were inspected for the same type of things that you mentioned in your story."

"I knew that people were chosen to be gassed based on age and things like that."

"Right, but there were other criteria used when quotas for the gas chambers needed to be filled. Prisoners were made to undress and the slightest skin blemish was a death sentence."

Mitch slowly shook her head. "It was a crazy time."

"Run by crazy people."

"I should call Rose and apologize. Would that help?"

"You don't need to do that. It might only embarrass her. She copes in ways only known to her. Besides, you don't have anything to apologize for, except maybe for not being psychic."

"Okay. But keep me apprised. I want to be able to invite Rose and Max over here a lot and I don't want to make the same mistake."

"I promise to keep you posted. Now, tell me the end of the story."

"Reb passed inspection. Finally. But the nursing staff didn't. We had to do another sponge bath, but there's no sign of pressure sores, thank goodness."

"What's the plan for tomorrow?"

"I haven't heard yet, but I'm sure I'll get my running orders from Chris."

"She didn't stick around long."

"She's a busy lady. Making the Governor happy takes a lot of effort."

"And yet, you make it look so easy!"

"It's all in the wrist!"

By the time the hospital returned to its normal hum, Reb had dropped off to sleep. Mitch camped out in Aunt BeBe's vacated room, but she slept fitfully. Maybe it was the fettuccini Alfredo, or the sesame chicken or the turtle cheesecake. Okay, so maybe she had overdone it a little. Her nerves were to blame. She was eating to calm herself and that would pass. Soon. It would have to. Mitch would need to be in shape to keep up with her new responsibilities.

Chris arrived the next morning, right after breakfast.

"Morning," she chirped. "That was some dinner party last night."

"Mitch outdid herself, as usual," Reb agreed. "What's on the schedule for today?"

"Today, we'll talk about your team."

"I get a team all to myself?"

"Not quite all to yourself."

"But it's probably going to feel that way, right?" Mitch piped up.

"The Governor will be outnumbered from time to time, but in reality, we're all pulling for her."

"So, who is on my team?"

"First, of course, is Doctor Morgan, the rehab physician."

"Didn't I meet him already?"

"He came in on the case soon after the paramedics brought you here. He has supervised your immobility as well as your mobility and prescribes medication. He will also order therapy as needed and will follow our case through to your discharge and beyond."

"Okay."

"Next, you will have two physical therapists. One male, on female. Joe and Anna."

Mitch began to look around for a pen to take notes.

"You won't need to write all this down," Chris read her mind. "I've prepared packets for you."

"Thanks."

"Your PTs will work with the physical aspects of your rehab, including exercise, wheelchair use, transfers and driving."

"Sounds good," Reb brightened up at the prospect of once again being able to drive.

"You've briefly met three of our best rehab nurses, Linda, Sebrina and Beth. They assist you with your hygiene, as you've already noticed. They will take over your case full time when you transfer to the rehab wing."

"I'm moving?"

"Rehab is on the first floor, in the Taylor Wing."

"I wasn't aware that I would need to relocate."

"We are preparing a room for you. It will, of course, be equipped with your necessary Governor-type items. Next, you will have an occupational therapist, Carla."

"But, I already have a job."

"As do most spinal-cord injured people. The OT helps in interesting ways, anything from helping you dress yourself using specially designed aides, to consulting with Mitch on ways to restructure your home. Speaking of which, I have an item of interest for you."

"Something interesting for me?" Rebecca sounded less than jovial.

"I have a check for you."

"An insurance check?"

"No. It's a donation from a corporation."

"You're sure it's not a campaign contribution?"

"A letter was sent as well. It mentions your injury."

Mitch's curiosity was aroused. This could qualify for the highlight of the week. "Can I see it?" she asked.

"Sure. I put it in a folder for you, along with other papers. But, let me get through my list first."

"Sure thing," Mitch agreed, but her eyes watched the envelope like it would any minute grow legs and walk away.

"Then, you have a dietitian. His name is Clark. He'll help you with nutrition, matters of digestion, and also monitors your prescriptions for possible interactions. He will also be available to your staff at the mansion as a consultant and perhaps he can even assist Mitch with any future dinner parties."

Mitch was going to comment on the cooking skills of the Governor's staff, but instead mumbled, "I need all the help I can get!" in her best self-effacing manner.

"You will also have a psychologist, a counselor, and a recreational therapist. Dr. Henry, Peggy and Tommy."

"So, including you," Mitch summed up, "That's an even dozen people on the team."

"And with you as part of the effort," Chris noted back to Mitch, "It's really a baker's dozen."

"Lucky thirteen," Mitch did the math. "Good thing we're not superstitious."

"That's all I had on my list today. Do you need anything else, Governor?"

"One more thing."

"What?"

"I need you to call me Rebecca. You've already seen my naked rear end. That qualifies us to be on a first name basis."

Chris nodded her head. "Got it, Rebecca."

"Consider yourself fortunate," Mitch couldn't resist a quip. "I didn't get to call her Rebecca until a good three weeks after I'd seen her naked behind."

"Four weeks!" Rebecca teased back.

"I stand corrected."

"You're sitting."

"I'm tired."

"Well," Chris stood up, "If that's all you need, Rebecca and Mitch, I'll go for now. Here's that folder of information." Chris handed everything to Mitch to sort out. After she breezed out, Mitch studied Rebecca. She looked overwhelmed, in spite of her brave façade in front of Chris.

"You okay?" Mitch asked.

"I will be. I need to check in with my staff. Is there anything you need before I get all tied up in work?"

"Just one thing. How did it go with Mary last night?"

"I won't lie to you, she has me worried. She's talking about quitting the Center."

"And then what?"

"She said she wants to help out with rehab."

"That would be great."

"But I really think she's resigning so she can move out east."

"To be with Hilary?"

"It has me worried."

"You mentioned that. Let me see if I can find out anything more. In the meantime, don't you work too hard!" Mitch leaned over and kissed her forehead. There hadn't been much in the way of affection between them lately, and for good reason. Mitch wasn't worried. Yet.

Trish followed her morning routine as she did most days in her new lifestyle as a wanna-be author. She slept in, got up, made coffee, took a shower and then checked her e-mail while still swallowed up in her robe. She wasn't quite yet addicted to the computer. Most die-hard computer nerds check their e-mail at each above-mentioned interval. Get up, check the e-mail. Make coffee, check the e-mail....

Besides, if there was mail for Trish, she liked the anticipation. After all, it was the only anticipation she was getting lately. Robbie was in touch.

Trish,

How can I ever thank you for inviting my parents to the hospital dinner party? They had a fabulous time! On another subject, I have been thinking about your book, and your search for someone to interview. Working in a nursing home, as I do, I see a lot of people who are of the

right age. Now, I don't want to get your hopes up, but I may have found a lead. Let me know if you are interested, okay? Thanks again,
Robbie

Trish had picked up her phone to dial Robbie the second she read "I may have found a lead." She got through to Robbie's answering machine and left a very plain, simple message. "This is Trish. I'm interested."
Then, a bit on the nervous side of anticipation, she went to the hospital to help.

Chapter 15

Mitch read the letter again. There had to be more.

Dear Governor Fairbanks,
We at SAIL Inc., wish to donate the sum of
$100,000.00
to your rehabilitation fund.

We wish you the best of luck.

SAIL Inc.

Well, SAIL Inc., sure hadn't wasted any ink, Mitch thought as she checked out the letterhead. SAIL, Inc., was operating from a post office box in Diamond Bar, California. You'd think with money like that to throw around, they could at least have a street address. They probably did, they just had the P.O. Box for convenience. All this, as well as the roster of team member's names were jumbling through Mitch's mind when both Mary and Trish showed up. It was a great excuse to have a mid-morning gay gals discussion in the hospital coffee shop.

"This is a list of your mom's team for rehab."
Mary whistled. "That's quite a group."
"I wonder if any of them are gay?" Trish mused.
"I see three offhand," Mary answered matter-of-factly. She had the Gay Who's Who in her head.
"You do?" Mitch said.
"Sure."
"What about the others?"

"I don't have gay x-ray vision. I can't see through the closet door."

"Well, I guess we'll know, if we're supposed to know," Mitch trailed off.

"I have some interesting news!" Trish announced.

"What?"

"I may have found a good source for my book."

"You had all but given up hope on that," Mitch looked pleased.

"I know. Now, nothing's for certain. It's only at the hope stage right now."

"What's next? After hope?"

"I have a call in to Robbie."

"Robbie found you a lead?"

"She thinks."

"Who's Robbie?" Mary asked.

"That's right! You haven't heard about Robbie!" Mitch exclaimed. "Imagine that!"

"Robbie, Roberta, is the daughter of Rose and Max."

"So, she lives here in Colorado."

"No, she lives in Arizona. She works at a nursing home complex."

"So, you're going to Arizona to do research?"

"I don't know yet. I'm still trying to talk to Robbie in person, I mean over the phone in person."

Mary gave Mitch a look that conveyed the sum and total of the situation. *"Trish has fallen hard, hasn't she!"*

Mitch just nodded. Real slow.

"So," chirped Trish, "I'd better go try to call her again!"

"Good idea," Mitch nodded. Again.

Trish took off down the hall, even though she had a cell phone right in her hand.

"Robbie?" Mary asked again.

"Roberta Goldstein."

"Looks like Judy is off the A-list for good."

"It happens."

"My mom told you about me and Hilary, didn't she?" Mary segued.

"She mentioned it briefly."

"Hilary is in therapy. She's working on her problem and no, we're not sleeping together."

"I'm glad to hear that. Your mom also mentioned that you're quitting your day job."

"I want to be here to help."

"I appreciate that. You're a darn sight easier to get along with than Aunt BeBe."

Mary chuckled. "She is something."

"Hey! I know something you could do to help out."

"Sure. What?"

"Find out everything you can on a company called SAIL, Inc. out of Diamond Bar, California."

"Why?"

"Because they sent an unsolicited donation to us. Any company who does something like that deserves a second look."

So, everyone had their homework assignment. Trish was checking leads with Robbie, Mary was researching SAIL, Inc., and Mitch was studying dietary guidelines for the upcoming Friday Afternoon Feast. The way she had it figured, Fridays were a great day to celebrate a week's worth of work. Okay, so maybe she had to get things a little more on the healthy side. There were lots of healthy options from her four previous restaurant choices, and if she arranged for one honest-to-goodness health food outlet to be in the mix, even Clark, the dietitian, might approve.

Mitch got on the phone and called around, requesting copies of menus from no less than seven health food restaurants. She asked that they be sent to her "ranch house" address and immediately thought to herself, "Oh geez, the ranch house!" What was she going to do about the structure? Could it be refurbished and remodeled, or should she just raze it and start all over? Decisions, decisions. That's why they had the team, to help with these quandaries. By lunchtime, Mary and Trish were gone, Reb was asleep and Chris was at loose ends. Mitch went in and sat down in Chris's office and asked her one question that had been in the back of her mind for a while. After fielding a few questions in return, Mitch got an affirmative.

When Reb awoke from her nap, she had a special visitor.
"Doozie!"
Mitch had a tenuous hold on one very excited dog.
"Come here, girl!"
Mitch placed Doozie in Reb's arms and watched both of their spirits rise markedly. After much conversation, all one-sided of course, Doozie settled in for a long stay.
"How did you get permission for Doozie to visit."
"I'm passing her off as a therapy dog. Seems to be working."
"She's a good visitor."
"Pets tend to be that."

They whiled away the time until dinner, ate, and then talked about the night. Rebecca assured Mitch that it would be absolutely okay to spend her nights at home now.
"I won't stay at the mansion," Mitch was stubborn.

"So, then, stay at the ranch house. Doozie loves it there, too. Then, I can call you direct and you can call me direct. I'll be fine and you'll be so much more comfortable."

"I surrender. You've convinced me."

"Good. I had it planned that way."

Mitch kissed Rebecca goodbye and then gathered up Doozie to go.

"See you in the morning."

"Goodnight."

Mostly because Doozie was with her, Mitch put on a brave face all the way home. It wasn't until Doozie was chasing down phantom shadows and scents out in the yard that tears began to trickle down Mitch's face. They flowed well over ten minutes. She had once disliked Jake when he was alive. Now that he had ripped a once-well Rebecca forever from Mitch's life, she utterly loathed him. The other driver, totally innocent and extremely penitent, would forever have Mitch's gratitude. They had called the paramedics straight away and saved Rebecca's life. Mitch would have given them a million-dollar reward, except she now worried about future expenses. So, instead, she called and thanked them personally. It pulled her out of her melancholy mood and, in better spirits, she called Mary.

"Any luck tracking down SAIL, Inc.?"

"Nothing on the Internet. I could do a library search."

"Whatever."

Then, Mitch tried to call Trish. The line was busy. Mitch put two and two together, or in this case, one and one.

When Trish had called Robbie from the hospital, she didn't catch her. Some days were like that. Finally, they connected in the evening.

"You've had a long day," Trish noted.

"I had some shopping to do after work."

"Did you buy anything frivolous?"

"Oh yeah, some frivolous meat and chicken and celery and rice."

"You're quite the wild shopper," Trish said, trying hard to not jump right to her question.

"I do my best. I got your message."

"So, you have a lead for me?"

"I may have. I don't want you to get your hopes up."

"I won't," Trish lied. "Tell me what you've found."

"I found Albert."

"Albert?"

"He's one of the residents at our facility."

"Really! How about that," Trish said. The phrase sounded so unoriginal that it embarrassed her.

"And he doesn't have any family left."

"Never married?"

"Never married. Of course, I shouldn't go into his personal file information."

"I understand," Trish agreed and then puzzled, asked, "How do you know if he would be a good subject for my interview?"

"He has a distinguishing mark."

"A mark?"

"A tattoo. A number tattoo."

"A concentration camp tattoo?"

"Right. At least, it's the same kind my parents have." Trish strained to recall.

"I don't think I've ever seen your parent's tattoos."

"They cover them most days."

"I see. Well, back to Albert, what do you suggest I do next?"

If Robbie had given the situation much thought, she didn't give Trish any inkling.

"You could always come and visit him."

"That would be a sensible thing to do. Let me think it over. Things have been day-to-day up here."

"Of course."

"What else should I know?" Trish asked more from instinct than curiosity.

"Just don't wait too long."

"I understand."

"I knew you would."

Trish called around until she found Mitch.

"You okay?" she asked first and foremost.

"Sure, why?"

"I just didn't know you were sleeping at the ranch."

"Reb suggested it. She thought I'd sleep better."

"She's right."

"She always is. What are you up to?"

"I'm trying to make a decision."

"And you need *my* advice?"

"More like your permission."

"My permission! That's a first."

"I finally got through to Robbie tonight and she has found someone she thinks I could interview. Some guy named Albert."

"That great news!"

"Except he's in Arizona."

"That's close. You got lucky."

"And not only that, he's a resident of the place where Robbie works."

"That makes sense."

"But I would need to go down there to do the interview."

"And you need me to help you pack your suitcase?"

"It's a bad time to go right now, with Rebecca in the hospital and all."

"You go do the interview. I have over a dozen people who are going to be on our rehab team. I will miss you, but don't not go on my account."

"Are you sure?"

"Absolutely. We will keep in touch and update you. We miss you already. Now, go."

"Okay. I'm packing."

"Good luck."

"You, too."

Trish packed as she made reservations at a discount motel chain on the outskirts of Phoenix. She reserved a week, beginning tomorrow night. Then, just because she was functioning solely on nervous energy, she put her luggage in the truck and took off. Traveling at night was restful to Trish. The weather was cooler, the highways were deserted, and truck stops with three-egg specials were open twenty-four hours a day. The last item was very helpful in breaking up the twelve plus hour drive. Six eggs later, Trish pulled into Phoenix. Her room was ready, miracle of miracles, and she stretched out for a quick nap. Midnight came quickly when you were sound asleep, and Trish had to decide whether to venture out for another egg-a-thon or make do with the snack machine in the motel lobby. A cola, a bag of chips and a candy bar was dinner and breakfast. Trish slipped into a sugar-induced stupor and slept until morning.

A hot shower never felt so good. By the time she emerged, the hours on the road were a distant memory. She dressed lightly for the torrid July heat, and ate a light breakfast at a spot near the motel. A bowl of oatmeal, a dish of cantaloupe, and a carafe of decaf was her idea of turning over a new leaf, nutrition wise. She settled the bill, left a generous tip, gassed up the truck and purchased a map of the city. It hadn't dawned on Trish until Albuquerque that Phoenix had to have its fair share of resident facilities for the elderly. So, rather than dropping in on the place where Robbie worked, which didn't seem right, being unannounced and all, she kept herself fruitfully occupied by becoming familiar with the city. She drove several of the major thoroughfares, roamed around downtown, and then patronized a shopping mall in the suburbs. By the time she got back to the motel, it was time for another shower and change of clothes. Then, dressed in a crisp new wardrobe, she dialed Robbie's number. To Trish's surprise, she picked up.

"Hello?"

"Hi there. It's Trish."

"I'm glad you called. What did you decide to do?"

"I'm in town."

"Here, in Phoenix?"

"Right."

"Well, then, by all means, come over for dinner."

Oh, like mother, like daughter, thought Trish.

"Are you sure? I mean, it wouldn't be a bother? I could bring a pizza?"

"I have a chicken in the oven. Do you need directions?"

"I need your address and some general directions. I have a map."

Robbie supplied specific directions and then warned Trish that she lived on the third floor of a rather confusing apartment complex.

"Better wear your hiking boots. There's no elevator."
"Okay. When do you want me to show up?"
"Five minutes from now?"
"Give me ten," Trish said after checking the map.
"Drive safely."
"Okay."

Trish had only to follow her nose once she got to the
apartment complex. The smell of chicken roasting was
unmistakably wafting from apartment 304. Robbie's door
was open, but Trish still knocked loudly. As Robbie
approached, Trish realized that her pictures didn't do her
justice. She had the gracious features of Rose and the full
figure to match. Her smile was radiant and as she directed
it toward Trish, the latter felt a familiar tingly warmth in
her knees.
"It's so nice to meet you in person."
"It's nice to be here," was all Trish could come up with on
short notice. Why hadn't she practiced something more
erudite during the long, solitary drive?
"You look hot. Come in and have some iced tea."
"Sounds great."
Robbie led the way through the apartment to a postage-
stamp size patio. There was room for either one chaise
lounge or two web lattice chairs. For whatever reason,
Robbie had two chairs, as if she had planned for company
well in advance.

The sun was still hours away from setting, but the patio was
on the shady side of the building. Robbie brought tea,
lemon and sugar. Trish indulged in all three and drank
thirstily. Two full glasses in less than five minutes.
"It's a good idea to drink a lot down here."

"I know I should drink water, but this tastes so good."

"Thanks," Robbie accepted the compliment gracefully.

"I really didn't plan to invite myself over for dinner."

"I'm glad you did, and it was a wonderful surprise. When you make up your mind, you really make up your mind."

"I don't believe in wasting time."

"So, where's your luggage?"

"At the motel."

"The motel! I won't hear of it. After dinner, you go and check out and bring your things here."

"I couldn't."

"I have a spare bedroom."

"It would be an imposition."

"I could have the sheets changed and the pillow fluffed by the time you get back."

"I really couldn't. I think I'd be able to work better at the motel. Writing can be like that."

"Well, okay. But any time you change your mind, the door's open."

"Thanks, really."

"And of course, you'll eat here. Dinner every night, rain or shine. There's more shine than rain, of course."

"Only if you allow me to pitch in and help. I will buy groceries and do my share of the cooking. Your mother was trying to teach me how to bake a cherry pie. I'm afraid I still need to practice quite a bit."

"You can use me as a guinea pig any time."

Trish looked at Robbie. Normally, a remark like that meant little, but it gave Trish a chill after all her study of the Holocaust. Was she beginning to be like Rose? Would a word here or there trigger a horrible concept from now on?

"Are you okay?" Robbie pierced the mood.

"Tell me more about Albert."

"Albert is Albert. He's a very old, very stubborn, very cranky man."

"What will I need in order to be able to see him?"

"His permission."

"Sounds easy enough."

Robbie had a look on her face that conveyed otherwise.

"What?"

"Albert is Albert."

"Meaning?"

"Nothing is easy where Albert is concerned."

"Well, I guess that nothing easy is worth having."

Robbie nodded agreement.

"I'll go check on dinner."

They shared a sumptuous meal of chicken stuffed with cornbread and pecans, honest to goodness mashed potatoes, roasting-pan gravy and creamed corn. It beat a bag of chips and a candy bar all to hell and back. After dinner, they took a walk around the apartment complex. It was quite gorgeous with palm trees, sparkling clean sidewalks and an Olympic-sized swimming pool.

"If I'd known about this, I would have packed my swimsuit."

"I have a couple of spares back at the apartment. Want to go and try one on?"

"I'd better not. Too soon after dinner."

"Come take a look at the club house."

Cold air blasted them as Robbie unlocked the first of a dual set of doors. Several rooms were set aside for card playing and meetings. Pool and Ping-Pong tables were deserted.

"Is it usually this quiet?"

"The weekends are busier."

They strolled around the grounds until the heat got to Trish. She would need to acclimate quickly if she hoped to work and play during her stay.

"Let's go get something cool to drink."

Robbie led the way through the shortcut and they were back upstairs in five minutes.

"It takes a few days."

"To what?"

"To get used to the heat."

"It shows?"

"Just a little, around the edges."

"Probably where I'm melting."

"So, you're going to drop in to visit Albert tomorrow?"

"I might as well get started. I've only reserved the motel for a week."

"Uh huh," Robbie said. Quietly.

Before Trish left, Robbie gave her a spare key and directions to work. "This will get you into the apartment and club house - just in case you want to try out that pool. Or the pool table."

"Thanks. Great. Dinner was wonderful," Trish said, backing out of the apartment.

"Thank you."

"Anytime."

If the parting was awkward, it didn't seem to matter to Robbie. Trish went out of her way to drive past the nursing center on her way back to the motel. Mostly to become more familiar with the neighborhood, and to keep from sitting alone in a strange motel room too long. Once back at the room, she started to seriously question her decision to pass on Robbie's spare bedroom. Bored and restless, she dialed Mitch, and caught her at home.

"You get there safe and sound?" Mitch inquired.

"I'm talking to you, aren't I?"

"Point well taken. You okay?" Mitch fished around a little more.

"Just a mixture of bored and nervous."

"Why?"

"I meet with Albert tomorrow."

"That's the retiree?"

"Right."

"So, I guess that means you meet Robbie as well?"

"Oh, we've already met."

"Really?"

"Yes. She cooked dinner for me. The woman can do things with a chicken that I've only read about in cookbooks."

Mitch chuckled. "Sounds like you won't starve."

"Not at this rate. But I'm going on and on. What's new up there?"

"Nothing. Reb starts rehab in a couple of days, just in time for the primary election."

"Oh hell! I forgot to vote!"

"That's okay. You've been preoccupied."

"Vote twice for me."

"Sure. Just send my things to Leavenworth. And give me the phone number of the motel."

After exchanging information, Trish signed off. She made a few notes, puttered around the motel grounds, looked askance at the dinky, kidney-shaped bowl masquerading as a swimming pool, and then turned in early.

For reasons known only to the gods of sleep, Trish woke up late. Not that it mattered much in a town half full of retired people. Oversleeping was a cottage industry around these parts. She drove fast and pulled into the parking lot of the Cypress Senior Resident Center about an hour before lunch. Robbie was manning a desk in the north wing.

"Good morning," Robbie greeted warmly. "How did you sleep?"

"Over, I'm afraid."

"You do look rested."

"And ready. Where's Albert?"

"Come on, I'll show you, but…."

"But what?"

"Don't expect too much on the first date. Okay?"

"I won't."

As they walked down the hall, Trish had that uncanny feeling that she was being watched. She was correct. Some stares were bold, some furtive, some vacant. It made her feel self-conscious but had no effect on Robbie. She had to be used to it by now. Robbie indicated Albert's doorway and then stepped aside.

"Aren't you going in with me?" Trish whispered, as if it were a funeral viewing instead of a visit.

"I'll be back in a few minutes. I have another resident to check on."

"Okay."

Trish inched into the room and then peeked around the privacy curtain.

"Hello?" she announced in a voice too quiet.

"Huh?"

"I said, 'Hello'!" Trish gained courage. After all, he didn't look like he was going to jump up and bite. In fact, she wondered if he could get up at all. He appeared to be in his seventies, with just a sprig or two of wispy white hair and frail, shaking hands.

"What did you say? Speak up. I can't hear you."

"I said, 'HELLO'!" Trish fairly hollered the greeting.

"Well, you don't need to yell. I'm not deaf!"

"Oh, okay."

"Who the hell are you?"

"My name is Trish Sull-"

"Get out!"

"Excuse me?"

"I don't know you. Get out!"

Trish backed slowly away and then went out to the hallway. The eyes of Cypress were upon her. Robbie came to her rescue before she could decide which way to bolt.

"How did it go?"

"Badly."

"How badly?"

"Very badly," Trish conceded defeat.

"Well, you'll do better tomorrow."

"Who said *anything* about tomorrow."

"I believe I did."

Trish studied the expression on Robbie's face. She believed in Trish. Perhaps it could become infectious and Trish could contract the disease.

"Why don't you make good use of that spare key. Go grab a swim and some rest at my place."

"I'll fix dinner as well."

"I look forward to it."

"That's because you've never tasted my cooking!"

"I'm always willing to try anything, once."

Robbie's calming effect soothed Trish. She drove to the grocery store to pick up a few things and only as an afterthought, picked out a swim suit in two minutes from a discount chain. She didn't have time to fool around, the perishables were waiting. The suit would do for a week. Trish carried the groceries up the three flights of stairs and guessed where to put everything. Then she spent a calming twenty-five minutes whipping up a meatloaf and then wrapped it and popped it in the refrigerator for future use. Then, she slipped into her new swim suit. It was modest and comfortable, not even remotely resembling anything in a swim suit edition of any magazine. She pinned the apartment key to her shoulder strap and set off. The pool was deserted and she dove in without preamble. The shock of the cool water washed away her frustration and she swam lap after lap until exhaustion. It didn't take too long, she was out of shape after a spring and summer of lethargy and research. Nevertheless, she found that she had acquired a minor sunburn and lectured herself on the walk back of the absolute necessity of using sunscreen from now on. Like, until she was ninety-nine! To her surprise, Robbie was home when Trish got back.

"Oh, hello!"

"Hi there. You look like a lobster."

"I forgot the lotion."

"There's sunburn medication in the bathroom cabinet. I started the casserole. It looks wonderful. 350 degrees okay?"

"Yeah, thanks, I'll go and change."

Trish took her time medicating herself and extended the process to include a beer. Robbie had changed out of her work clothes, opting for slacks and blouse. She was sipping lemonade on the patio.

"I didn't even ask if you like meatloaf."

"I love it. There aren't too many food groups that I don't like, as you can tell by my figure."

"You have a very nice figure," Trish said candidly.

The remark made Robbie blush. She hurriedly changed the subject. "So, tell me, what's it like to have a governor for a best friend?"

"It's unreal. It really is. It's like being plugged in to power."

"And everything they say about her is true?"

"Gee, I hope not! Imagine a life where everything they say about you is true!"

"I should narrow the scope of my questions. Is everything my parents say about her true?"

"Oh, absolutely. Your parents are two of the most honest people I know."

"They are good people."

Trish wanted to elaborate, to tell Robbie how brave her parents were, especially her mother. The story of war-hero Rose would be buried with her. The same, it seems, would happen with Albert if Trish wasn't careful.

"What should I do about Albert?"

"Just go in tomorrow and try again."

"He said he doesn't know me."

"That's true, except he does, *now*. Build on that."

Trish pursed her lips.

"That might just work."

The meatloaf was sinfully delicious. Trish slathered her portion with a heavy dose of ketchup, a habit carried over from childhood. A nagging, unasked question was dogging Trish's concentration. It wasn't until the conversation drifted back to Rebecca and Mitch did Trish remember. How could she inquire of Robbie if her parents had discussed Trish at any great length without sounding conceited. Or concerned.

"What did your folks tell you about me?" tumbled out of Trish before she could think twice.
Robbie looked up and started to speak. Then, she hesitated.
Trish held her breath.
"They told me you were a writer and an important person."
"Well, they told me you are a wonderful daughter, and they were right about that."
Again, a blush.
"And beautiful," Trish added with glee.
"Stop it. I'll get all swell headed," Robbie said as she began to clear the table.
"I'll help you with the dishes."
Together they loaded the dishwasher and scrubbed the stove and counters. It took all of ten minutes.
"You want some coffee?"
"No, thanks. I have to get home. Get some sleep."
"Okay."
Trish resisted the urge to dawdle and glance over her shoulder. She felt like she was thirteen all over again. Wishing that Robbie was watching and too afraid to check it out. Once back at the motel, she fell asleep, simply from sheer boredom. It helped fend off the acute loneliness.

The next morning, hazy stillness greeted Trish as she stepped out of the motel room. She debated eating a snack versus a full breakfast. Breakfast won the vote, not so much for the expanded menu selections, as for the time it afforded her to make notes. After she had scribbled a line or two, she realized the snack would have been a viable option. Even so, there seemed to be no need to rush. It wasn't as if Albert was spinning hour-long stories. What had Robbie suggested? Build on what little she had. Okay. She had met Albert. Albert knew her. She knew Albert. Other people in nursing homes could only hope to have company. Albert's first instinct was to toss people out. Trish finished her breakfast, determined to open the door wider between herself and Albert.

She drove to Cypress, walked in the front door and right to Albert's room. Boldly. Just because she could. Besides, Robbie was busy.

"Hello, Albert," she greeted breezily. And loudly.

"Who are you?"

"Don't you remember me!"

"I'm seventy-five years old! I don't remember what I had for breakfast, young lady!"

"I had waffles," Trish confessed. Why, she didn't know.

"You're not seventy-five. Now, get the hell out of my room."

"You would throw me, your friend Trish, out of your room?"

"I'd throw the mayor of Phoenix out of my room when he shows up."

"Has he?"

"Has he what?"

"Shown up?"

"You expect me to remember!"

Trish smiled. For some unfathomable reason, this felt like progress.

"Go away!"

"Okay, I'll let you rest, but I'll be back tomorrow and Albert--" Trish paused for emphasis, "tomorrow, I'll want to know what you had for breakfast."

He waved his hand in dismissal. Taking her cue, Trish left the facility. Back at the motel, she made notes of their conversation. Albert said he was seventy-five, and frankly, he looked every bit of it. He claimed to have faulty memory, which may or may not be true. How many times did memory lapses occur out of convenience? Several presidents came to mind.

Trish found herself staring out of focus at her notes. Time for a stretch. She hopped in the truck and drove to a department store famous for household goods. She wanted to buy a coffee pot for the motel room, and ended up with several other goodies as well, including cups, saucers, matching tablecloth and napkins, a medium price range set of flatware (just for the spoons, mind you) three bath towels, fifteen bars of soap (packaged that way on special) two pillows, two pillow cases, and a toaster. If the motel manager thought she was moving in for the long haul, they only need call Mitch in Colorado for assurances that in Trish's case, this was just a minor shopping spree. Wait until she really got the itch.

It was still early afternoon by the time Trish had unloaded her purchases, set up everything electric, and personalized the bathroom. It would only take a modest tip for the cleaning crew to leave her stuff alone, she hoped. Next, she hit the grocery store. Again. She bought some things in quantity that she knew how to cook, like bagels for instance. Pop those in the toaster and breakfast is served. Enough of the waffle and syrup diet if Trish wanted to live as long as Albert. Her thoughts turned to the man. He didn't strike her as a Holocaust survivor, but neither had Max or Rose. Especially plump, good-natured Rose. And how Robbie took after her mother! With her mind mostly on Robbie, Trish absentmindedly bought almost every kind of canned vegetable, which with all the varieties out there, amounted to quite the pile of cans in her shopping cart. She stocked up on soup, no pun intended, and made a point to buy the cream kind that, with a few more things added, such as, meat, chicken, pasta, rice and five or so other ingredients, could be transformed into a main dish. Okay, so it wasn't a *miraculous* transformation. It still worked in a pinch. Next, Trish pondered buying frozen foods. It wasn't that Robbie didn't have a freezer. The refrigerator had one built in right on top. The pondering was more about whether or not it would seem presumptuous on her part to stock it. Trish weighed the circumstances. Robbie had offered her a room, but freezer space was an entirely different matter. She passed on anything that required refrigeration, except for the things she needed for tonight's feast, which was hamburgers in mushroom gravy with potatoes and corn. Diner food at its best.

Trish started dinner at three and then watched TV until Robbie pulled around five.
"Sorry I'm late."
"Is this late for you?"
"Report took a little longer than expected. Did you cook again? Smells great! What is it?"
"Meat and potatoes and gravy."
"Comfort food. My favorite."
"It's ready when you are."
"Which should be in about ten minutes."
Trish set the table while Robbie changed out of her "greens." That's what she called her work attire, even though most days it wasn't green at all but a floral or

247

checkered pattern. "Lively" was the word that came to mind when describing Robbie's appearance. It wasn't surprising, therefore, to find that Robbie's taste in street clothes bordered on the mundane. Plain white, deep blue, black and brown were the primary off-duty colors. Which, just in case anyone was wondering, Trish thought Robbie looked gorgeous in.

"So, you didn't come to Cypress today?"

"I was there."

"I didn't see you."

"I wasn't there very long."

"Did Albert toss you out again?"

"We managed to talk a little more than yesterday. I took your advice."

"I don't remember giving any."

"You told me to build on our conversations."

"I guess I did."

"Are you okay?"

"I'm just tired from the day."

"I understand. Let's eat and then I'll go home."

"I said I was tired. That doesn't mean I'm tired of you."

"Well, okay. But I'll do the dishes."

They were silent through the first half of dinner.

"What's on your mind, Trish?" Robbie asked, apparently catching her breath from her long day.

Trish looked up, caught unawares by the question.

"Nothing's wrong."

"Then why are you fidgeting?"

"I was fidgeting?"

"Something bothering you?"

"I was just wondering what to cook for dinner tomorrow."

"I thought tomorrow was my turn."

"Well, I seem to have more free time than you do. But I don't want to take over. You know the old saying, 'A woman's kitchen is her castle.'"

"That's not an old saying."

"It is where I come from."

Robbie tried another tack. "What did you do after your visit with Albert?"

"I went to the grocery store."

"And…?"

"I bought stuff. A lot of stuff."

"Stuff?"

"I bought a bunch of groceries," Trish said, feeling more like a child and having no earthly idea why.

"That's sensible."

"They're back at the motel."

"Now, *that's* interesting."

"*Because* I didn't want to presume."

"Now I see," Robbie gained insight. "For goodness sake, Trish, presume away! You should bring them over. I'm sure the motel room is crowded enough already."

"It kind of is," Trish smiled with relief. "Especially with the coffee pot and toaster."

"Sounds like you're setting up a restaurant!"

"I thought about a waffle maker, but you *know* how batter can drip."

Robbie chuckled at the thought of Trish making waffles at the motel.

"You know," she announced after dinner, "I'm not as tired as I thought I was."

"Then why don't we go for a swim?"

"Why don't we go for a walk instead."

"Do you use the pool much?" Trish asked directly.

"Once is a while. Late in the evening. It's quieter then."

249

"Sounds lovely."

Trish cleared the table, glowing in this new-found information. If ever she was to see Robbie in her swimsuit, it would be late in the evening. The images flooded her mind and her hands worked quickly to hurry through the chores. In the meantime, Robbie called Cypress. After a brief chat, she informed Trish, "I'll have to cancel our plans. I need to go back into work for a while."

"Oh, Okay. That's fine. I'll just head back to the convenience store that's masquerading as my motel room," Trish joked, hiding well her disappointment.

"Sure," Robbie answered, completely distracted.

Trish left as Robbie changed into her greens.

The motel room actually felt a little more welcoming now that it was full of homey stuff. Not as much fun as a midnight swim with Robbie, but there's just some things you can't rush.

Chapter 16

The first day of rehab was tolerable. The Honorable
Governor was feeling just a little bit too satisfied with her
efforts. You know, like that first day on the weight
machine. Then, that second day arrives…and it was hell on
earth. Rebecca hadn't even *cared* to discuss the looming
day three with Mitch, so they had eaten dinner in silence.
Mitch had watched Reb move with grimaces, and decided
to try and get her mind off all things rehab.
"I'm planning a victory party for Tuesday. Got any
requests?"
"Can I request that you cancel it?"
"Nope, sorry, that's not one of the options. But I will keep
it down to a mild roar. A few hundred of our most intimate
friends, maybe?"
"You've got to be kidding."
"Yeah, but just a tad. We do need to do something for your
campaign staff. They have worked hard."
Jake did manage to build up quite a corps of volunteers
before…."
"Before the accident."
"Right. I'm just not sure the hospital staff is going to be
thrilled with a horn-blowing party."
"Let me see what I can arrange. Maybe there's a meeting
room we can borrow. And then, I'll cancel the order for ten
thousand horns."
"I'll leave it in your capable hands."
"Do you want to talk about today, yet?"
"No."
"Not even a little?"
"No!"

Mitch shrugged her shoulders. She didn't feel like she was being much support.

"Want to hear about my day?"

"Sure," Reb answered dully.

"Mary and I-"

"Where is Mary?" Reb pounced mid sentence.

"That's what I'm trying to tell you."

"Is she with Hilary?"

Mitch silently counted to three. Sometimes the governor could be so ahead of everything.

"Is Hilary out here on another vacation?"

"Not that I know of."

"Well, what then?"

"You know, I'd actually finish this story if I could just get the chance to begin it!"

"Okay. Mary and you...."

"Mary and I have been looking into this donation by the SAIL Corporation."

"Why?"

"You know, I don't know exactly why, but I've just had this funny feeling about it."

"The donation or the corporation?"

"Both, and in that order. A donation comes in from out of the blue from a corporation that has a post office box number."

"Did you cash the check yet?"

"No. It has a sixty-day void directive."

"What is your main concern?"

"What if it's got an unsavory past?"

"The corporation?"

"Right. I mean, they could be making kiddie porn or something equally distasteful."

"Okay, so I have half the story. What about the 'Mary' half of the story?"

"I sent her on a mission."

"A mission?" Reb asked with that tone of voice that indicated that she was about to explode.

"A small mission."

"How small?"

"I sent her to Diamond Bar, California."

"Diamond Bar, California? Why?"

"Two reasons. First, it's about as far away from Hilary as I could think to send her in the continental United States."

"And second?"

"That's where SAIL Inc. has its P.O. Box."

"And now, just so I have this straight, you have sent Mary halfway across the country to investigate a corporation that, for all you know, makes kiddie porn?"

"Well, you wanted me to take her mind off Hilary, and besides, California isn't exactly half-way across the country."

"Why didn't you just suggest a hobby!"

"What, like finger-painting?" Mitch scoffed.

"When did she leave?"

"This morning."

"Without saying goodbye?"

"You were baking a cake in rehab."

"I was lifting weights today."

"You were? Two days in a row you've lifted weights? God, you're good."

"Damn, you're sneaky," Reb said without irritation. Mitch had tricked her into discussing the day after all. Which was something she had really wanted to do anyway. Even if just a little.

"I know. And I know that you have some super sore muscles and I think you are so brave to put up with the pain."

"Should I worry about Mary? Tell me honestly."

"I'll tell you when to worry. Don't worry now. Just rest all those big, huge sexy muscles you're developing."

"Shut up."

Mary's flight went without incident, but the drive from LAX to Diamond Bar was another matter. Mitch had told Mary to spare no expense, which extended from car rental through hotel room. Mary had rented a Ford Explorer, knowing that time spent on the highways of California would be at times sluggish and otherwise fast and furious. Hence, the tenuous drive to the Diamond Bar Post Office. The box was easy to locate, the real problem was that there were several hundred there to keep it company. The postal workers could be no help. In fact, Mary spent as little time as possible on this visit to avoid arousing suspicion. If she was approached, she had a plan all worked out. She would inquire about renting a box herself. Nothing more. Nothing less. It didn't come to that. Every employee in the place was far too busy with work to monitor the meandering of one person. Mary drove to the hotel and called the phone number Mitch had given to her. Rebecca, with effort, picked up the phone. "Hello?"

"Hi, Mom."

"Mitch told me you went to California."

"That's right. I just checked into the hotel. It's really nice. Are you okay?"

"I don't want you to be in any danger."

"I went to a post office. No danger there. How was your therapy session?" Mary changed the subject.

"Tiring. Do you want to check in with the head spy?"

Mary giggled. "Sure."

Reb handed the phone to Mitch. "It's for you, Double Oh Seven."

"Thanks."

Mary filled Mitch in on what little she had accomplished her first day and awaited further orders. Mitch brainstormed out loud.

"Is there a way you can watch the post office from your car without some ambitious citizen calling the police?"

"I suppose I could pass myself off as a lost tourist. You know, have a map unfolded and ready."

"That might work for an hour or two, tops."

"Got a better idea?"

"While you're posing as a tourist, look around to see if there's a motel or house or coffee shop or apartment where you could hang out and watch. If you need to buy a telescope or binoculars, just charge it to me."

"I can just see me in a Starbucks with a telescope."

"Get me a triple-shot mocha while you're there!"

"Does my mom want to talk to me again?"

"You want to talk to Double Oh Eight?" Mitch winked at Reb.

"Sure."

Mother and daughter chatted for a few minutes before Rebecca got tired. She hung up the phone and closed her eyes.

"Going to sleep?"

"Only if you'll let me."

Mitch took her cue and wandered home. Doozie needed a long walk, and so did Mitch.

Trish arrived at Cypress a little after breakfast. If she wanted Albert to remember breakfast, the least she could do was give him a fighting chance. Eyes still followed her, but it was a bit more comfortable this time. Even a smile or two sprang up. Some folks were glad to see her again. She went to Albert's room and before she could even say "hello" he said, "Oatmeal!"

"Oatmeal, for breakfast?" Trish clarified.

"Right!" he beamed from ear to ear.

"Good," Trish nodded.

"What do you want?" Albert asked, now quite over his memory test.

"I want to know about you."

"What is it you want to know about me?" he looked suddenly suspicious.

"Were you in the war?"

At the word "war" he froze.

"Get out!"

"You don't want to talk about the war today?"

"I don't want to talk about the war ever! Get out!"

Trish nodded agreeably, but warned him in her best schoolmarm voice, "I'm coming back tomorrow and every day until you tell me your story about the war."

With that brave pronouncement, Trish walked confidently out of the room. It was her best bluff in ages. Robbie was nowhere to be seen, so Trish followed her suggestion. She went to the motel and loaded up the groceries. By noon, she was hauling sacks of canned goods up three flights of stairs. The door was open. Robbie was drinking coffee at the table.

"Morning!" Trish greeted, caught off guard by her presence.

"Hi," Robbie said wearily.

"Did you work all night?"

"I lost a patient last night."

The euphemism for death was not wasted on Trish. "I'm sorry to hear that."

"You'd think that being in this line of work would make it easier."

"I'm glad it hasn't."

"Why?"

"When you become unemotional or unaffected by death, you lose a big part of your humanity."

"Well, I've still got that part."

"Good. Do you need to go into work today?"

"I have the day off. I traded with someone."

"Let's take that swim."

"Now?"

"Sure."

"It's hot!"

"So, we can take a dip and then lay around in the shade. You can take a nap in the chaise lounge."

"Maybe for a few minutes."

"Great!"

Finally, Trish had succeeded in blasting away whatever barriers stood between Robbie and her swimsuit. When she changed and emerged modestly from the bedroom, Trish could only observe the entrance with stunned silence. She was absolutely gorgeous. Good thing Trish had a slight sunburn, it hid her blush well. They had the pool to themselves and paddled around like sea otters. When they emerged to cool off, Trish scrounged up enough cash to buy two cans of cola from the poolside machine. They relaxed and chatted.

"I didn't ask about Albert. How is it going?"

"I got ordered out. Again."

"I can tell you're getting used to it."

"He sure has strong feelings about the war."

"Wouldn't you if you were in the Holocaust?"

"More than I once thought possible."

"Thanks for doing the shopping."

"You're welcome." It was obvious that Robbie's lack of sleep was getting the best of her. After one more quick dip, they went upstairs and heated up leftovers for lunch. Then, to no one's surprise, Trish, not Robbie, fell sound asleep on the couch. Robbie turned off the TV and went to bed.

Trish stirred awake when she heard the coffee pot gurgle. She struggled for a second or two to get her bearings. Robbie's couch was so snug that she lingered for a moment, still pretending to be asleep after she remembered where she was. Which worked. She dozed off for another fifteen minutes to the soothing sounds of water running in the other room. Then, as Robbie walked through the apartment, Trish sat up.

"I didn't mean to wake you," she said softly. "Go back to sleep."

"You didn't. I can't. I have a bladder that can tell time." Trish took care of that issue and then joined Robbie in a quick cup of coffee. Work was awaiting both of them. They drove separately to Cypress and Trish arrived in Albert's room as early as the day before. He must have remembered their conversation about the war. He was tense and surly.

258

"Why do you want to know about the war?" he demanded right off the bat. No "hello." No "Oatmeal."

"Because I'm writing a book about Holocaust survivors."

"And what's that got to do with me?"

"You have a camp tattoo. I know you were a prisoner."

He glanced down at his forearm and then put his arm under the sheet. Too late.

"And you just decided to write this book?"

"I've been thinking about it for a while."

"Well, stop thinking about it! You can't write a book about something you don't know about! Or survived."

"I still want to try and understand."

"You want to *understand*?" he mimicked with sarcasm.

"I'd like to try," Trish said, ignoring his baiting.

"Okay. You want to understand. You want to know? Put your pocketbook and paper down and stand at attention."

"Excuse me?"

"I said stand at attention. And shut your mouth."

Trish considered his demands for a moment and then followed directions. Even being in good physical condition, Trish still felt the ache in her lower back and feet after an hour of standing still. When Albert dropped off to sleep, Trish quietly gathered her things and crept out.

Robbie caught up with her in the hallway, which was no great accomplishment with Trish still working out the cramps in her calf muscles.

"You were in there a long time. That's good!"

"I'm not so sure. I spent most of the time standing at attention."

Robbie looked concerned at this revelation.

"You did what?"

"I guess I'm pretending I've joined the army or something."

"Why?"

"That's for Albert to know and for me to find out. I expect an answer by tomorrow. He's sleeping right now."

"Why don't you go home and take a hot bath."

"Good idea."

Mary had awakened early as well to begin her first full day of impersonating Nancy Drew. Didn't people check their mail before work? She watched in growing frustration as stranger after stranger came and went. It was impossible to tell who went to which box. No one resembled a criminal, or even exuded suspicious behavior. Except Mary, of course. By ten, she had parked the rental car and walked around the neighborhood. There was one apartment house that had a good vantage point of the front of the postal facility, so she inquired about vacancies. One was available at the correct side of the building, but it was one of the largest apartments with a hefty price tag to boot latched to a year lease agreement. Mary breathed deeply as she signed her name on the line after stipulating that she needed immediate occupancy. Now, about that telescope....

By three p.m., surveillance central, code name Diamond Bar Tower, was up and functional. It wasn't perfect, but at least Mary was off the street. She checked in with Mitch, who was waiting for Reb to finish up the day's therapy.

"I got an apartment."

"Send me the bill."

"It's a whopper."

"Let me worry about that."

"I can observe the post office from here."

"Good."

"Except, I'm still not sure what I'm looking for."

"Leave that to me. Did you get a camera with a telescope lens as well?"

"No."

"Get one, and have it ready."

"Okay. Anything else?"

"Just keep in touch."

"Will do. Hug my mother for me."

"Consider it done."

Not only was this day three of rehab, but it was also day one of "group night" as well. This was the time when rehab residents and their support people attend a workshop. Tonight's topic was bowel and bladder. Mitch could hardly wait. She hadn't been this embarrassed since biology class.

Thankfully, the speaker understood all too well the unease of the crowd. She found it best to acknowledge the discomfort levels of the participants first and only then discuss the topic in its specifics. By the time the session wrapped up, Mitch knew more than she ever cared to know about the topic. She also, however, felt more able to help Rebecca with her adjustment to her new life. If a catheter needed to be checked, Mitch could easily be trained to do it. If a change in dietary habits was called for, Mitch could arrange it. For the first time since the accident, Mitch felt empowered. Rebecca was, by contrast, glum and moody. By the time they got back to the room, she was on the verge of tears. Her arms ached from her exercises, so much so that she needed extra help getting into bed. After everyone else had drifted away, Mitch attempted to assuage whatever else was paining the love of her life.

"For putting in such a long day, you're doing great."

"Leave me alone."

"Nope."

Rebecca shot a look at Mitch. She tried to appear miffed, but it fell far short.

"What do you mean, 'Nope'?" she said in her best gruff voice.

"I mean 'Nope.' I'm not leaving you alone right now. You can order your staff around, but me? I'm immune to that."

"If I said 'Please,' would you leave me alone?"

"In a few minutes. But first, Mary said that I had to give you a hug for her."

Rebecca gave the impression that she was thinking this over long and hard.

"Okay."

Mitch gathered a weary Rebecca in her arms, gently at first and then tighter as she felt the shaking that so often precedes tears. Mitch held on until she felt Reb relax a bit.

"You feel better?"

"I don't want to cry."

"You have to cry. It's a vital part of the healing process."

"It makes me look weak and childish."

"No, it doesn't. It makes you a little soggy and a lot gorgeous."

"You stop with the flattery," Reb remarked with absolutely no conviction.

"Make me."

"Can I go to sleep now?"

"Sure." Mitch kissed her on the forehead. "Goodnight."

Mary had had enough of this already! Siting around watching people through a telescope was next to the last thing on the list of the most boring ways to pass the time. Watching paint dry would be an improvement. Whatever illusion she had held previously that somehow this would be more interesting by virtue of the fact that she was doing this in California was dead wrong. She nodded off to sleep three times watching through the telescope before she decided to lie down, mostly to avoid eye injury by poking her eyeball into the lens on the way to the floor. After her nap, she called Mitch.

"This sucks."

"I guess that means you're not having any fun."

"I'm going to develop amblyopia at this rate."

"I've been thinking this over and I think I have a plan."

"The last time you had a plan we all ended up in Texas."

"Well, it worked, didn't it."

"Depends on how you define 'worked.'"

"Oh ye of little faith."

"What's your idea."

"What color can the human eye see at a great distance."

"Red," Mary answered quickly.

"Yellow."

"Red!"

"No, it's yellow," Mitch argued for her choice.

"Okay, for God's sake, let's compromise. How about orange?"

"Orange. Fine. Orange. Would you be able to see orange from where you are?"

"Well, I guess it would depend on the size of whatever was orange."

"How about a bright orange box, say, about a foot square?"

"Yes, I'm sure I could see a bright foot square orange box."

"Okay. I'm going to mail such a box to the P.O. Box address of SAIL. Whoever walks out of the post office with said box is our man."

Trish sauntered into Albert's room at ten on the dot the next morning.
"Hello."
"I don't talk to dead people."
"The remark stupefied Trish. Great. Now he couldn't tell if someone was alive or dead.
"What are you talking about?"
"You are dead."
Trish looked down at herself. As far as she could tell, she was still in her skin and her bones were still holding her up and she was on the right side of the grass.
"I don't look dead."
"This is no joking matter."
"Okay, so, why am I dead?"
"When I woke up yesterday, you were gone."
"You went to sleep."
"I told you to stand at attention, didn't I!"
"And I did. For a good long hour or more!"
"I didn't tell you to leave. If you were a Jew in a camp, you would be dead."
The point of the discussion was beginning to dawn on Trish. Albert was harking back to the prisoner roll calls that were the scourge of the camps. It wasn't enough to expect people to slave endless hours on a starvation diet. No, they also had to stand, sometimes for hours on end while they were being tallied. In the insanity that permeated the Nazi brain, they were fanatics for numbers. One missing prisoner, or even a simple miscount, delayed

the roll call process for hours. Prisoners too weak to stand were shot to death on the spot. The dead were piled up as roll call continued. Dead or alive, they were tallied over and over.

"You don't understand anything," Albert declared his version of truth.

"Then, help me understand," Trish dared him.

"Stand at attention until I tell you otherwise."

Trish set her things aside and stood at attention. Her back muscles remembered yesterday's endeavor instantly, but she held out for two hours before she had to go down the hall to the restroom. When she came back, Albert announced again, "You are dead."

"I needed to use the restroom."

"Not during roll call, you don't."

"You mean that during roll call, no one was, uh, excused?"

"No. Not unless they wanted to die. What do you think it was, Kindergarten? Go away."

"I'll be back tomorrow."

"Dead people don't come back."

Trish walked out slowly, working the soreness out of her knees with each step. It hurt. Badly. Albert was making her understand. Almost too well.

There was no doubt about it, Rebecca was getting stronger. And more stubborn, if that was even possible. It was two days until the primary election and she was demanding changes in the buffet menu. And this from a woman who was ready to cancel the party the minute Mitch brought the subject up just days ago.

"Just because I'm on a strict diet doesn't mean that the staff has to suffer. I want five-hundred lobster puffs."

"*Just* five-hundred?" Mitch asked with a mixture of mock surprise and sarcasm in her voice. "*Only* five-hundred?"

"*And*," Reb continued, unimpeded, "those bacon wrapped livers and deep fried wontons stuffed with cream cheese."

"Good thing the party's at the hospital! Folks might be going straight from the buffet table to the operating table with food like that!"

"Are you going to call the caterer or are you going to make me do it?"

"It would be good exercise for your upper arms, not to mention your jaw."

"Hand me the phone."

It didn't take as much talking as Mitch had expected. From what she could surmise listening to the one-sided conversation, it seemed that the party on the other end of the phone was saying a whole lot of, "Yes, Governor Fairbanks." No wonder Reb was so crazy about Mitch. Mitch would still say "No." From time to time.

"There. That's taken care of. Anything else?"

"Gee, I'm all out of tall buildings to leap in a single bound, Superwoman Fairbanks."

"Calling caterers I can do. Leaping is off the list for now." Mitch savored the sound of the last two words. Hidden in them was a sign of hope that had been buried for too long. She didn't make a big deal about it, but her face gave her away. It had a habit of doing that.

"What are you thinking about?"

"Five-hundred lobster puffs," was Mitch's cryptic reply. "It's the least I can do for volunteers who helped, even if it was in a losing effort."

"What makes you think you're going to lose?"

"How can I win? I'm in rehab, for God's sake!"

"So?"

266

"Nobody's going to vote for a crippled lesbian."

"I will."

"You don't count."

"Actually, I do. I already voted early."

"And so, I'll have one vote."

"And five-hundred lobster puffs."

"Where were you this morning?" Reb asked, suddenly curious.

"I was out setting lobster traps for the caterer."

"You're certainly in rare form today. Either that or you're up to something."

"I mailed a parcel today. The line at the post office was long."

"What kind of parcel?"

"An orange parcel."

"Do I even want to know about this?"

"Well, I mailed it express overnight. Mary is tired of being in California."

"You mailed something to Mary in a orange box?"

"No. I mailed an orange box to the mysterious P.O. box holder. So, when he shows up, Mary can take pictures."

"Of someone carrying out an orange box."

"Right."

"What did you put in the box?"

"A basketball."

"Okay, so let me get this straight. You put a basketball in an orange box and mailed it to a post office box so that my daughter can take pictures when someone picks it up."

"That's the plan."

"And you think I'm weird for ordering five-hundred lobster puffs."

"Hey, it could work."

"Mary isn't going to be here for the party, is she?"

267

"Keep the faith."

Chris came in on the tail-end of the conversation.
"How are things today?"
"Mitch is mailing basketballs to California," Reb snitched.
"And she's ordering lobster puffs out the wazoo!" Mitch pointed to Reb just for the emphasis factor.
"Why are we doing all this?"
"The lobster puffs are for the party," Reb justified her actions well.
"And the basketball is lightweight!" Mitch defended her endeavor.
"Why did it need to be lightweight?" Chris bit.
"You think I'm springing for extra postage!"

Chris went no farther down that road and instead opened a topic all her own.
"I know you might think this is early for this discussion, but we should begin to talk about wheelchairs."
"What about them?" Reb asked as Mitch sat down.
"I've talked to your entire team and the consensus is that you will need a wheelchair."
"I expected that," Reb stated matter-of-factly. Too matter-of-factly for Mitch, but that would be their little secret for now.
"Once you've accepted that as a fact of life, you still need to make a decision as to what kind of wheelchair you want."
"We want the best," Mitch jumped right in the middle of the discussion.
"She always wants the best," Reb explained, dead pan.
"I gathered."
"I want Rebecca to have the Cadillac of wheelchairs."

268

"How about the Mercedes of wheelchairs?"

"Hey, I have an idea, how about the Corvette of wheelchairs? Zero to sixty in record time?"

Chris interrupted the car discussion.

"Sounds like you two at least agree that you want something good. So, you'll be glad to know that wheelchairs can be custom made. Soon, you, Rebecca, will be measured for a custom fit and the chair will be manufactured to your specifications."

"What's the downside?" Mitch knew a little about how Chris structured these discussions and felt it necessary to ask about the negatives.

"It takes time to do that. The way you're going, you might be released from rehab before it's ready."

"Will I get a loaner in the meantime?"

"Oh, I thought we'd just have Mitch here carry you around until delivery."

With that. Mitch stood up and flexed her arm muscles as best she could with her own damaged limb.

"On second thought, maybe we'll just rent in the interim," Reb shook her head.

"Now, there's still one decision to make, and I do suggest strongly that you give this long and serious consideration. You need to decide if you want a manual or powered chair."

As Rebecca answered "manual" Mitch simultaneously said "powered."

"Manual," Reb assured Chris with a regal nod of her head.

"Powered," insisted Mitch with an equal amount of authority.

"Manual," Reb said to Mitch.

"Powered," Mitch held up her hands to make her point, like somehow that would help.

"I'll leave the two of you to mull it over," Chris offered.

"Thanks, Chris," Rebecca said.

Chris was barely out the door when the debate resumed.

"I'm strong enough to handle a manual chair. There's no way I'm going to allow my upper body strength to atrophy."

"You might want a powered chair to avoid fatigue."

"I'm not going to be tired."

Mitch thought of two or three pointed rebuttals, but decided against them. No use bringing fatigue into the argument now. Now that Reb had her fighting spirit back, it was more important for Mitch to be supportive than to win the argument. Geez, first it was lobster puffs and now this.

"I have an idea for a compromise."

"You've been around politics too long."

"Let's get one of each."

"I'm not sure the insurance covers one of each."

"Hey, we're looking for ways to spend the money from SAIL Inc, right? This could be a good use for the funds."

"Let's wait and see who picks up the basketball."

"Whatever you say, Coach Fairbanks."

Chapter 17

If you looked up the word "determined" in the dictionary,
you could very well find a picture of Trish for an
illustration. Here she was, back again, in Albert's room.
He must be bedridden, he was never anywhere but in bed.

"Good morning, Albert."
"Go away, dead person."
This was wearing very thin on Trish's nerves.
"I'm not dead. Neither are you. I want to know how you
survived."
"I survived because I stood when the Nazis told me to stand
and I worked when the Nazis told me to work and when
they shot my friend next to me in line, I didn't move."
"You just stood and watched?"
"You got a better idea?"
"I would have tried to help."
"No, you wouldn't!"
"Yes, I would!"
"And they would have shot and killed you, too!" he lifted
an arm and shook his bony, arthritic finger at her.
"That's better than letting Nazi murderers kill my friend!"
"And then you would be dead, as well!"
Albert had worked himself into a shouting match.
"At least I wouldn't have died in vain."
"And you wouldn't be alive to bear witness, either."
Trish thought back to the Hall of Witnesses at the
Holocaust Museum. What would we know if everyone had
been exterminated per Hitler's plan? She remembered the
accounts videotaped for all to view. A thought struck her.
"Albert, what good did it do for you to survive to bear
witness if you don't ever tell your story?"

This quiet reasoning took the air out of Albert's sails. He seemed to deflate before her eyes and lapse into brooding silence.

"I need to sleep," he said with unsure voice that signaled tears were there to cry.

Trish left him to rest, to ponder, and to weep.

Robbie pulled Trish aside in the hall.

"We heard the shouting all the way down the hall. What on earth is going on?"

"Albert and I are finally coming to terms."

"Loudly, it seems!"

"He started it," Trish stood up for herself.

"Sounds like a playground defense to me."

"Hey, you do your research your way and I'll do mine my way."

Trish left the building, not really caring at that point who was watching. Between her frustration with Albert and her ubiquitous homesickness, she was afraid of snapping, particularly at people who didn't deserve it.

After she drove around in her truck for a while, she realized something. She didn't feel like shopping, cooking, swimming, writing, sleeping or eating. She felt like voting. With that settled, she drove to the airport, parked her truck in a secured lot and flew standby to Denver. She was at her place by three and at the rehab center by dinner time. Reb and Trish hugged and chatted like Trish had never left.

"How are things in Phoenix?"

"Hot."

"Too hot?"

"I needed a break."

Trish filled Reb in on the daily drill with Albert.

"He sounds like a man filled with pain," Reb said quietly.

272

"It is hard to get through to him."

Suddenly, they heard Mitch's approach. With her lilting "hellos!" to the staff, she was hard to miss.

"Look who came to dinner," Reb announced as she indicated Trish's presence.

"Trish! Look at you, all sunburned and everything!" Mitch exclaimed joyfully and she pulled her close but not too tight, on account of the sunburn. "Are you back to stay?"

"I'm just taking a breather. Besides, I wanted to vote. Remember, I forgot."

"And you'll be here for the party as well," Reb added with forcefulness.

"Yeah, the party!" Mitch agreed. "Reb did the menu. Hope you like lobster puffs?"

"They are my absolute favorite," Trish smiled. It was so good to be around people who appreciated your very presence.

"They're her favorite," Reb repeated the remark, directing one of her, "See, didn't I tell you," looks at Mitch. Mitch just nodded and rolled her eyes in pretend surrender.

"So, you'll vote first thing tomorrow and then we'll hang out and party and celebrate Reb's victory."

"And then I do need to go back to Phoenix. If only to check out and come back home for good."

"What? Things aren't going so well?"

"I'll tell you tomorrow. What's for dinner?"

"Anything but lobster puffs," Mitch giggled, just happy to have Trish in the room. It made everything a little less overwhelming.

Mary was just about ready to call it quits for the day. She had spied on every person going into and out of the post office. Her bathroom breaks had been like Olympic events: in, over, out. Meals, such as they were, had been hand held and taken in the chair as she peered at the customers. One after the other. In. Out. In. Out. Closing time was in ten minutes. It may have just been a blur the first time, but Mary sat upright. Something about the blur seemed familiar. She felt her blood tingle at this prospect. She readied the camera and prepared to take pictures. As the bearer of the orange box came out, Mary began snapping pictures, one after the other, including the car and license plate. When she finally realized who she had caught on film, the only words that came to mind were, "Well, I'll be damned!" Good thing her mother wasn't here. Such language!

Mary bolted down the stairs and pointed her rental car in the general direction of her prey. Not many people drive a metallic blue Porsche, with a silver racing stripe and vanity license plate with their name on it. Even so, Mary had a hard time catching up and then, just when she had the car in her sights, it was swallowed up by the hallowed grounds of a gated community. A serious gated community, not one of those faux sentry buildings erected for show. This sentry post had a guard with an honest-to-God gun. Mary documented the location anyway and then went back to the apartment to pack. She called the airlines and got a first class reservation for the following day. It wasn't soon enough, but it would have to do. Besides, it would give her time to get printed copies of her photography. She dialed the hospital and got Mitch on the second ring.
"Hi there!" Mary said.
"You sound chipper. What's new? Did you follow the orange box?"

"I sure did, and you're not going to believe this."

"Tell me."

"I'm flying back tomorrow. I'll have copies by then."

"Copies of what?" Sometimes, the modern world went by too fast for Mitch.

"Pictures of the mystery donor."

"Good work."

"Oh and one more thing, the answer is in the corporate name. I'll see you tomorrow."

Mary hung up before Mitch could ask for clarification. What had she said? The answer was in the name. Was it a play on words? SAIL rhymed with SALE. Was that it? Who did she know in sales? A few liquor salesmen came to mind from her days at the Lucky U. But not in California. Maybe SAIL meant boat? Did she know anyone named Boat? Or Tug, for that matter? Wasn't there a famous actor or musician named Tug? Why would he be giving money away?

"What are you thinking?" Reb asked after noting Mitch's meditation.

"Mary will be here tomorrow for the party."

"Aren't you glad I called the caterer now?" Reb asked for compliments so readily these days.

"Ecstatic," Mitch replied absently, still pondering Mary's call. Tug. Boat. Sale. God, this was maddening.

"Why don't you go home," Reb suggested bluntly.

"Tomorrow will be a busy day."

"Okay."

Mitch gave Reb what she mentally referred to as the usual rehab kiss. What it lacked in passion, it made up for in love.

Trish had long since gone home to gather her wits about her and to make an important phone call.

"Hi, Robbie, It's Trish."

"Are you okay?"

"I'm back in Denver for a day or two."

"I wondered where you had gone."

"It was a spontaneous decision. I didn't worry you, did I?" Trish asked the question before she had decided what answer she wanted to hear.

"I just hoped you hadn't become too discouraged about Albert. Whatever you're doing seems to be having an overall positive effect on him."

"It is?" Trish asked, surprised at this news.

"He seems livelier."

"I guess a screaming match is always good for the adrenal system."

"It does tend to perk some people up."

"Well, lively is one thing. Cooperative is another. I still don't know if he'll agree to help me with my book."

"I'm no expert on such matters, but I think you've made too much progress to stop now."

Overall, Trish was encouraged. Robbie was so good at this.

"I need to come back down anyway. My stuff is still at the motel."

"You didn't check out?"

"No. I still have the room for a day or two."

"You know, if Albert does decide to tell his story, you'll need that room for a while."

"Maybe they have a monthly plan?"

"Maybe so. Well, I'll keep an eye out for you."

"Thanks. And, Robbie?"

"Yes?"

"I appreciate all your help."

"Anytime."

The next day, Mitch was twitchy. There was no other word to describe it. She blamed most of the condition on the election. Good Lord, if she got this nervous over a primary election, imagine her trepidation when the general election rolled around. If it rolled around for Reb.

"You look worn out! It's only 8 a.m."

"I was dreaming all night about boats."

"Boats! It's a wonder you don't look seasick as well. Why are you dreaming about boats?"

"Mary said that the answer to the mystery about the donation was in the name."

"The name? Boat isn't the name. Sail is the name."

"Okay, genius, so what's in the word 'sail'?"

Rebecca peered at Mitch with an inscrutable expression. Most folks should never play poker with the governor.

"You know something I don't?"

Reb was rescued from answering either way by the arrival of the occupational therapist.

"Unscramble the letters," was her only parting comment. Mitch sat down and began the task. After all, there were only four of them. How long could this take. Okay, "S" at the beginning with all the other letters switched made for interesting words. SIAL, SILA, SALI. Did they know anyone named Sali? Sally. Nope, had to be Sali.

Mitch closed her eyes. She hated this. She was never good at crossword puzzles and usually broke out in hives at the slightest hint of jumbled letter challenges. Maybe she was borderline dyslexic? Or was it lyxdesec?

The problem went to the back burner of her mind and then, miraculously sprung back to the front, all solved. Neat and nice and tidy.

"It can't be!" she breathed out loud. "It just can't be!"

Reb, damn her, had it figured out immediately. Fine. She was probably some spelling-bee champion back in Kansas. She sure had a quick mind. They had to be wrong. Maybe they were both wrong. Only Mary and the photos could answer the question, and the possibility made her even jumpier. She called Trish, waking her up.

"What?" Trish sounded irritable.

"Were you asleep?"

"Yeah. I'm getting over jet lag."

"From Phoenix?"

"What do you want?"

"I want to buy you breakfast."

"Make it lunch and you got yourself a deal."

"Let's do brunch at the Bramble Bush. In an hour. I'll make reservations."

"Okay, alright, already. This had better be good."

"Oh, honey, it is."

An hour later, Trish was parked in front of a steaming cup of mocha. Mitch was sipping orange juice.

"Did you vote yet?"

"In my sleep?" Trish retorted.

"Sorry. I'm just on edge today."

"I noticed. What's up?"

"It started with a donation."

"A donation, to what, Reb's campaign?" Trish was warming up to the story.

"No, to Reb's medical bills."

"So, why is that a problem?"

278

"It was unsolicited."

"It just showed up, you mean."

"Right out of the blue."

"Pennies from heaven, to coin a phrase."

"Yeah, something like that. So, I had Mary check it out, which was no easy feat. She's been in California, following a basketball."

"Hold on a second. Tell me the truth. Am I awake or is this some weird dream starring you?"

"You want me to pinch you?"

"Not in front of everyone!"

"So, Mary found the anonymous donor."

"And is it someone special?"

"Who do you know that has money to throw around?"

"It's a Republican!"

"You know, I never asked," Mitch admitted.

"You talked to them?"

"Her. It's a her."

"Okay, so it's a *her* and you never asked her political persuasion and she's got money to throw around. In California. Melissa Etheridge! Did I guess right?"

"Don't you think Melissa Etheridge would be a Democrat?"

"I suppose so, but that doesn't mean you've never asked her. God, isn't that something. You know Melissa Etheridge. Can you get concert tickets?"

"No, I don't know Melissa Etheridge. Sheesh. I mean, sure, I know who she is. But that's not our donor. Think again."

Trish closed her eyes, trying to brush away all the mental cobwebs.

"Oh, I get it now!"

"Ah ha, right?"

279

"Holy God in heaven, what are you going to do?"

"I don't know yet."

"Keep me posted!"

They both cleaned their plates as Trish caught Mitch up on the Albert saga.

"You stood for *how long*?"

"Just three hours total."

"I see."

"You're bothered by it, I can tell."

"I just don't think you should have to put up with that sort of crap."

"Jews were forced to stand for hours on end in the camps. Sometimes five or ten hours and more."

"Right. But Phoenix isn't Nazi Germany and Albert isn't Hitler."

"I think it helped me understand."

"Did it help Albert understand?"

"I don't know. I'm not sure anyone does."

"Then I suggest that you refrain from participating in any more of these challenges. Your heart is open to understanding. That's all anyone needs."

Trish nodded. Mitch hoped it was in agreement,

"So, changing the subject, today is Reb's big day."

"Yes! She's fine and I'm a wreck."

"If she wins in November, you'll have to move to Washington D. C."

"I know."

"How do you feel about that?"

"I'd follow her to the Big Dipper."

"You're crazy about her."

"Still and always."

"Can I ask you something personal?"

"Anything. You know that."

"The injury has to affect your relationship, doesn't it?"

"It doesn't affect our total relationship, just one aspect of it."

"She can't feel a thing, can she?"

"Not below her waist."

"I'm only asking because I want to understand and just to let you know that you can talk to me anytime you need to vent."

"I appreciate that. Even long distance, to Phoenix?"

"Especially long distance to Phoenix."

"You haven't said much about Robbie."

"I'm in love."

"That much is evident. How does she feel?"

"She's not as evident as I am, apparently."

"Well, when do you plan to find out?"

"Soon. I'm not the dawdling kind."

"It's fun. You should try it someday," Mitch winked.

"Hush up and pay the check."

They stopped by the ranch house to check on Doozie and the contractors. It sounded like a rock group. Right after consulting with the rehab team, Mitch had called around to begin the process of remodeling the ramshackle house to comply with ADA specifications. Along the way, she also had about three or four bright ideas of her own, like, for instance, new wiring and new plumbing and a new driveway. Always willing to support the hard-working gay community, Mitch met with a gay contracting company at the hospital. They prepared blueprint upon blueprint as Mitch signed contracts and checks. Who could resist? They all looked so dashing in their tool belts. Even the guys.

It hadn't taken the brains of Frank Lloyd Wright to understand that a remodeling job could soon develop into major renovation when working with property as dilapidated as this. Every time Mitch went home, another wall was torn down. It was okay until the bathroom was stripped of its sheltering slabs of sheet rock.

"Something tells me I'm going to need a motel room soon."
"Stay at my place," Trish offered.
"You sure?"
"Absolutely."

They donned hard hats and discussed things at length with Delia, who explained, "We had to strip most of the interior walls to make the house wheel chair accessible as well as to rewire. The weight-bearing walls are in convenient places. Lucky you. The floor needs to be replaced and given additional support. Termites. You still have time to select the hardwood flooring that you want. The bathroom will need to be expanded to accommodate the wheelchair shower stall as well as the new toilet, basin and hand grip bars. It will be terrific when it's done."
"Sounds marvelous."
"The kitchen will be a wonder as well. Wheelchair accessible counters and appliances. And regular-height counters as well, just in case it's your turn to cook."
"A dual-accessible kitchen. How very unique."
"Exactly." Delia nodded her most efficient nod. "So, are you planning to vacate the premises for a while? Things are going to get awfully dusty."
"I think so."
"Well, you be sure to bring Doozie along when you visit. She's our favorite pup."

"Okay. "

"We'll work as fast as possible. We know you want to be back in your home."

"Don't rush on my account."

"Thanks."

As Trish got in the car, she confirmed Mitch's original thoughts. "She sure looks nice in that tool belt!"
They traveled across town, stopping first at Trish's polling place, and then arriving at the rehab center just after noon. The rehab team had promised in advance to release Reb early for her election party preparations. By the time Mitch, Trish and Doozie were settled in, Reb was bathed and coiffured, looking every bit the distinguished head of state.

"You look lovely," Mitch assured Reb, although the look was too stilted for it to be Mitch's favorite. The governor she had fallen in love with had wind blowing through her hair in the desert. "Have the news crews been by yet?"

"No," Reb replied. "I don't expect them until after the polls close."

"So, you have time for a nap."

"I don't think I could sleep and besides, it would muss up my hair."

"Well, if you're not going to take your nap, can I have it?"
Mitch didn't want to discuss mussing up hair right this exact minute in time.

"Sure. Go stretch out in the lounge."

"I think I will."
Mitch left Trish in Rebecca's custody, or vice-verse, for that matter. Once on their own, they taste tested the food when it was delivered. The lobster puffs were delectable.

"One down, 499 to go," Reb said as she served the first one to Trish.

"Two down, 498 to go," as she partook of the treat herself. Doozie couldn't talk but made short work of her sample.

Trish closed her eyes and moaned softly over the wantons. "Thanks for the invitation to the party. I know I didn't work on your campaign."

"You voted, that's good enough for me. Besides, you are so good for Mitch. I think she's going bonkers between my rehab and the home remodeling project."

"I told her to move into my place for a while. Hopefully, my Phoenix project will continue."

"It's like we're playing musical houses."

"And one day, very soon, your house will be in Washington D. C."

"We'll see."

Volunteers and staff began to drift in around five. The lobster puffs were gone by five-thirty. A great big unspoken, "I told you so," passed from the glowingly beautiful Governor to the humble sheepish significant other.

"I'll personally order five thousand for your victory party in November," Mitch vowed.

"Let's get through tonight first."

Primary elections usually received pretty ho-hum coverage from the media. A couple of contested races were the usual fodder. Reb's run added a spark to an otherwise boring election. As hard as Jake had tried to squelch Democrat opposition, there had been two other candidates vying for the spot. Reb was the most qualified, but the other two weren't gay. Most voters, when asked, saw those criteria as a toss up on a good day.

284

It was Mitch's opinion that such polls should be outlawed anyway. Her view was that they interfered with the decision-making process of the voters. Too much peer pressure, not nearly enough voter participation.

Mary breezed in about six forty-five. She always did have a knack for timing. Trish gathered another chair so Mary and Mitch could sit and watch TV. Others milled around, possibly looking for stray lobster puffs. No chance.

Technology was a wonderful thing. By seven-thirty, ninety percent of the vote was tallied and flashed across the screen. Cheers erupted throughout the halls. Rebecca had sole possession of a spot on the November ballot. As people pressed forward to congratulate her, Mitch made herself scarce. She huddled with the caterers to secure their services for the next election gala. They put it in ink on their planners. She helped them clean and pack things up and then presented them with a bonus check and a retainer. She then personally thanked as many people as possible before the festivities wound down. Soon, it was just Reb, Mitch, Mary, Trish and Doozie.
"You did it, you lesbian you!" Mitch finally got within hugging distance of Rebecca.
"I sure did!"
"I'm so proud of you."
"Thanks for all your love."
"All the time, every day."
They held each other for a moment. Ah, the spoils of victory.

"So, anybody want to see pictures of my California vacation?" Mary piped up, truly bursting at the seams with this news. Too bad no one was going to be surprised.

"Sure," Mitch said, calmly.

Mary produced an envelope with photos. They each received a copy of the photo and then looked from one to the other.

"What are we going to do now?" Mitch asked.

"Cash the check!" Trish affirmed.

"I agree," Reb said.

"Has everyone forgotten that there's probably still a bench warrant out for her arrest?"

"Oh, yeah," Trish nodded.

Once again, they all looked at their very own picture of the stunningly beautiful Lisa.

"I have an idea," Mary announced.

"Let's hear it," Mitch prodded.

"Since I still have the apartment and I know where she lives, maybe I could go back and do some more snooping around."

Mitch nodded slowly. After all, this idea was originally intended to distract Mary and keep her mind off Hilary. So far, so good.

"Sounds reasonable."

Reb shrugged her shoulders. She was tired from the day and didn't put up any objections. The meeting broke up soon thereafter. Finally, Mitch and Reb were alone.

"So, how does it feel to be almost a senator?"

"It feels almosty. I am worried about something."

"What? Whether the "Save the Lobster" group attended tonight's party?"

"No. I'm worried about you. With Trish in Arizona and Mary in California, that leaves a lot of responsibility squarely on your shoulders."

"Oh, I've got all that figured out."

"You do?" Reb didn't sound too terribly convinced.

"Yeah. I'm going to ask your sister to come back out and help."

"You *can't* be serious!"

"I am serious. I'll stay at Trish's and BeBe can stay at the mansion and terrorize everyone there. We can split the chores and help you get through rehab."

"She's an overbearing, homophobic pain in the neck."

"She's family."

"She wanted to ban you from the hospital."

"That doesn't mean I should follow her lead. She deserves a second chance. But, if it makes you worry, I'll leave it up to you."

"I've never met anyone as forgiving as you."

"I could've been a priest."

"Maybe in a hundred years."

"I'll think about BeBe. You get some sleep."

"You, too."

Mary decided to drive to California this time. Rebecca, the mother that she was, hid her panic well. Especially after Mary planned two overnight stops along the way, Green River, Utah and Mesquite, Nevada. It would take her that long to come up with a good plan for cornering Lisa. Both nights were enjoyable; plenty of food, swimming and sleep. Indulging in gambling fever at Mesquite wasn't so bad, either. Before she left Denver, she had asked Mitch if she could borrow some of her art supplies.

"You'd be taking up painting?" Mitch had asked.

"It makes loitering look less suspicious."

"There's a lot to loan out. Take your pick."

When Mary arrived two days later at her vacant apartment, there was plenty to unload.

Aunt BeBe must have been one of those people who had a bag packed all the time. From all the cajoling Reb had to do to talk her into coming back for a visit, Mitch didn't expect her for a month. Now, here Mitch was, waiting at the terminal gate for the Terror from the East, or perhaps the Mid-west? This idea, all of a sudden, was feeling less brilliant. Magnanimous on paper was one thing. In person, it was a whole other story. Reb had extracted a promise from BeBe before giving her permission to touch down that she had to speak to Mitch with civility. At all times.

Mitch caught the first glimpse of her as she marched up the walkway. She appeared as determined as ever to impose herself. Mitch steeled herself for the greeting.

"Hello, BeBe!" she said as cheerfully as her stomach would allow.

"Good day."

"We'd better go get your luggage."

"I know my way around."

"That's right, you've done this before."

"And without your help."

Silence stretched between them like bubble gum stuck to a shoe on a hot summer's day. They gathered the bags, all four of them. The fine line between visiting and moving in seemed to be a finish line that Aunt BeBe was heading toward full throttle. But every time Aunt BeBe glanced

over, which wasn't often, a warm smile radiated from
Mitch. Mitch was grateful just for the distraction. Rehab
was becoming maddeningly routine.

"Rebecca has made remarkable progress since you last saw
her," Mitch felt obligated to report as she nosed her car
through heavy commuter traffic. BeBe only nodded. She
was already up to eleven words. Mitch could be patient.

"And she won the primary election."

No response.

"And we're picking out wheelchairs together."

"She will walk again someday."

Mitch looked over and said, "From your lips to God's
ears."

BeBe appeared stunned that a lesbian would have the nerve
to talk about God, but she let the remark pass after a stern
look.

"But in the meantime, she's going to need a wheelchair."

BeBe must have felt that she had spoken her peace on the
matter. They arrived in rehab quietly. Reb was still in
session, so Mitch left BeBe to her own devices while she
took her luggage over to the mansion.

A year ago, Mitch would have approached this turn of
events with glee. If ever people deserved each other, it was
the staff of the mansion and Aunt BeBe. BeBe gave the
correct impression that she could shake the shutters when
she felt it necessary. After a month of her, the staff would
be begging Mitch to come back. Yeah. Right.

Even as Mitch unpacked the clothing, she felt dislocation.
Without Rebecca's presence, the mansion felt dead to her.
The air was heavy, the colors dark, the hallways

foreboding. A castle without its queen, Reb. Or court jester, Mitch.

There were signs that someone had given more than passing interest to making the structure handicap accessible, but they weren't nearly as far along as Mitch and her gay construction crew at the ranch house. So there. After unpacking BeBe's suitcases, Mitch headed over to "Construction Central" to see how things were progressing. And to visit Doozie. Poor Dooz. She had become a victim of circumstances over the past weeks. As lenient as the rehab center had been, Doozie still didn't get enough time with Reb and Mitch. Her days at the mansion were not in the least bit stimulating, and now completely out of the question, and the ranch house was a confusion of noises and smells that, on one hand were fun to investigate, they still interfered mightily with her naps. Every time someone ran a drill or electric saw, Doozie howled along. The crew treated her well, but it was still a far cry from her previous life. If Mitch stayed over at Trish's, it would be a calm place for them both. So, the plan was to keep an eye on construction during the day, visit the governor in the evening and sleep in the bachelorette pad at night.

Mitch gathered up an armful of Doozie and headed to the hospital. Reb would just about be finished for the day and then, it was group-workshop evening. Wonder what the topic would be tonight, and maybe Aunt BeBe could go as well? Deciding to tread lightly on that concept, Mitch carried Doozie into the room.
"What is *that* thing?" was the greeting blasted out by BeBe before Mitch could even get a polite, "Hello," out of her mouth.

"This is Doozie, the Wonder Therapy Dog," Mitch explained as she went over to peck Reb on the forehead. "You look great today."

"I look great everyday."

Mitch crinkled up in a smile. She did. She really did. "Must have been a good day."

"It was."

"You'd better get that dog out of here," BeBe interrupted Mitch and Rebecca's feel good moment of the day. Damn her. What timing.

"Why?"

"Because *it* doesn't belong here!"

"Why not?"

"Because *it's* a dog!"

Mitch couldn't argue with that news flash, but she did quibble. "She's a her."

"What?"

"Doozie is a female."

"Oh, so she's a bitch."

Okay, so Mitch only had to practically bite her tongue in two to keep from saying, "It takes one to know one."

Rebecca, brilliant woman that she was, could see Mitch's restraint. It wasn't hard to see the red begin to creep up her neck.

"Give Doozie to me."

Mitch put the wiggley bundle of dog next to Reb. For some reason, every time Doozie and Reb got together, they both settled down. The change was visible and instant. Reb would absentmindedly scratch Doozie's ears and Doozie would use Reb's left breast for a pillow. For a dog, she was one lucky canine.

Meanwhile, BeBe was still having kittens.

"Never heard tell such a thing as a *dog* being in a hospital that's *supposed* to be clean."

"Doozie's clean," Mitch defended. That red was still on the creep.

"It's dusty."

"Oh, that's just sheet rock dust. That's clean dirt. Besides, it's not like we're in the operating room."

"It's still a filthy dog, and it doesn't belong here."

Mitch took a moment to assess the situation before falling into the obviously bottomless pit of arguing further with BeBe. Aunt BeBe was just one of those type of people who considered it far more important to win an argument than to acknowledge the common sense being made on the other side. Couldn't she see that there were two perfectly contented beings in her midst? Reb and Doozie were so happy together. So symbiotic. Compared to them, Madonna and child appeared agitated. The artwork, that is. Not the pop star.

"Sit down, Sweetie, and I'll tell you my news," Reb said to Mitch. Not wanting to be left out, BeBe sat as well upon issuance of the command. Good girl.

"I talked to Jeff today."

"That's her husband," Aunt BeBe put in, for Mitch's edification.

"I think we've met," Mitch nodded, wondering why BeBe hadn't remembered seeing Mitch and Jeff in the waiting room just weeks ago.

"The ex-husband," Reb clarified.

"Not in the eyes of God!"

This was going to be a long story if it was going to continually be derailed by BeBe the caboose.

"So, Jeff was here?" Mitch pulled things back to center.

"We talked on the phone."

"Okay."

"He's going to stop by tonight."

"That's great!" Aunt BeBe launched out of her chair. "He *is* my favorite brother-in-law," BeBe put special emphasis on the verb tense.

"He *was* your *only* brother-in-law," Reb made two points at once.

"I can *hardly* wait to see him again."

Mitch didn't say it out loud, but she was thinking that someone should maybe call Jeff and warn him? Instead, she asked innocently, "Does Jeff know that Aunt BeBe has been so kind as to make a return visit…for an extended vacation?"

"I forgot to mention it."

Oh, the poor dear man. Matchmaker BeBe was tuning up to orchestrate a reconciliation and nobody was warning bachelor number one to bring his earplugs. This tune wasn't going to carry from here to the porch.

"Well, there must be more to that news?" Mitch prodded.

"He said he wanted to talk about the campaign."

Mitch's heart immediately shed ten pounds. What a relief.

"That's great news!" Mitch smiled in earnest.

"Surely, you're not going to continue to run for Senate, are you?" Aunt BeBe was going to go into second stage separation and throttle up over this one. She'd be orbiting the hospital in five minutes at this rate.

"Why not?" Reb asked bluntly.

"Well, because," BeBe blustered and then stopped as if that covered it. There were only two things that BeBe could be

293

blustering about, and right now, Mitch didn't care to hear the Gospel according the Aunt BeBe on either topic. Reb did.

"Because why?"

"Because you're *sick*, Honey."

"I'll be *well* by Election Day."

"You don't know that."

This from a woman who inferred that Reb would soon be walking again. Mitch silently wondered what the mixed message was here.

"What else?" Reb pressed the point.

"Well, you know," Aunt BeBe said knowingly.

"What?" Reb dared her to answer.

"People don't want *your kind* in office."

Mitch waited patiently for the awful truth to dawn on Reb. Not the awful truth that Aunt BeBe was indeed homophobic. Instead, the truth about how Reb had those same thoughts during her primary jitters. She had called herself a "crippled lesbian," but it came out sounding the same, even if you considered the camouflaged language employed by BeBe.

"I won the primary!"

"Well, everyone knows that Democrats will vote for anybody."

Gee, when BeBe said it that way, you could almost substitute the words, "vermin," or "cretins," for the word "Democrats."

"I'm giving people a clear choice," Reb practiced her speech on both of them.

"And when you lose, you'll still be Governor, dear."

Aunt BeBe sure had a way with words. Maybe Jeff could find a place for her on the campaign, like, chief in charge of sabotage? Speaking of Jeff, here he was now. Timing was important for any campaign manager. He was good.

"Hi, everybody. Aunt BeBe! Nobody told me you were going to be here! How wonderful!"

As he gave her a hug, he intentionally crossed his eyes at Mitch and Reb. It was one of his better mugs.

"How is my favorite brother-in-law!"

"Ex-brother-in-law and I'm fine. I brought dinner."

Considering the fact that he was empty handed, this was intriguing news.

"They are sorting it out in the staff lounge. They said they would come and get me when it was ready.

"Is it sinful stuff?" Reb asked hopefully.

"Mitch gave me a copy of the dietary guidelines," he grimaced.

"Oh, darn," Reb teased.

After all the complications of the divorce had settled down, Mitch had encouraged Reb to stay on good terms with Jeff. Naturally, it hadn't been a walk in the park. There had been unspoken issues between them for years, but it was important to foster support for Mary and for each other in times of crisis. There was nothing worse than relatives who carried grudges and feuds into hospital waiting rooms. All across America, people died every year while their loved ones sat in cold silence fifty feet away. Besides, Reb was getting a little more lovable, so that helped the process. Once upon a time, she had been somewhat like her sister, hard and unyielding. At least the condition had been reversible, in her case.

"Miiiiitch."

"What?" Mitch snapped to.

"That's some deep thought you were in!"

"Not the shallow end of the pool by any means. I was thinking about Mary."

"Is she still sleuthing in California?" Jeff asked. Apparently, he and Reb had been on the phone quite a while.

"Yes, and you'll never guess who she found."

"Rebecca told me already."

Mitch smiled. BeBe frowned. Dinner was served.

Trish hadn't had the luxury of dragging her feet when she went back to Phoenix. Time was ticking on her motel reservation and they couldn't renew the reservation for the room. Seems there was a convention of morticians and a softball tournament converging nearby. Every cheap motel room was booked. Solid. What wasn't booked solid was the apartment complex where Robbie resided. There was one unfurnished three-bedroom apartment for rent. One. For six months. The rate things were going with Albert, it might take six years. Six years he probably didn't have. So, unbeknownst to Robbie, Trish signed the lease and moved in. Now, that buying spree didn't seem quite so ridiculous. The coffee pot and toaster fit perfectly on the counter. The soap was exquisite in the bathroom. Gee, why hadn't she thought to buy a bed while she was at it. And a chair. And a TV tray for her books and pens. It wouldn't work to have Mitch ship some things from her place in Denver. She would need those herself. Besides, Mitch had her hands full. So Trish went back to the mall and bought an air mattress, a set of four hardwood TV trays, a patio chair, a hanging lamp and a clock radio. With her change, she splurged on a triple cheeseburger, onion rings and a strawberry shake. She ate as she drove and was through the cheeseburger and half the rings when she pulled up to the apartment. Moving in took four trips and then she washed down the rest of the onion rings with the shake. It was now time to consider options. She could visit Albert, swim, or test the air mattress. The third choice seemed logical and the inevitable happened about five minutes into the test.

Chapter 18

Enough already. Mary had painted and waited and lurked and consumed enough coffee to float the Queen Mary and she still hadn't cornered the elusive Lisa. In her newly acquired charmed lifestyle, Lisa drove from restricted area to restricted area like she was with the CIA. Mary couldn't get an even break, so after two days of nerve-wracking surveillance, she saw an opening and jumped. Lisa was having lunch in a normal restaurant, not the usual restrictive Country Club, just your average diner. Mary went into the establishment and breezed by the hostess. She had her prey in her sights and was standing at the table before Lisa had a chance to bolt. Mary was ready for anything, like for instance, a good fight.

"About time you caught up, Mary," Lisa said without even a glance upward or a drip of surprise in her voice. "Have a seat. I'll buy you lunch."

Somewhat deflated, Mary followed instructions. "You saw me?"

"Stevie Wonder could have seen you," Lisa said as she brought her eyes to Mary's. They were clear and bright. No hint of lost night's sleep here.

"You left Mitch in the lurch, you know that, don't you?"

"I took a vacation. Borrowed some money that she said all along that I could have. There's nothing wrong with that."

"She ended up in jail because of you!"

Finally, a remark that pierced the otherwise bored façade.

"Jail?" Lisa's eyebrows shot up.

"Yeah! Jail. Like, bars and cots and bail!"

"Why?"

"The judge in your lover's custody case held her in contempt when you two didn't show."

298

"Hey, don't forget that she was your friend, too! And besides, she wasn't my lover."

"Where is she, anyway?"

"She took off."

"With your money?"

"Part of it."

"The part you left lying around?"

"Something like that."

Mary couldn't help it. She gloated. "So, now you know what it feels like."

Further "I told you so," comments were delayed by the arrival of the waitress. Mary ordered soup. Clear, not cream. Lisa ordered three times as much food as the usual one-hundred pound woman would have ordered. The waitress almost got writer's cramp, but managed to get it all down. When she left, Lisa looked squarely into Mary's eyes. She asked, "Is that going to be enough for you?"

Mary thought about the question. Was it about gloating or soup? She settled down a bit, but continued the narrative. "And Mitch is losing the Lucky U."

"What happened?"

"When my mother forced the judge to release Mitch, someone started looking into the business deals of Marge. Everything is all tied up in legal wrangling, and Mitch is just giving up."

"That's too bad. I'm really sorry to hear that. I would have sent money if I had known."

"We don't need your charity."

"Was it you or Mitch who thought up the basketball trick?"

"Mitch."

"Well, even the Harlem Globetrotters would have approved."

"She wanted to know if the check was legit before she cashed it. When we found out that *you* were involved, we knew that a full-scale investigation was in order."

Lisa studied Mary for a full minute. Silently. Mary began to fidget after the first thirty seconds.

"You're still mad about Texas, aren't you?"

"I am not!" Mary snapped.

Lisa shook her head and smiled. "God, I thought you'd be over that by now."

Soup for Mary and salad for Lisa arrived. Klunk. Klunk. "Lunch be out in a jif," the waitress said like it was a headline news item.

Nobody made a move for their food.

"You all had your little role to play in Texas. Just because you ended up being the maid doesn't mean you need to be sore about it the rest of your life. You were a great maid, after all."

"Just hush up and eat, okay?" Mary requested.

"Okay. So, have you heard from Hilary lately?"

Lisa never did know the meaning of "hush up."

"We talk."

"And that's all?"

"That's not your concern."

"Maybe it is and maybe it isn't."

"It isn't."

"So, where is she now?"

Time to add "isn't" to the list, right below "hush up."

"In school," Mary answered. It just seemed easier at this point to surrender to Lisa's curiosity.

"That's good. And, how's the Center?"

"I'm resigning."

"Why?"

"You remember? My mother? The accident?"

"Well, she must be doing okay if you're out here in California painting and drinking coffee and peeping at people through telescopes."

"I'm doing this as a favor to Mitch."

"I guess I should give the old girl a call. Hey, here's a good idea. Come for dinner."

"Excuse me?" Mary said, not sure what the connection, if any, was between Lisa's thoughts.

"Come to dinner, tonight, my place."

"There's a guard at your place."

"Just pull up at six and flash your I.D. I'll take care of the rest."

Lunch arrived for Lisa. All three plates. Klunk. Klunk. Klunk. Mary had long since finished her soup and the sight of solid food gave her a case of the calorie twinges.

"Let's see, this one I ordered for you. I remembered that you like hot turkey sandwiches," Lisa said as she maneuvered the plate in front of Mary. Only sheepishness on Mary's part caused her to hesitate.

"Dig in. It's a long time until dinner."

"Thanks."

"So, tell me what's going on with your mom."

"It was all over the news."

"What haven't they printed?"

Mary studied Lisa to ascertain if it was true concern or prurient interest that spawned the questions. She decided it was the former and continued.

"Her campaign manager caused the accident."

"Really! On purpose?"

"It was more a case of unsolicited sexual advances."

"Oh, my God. He died, didn't he?"

"Yup," Mary said matter-of-factly.

"And your mom is paralyzed for life."

301

"So far. We're still hoping for a miracle."
Lisa nodded, knowing about hope and miracles. Mary saw compassion leaking out from Lisa's usual tough countenance and wondered if she had just missed seeing it other times. She shook her head to clear her thoughts.

Lisa made short work of her club sandwich and then picked at her veggie omelet. It wasn't like her to lose her appetite, but maybe it was just the heat. Diners could be warm places indeed. She paid the tab, boxed up the leftovers and then walked Mary to her car.
"Dinner at six."
"Okay."

Mary had packed light in the clothing department when she headed west. Now, she fretted that she didn't have something appropriate to wear to dinner. How could that be, though? She was dining with a fugitive from the law. Stripes were out. The exclusivity of the neighborhood was truly behind her nervousness. She hadn't actually seen the houses from the street, but she assumed they were magnificent. But, was that really what was bothering her? The nosiness of neighbors never bothered her before. Mary knew the root of her anxiety. She wanted to look nice. Nice and happy. Nice and secure. Nice and…nice. She shopped for two hours and settled on beige cargo pants and a white, loose-fitting broadcloth shirt. She looked like she was ready to sail the seven seas. Except that she didn't have the earring.

At six, she pulled up to the gate. Its resemblance to a prison was an irony not lost on Mary. If Mitch had pressed charged when she should have, long ago, this would have been prison for real. Would Mary have visited then?

As promised, the guard waved her through after a check of her driver's license. After coasting about twenty feet, Mary slowed to a stop. The only thing she could see was a road with a fork in it. The guard was at her window before she could decide which way to go.
"Just veer right,"
"Thanks."
Mary veered as directed and then drove up and around until she pulled up in front of a house that was about three times bigger than the Governor's Mansion back home. Two people awaited her arrival. A valet attendant and a butler, she was guessing. At least, that's how they were dressed. The valet attendant held her door and the butler greeted her with aloof posture.
"Good evening, Ms. Fairbanks. Please follow me."
If Mary had worried about the neighbor's passing judgment on her wardrobe, she needn't have given it a second thought. There were no other neighbors. Mary jammed her hands in her pockets and strode three paces behind her leader until they were through the front door and standing in the foyer.
"Will the library be to your liking?"
Mary missed the meaning of the question, so wrapped up in taking in her surroundings. The chandelier alone must have been worth thousands. Let's not even go into the value of the Italian tile.
"Excuse me?"
"Would you care to wait in the library?"
When he said it, he added a syllable. As if that would make it sound more significant.

"Madam has asked me to have you wait there. She will be down. Later."

"What are my other choices?" Mary asked, resisting the status quo. Maybe she wanted to wait in the kitchen. Or the study. Or the hall closet.

"Choices?" he asked, now going into what could only be described as butler tizzy.

"Yeah, like, do you have a room with a TV? If I have to wait a long time, I'd like to watch the news. Or a movie?"

"It shouldn't be a long wait, Miss. Madam does prefer to greet in the library." Now, it had only three syllables. What was with this guy? He was beginning to sound like a school principal.

"Maybe I should just forget about dinner. I really don't care to cool my heels in the library waiting for Madam. Thanks all the same."

Mary turned to exit. She was somewhat puzzled herself by her sudden prickliness, but felt instinctively that this was the right choice. She walked down to where she had left the car, and found the valet preparing to wash it.

"What are you doing?"

"Washing your car, Mum."

"Thanks, but no thanks. I just want to go now. Can you arrange that?"

"The keys are in the shed. I can just go over and get them for you, but if you care to wait ten minutes, I can have it washed."

"Just get the keys."

"Yes, Mum."

He retrieved the key chain from the shed and handed it to Mary. She opened the door and was ready to get in when she heard Lisa call out.

"Hey, Mary. Where are you going?"

Mary turned around. Lisa was right next to her. She must have run all the way, she was all out of breath and rosy cheeked.

"Anywhere but the library."

"The library?"

"I don't like to wait around in rooms full of books."

"Did I miss something?" Lisa stood closer.

Mary couldn't back away, she was constrained between the car door and the car.

"Your butler was bound and determined to stash me in the library."

"And that's what you're all huffy about?" Lisa asked with just a hint of a smile. She was now breathing steady, and Mary wasn't, what with the close proximity. Lisa was radiant, smelling of roses.

"I'm just on edge," Mary explained in a voice that wasn't hers. "I didn't expect all this."

"I'm sorry I didn't give you more warning. Come on back in. I won't even make you go near the library. You can go anywhere your heart desires."

It may have been the time when most people would back off, but Lisa stayed close while Mary struggled with the decision.

"I have a hot tub," Lisa tempted.

"I didn't bring my suit."

"I have one for you."

"You do not."

"I do too, and you'll look lovely in it, although what you're wearing now is very nice."

"I suppose I could go for a dip in the hot tub. I don't think I'd melt."

"Good. Only, one thing."

"What?"

"Don't go around telling people that the first thing I talked you into was taking off your clothes."

Lisa tugged playfully at the sleeve of Mary's blouse and then led her back into the sprawling mansion. If the truth were known, the first thing Lisa talked Mary into was a glass of wine. A two-hundred dollar glass of wine. Lisa poured it herself. The butler was nowhere to be seen. Then, glass in hand, Lisa showed Mary the vast array of brand new swim suits. Mary selected a modest one-piece affair and slipped it on while Lisa went to her room to change. The tub was gloriously hot and bubbly and Mary stepped in while awaiting Lisa. She appeared after a moment. Mary's eyes followed her every move as she descended the steps. If Lisa noticed the attentiveness, she had the good grace not to mention it.

"I should apologize to your butler."

"He's gone for the night. Besides, I don't think that's necessary. It sounds to me like he wasn't listening very closely to your wishes."

"So, he's gone?"

"Right. He usually serves dinner, but I told him I could handle things tonight."

"I don't know why I snapped," Mary said as she relaxed into the water. Between the water and wine, she felt almost sacramental.

"You've been under a lot of pressure lately. All things considered, I think you're doing very well."

"When are you going to tell me how you managed all this," Mary waved her wine glass around to indicate the entire scheme of things.

"I got lucky."

"This cost more than two million and from what you say, you didn't even have the full two million to start with."

"That's right."

"So, what happened?" Mary wasn't ready to let go. Mitch wanted legal particulars, if possible.

"I made a wise investment."

"In what?"

"Do you know much about this area?"

"You mean California or Diamond Bar?"

"Diamond Bar."

"You found a diamond mine!"

"No, sorry. No diamonds. No gold mines. No oil."

"What then?

"Cal Poly is in this area. Let's just say I found brains."

"You went to the university?"

"No, but I did find someone who graduated from there with a bright idea."

"And you invested in it."

"Bankrolled would be a better description."

"What was the idea?"

"It's proprietary."

"Is it legal?"

"Oh sure, I've gone straight. At least, in that way."

Lisa turned her radiance up a notch. Mary began to feel the warmth. The glow beginning somewhere in her knees and threatening to travel northward. So, this is why she felt like bolting an hour ago. It had nothing to do with the library. Or the butler.

"Are you okay?" Lisa asked like she knew the real and complete answer. The truth, the whole truth and nothing but.

"I am getting a little warm."

"Hot tubs and wine have that effect. Do you want to go in and have dinner?"

"That would probably be a wise idea."

Dinner was lobster, steamed broccoli and wild rice. Mary cleaned her plate like lunch was a far distant memory. It helped soak up the alcohol. There was German chocolate cake for dessert but that was put on hold until after a tour of the house. After the dip in the hot tub and prior to dinner, they had both changed into white cotton terry robes. Now, as they padded quietly through the house, they could have easily passed for ghosts on a twilight haunting. They toured around the first floor, including the library.

"Now, this wouldn't have been so bad to wait in, would it?" Lisa touched Mary's hand. Sparks jumped between them, both real and sexual.

"I would have managed," Mary admitted, squeezing Lisa's hand gently in return.

"Come upstairs. You won't believe the woodwork." They were both reluctant to break their physical connection. It had, after all, taken quite a number of months to finally get to the hand-holding stage. The upstairs was every bit as breathtaking as the downstairs, but Mary might just as well have been wearing blinders. As she watched Lisa describe items of decoration here and there, she rarely looked away. She hadn't remembered Lisa being quite so magnetic during their other times together, but then again, Mary had been under the influence of Hilary at the time.

"And the Martians brought this vase from Venus," Lisa wound up her narrative.

"Uh huh...What?" Mary caught the tail end of the yarn and then said, "Everyone knows Martians come from Mars!"

"And what planet are you visiting?" Lisa teased with a coy smile.

"California," Mary smiled back.

They had been holding hands during the tour and now Lisa took hold of Mary's other hand. If their first touch had created the spark, this new connection completed the circuit. Sexual energy now coursed through both of them, drawing them closer. Bravely, Mary leaned into a kiss and found instant pleasure when she met Lisa halfway.

Knowing that the tease was half the fun, Lisa gave and then pulled back. Mary checked to see why and found that Lisa was ready to shed her robe. The entire action took two seconds and then Mary wrapped Lisa in a snug embrace. This time, there would be no pulling back, but with her own brand of teasing, Mary kissed Lisa everywhere on her face and neck first, saving her lips for last. Lisa couldn't endure any more evasion and caught up with Mary's lips. The parting made her moan with passion.

"I've waited a long time for you," Lisa whispered as she slowly pushed Mary's robe from her shoulders.

"Well, now that you have me, what are you going to do with me?"

"Stuff you've only read about in books."

Mary hadn't read *that* book. Maybe she should have waited in the library? Lisa was snuggled close to Mary, who hadn't moved off her back since Lisa had put the finishing kisses on Mary's second orgasm. She was already one ahead. Lisa didn't seem to mind.

"You were great," Mary made the understatement of the millenium.

"I was great, wasn't I."

Mary chuckled and then tried to move again.

"Where do you think you're going?"

"I thought I'd go look at that vase you got from the Venutians."

Lisa moved quickly to straddle her.

"I'm not letting you out of this bed."

Mary, ever the creative one, took advantage of the situation by slowly stroking Lisa right about at her straddle point. She didn't exactly stay still for the touch, but Mary followed her own pace, which reduced Lisa to a helpless bundle of desire. A lot like the first time. After Lisa relaxed into Mary's arms, sleep overcame her. Mary stayed awake for a few minutes thinking. Her first affair was news she felt she had to break gently to her mother. This relationship was now news that she would need to break gently to Mitch.

Mary awoke to find Lisa already gone. This was Lisa's normal routine. Lounging around in bed in the morning just wasn't her style. She saved that for the night. But, when pressed for details of what Lisa did with her time, Mary was unable to categorize much of anything. No one could do as little as Lisa appeared to be doing and make the kind of money she needed to finance this new lifestyle. If their relationship were to flourish, Mary would need to know more.

"Good morning, sleepyhead," Lisa found Mary in the library, taking her morning coffee.

"Hi there, yourself," Mary greeted back.

"Trying to find that special book?" Lisa had that tease in her voice again. The one Mary lived for now. This morning, however, she resisted being distracted.

"I want to ask you something."

"Sure," Lisa sat next to her on the couch.

"I need more information on how you earn your money. I'll be the most faithful, loving, caring, generous lover on the planet, but I refuse to be a Mafia wife."

"What's a Mafia wife?"

"You know, a wife who looks the other way and doesn't ask questions. I won't do that."

"Do you still think I'm doing something illegal?" Lisa didn't try to keep the honest hurt out of her voice.

Mary took quick and decisive action to prevent her from walking out. She embraced her gently but firmly. "I don't think you're doing anything illegal, but how can I really know anything when all you tell me is that it's proprietary?"

"That's all I can say. Truly."

Mary exhaled slowly and didn't voice a reply.

"You don't believe me."

"If it isn't illegal, what's the big deal?"

"I think that's an apt description. It is a big deal."

Mary thought about the words and then looked into Lisa's eyes. What had she gotten herself into? Who keeps secrets besides organized crime?

"Now, are you going to hold on to me with a death grip or can we go and eat breakfast?"

"I'm not very hungry."

"Oh?" Lisa cocked an impish eyebrow.

"And I'm not that, either."

"Okay, so, what are you?"

"I'm going back to Denver."

"I understand."

"I need to check in with my Mom."

"I agree."

"And help out."

"Absolutely."

Lisa couldn't have been more understanding. Damn her anyway. She did want one more kiss before Mary drove away. Mary had wondered briefly if, given the opportunity, would she have changed anything about her time spent with Lisa. The parting kiss removed all traces of that mindset. She was hooked and didn't want to fight it. Mary pointed the truck east and left town without packing anything from the apartment.

Chapter 19

Jeff had found his niche. He was both a great campaign
manager and someone Mitch trusted. That made all the
difference to the team, of which Mitch was now a part of
again. After the primary victory, the volunteers were
reenergized and ready for battle. Normally, the district that
Rebecca lived in was traditionally Democratic where
Senate elections were concerned, but when you were a gay
candidate, nothing could be taken for granted. If the
Republicans were afraid to play the rehab card, none shied
away from sitting down at the high-stakes homophobic
table. It was always the same drum beat no matter who
was leading the band. A familiar theme was, "Who wanted
their children indoctrinated into the deviant homosexual
lifestyle starting in Kindergarten!" This was one of the
more moderate slogans repeated by Reb's challenger.
Never once in her life had Rebecca touted this plan. Heck,
the woman hadn't even been able to say "oral sex" until she
was halfway through her projected life span, let alone
champion a curriculum on the subject. However, that
didn't matter in politics, and if that wasn't bad enough, all
the kooks came out of the woodwork as well. Jeff had been
scouting the opposition diligently and showed Mitch two
separate flyers that he picked up in a street corner in
Downtown Denver. The first had to do with cannibalism;
the second, vampires. Mitch read through both epistles.
The first accused gay men of being cannibalistic in their
sex acts. Literally. Mitch looked up at Jeff with absolute
amazement.
"Keep reading, it just gets worse," he shook his head.
It seemed that the author of the missive had decided that
since oral sex between males could include the ingestion of

sperm, gay men had sex this way so that they could satisfy their urge for eating human beings. What went unsaid was that the sperm only contained half the genetic material needed to make a human being, but I guess being half a cannibal was bad enough? It sounded half-baked. The second letter suggested that since gay men had oral sex (gosh, everyone was all hung up on sex this week!) then they must be vampires. Mitch scanned the document, trying not to laugh. Apparently sperm and semen had microscopic traces of blood. Therefore, gay men had this insatiable desire for drinking human blood. Yeah, right.

"Somebody's really staying up late at night dreaming this stuff up."
"It's being mailed, e-mailed, faxed, and generally hand distributed all over the state. The only thing they haven't done is drop it out of airplanes."
"Julius Streicher would have been proud."
"Who?"
"Julius Streicker was a Nazi who used the power of false and inflammatory literature like this to destroy Jews in Europe during World War II. He published a magazine called Der Stuermer which depicted Jews in hateful ways. It was very effective and people who might not have otherwise hated the Jews were swayed by the so-called literature."
"You sure know your history."
"Trish is helping me brush up on history lessons they never taught in school. Anyway, once people believe that a group of people, minority or otherwise, is responsible for all the ills of society, a skilled fascist can do any amount of unimaginable harm."

Jeff mulled this over. Mitch enjoyed watching him think. It was his most handsome pose, a lot like the portrait of JFK displayed in the White House. Suddenly he looked up and asked, "What happened to Julius Streicher?"

"He was hanged. Sentenced to death on Count Four by the Nuremberg Court."

"What was Count Four?"

"Crimes against humanity. The court decided that publishing such vitriol does cause pain and suffering, no matter how the authors might prefer to hide behind freedom of speech."

Jeff nodded his head in his best Kennedyesque way.

"Anything else I should know?"

Mitch shook her head and then changed her mind. "There is one more interesting footnote. During the Nuremberg Trials, no one wanted to be near Streicher. You know, sit at the same table and eat with him. They called him the 'Jew baiter.'"

"You mean even his fellow Nazis didn't want anything to do with him?"

"That's right."

Jeff had an idea. Mitch could tell because whenever he got an idea, his eyes sparkled. Now, after working with him for a few days, Mitch could see why Rebecca would have been attracted to him so many years ago.

"What are you thinking?"

"Don't you think that the average voter would disdain this kind of propaganda if they knew it existed?"

"If I had to bet, I'd say yes."

"And wouldn't it be considered a positive public service if our campaign unmasked this trash for what it really is?"

"It would be a bold move."

"We're not going to win this campaign through meekness."

315

"You're going to publicize this stuff?"

"Press conference tomorrow. Say, ten in the morning?"

"Make it nine. Some local news starts at eleven."

It sure beat renting an airplane. By one minute after noon in Denver the following morning, everyone within hearing distance of a TV or radio heard about the flyers. By five, the opposition was howling at what they dubbed the "cheap tactics" used by the Fairbanks's campaign and denied knowing anything about the literature. The general public ferreted out the hypocrisy and by the following day, Reb inched up in the polls.

"We're up three points," Jeff announced.

"I still don't trust those things."

"Well, Rebecca needs to know either way."

"You tell her. It was your stroke of genius."

"I couldn't have done it without your help. Do me a favor and keep doing that historical research. It might come in handy someday."

After the argument with Albert, Trish was unsure whether they would ever again be on cordial terms. Not that they even had been. Having been ordered out of his room practically every day, she was beginning to feel the crush of futility weighing on her mind. Max's story had been told so often it was almost in the public domain. Rose's story would forever remain silent now that Trish had sworn the oath. She was running out of options for her book, and felt that she was also wearing out her welcome with Robbie. How could she help but? Robbie had been a perfect hostess during her stay. Meals were cooked. Jokes were told. It was the picture of tranquility, an oasis where she

316

could sort through the prospects of her budding career as a writer. As difficult as selling real estate had been, it was nothing compared to this struggle.

She inhaled twice. Deeply. Then, she entered Albert's room. He was awake. That was a good sign.
"Good morning," she gave her usual greeting.
"Good morning," he echoed back. Something was different.
"How are you?"
"I am dying, and how are you?"
Trish nodded. "I guess we're all dying?"
"So, where have you been. I've been waiting."
"You have?" Trish asked honestly. This was a new twist of events.
"Did you bring your pencil and paper?"
"I have a steno notebook."
"Sit down."
"Thank you."
"And a pencil?"
"I have a pen."
"What if you make a mistake?"
"I'll deal with it."
"You have earned the right to hear my story."
"That's good news."
"You think so?"
"I think so."
"In 1939, in Poland, I was seized."
Trish flipped open her notebook quickly in order to not miss the chance of a lifetime.
"You were seized in Poland in 1939."
"Are you going to repeat everything I say? If you do, this will take a long time. Time I don't have."

"I'll try to refrain from interrupting, but I will probably ask questions here and there."

As she was saying this, Trish scrounged up a spare pen. Not running out of ink was the top priority of the morning.

"I was dragged from my house, taken to a train station, and after an all-night ride in a cattle car, disembarked at Auschwitz. From the first moment I set foot on the ground, I knew it was a horrible place."

Albert stopped talking long enough to steal a glance at Trish, who had stopped writing.

"What? You don't like my story so far?" he asked.

Trish watched him carefully, and to her surprise, the corners of his mouth upturned ever so slowly. A smile. A very slight smile, but a smile nonetheless.

"I suppose I *would* like the story so far, if it were true," she stated bravely. Or foolishly, if she had misread his sense of humor.

"You think I'm telling you a lie?"

"I would never call you a liar, Albert. I just don't understand how you could have been taken out of Poland in 1939 and interred at Auschwitz, when Auschwitz wasn't even a concentration camp until 1940. The first deportations to Auschwitz occurred June 14, 1940. The first deportees were prisoners from a place called Tarnow. So, if you were taken from Poland in 1939 and put on a train, that would have been an awfully long train ride. Help me out with the math, six months? A year?"

"Ah, so you are correct," Albert nodded and then winked.

Trish about fell off her chair. He was teasing her. A dying, gay, tortured soul of a man was teasing her. And, about of all things, the Holocaust.

"Being correct about one detail isn't good enough. I want to know more."

318

"What would have happened to a person taken from Poland in 1939 if there was no Auschwitz to go to?"

"How would I know?"

"Take an educated guess," he prodded.

"Well, my first guess would be that they were just killed on the spot."

"That's a good guess. You have been studying. Tell me another possibility."

Trish racked her brain for some of that historical data that she had soaked up in her reading. Remembering about Auschwitz was just a lucky happenstance. Now, the real test had begun.

"I think I remember reading that some were sent to fortify the German front on the Russian borders."

"That happened, although not at first, I should think. After all, Hitler and Russia were working on a secret pact. And what of the others?"

"Isn't that when the ghettos were formed?"

"That's correct. The towns of Wloclawek, Kutno, Ozorkow, Pabianice, Zdunska Wola, Zelow, Belchatow, Wielum and of course the legendary town of Lodz were all places that Jews were forced into, after being stripped of most of their possessions."

"But not everyone. What about able-bodied persons? Weren't they selected to do labor?"

"That was another possibility, yes, and depending upon where you lived, you might have been sent to one of the other concentration camps. You know, there was more than one concentration camp in Europe!"

"Of course."

"For instance, the Jews in the town of Danzig were deported to Stutthof. That was a notorious place, and yet people survived it."

"So, is that where you ended up?" Trish tried to get back on track. After all, Albert was the one who kept noting his lack of time left on Earth.

"No."

"No?"

"No."

"So, where?" Trish asked.

"Do you know the name of the last concentration camp to be liberated by the Americans?"

"No, not offhand."

"When you find out, come back."

With that homework assignment, Albert closed his eyes. He was obviously needing to catch up on that nap that he had foregone awaiting Trish's arrival. She walked out. Another day, she would have been angry. Today, she was determined. At least she knew what she was searching for, or rather, researching. Concentrating so hard on her assignment, she nearly collided with Robbie in the hallway.

"Oh, my goodness, I'm so sorry," Trish said. Thank the stars Robbie hadn't been carrying a tray of medications or pureed turnips. It would have been a royal mess. Luckily, she was just carrying herself, as Trish's adopted mother would have said. And carry herself she did so well.

"That's alright. You were about a zillion light years away. What are you thinking about?"

"Albert and I have had a breakthrough."

"Let's celebrate over dinner!" Robbie blurted out.

"I need to do some research."

"You need to eat. I'll cook and you read."

"No," Trish said suddenly, resolutely. "You've cooked enough. It's my treat! Dinner out! I can study into the night while you sleep."

"Now, that's an offer I can't pass up."

"Good! I'll see you later."

When later rolled around, Trish was deep in study, so Robbie walked quietly through the apartment. Out of the corner of her eye, Trish noticed the thoughtfulness and called out, "I've made reservations for seven at Chez Something!"

"Chez Something?" Robbie inquired.

"Yeah, that French restaurant, Chez Oobie Doobie or whatever it's called."

"Chez DuPois?"

"That's it!"

"My God, Trish! When you make reservations, you make *reservations*!"

"I knew you liked French food."

"Of course I do. But I'd settle for French fries. This Chez DuPois is very expensive."

"Is it?" Trish asked, giving the impression of one who doesn't care about finances when caught up in the moment of celebration.

"Maybe we should go to the Dairy Queen instead?"

"Chez DuPois at seven."

Robbie's only other comment was, "I wonder if I have time to get my hair done?"

Dinner at seven was such an illusion at a place like Chez DuPois. You were seated at seven, promptly and without the need of a twenty-dollar tip to ease the process. Then, somebody who wore kid gloves over their kid gloves approaches your table with a wine list the size of a short story. Hanging around Mitch and the Lucky U all those years was finally beginning to pay off. Trish expertly

321

ordered wine after conferring with Robbie as to her preferences. Only then did they have a chance to survey their surroundings and make the properly quiet remarks.

"This place is gorgeous!" crooned Robbie.

"It's like a library."

"Or maybe more like a place of worship."

Trish nodded. After all, as time had passed, anywhere she was with Robbie was a place of worship. She was slowly but surely beginning to succumb to the fact that she adored this wonderful, kind, gentle professional nurse, and would have asked for a prescription for love sickness had it been available. The last thing she needed right now was a distraction. Writing with Albert was challenging enough.

"What are you thinking?" Robbie asked.

"A hundred thousand million things."

"Just a hundred thousand million things?"

"Maybe more, maybe less."

"Any of those thought about me?"

Trish nodded.

"Good or bad?"

How was Trish going to answer this one? "All good."

"Not even one bad?" Robbie sounded disappointed.

Maybe.

Trish looked into her eyes and saw the twinkling mischief. Okay, maybe one bad thought, if you're Catholic, anyway. In the Catholic church you could get into trouble for what you were thinking, not just doing. More than once, Trish had visited the confessional to admit to impure thoughts. Uh huh.

"I'm thinking that I've met a woman who is more beautiful than you."

"And who was that?"

"Your mother."

322

Robbie laughed. "You are full of what the Irish call blarney."

"Not in this case."

"Which doesn't mean that I don't think my mother is beautiful. Lord knows she is. But have you looked in the mirror lately?"

"Why?"

"You are absolutely gorgeous."

"Okay. Third in line behind you and your mother."

"Stop it before I blush!"

"Drink some wine and then no one will think a thing about it."

"And if I drink too much, I won't think another thing period."

Wine was savored along with some cheese-based appetizers brought to their table. They fell into easy conversation as waiters in tuxedos hovered noiselessly about. Sinful dinners were devoured, and dessert was more rich than anything available at Dairy Queen.

"You haven't told me what the breakthrough was with Albert," Robbie asked over coffee.

"He's finally talking. He kidded around at first to see if I was paying attention."

"How did he do that?"

"He tried to tell me a story that wasn't true. The dates didn't make sense."

"So, he was testing you. Again?"

"And I guess I'm finally passing for a change."

"You have put up with a lot from him. I sometimes wonder if I did the right thing, suggesting that you come here to try for the interview."

"You did the exact right thing."

"Not very often in your life do you get accused of doing the exact right thing. I shall hold this day up as a shining beacon to all my future days."

"I will, too," Trish said.

"Because of Albert?"

"Because of you," Trish said before she could stop herself. Robbie looked into Trish's eyes.

"Why me?"

"Because I'm falling in love with you."

Robbie stopped everything she was doing, except breathing. Then she said, "You can't be doing that."

"Why not?"

"It isn't possible."

Trish gazed at Robbie for a moment. Had she gotten this all wrong? How insulated had Robbie been? After all, she had known before most that Albert was gay. Hadn't she figured it all out by now? Why it was so important to Trish to interview a gay survivor of the Holocaust. Stupefied, Trish said the only real thing that popped into her mind.

"I'm gay, you know."

"I know."

"And gay people do fall in love."

"I know."

"So, it is possible."

"For you, not for me."

"I did not assume you were gay. I'm just telling you how I feel."

"Thanks for sharing."

"You're welcome."

Hiding behind these polite phrases was a flurry of unsaid feelings. Robbie didn't appear to want to budge. Trish wasn't about to push. If she was anything like her mother, it would take time.

They parted ways after dinner. Trish spent her time wisely, concentrating on the challenge Albert gave her long enough to come up with the correct answer. Mauthausen. Then her mind wandered back to the dinner conversations. Robbie had said a lot of things, but it was the one thing she didn't say that stuck out in Trish's memory. She never said she *wasn't* gay. That would have been easy enough. Heck, Trish knew lesbians who claimed to be straight to avoid going out on a date with one woman or another; and straight women who likewise claimed to be gay to avoid certain men. All Robbie had said was that it wasn't possible. What an interesting answer. Trish burned to know more, but she also knew to begin full-scale research about Mauthausen. Albert would be ready for more trick questions, to be sure. Robbie would have to be on her back burner. At least, for a little while.

"Mauthausen," Trish said to Albert instead of her usual "Good morning."
He repeated, "Mauthausen. What about Mauthausen?"
"You were in Mauthausen."
"I wasn't in Mauthausen."
Trish began to worry. What was going on in Albert's mind.
"You asked me to find out the last camp that was liberated by the Americans. That camp was Mauthausen."
"Of course it was. I wasn't there, though."
"I thought you were."
"Boy, are you confused," Albert stated maddeningly.
"Well, where were you, then?"
"I was in one of the first camps built by Himmler."

Trish prayed that this wasn't going to lead to another round of research. The clues were becoming more and more vague.

"Sachsenhausen."

"Another notorious place. So, how did you survive."

"By lying."

"Lying?"

"I lied, at least I tried to, as the youngsters say today, about my sexuality. That is what they say, right?"

"Among other things."

"I figured, I wasn't the first homosexual man to lie about it to save myself and by God, I'm not the last! They think they got it bad today! Today, you might lose your job. Big deal!"

"Some people still lose their lives by being gay."

"One or two."

"One or two too many."

Albert nodded. "I'm sorry. I think sometimes that I'm the only gay man who has suffered."

Trish had to sit down. It was the first time he had ever apologized. The shock was stunning.

"You going female on me?"

Somehow, hearing Humphrey Bogart-type dialogue from Albert struck her as funny.

"How could I possibly do that?"

"You seem about to faint. You want a really good excuse?"

"An excuse?"

"An excuse to faint."

"I'm not sure."

"The Nazis made sure I'd never have any children. Ever. Want to see?"

"No!" Trish assured him.

"So it would bother you?"

"Of course it would bother me!"

"Suit yourself, but boy, you talk about a loss of blood. And the way they go about it. I don't think any of those Nazis had one good sharp knife between them. Ms. Weingarten. Ms. Weingarten…?"

It was a little too late to worry now. Trish had fainted clear off the chair. When she came to, someone had taken care to place her in a bed in an empty room and Robbie was there to administer to her.

"What happened?" Trish said as she tried and failed to raise her head.

"Seems you went down for the count."

"My head hurts."

"Of course it does. You landed on the floor."

"Do you have something for the pain?"

"Yes, but you can't have anything."

"Why not?"

"Because we're checking you for concussion. A pain killer will mask the symptoms and we wouldn't want that."

Why did everyone become a "we" when they were in the hospital?

"We're better now and we would like to sit up."

"Take it easy. It isn't a contest."

"You don't suppose I'm allergic to French food, do you?" Trish tried a smile. Even that hurt.

"Probably would have found out before now."

"We need to talk." Trish stated firmly. And she did mean "we."

"I need to get back to the other patients."

"Tonight then?"

"You know where I live."

Trish thought over that turn of phrase in her mind. "Do I really know where you live?" she asked the walls after Robbie had left the room.

After two false starts, Trish was back on her feet. She considered for only a moment or two checking back in with Albert, but had now remembered the conversation that sent her to the floor in the first place and thought the better of it. Instead, she went to the library to check out a few more books and then picked up Chinese food on her way back to Robbie's. They ate and talked about Trish's state of health until Trish could stand it no more.

"I want to talk about last night."

"Last night was last night."

"There's no disputing that," Trish nodded. "Tell me what you meant when you said things weren't possible."

"Some things are possible. Some aren't."

"I love you. That's possible."

Robbie looked imploringly at Trish.

"How can you know that? We've only just met."

"Ask my friends in Denver. I have been in love with you from the first."

"You told them?"

"I didn't need to. They knew it just by looking at me."

"You must have pretty good friends."

"I do. But I didn't know what to do. Just because I was attracted to you, didn't mean you were able to return my affection."

Trish waited for Robbie to respond. A definitive "no" would have been hard to bear.

"Are you able to do that?" Trish followed up when Robbie remained silent.

"I like you a lot."

"As a friend?"

"It could be more. That isn't the problem, I don't think."
Trish felt her heart begin to rise up and take note. There
was a possibility. That's all she wanted.

"So, you could have feelings for me?" Trish asked with a
new, sudden lilt in her voice.

"Life is complicated."

"Of course it is," Trish agreed readily.

"And I've never had this type of relationship."

"I understand."

"In fact, I've never had any type of relationship."

"I see."

"And so I'm not sure about myself, in several senses of the
word, so to speak."

Trish recognized the chatter as nerve driven, and listened
for ways to calm Robbie.

"Why do you suppose you've not yet had a relationship?"

"Take a look at me."

"I have. Many times."

"I'm just not a cover-girl type."

It was true, Trish thought to herself. Robbie was a little on
the pudgy side, but her eyes were captivating. So what if
the rest of the world wanted Calista Flockhart look-a-likes
for bedroom companions. Trish would be more than
interested in Robbie. A lot more.

"I don't want a cover-girl type."

"Everybody wants a cover-girl type."

"I'm not just everybody."

"No, you're not," Robbie smiled at Trish, who felt her heart
become liquid. "But there's another complication."

"Name it. I can take on anything."

"My parents."

"Your parents seem okay with some things."

"My parents want grandchildren."

"Most parents want grandchildren."

"But mine *really* want grandchildren. The more the better. It's part of the Holocaust mentality. They survived the Holocaust, the most widespread destruction of the Jewish population in recorded history, and they feel this need to keep the Jewish culture alive. That means grandchildren."

"You want to have children?" Trish asked fearlessly.

"I do. I did. It's something that is important to me. But it just hadn't happened yet. And I'm not getting any younger. And I haven't found any man who is willing to walk down the aisle with me."

"I'll do it," Trish said matter-of-factly.

"You'll do what?"

"How many children do you want to have?"

Robbie studied Trish's eyes. There was no silliness. No kidding-around look.

"You're serious!"

"Of course I'm serious. How many children do you want? Two? Four? A baseball team?"

"You shouldn't tease about things like this."

"Who's teasing. I'm dead serious. You and I could have children. Of course, we would need a donor. A nice Jewish donor, right?"

"That would be a necessity on both counts."

"But I'm sure that's possible. Then, we just start having children. Do you want to give birth? Of course you would. What a question. It's your parents that want the grandchildren."

Now it was Robbie's turn to recognize the nervous chatter coming out of Trish.

"Hey, Trish. Slow down."

Trish laughed and then relaxed. She held Robbie closer. Good grief, they hadn't even kissed yet and already they were planning the layette.

"I'm sorry. I just know that we can overcome anything as long as we know how we feel about each other."

"I've tried to fight how I feel about you for a while now."

"So, stop fighting it."

Robbie looked at Trish. So close. So loving. So ready to kiss. She closed her eyes and felt the soft pressure of Trish's lips on her own and immediately felt the heat rise in her body. Trish was a perfect lady, polite as a virgin on the first kiss. The second was an entirely different matter. Robbie was open to more than one chaste kiss. Much more open.

Mary arrived back in Denver just in time to have her opinion known on the wheelchair controversy. On the evening of the second scheduled workshop, when Jeff had arrived with dinner, Mitch and Reb had skipped the seminar which, coincidentally enough, was about wheelchairs. Chris had all but visibly breathed a sigh of relief. She had visions of a "manual" versus "powered" smack-down wrestling match between Mitch and Reb dancing in her case-manager's head. But now, the time to decide had come.

"I think a manual would help me keep my upper body strong."

"But think about all those miles of sidewalk in Washington, D.C." Mitch intoned.

"I could still go faster in a manual."

"What about uphill?" Mary pointed out.

"Powered would be easier uphill," Chris noted.

"Let's just break down and get both," Mitch said, in the mood for a truce. "We could take that donation from Lisa and pop for two chairs. Regular and unleaded. Right, Mary?"

Everyone looked at Mary like she was the scribe of the hour. "I guess so."

The matter was settled. Everyone was happy. As the group was filing out of the room, Mary tried to follow along like it was a parade.

"Not so fast," Mitch pulled her back in. "Come back here and tell us about California."

"It was fine."

"Are you sure?" Mitch probed. Something was lurking under the surface.

"Why wouldn't it be?" Mary replied.

Now, Mitch knew she was on to something.

"Well, you just had sort of a funny look on your face when I mentioned the donation. Is the check good?"

"Oh, yeah. And there's plenty more where that came from."

"You mean, she's giving more?" Reb quizzed her daughter with pinpoint accuracy.

"I'm sure she would," Mary hedged.

"Is she still in legal trouble?"

"I forgot to ask."

"Well, what exactly were you doing while you were supposed to be snooping?"

Mary looked from her mother to Mitch and then back again. Mitch felt a twitch in her gut, like something important was about to be said.

"Maybe I'll leave the two of you alone to talk," Mitch said in an accidental falsetto.

"Oh, no, you don't!" Mary commanded instantly. "You started this, so you're staying right here."

Mitch froze to her spot.

"Lisa and I are a couple," Mary blurted out.

"A couple of what?" Reb asked.

Mitch worked very hard to stifle an inappropriate giggle. Why she was humored was anyone's guess.

"We slept together, Mother."

Now, everything was beginning to make sense.

"You and Lisa?"

"Me and Lisa."

"I thought you couldn't stand the sight of the woman."

"Well, you know, Reb-" Mitch started to say something before Reb interrupted, "*YOU* stay out of this!"

"That works for me," Mitch nodded agreement. "I'm just going to go to the coffee shop now. For about three hours."

She made good her escape this time. The halls were silent this evening. Midweek was usually quiet in the rehab center. The coffee shop was deserted. Mitch bought enough snack food for two. Mary would be along shortly. But, the longer, the better. Mary was there mid second cookie.

"Have a seat."

"Thanks."

"Are you going to be okay?"

"I'm fine. Mom is still monitoring her blood pressure, I'm sure."

"Well, you must admit, it is a surprise. You? Lisa?"

"It was like something just went off."

"I'm sure it did," Mitch smiled knowingly

"I don't mean that. Although, that happened, too. Boy, oh, boy, did that happen."

"Have a half a cookie to keep up your strength. Trust me."

"I know my mother will eventually be okay with this, but how about you?"

"Me!?"

"She is *your* ex."

"You have my blessing. I'll throw in a bottle of vitamins for good measure."

"Thanks," Mary said, still not satisfied.

"What else aren't you telling me?"

"It's more like what Lisa's not telling me."

"What's up?"

"You should see the place she's living in."

"Pretty bad?"

"Oh, hell, no! It's a freaking mansion with a butler who buttles and a car-washing fanatic for a valet."

"Does she have a maid?"

Mary checked to see if Mitch was smirking. She was smirk free.

"We talked about Texas and Hilary and basketballs. What we didn't talk about was where exactly she got this new batch of income."

"Not at all?"

"She mentioned Cal Poly and bankrolling an idea."

"Sounds legit to me. Must have been one helluva good idea."

"Who keeps secrets?"

"Is this a riddle? Let's see, three people if two are dead, right?"

"Seriously."

"Seriously? Well, criminals, industry and the government."

"So, she could really be above board on this. I mean, maybe she invested in something that is used in manufacturing or defense and had to sign an oath of confidentiality."

"Or take a vow of silence."

"That's for cloistered nuns. I guarantee she hasn't become one of those. Although she is very isolated."

"Not so isolated that she doesn't pick up her own mail."

"Or eat at the local diner," conceded Mary. "She ordered a hot turkey sandwich for me."

"Well, if that isn't love, I don't know what is."

"You aren't going to be jealous, are you?"

"No, I'm not. I have the love of my life upstairs. I'd better get back. What are you going to do?"

"I'm not sure."

"You want my advice?"

"Sure."

"Pack your bags and move to Diamond Bar."

"What about my Mom?"

"I can handle your mom."

Mary headed home to locate more luggage. Mitch went back to Reb's room. She had been crying. Mary hadn't said anything about tears.

"You okay?" Mitch sat close and held hands.

"Well, we sure got her mind off Hilary," Reb snuffled through a tissue.

There was hope. Reb had a grasp on humor.

"Worked like a charm, didn't it," Mitch nodded.

"I think she's going to move out there."

"Probably," Mitch agreed without admitting to suggesting it to Mary five minutes ago.

"I hope she's not making a mistake."

"She might be. She might not. Lisa might break her heart eight ways from Sunday, but I can guarantee one thing."

"What can you guarantee?" Reb dried her eyes.

"Lisa will never, ever hit Mary. She's not the hitting kind."

"No, she's just the cheating, stealing, skipping out on a warrant kind."

"Well, everybody has their little flaws."

"You know, it's a good thing we're gay."

"Why is that?" Mitch raised her eyebrows, wondering where this was going.

"Because if we were straight, someone would pen our life story for a soap opera."

Chapter 20

Trish didn't know which to do first. Begin writing Albert's
story, tell Mitch about the stunning developments in her
romantic life, or ask Robbie's parents for their blessing.
She decided to leave the last two items to fate. If Mitch
called, she would talk to her. When Robbie wanted to run
"Plan A" by her parents, Trish would follow her lead. That
left Albert.
"So, now you know how a seventy-year-old homosexual
man kept from getting HIV."
Trish nodded somberly. Albert had survived. His ability to
have issue didn't.
"Did I tell you about the Saxon stance yet?"
"No, you didn't."
"You remember how hard it was to stand for roll call?"
"My feet still hurt."
"So, do this. Stand up."
Trish looked wary.
"It's okay. I just want you to know what this was."
"Okay."
Trish put her notebook and pen aside and stood up.
"Now, put your arms behind your head, like you were in a
resting position if you were lying down."
"Got it."
"Now, you must hold your elbows as far back as you can."
Trish tried it. It pulled her muscles tight and made her want
to bow her head forward."
"Keep your head up. Look straight ahead."
"It hurts a little."
"After four hours, you can't feel your arms. In winter, you
get frostbite."
"Why did you have to do this?"

337

"Because crazy people were in charge of our world. You may sit back down now."

Trish lowered her arms. She wouldn't have made it ten minutes.

"I suppose if you lowered your arms, they shot you."

"Didn't matter. If you wiggled, they shot you. If you shifted your weight from foot to foot, they shot you. They would beat us with truncheons and shoot those who fell. If they were lucky, it was a mercy shot. But sometimes not. One night, they took one of my five bunkmates and dragged him to the front of the camp. They knew where to shoot to inflict pain, but not to kill. The knees were a choice often made. They wounded both of his knees and then threw him on some razor wire. It was not live."

"It was not live?"

"The wire. It was not electrified. They left him to die. It took two days. He couldn't free himself and where would he go even if he could."

Trish had long since stopped writing. She didn't expect to forget this for a lifetime.

"They just left him there?"

"We stood roll call, morning and night, morning and night before he died. I still hear his screams in my sleep."

"Why did they do that to him? Why was he the one?"

"Because he was the fifth person in the row. They killed every fifth that night. They made him linger, why I don't know. Maybe to warn us not to be in the wrong place next time."

"What number were you that night?"

"I was fourth."

Trish closed her eyes to absorb the horror.

"Are you going to faint again?"

"I'm fine."

338

"You better go home, get some rest."

"I can work a little longer."

"Maybe you can but I can't. Go home. Eat. Sleep."

"Okay."

Robbie caught up with Trish in the lobby. "How is it going?"

"Albert remembers a lot of detail. Sometimes, too much."

"He seems to be finding comfort in telling his story."

"Even so, it still takes a lot out of him."

"And you, too. Take it easy today. Remember, it's my turn to cook dinner."

"I know. It's the highlight of my day. That, and your kisses," Trish finished the sentence quietly.

"Shhhh. Don't tell everybody."

"I won't. You're a secret I'm keeping all to myself."

Reb was getting buff, no doubt about it. Her main goal with her upper body strength was to be able to transfer herself from bed to wheelchair to regular chair to toilet seat. The trick was in the method of transfer. It was far better to be able to lift her weight as much as possible as opposed to throwing her weight. Mitch practically had to duck when she teased Rebecca about being good at throwing her weight around. The slipper missed her by a good foot, no pun intended. Good thing Aunt BeBe wasn't on duty at the time. She would have scolded them both.

"Come on, you've got two slippers. Give it another shot."

"Oh, I plan to, just not when you're expecting it."

"Nothing new about that."

Mitch handed the first slipper back to Reb. She needed it to wear to their evening workshop. Since they missed the last seminar, Mitch felt it was important to go tonight, even if Reb did look a tad weary.

"What's tonight's topic?" Mitch asked.

"I honestly don't know."

They walked and wheeled down the hall, scooting in right on time. For a change, the room was packed and they ended up in the back. Mitch sat in a regular chair and Reb wheeled up next to her. Class was now in session.

"What a wonderful crowd we have tonight," the speaker began. "But it's no surprise, considering the discussion topic. Tonight, as planned, we are going to talk about sex." Reb looked over at Mitch who shrugged her shoulders. So much for previewing the agenda.

"This is a topic that is sometimes difficult to talk about, but we know from experience that once the topic of sexual ability and relations is brought up, it makes it easier for couples to talk about it. So, let's begin by going around the room...."

Reb tapped Mitch's arm. "I need to go back to my room."

"Did you forget something? I can go get it for you?"

"No, I'm getting a headache."

"You do look pale."

"Just take me back, okay."

"Sure."

Mitch wheeled Reb out of the room as inconspicuously as possible, although people still turned to stare. Governors always attracted attention when they arrived, but disappearances usually caused even more speculation.

They were settled in the room before a nurse checked in on them.

"Do you need anything?"

"Something for a headache," Mitch requested.

"I'll go check the chart, see what's ordered."

"Thanks."

Mitch watched Reb settle in with paperwork. She had regained the color in her face and was steady of hand as she made notes for work.

"How's the headache?"

"Better already."

"Miraculous recovery."

"It happens," Reb was evading passively.

"When the nurse brings the aspirin, save it for me."

"Sure."

Tomorrow. That's when Mitch would talk about sex. With Reb. Then, it would be the right time.

Albert was sound asleep. Trish waited patiently in the chair, reading still another book about documents of the Third Reich. Someone had once told her that if you took out the word Jews and substituted the word Gays, you could easily find exactly the same kind of wording in modern anti-gay literature as had existed in anti-Jewish literature in Nazi Germany. As the Jews were the enemy of Hitler, so are gay people of today seen as enemies of America by those who need a convenient scapegoat. What had gotten lost in the discussion was that Hitler's regime also had created special laws against male homosexuals. The German criminal code contained a paragraph that made homosexual relations a criminal offense, in effect, a law against sodomy. It was Paragraph 175. When Hitler's power increased, Paragraph 175, and anti-gay prejudice in turn, was strengthened. Himmler believed that homosexuals were a threat to the purity of the Aryan race, so Paragraph 175 was expanded to include homosexual intent. A mere touch between two men, gossip, or

341

innuendo alone were enough to persecute. If someone had a gay friend who they kept in touch with, this also was grounds for interment in a prison or concentration camp for both parties.

"What are you reading?" Albert had stirred awake and watched Trish quietly until now.

"What does the number 175 mean to you?"

"It means hatred."

"You know about it."

"*Know* about it! I lived it! You were called a 175er. Your barracks were called 175 block. Other prisoners, if you were lucky, called you a 175."

"If you were lucky?"

"When I first went to the camps, we had to wear the letter A on our uniforms. It stood for something which is not polite to say."

"You would probably hear the words in any high school in the country."

"Kids these days have filthy mouths."

"Some kids."

"The triangles came later."

"Pink triangles," Trish nodded.

"And others. Do you know them by heart," Albert asked thoughtfully.

"Yellow for Jews. Red for criminals?"

"Red was for political prisoners. Green was for criminals. What about black?"

"I don't know."

"Sometimes, we 175ers wore black because that designated anti-socials. How about purple?"

"Jehovah's Witnesses!" Trish remembered.

342

"And brown for Gypsies and blue for emigrants," Albert
finished his list. "Now, what happened if you were
designated as a Jewish political?"

"I don't know."

"You wore two triangles, two different colors and together
they formed a Star of David."

"How do you remember all this?"

"How do you forget," he sighed his answer.

Trish nodded. Good point.

"One more thing. Do you know what they did to the pink
triangles? They made them bigger," Albert went right
ahead, answering his own question. "And this was so
everyone could guard against what they called the "Butt-"
Albert pulled up short.

"Another one of those high school words?"

"It was so a guard wouldn't feel threatened!" Albert snorted
out the words. "Imagine a man with a machine gun feeling
threatened!"

"Unbelievable."

"And if you got within a certain distance of a guard, you
got twenty-five on the horse."

Trish began to feel her mouth go dry. She had read a few
pages about this and knew the reference. It had nothing to
do with animals, except of course, the Nazis who inflicted
the torture.

"Did that ever happen to you?" Trish felt obligated to ask,
but dreaded the answer.

"Would you care to see the scars?"

"No. Thanks, but no. Why were you punished?"

"My cap blew off during roll call one day. And for that
horrible transgression against the Third Reich, I was
stripped naked, tied to a rough wood board so that my head
was down and my exposed buttocks were up for all to see.

343

When they draw your legs up in order to stretch your flesh to the limit, it becomes such a painful and humiliating pose that you cannot imagine it could get worse. But it does."

"You don't have to talk about it if you--"

"Do you want to hear my story or don't you?" he said calmly.

"Go on," Trish nodded, feeling her temples throb as she wrote.

"And so they bring a whip and flail your skin. And you count the blows. One, two, three. If you don't count it right, they start over. My twenty-five on the horse was thirty-three before they were happy. And then, because they were the master race, they took pity on me and treated my wounds on the spot by dousing them with iodine."

"Oh, my God," Trish inhaled and then tried to concentrate on breathing more steadily.

"I screamed myself hoarse and bled in my pants through the remainder of roll call."

"You still had to stand roll call?"

"It wasn't a finishing school, Ms. Weingarten. It was a death camp."

"And yet, you survived."

"A matter of chance. That's all."

Trish didn't believe this. Those who survived found ways to circumvent the rules. Whatever rules Albert broke in order to live were a crucial part of the story. For now, Trish could only wonder. He had fallen asleep.

Mary flashed her I.D. at the gate and once again gained admittance into the world of Lisa. She was waiting in the driveway this time, not wanting to chance a repeat of their previous library misunderstanding. In front of God, the

344

valet and the butler, Lisa pulled Mary into an intimate embrace and kissed her.

"I missed you," Lisa murmured.

"I've only been gone a couple of days."

"I ached for you every single second."

"Well, then, don't just tell me about it…."

"Come in," Lisa backed away. "Lunch is ready. You'll probably want to freshen up after your trip."

Lisa led the way back into the house and through the hallway to the master bedroom. It only took three kisses before Lisa extracted herself from Mary.

"You get cleaned up. I'll go check on lunch."

"If I get lost, come and find me."

"We're eating in the solarium."

"Sounds lovely."

Mary decided to take her sweet time showering and washing her hair. When she emerged from the shower, her clothes were gone and in their place was a chenille robe, as red as blood. Guaranteed to make any white item pink in the laundry. So? It was going to be another robe adventure, was it? Mary went downstairs and found the sun room with no problem. It was light. Lisa was waiting. Unperturbed. Sipping champagne.

"Do you like champagne?"

"What are we celebrating?" Mary took the glass offered.

"A beautiful life together."

"That sounds like a proposal," Mary commented off-the-cuff.

"It is."

With a smooth motion, Lisa extracted a long, narrow box from her robe pocket. Mary was now just a tab self-conscious that she had made light of the moment.

"What have you done?"

"I searched the face of the earth and three jewelry stores for this. It is an inadequate expression at best."
Lisa held out the box with both hands.
"Maybe I'd better sit down first."
"Come over to the sofa."
They sat close together, robe next to robe.
"Are you just trying to butter me up?"
"If that was my plan, I would have bought a cow."
Mary laughed, still a little nervous. With everything. The gift. The champagne. The opulent lifestyle. The precipitous love affair.
"What are you thinking?" Lisa asked.
"I didn't get you anything."
"You don't need to. Your precious love is all I need."
Mary opened the box carefully. Inside was a dazzling bracelet laden with diamonds and rubies. It had to easily have cost tens of thousands of dollars.
"Oh, my," was all that Mary could manage for a moment, so Lisa picked up on the conversation.
"It took me a little while to decide on the rubies. Some people like them. Some don't."
"They are exquisite," Mary finally found her voice, and it was filled with awe.
"So, it's okay?" Lisa was curious in a devil-may-care way.
"This is way beyond okay. It's too much, Lisa. How can I possibly accept this?"
"Here. Put it on," Lisa helped with the clasp. It fit perfectly and felt utterly glamorous.
"I could never give you a gift in return that would even come close to this."
"I have an idea," Lisa ventured.
Mary studied her countenance for hint of a tease. "What's on your mind?"

"You can forgive me for Texas and all my other past transgressions."

"I already have. We wouldn't have been together in the first place otherwise."

"Oh," Lisa tried to sound off guard. "Well, how about this, then…will you spend the rest of your life with me?"

"You're serious about this, aren't you?"

"I've loved you since the day I met you. Unfortunately, you were preoccupied at the time."

"And so were you."

"Then, when Hilary began to hurt you, it was all I could do to stay out of things."

"You left town, as I recall."

"I needed time to think."

"You did more than that."

"I did a lot of thinking."

Mary fell silent. It wasn't like her to be so querulous after getting a multi-thousand dollar gift. "Yes," she answered. Finally.

"Yes? Yes! The big Y-E-S."

"The big yes."

"Oh, my goodness, you mean it?"

"I mean it."

"Omigod! That's wonderful. That's terrific! What do we do first?"

Mary gazed at Lisa. "We did it already."

"Oh, I know. And it was heavenly. But, don't you want something a bit more on the formal side?"

"Like making love in tuxedos?"

"No! Like having a ceremony. A gathering. Oh, wait…you haven't told your mom, yet, have you?"

"Yes, I did. And Mitch as well."

"What did Mitch say?"

"She suggested vitamins. Multipurpose," Mary extemporized.

"And your mom is okay about this?"

"She will be. Eventually. Have you stopped to think how you and Mitch would be related if all these marriages were blessed by law?"

Lisa didn't take long to figure it out.

"I slept with my future mother-in-law."

"And enjoyed it. Not too many people can say that."

"Especially with a straight face."

Lunch arrived. It consisted once again of lobster with drawn butter, French fries, grapes and chocolate nut clusters. The feast at first blush appeared odd, until Mary realized that it was all finger food. Lisa's plan was to feed Mary like some goddess. They had all sorts of adventures with the butter, and some even ended up on the lobster.

Albert was awake and reading a newspaper. This was a first. Trish settled into her chair while he finished the article.

"How are you?"

"I'm not in the obituaries. Let's get to work."

"Okay. Where were we?" Trish scanned her notes.

"You were wondering how I survived."

"Ah, yes. So. How did you survive?"

"I did favors for the wife of one of the officers."

"What did you do? Bring her tea?"

"It was more involved than that."

"Tea and crumpets?"

"She wanted certain sexual things."

Instantly and subconsciously, Trish furrowed her brow.

"You don't approve."

348

"That's not it at all. I just don't quite understand."

"She wanted what she so callously termed 'queer sex' from me."

"Did her husband know?"

"He did not. I would be dead otherwise. Her logic was that anything her husband refused her, she would find elsewhere. None of the other officers were willing to fulfill her wants. They would be dead, as well."

"I see."

"And so you lose all respect for me."

"No, I haven't. I just had no idea that prisoners had access to wives."

"Many things were arranged. You were correct about one thing, it did begin with tea. When I first went to the camp, there was a period of time where we did the most difficult work imaginable. It was probably about ten times harder than any American boot camp could be. We carried heavy loads, constantly under the whip. So, when you were picked from a group to do something different, you didn't care to question fate. I was assigned to be the domestic servant for the wife. Had I not done this, I would have died within a month or two. When I first started the work, I still suffered from malnutrition. I was soon able to procure more rations. The wife did it, actually. It was convenient blackmail."

"It was like sexual extortion."

"Except that the sex hadn't started yet. I was still too lowly for her. It took a while to gain even a little weight."

Albert closed his eyes, as if to blink away the mental images. Trish waited, respectfully.

"And so I got a little fatter," he laughed a small laugh. Like it hurt. "What I got was a little less starved to death."

"And then you gave her what she wanted."

"Not without a struggle."

"She liked that as well?" Trish was trying hard to understand his train of thought.

"No, not that! Once I found out what was expected of me, I resisted. I was, after all, a self-respecting gay man! I don't cheapen myself for anyone. Not even a Nazi wife. At first...."

"But it happened, eventually?"

"She was going to have me put on the tree."

"Put in a tree?"

"Stand up. Go on. It's just so you'll know."

Trish stood up.

"Now, put both hands behind your back, like someone was going to handcuff you."

"Okay," Trish said, "But no one ever has."

"Now, imagine your hands are tied together and then you are raised off the ground by the rope."

Trish tested the stretch and felt the beginnings of pain.

"It would be unbearable."

"It was."

"You mean, it happened to you?"

"I managed to endure an hour. Some men hanged that way for entire days. The screams were piercing, haunting, beyond belief. Everyone in camp knew when someone was on the tree. Even the citizens. The farmers. The townsfolk."

"Camps were that close to towns?"

"Close enough in some cases. And the people were either hostile or scared out of their wits, so strong was the propaganda and power of the swastika."

"So, you hanged there, with your arms twisted behind you."

"Yes. When she demanded my attentiveness, the wife, she said that if I refused her request, she would have me flogged on the tree as well next time. That would have meant death or at the very least, crippling disability."

"So, you gave her what she wanted."

"Quickly. I was sick to my stomach afterwards. After every time."

Trish ran out of questions and simply waited for Albert to continue.

"She soon tired of me. As far as *that* was concerned. But as a domestic slave, she still found ways to exacerbate my misery. They had a small farm on the compound where they had animals. Germany was at war, after all, and everyone needed to use resources wisely. I became the 'manure boy.'"

"What did that entail?"

"I moved manure from the animal pens to the garden area."

"Not the greatest work, but better than some things."

"You are sitting there probably thinking that I had a wheelbarrow and shovel and hat and overalls and a bit of alfalfa propped between my teeth. A beautiful, bucolic scene?"

"I guess I thought so."

"There were no shovels or wheelbarrows for the men with pink triangles. Or Jews. Or anyone else that I knew. You gathered manure in your hands or the front of your shirt, much like a farmer's wife would gather tomatoes in her apron, and then you ran full speed to the garden. Then, after four hours of that, a five-minute lunch break and then you worked the manure into the earth by hand, which was all but impossible with the hard clay earth. During this eight hours of work, you were never allowed to stand up. By the first week, your knee bones were practically coming through your skin and your fingers were split and swollen. Infected." Albert's voice trailed off and he rubbed his

351

hands on the sheet as if to clear off dirt and pus that was no longer on his hands or under his fingernails.

"How long did you do this?"

"Twelve hours a day."

"How many weeks?"

"Three months. Then, I was ordered to go back to work in the house, which really isn't the right word. I was now to be the *pet* of the household."

"The pet?" Trish asked as if she hadn't heard correctly.

"Even Nazi tyrants needed pets," Albert explained wearily. He was wearing out.

"Do you want to stop for today."

"Could we? I shall promise to do twice as much tomorrow."

"You can have all the time you need to rest."

Trish gathered her things and then, for reasons she didn't consciously understand, patted Albert on his shoulder. She had never touched him. He had never touched her. He took her hand and gave it a squeeze. Bonding had crept up on them, shadowing them through their mutual journey down memory lane. Neither was surprised.

She should have transcribed her notes, but when she returned to the apartment, she stretched out on her air mattress. It was a hundred times more comfortable than anything the inmates of the camps had had for a bed. She closed her eyes in a fruitless attempt to avoid dwelling on Albert's story. It wouldn't leave her thoughts and she began to wonder about her own possible staying power under similar circumstances. Wasn't it enough to work twelve-hour days without adequate food or tools? Why was it necessary to further degrade a human being? It was more than ideology. It was pure insanity. Those who take lightly the suggestions by some that all gay and lesbian citizens be rounded up in America and placed in similar detention centers should be doused with the necessary number of buckets of water until they wake up from their naïve dreamer's paradise.

It was with this goal in mind that Trish began the arduous task of organizing her notes. In the back of her mind, she made a mental note to delve into the necessary legal issues and rights involved in publishing this biography. She assumed Albert would not object, but paperwork was paperwork, and lawyers would be needed.

Reb was nearly hidden behind stacks of folders when Mitch breezed in to have dinner with her.
"Are you in here somewhere?" Mitch yoo-hooed.
"Over here, Dr. Livingston."
"What is all this?"
"Work. You do remember the concept of work, don't you?"
"Vaguely."
"I'll be done in about an hour. Why don't you go see if Jeff needs something."
It was less of an order than a suggestion, but it still felt like a dismissal. Mitch bristled, but hid her reaction well.
"Where is Jeff?"
Reb looked up. Okay, so maybe Mitch had forgotten to clue her voice in on the anti-bristle plan of action."
"You okay?"
"Peachy."
Reb wasn't buying it.
"What's the problem?"
"I don't have a problem."

"Sure you do."

Damn Governors and their psychic abilities anyway.

"What happened the other night at the seminar?" Mitch asked.

Reb did her best to look puzzled. It was as convincing as Mitch's traitorous voice.

"I don't know what you mean."

"Sure, you do."

"Look, I need to get all of this work done tonight. I don't have time for guessing games."

"Fine."

Mitch walked out, leaving Rebecca to her reams and reams of paperwork. Instead of seeking out Jeff, however, she asked around and then located Chris hard at work in her office as well.

"Hi, Mitch," Chris glanced up. "What can I help you with?"

"I need a favor. A big favor."

After a fifteen minute discussion, only because they talked fast, Mitch got her way. It was one heck of a favor, but Chris, ever the willing co-conspirator, was always up for any plan that would take Reb one step closer to wellness.

"You take care of your part and I'll take care of the rest," Chris agreed.

Mitch nodded. "You got yourself a deal."

By the time Mitch paged Jeff, he was heading to the rehab center. Their cell phone chat was brief.

"I'm supposed to be helping you."

"Always good to hear that."

He was so much nicer to work with than the late Mr. McManus. Also less of a romantic threat, unless Aunt BeBe got her way.

"I'll see you down here."
"In five."

Mitch headed back to Reb's room. The stack of paperwork was about half done.
"I tracked down Jeff. He'll be here soon."
"You'll need to work somewhere besides here."
"Here here?" Mitch indicated the current surroundings.
"I need peace and quiet to get this done."
"Sure," Mitch smiled calmly. Her little talk with Chris had improved her mood tremendously. "We'll just grab a table in the coffee shop."

Jeff was the most organized man in the universe. You had to be to run a political campaign of this magnitude on a coffee table. After Rebecca's accident, the campaign effort had waned. This was understandable. What Jeff had done to date after his appointment was miraculous. He had already tripled the volunteer staff, crunched useful database information, and created issue-oriented flyers, brochures, and TV spots. Because he worked so hard, it took a huge burden off Rebecca.

"So, we still need to raise more money, but I managed to buy spots in September. Not as many as our opponent, but all of our fundraising has been legal. Jake, for all his other weaknesses, was a stickler about that."
"Am I limited on how much I can donate legally?"
"Yes."
"But Rebecca isn't? Right?" Mitch tried to stay out of these discussions unless absolutely necessary.
"Rebecca could spend every last cent she has to run for office. I'm reluctant to suggest that strategy, however,

355

since she will probably need money to cover her future medical needs."

"I will cover those."

"You don't need to. After all, Rebecca has plenty of assets."

Mitch nodded like she knew this, but her darn old face gave her away. Again.

"Do you have *any* idea of Rebecca's net worth?" Jeff asked pointedly.

"Well, she just always said that she needed to keep her day job."

"Is that what she told you?" Jeff seemed bemused.

"In similar words," Mitch clarified, unsure of what next turn would occur in the bizarre conversation. Jeff was stymied as well, like he had let some mangy cat out of a bag.

"What are you thinking?" Mitch asked point blank.

"I just didn't know that she kept this from you."

The last two words hit home, but Mitch had already used up her quota of bristles for the day, so she just replied cryptically, "She's not the only one who has secrets."

Dinner was uneventful, as uneventful as things could be whenever Aunt BeBe was involved. She made no bones about it, she was the matchmaker and Reb and Jeff were her designated matchmakees, if that was even a word. Mitch might just as well have been invisible, which suited her mood. Between Aunt BeBe's antics, Jeff's money revelation, and Reb's unwillingness to discuss sex, it was just another day in paradise.

"You were pretty quiet at dinner," Reb remarked when the three-ring circus broke up for the night. Maybe she was feeling a little bit on the guilty side. Maybe she needed to.

"It showed?" Mitch remarked tiredly.

"Don't forget that it was your idea to invite Aunt BeBe back."

"She does keep us on our toes."

"Jeff and I talked things over. We both know what she's up to. You don't need to worry."

"I wasn't and I'm not."

"Good. Well, have you heard from Mary?"

"No. I haven't heard from anybody lately. I think I'll go home and make a few phone calls."

Mitch had calls to make, and not just to Mary.

Chapter 21

Mary slept soundly and awoke to find Lisa still in bed with
her. Usually, she was up and working. Not today. Mary
snuggled close, resting her head on Lisa's shoulder. After
only a few days of sharing Lisa's bed, Mary felt completely
at home. She played the mental comparison game between
Lisa and Hilary. She had enjoyed sex with Hilary, no doubt
about it, until the abuse had started. But with Lisa, she had
transcended all prior experience. What puzzled her was
how? How did Lisa do the same things, essentially, that
Hilary had done, but with so much more spark. It was as if
a light shone from Lisa, and when she directed her radiance
at Mary, it transfixed her. There was no nervousness. No
self-consciousness. In place of this was a bond so strong
that Mary felt one with Lisa. Is this what everyone meant
when they talked about finding their "soul mate?" Mary
snuggled even closer.

"What are you doing?" Lisa asked benignly.

"I'm trying to get inside you."

"You already did that. Last night. You amazing woman,
you."

"Oh, no. You're the amazing one," Mary said as she
propped herself up on one elbow.

"Why? Because I lay here helpless to your touch?"

"That's part of it," Mary said as she began to run her index
finger on Lisa's skin. She wasn't touching any essential
places, and yet Lisa stirred.

"Are you going to tease me *all* day?" she inquired.

"Only if you want me to," Mary answered with an
agreeable smile.

"Your finger's going to get awfully tired."

"Well, when that happens, I'll just have to find a way to improvise, now, won't I?"

"I can only hope," Lisa pulled Mary closer. As they kissed, Lisa freed up her hands to tempt Mary with stirrings of her own but Mary was too quick for her. She traveled downward out of reach. Lisa would just have to suffer through being the sole center of attention for a while. Which, she did quite well and could only murmur quiet appreciation as Mary slowly kissed her way back up Lisa's spent body after bringing her to one very slow, very sweet climax.

"I'm going to return the favor," Lisa assured Mary. "When I recover from this orgasm. In about six weeks." She finished the sentence with effort.

"You just take your time. I'm not going anywhere."

"Imagine spending your entire life in bed. Wouldn't that be great!" Lisa exclaimed without thinking and then immediately realized what she had said.

"I'm sorry. I didn't think. I wasn't thinking about your mom."

Mary put a finger to Lisa's lips. "Shhhhh." she said calmly. "I know what you meant, and it's okay. Besides, my mom isn't going to spend her life in bed. She's very lucky in that regard, although it's tough to convince her of that."

"Well, if anyone can, it's Mitch," Lisa stated with conviction.

"You think so?"

"Heck yes. Why, Mitch could convince a zebra that it needed more stripes."

"She convinced me to come back out here to be with you."

"Genius, the woman is pure genius."

"It takes more than brains to be a good friend."

"Or a good lover," Lisa approached the topic she wanted to address. "Hilary really did a number on you, didn't she."

"You were there."

"I was on the periphery. Remember? I cooked. I cleaned. I worked at the Center. And you were in an untouchable shell."

"I'm sorry if you felt excluded."

"You don't need to apologize. I just wanted you to know that what happened between you and Hilary affected me deeply. It made me grow up a little and appreciate the people in my life. I couldn't imagine being intimate with someone who had hurt me."

"It's a contradiction that I couldn't live with either."

"When did the abuse begin?"

"At the last."

"But there was psychological abuse earlier, wasn't there."

Mary gave Lisa a studied look. "You were paying attention, weren't you!"

"Closer than you knew."

"It started innocuously. Pressure, sarcasm, bargains, schedules and demands on my time that, upon reflection, were designed to isolate me from friends and family."

"Which is classic behavior for a control freak."

"She's in therapy."

"Good for her," Lisa intoned quietly.

"And I'm here."

"Good for me!" Lisa grinned.

"And I love you, so, please, don't worry that I'll pull up stakes and move to New York."

"I'm actually more concerned that you're so far away from your Mom. How can I help?"

"I don't know. You're still a wanted fugitive in Colorado."

"No, I'm not!" Lisa exclaimed.

"You're not?"

"Nah, I took care of that problem."

"How?"

"I had the ticket fixed," Lisa evaded smoothly.

"How?" Mary persisted.

"Friends helped me."

"What friends?"

"Friends who realized the horrible miscarriage of justice by that sorry excuse for a judge."

"Friends that the Governor or her daughter wouldn't know about?"

"I'll introduce you someday."

"Okay. Now that I've answered all your questions, it's my turn. What do you do for a living?"

"I invest and then monitor my investments."

"What kind of investments?"

"Really smart ones."

"If I pulled out a Bible, would you swear to God that whatever it is that you do isn't illegal."

"Absolutely. As long as you didn't force me to read it first. All that condemnation really turns me off."

"So, why is it such a secret?"

"Because it's innovative. New ideas need to be safeguarded."

"Can you give me a hint?"

"It's polymers."

"Polymers aren't a secret."

"Uses for them can be."

"And you're in on the ground floor of this deal."

"I'm the cornerstone."

"A rich, respectable, law-abiding citizen."

"That's me."

"Sounds like I should take you home to meet my mother."

Lisa giggled. "Make those airline reservations. I don't own a jet. Yet."

"First thing tomorrow."

The phone jangled right in the middle of dessert. Robbie answered while Trish poured more coffee. They had connected up for dinner and Trish was ready to confess to Robbie that she had rented the apartment when the phone rang. Being saved by the bell wasn't the Godsend it first appeared.

"It's Albert," Robbie said to Trish.

"On the phone? Does he want to talk to me?"

"He's not on the phone," Robbie clarified. "He's in the hospital."

"Oh, no!" Trish said. Is he going to be okay?"

Robbie held her finger up as she listened to the voice on the other end of the phone. She nodded. She nodded again.

"Okay, thanks." She hung up.

"What?"

"He's in stable condition."

"Can I go see him?"

"I could probably get you in to see him, but I think he needs his rest tonight."

"Of course. I agree. What happened to him?"

"He had a mild heart attack."

"That sounds serious."

"At his age, it is. He's in serious but stable condition. The stable part is good news. We can go in first thing tomorrow. I can call you over at the motel if there's a problem later tonight."

"Actually, that won't work."

"Why not?"

"I moved."

"Really? What motel are you staying at now?"

"I moved into apartment 307."

"You mean, here, in this complex?"

"Yes. Are you angry?"

"No, not at all. Why would I be?"

"I guess I thought that since you offered me your spare room at the beginning of my visit, you would be upset if I once again passed on the opportunity."

"I would never be angry at you for something like that. I understand that writers need their space. Besides, when we get around to visiting my parents and talking to them about our future plans, us living apart will be an asset in their eyes."

"You're right. Will I be expected to ask for their blessing or permission?"

"Ask for neither. What I do want is for you to be very patient with two people who were raised in a world where it was socially acceptable to loath gay people."

"Your parents were raised in a world where it was okay to hate a lot of minority groups. If anyone should understand the injustice of prejudice, they should."

"And yet, some preconceived notions are tough to dispel. Especially where sexual orientation is involved. Just give them a lot of space, okay?"

"Okay, no problem," Trish agreed. She knew all about giving Rose and Max a lot of space. Besides, who else had the advantage of meeting the parents of their true love prior to meeting the true love proper?"

"I'd invite you over for coffee tomorrow morning, but I only have one chair."

"What do you sleep on?"

"An air mattress."

"At least allow me to loan you my spare bed."

"You might spoil me."

"Is it important to lead a Spartan life when writing?"

"I wouldn't know. I'm not a writer. Not yet."

"You will be. I have faith in you."

Trish smiled, "Well, you know the old saying, 'Behind every successful writer is someone who has a real job."

Robbie chuckled easily. "Let me walk you home."

They savored their time together. It was all they could do to keep from holding hands while they strolled across the complex. That was just something gay people got used to. It was not at all uncommon for gay couples to be ejected unceremoniously from shopping malls, baseball games and restaurants for the horrible crime of public displays of affection. If that wasn't enough, they were also followed and assaulted by self-righteous psychopaths. So it was always a case of safety first in these instances. Robbie glanced around Trish's new digs. It took about ten seconds to take in the view.

"Let's go back and get that spare bed."

"No, not now. I'm fine. Really. Besides, I'm not going to haul a mattress and box springs clear across the property."

"I'll hire someone."

"Let's worry about it after we find out more about Albert."

"Okay. Should I stop by in the morning?"

"I'll have the coffee perking."

When Mary had said, "First thing tomorrow," she meant it. She was out of bed and on the phone while Lisa still slept. Reservations, first class, were secured with Mary's credit card. They would need to pack quickly. The flight was at noon. Mary wandered back to the bedroom, quietly puttering about in search of luggage.

"Hey, you," Lisa greeted without opening her eyes.

"Hi, good morning. I made those reservations."

"The luggage is in the hall closet."

"There's about twelve doors. Which one should I try first?"

"How about this one?" Lisa indicated the spot next to her on the bed.

"And what door is that?" Mary inquired with a smile.

"The door to my heart."

"The flight leaves at noon."

"Plenty of time. Come over here. I want to show you something."

"Oh, really!" Mary perched on the side of the bed, well out of arm's reach. Lisa rummaged around in her nightstand and produced a box.

"What's that?"

"Open it up, see for yourself," Lisa pushed the box close to Mary.

The size of the box seemed to rule out a ring. Or a pony. She creaked it open and found herself reacting once again. Inside was the matching necklace of the bracelet, except that the necklace had more diamonds, less rubies. Eminently tasteful for dinner parties at the abodes of billionaires.

"Lisa, this is way too much!"

"It's just the beginning of what I want to give to you. You deserve nothing but the finest."

"I have you, don't I?" Mary inched close enough to bestow a kiss, but remained above the covers.

"You want me to get the luggage, don't you?" Lisa read her mind.

365

"I am nervous about the trip."

"That's understandable. I'm sure your Mom isn't exactly thrilled with our relationship."

"She just isn't quite used to it, yet," Mary sounded like she had more to say.

"What are you thinking?"

"Do you want me to be blunt?"

"Never anything but."

"Necklaces and bracelets are wonderful, but that's not what impresses my Mother."

"Honesty impresses your Mother. That's why she's so head over heels for Mitch."

"She will want to know that you've changed. Turned over a new leaf. Diamonds and rubies won't convey that message to her."

"Good. I wasn't planning on giving her any," Lisa teased.

"You know what I mean."

"You just let me worry about your Mom. I'll have the staff do the packing."

"I don't have much. I can do it myself."

"That's what I love about you. You're not one bit spoiled by your upbringing."

"Having a staff gets real old real quick."

"So does scrubbing toilets."

The hospital was as quiet as the proverbial morgue, which really wasn't the best comparison down here in Retirement Land. More deaths than births were listed in the newspaper. Albert wasn't in print, yet. Still, she checked.

"Hi, Albert," Trish said with nothing short of reverence in her voice.

"And where have you been?" he retorted quickly.

"I had to get permission to see you. They said you had a heart attack."

"Heart attack, smart attack," he scoffed. "I had a *spell*."

"Okay," Trish nodded agreeably. "You look pretty good for someone who's had a spell."

"I want out of here. Can you make that happen?"

Trish pursed her lips. "Probably not. Besides, what's the rush?"

"People die in hospitals. I can't stay here. Find my pants. Those nurses hid them from me."

"You really are anxious about this. Why?"

"Hospitals are bad places. People go in and they die. It's too much trouble to keep them alive."

It dawned on Trish that Albert's fears were a throwback to the war years as opposed to a more timely fear of HMO malpractice.

"Tell me about the camp hospitals." Trish probed gently.

"In a place where people were tortured and murdered on an hourly basis, what do you think the hospital would be like?" Albert demonstrated a healthy command of sarcasm for someone so ill.

"Not any better?"

"You would be correct. I never ended up there, but friends did. People died in line waiting to get in. Others died from injections. Some of those with the pink triangle were subjected to experiments in order to *cure* us."

"I thought you had a hospital stay during the war? You said you had some surgery done?"

Albert had to think for a moment to know what Trish was referring to.

"Oh that! That wasn't done in the surgery. That was done one day late in the war and not by any doctor, I can promise you that."

367

Trish didn't want to hear more about Albert's castration, and was frankly sorry to have mentioned it at all. It's just that she was confused by his story.

"Tell me what you knew about the other so-called medical experiments?"

"Some were injected with male hormones, much more than the body could deal with. It was just another cruel procedure, no one lived long enough to give credence to the alleged scientific basis. You think the Nazi doctors planned to follow the man around after the war and keep tabs on whether he had sex with women? Some experiment! It was simply one more excuse for injecting a tortured man with a harmful concoction. They did it for fun."

"So, you managed to stay out of the hospital. How?"

"I was doing house duty."

"That's right. You had the gardening detail."

"And then I was a guard dog."

"A guard dog?"

"Remember? I was the servant of the wife? Well, she wanted a pet. She got a pet. I was put on a chain, like a dog, and had to remain on all fours to guard the property. I had to bark at anyone walking by. If the day was fairly warm, I was naked. If it was cold, they usually allowed me to wear my prison uniform. I wore the knees out in a week. And they laughed at me. A lot."

"It must have been unbearable."

"There were worse things to do. I just had to bark. And to hold my own with the other guard dogs."

"They had other men doing this as well?"

"No, there were other real dogs. You've seen pictures, no doubt, of the Nazi guard dogs?"

"They looked vicious."

"They could be. It took a while to get on their good side. They were nicer to me than the Nazis were. After all, they were only trained to be mean. The Nazis were born that way."

"Where did you sleep?"

"With the dogs in an enclosed porch. Most days it was tolerable. The dogs were groomed impeccably and I was hosed off and deloused when necessary."

Trish struggled to comprehend life as a pet to fanatics and then marveled at Albert's composure during the retelling. It must have just been a spell as opposed to a heart attack.

"It must have been humiliating."

"It was staying alive, and eating. It was more than others could manage."

"What about your pride?"

"I saved it up for now. I knew I would need it in my old age. I was right, wasn't I?"

Trish thought it over and then nodded sagely. In a society that generally devalued the elderly, pride was a terrific asset to have in abundance.

"And so, you're feeling better today?" Trish eased off the main topic.

"I'm ready to go home. But they keep listening…and thumping… and checking my medical records. You'd think they'd leave an old man to rest."

"I should think so. I'd better go myself now so you can catch up on your sleep."

"I'm safe here, aren't I?" he looked to Trish for reassurances.

"You're in the lap of luxury. For goodness sake, take a nap."

She squeezed his hand and left. Not even a heart attack had gotten the best of him.

The flight was uneventful, a fact which helped to ease Mary's nerves. A little. Scant little. Lisa, by contrast, was unaffected. Somewhere along the line, she had developed nerves of steel, perhaps insulated by a layer of wealth. How could someone so cool turn so hot instantly? Mary put the thought out of her mind. It was distracting her in ways she didn't need right this minute. They arrived at Reb's rehab room just ahead of Mitch and Reb. It had been a "together" day for Mitch and Reb, which meant that Mitch had taken an active role in today's therapy regimen. This had been the norm more and more lately. They both looked tired, yet satisfied. Therapy agreed with them.

"Hello, you two," Rebecca greeted as she wheeled up to the side of the bed. She sounded chipper.

"Hi, Mom. How are you doing?"

"I'm getting better."

Mitch only nodded. She had managed to smile once in Lisa's general direction and then pretended to be totally absorbed by Rebecca's impending transition from wheelchair to bed. Her concentration did not go unnoticed.

"Don't look so worried. I've practiced all day."

"Okay, but remember, you might be tired."

"I feel fine."

With that pronouncement, Rebecca used her new skills to arrange herself in bed. Mitch nodded approvingly, trying her best not to show much more emotion. Every accomplishment by Rebecca pulled Mitch's emotions more front and center, usually to her consternation.

"There," Rebecca said matter-of-factly.

Mitch busied herself with furniture rearrangement. A chair for everyone and everyone in their chair. For four people with intimate knowledge of each other, they were certainly quiet. Reb broke the ice.

"We should talk fast, your Aunt BeBe is going to be here any minute."

"Aunt BeBe?" Lisa asked in Mary's ear.

"She's the family's Kansas version of Dr. Laura."

"And she has a mean right cross," Mitch added.

"I see, well, then," Lisa jumped right in, "I love your daughter and I'd marry her if I could."

"What about your criminal record?" Reb came back quickly.

"It's been expunged."

"Really?"

"You're the Governor. Check for yourself."

"I'll take your word for it. Where are the two of you going to live?"

"Who's going to live where?" Aunt BeBe made her presence known, in her best nosy fashion to boot.

Mitch didn't say it out loud, but to herself she thought, "The Inquisition begins anew."

She got up and offered her chair to Aunt BeBe. She didn't sit.

"Hello, Aunt BeBe," Mary said and then followed up with, "I'd like you to meet my lover, Lisa."

Lisa extended her hand but rather than accept it as the polite sign that it was, BeBe staggered back into the chair held so gallantly by Mitch. Caught her just right. An inch short and Aunt BeBe would be in a heap on the floor.

"You mean…," Aunt BeBe stammered, "you, too?"

"Us two. Yes, us, too," Mary answered all possible questions.

371

"How did *this* happen?" Aunt BeBe shot glares from Mary to Rebecca and then realized that she was outnumbered. Four to one.

"It just happens, Aunt BeBe," Mary explained in that wonderful way most young adults explain things to the family curmudgeon.

"It doesn't happen to *my* family!" she stood to leave.

"Don't go, Aunt BeBe," Mary said.

"I have to go," she said with a cold voice and then walked out.

Mitch checked Reb for a reaction.

"I'll go after her," Mitch volunteered. "You three just keep chatting."

Aunt BeBe wasn't hard to catch. She didn't exactly have the physique of a runner. They shared a quiet elevator ride with a priest. When they exited the elevator at lobby level, Mitch tried to restart a conversation.

"You'll need to talk about this sooner or later, BeBe."

"Not to the likes of you!"

"Then, who?"

"I don't know," BeBe said, sounding winded as she walked. "I'll find someone."

"I have an idea," Mitch piped up, thinking quickly. "We can go sit in the chapel. Have you been there yet?"

Aunt BeBe slowed to a stop. Apparently the idea of sitting down appealed to her.

"I haven't had time to sit around with all my responsibilities at the mansion."

Mitch nodded humbly. She knew all about that mansion stuff.

"Come on. I'll take you there."

BeBe appeared skeptical that Mitch would know the way to a religious place, but she followed, drawn first and foremost by the lure of a seat. Mitch held the door for her and they settled side by side in the second pew. The first pew was presumptuous, but no one was there to judge. Except, of course, the landlord. They sat for a few moments in meditation. Mitch was counting Hail Marys on her fingers. She was up to fifteen before she felt the gaze of BeBe upon her.

"What are you doing?"

"I'm praying the rosary."

"You know the rosary?"

"I'm working on a Novena for Rebecca. I'm up to day twelve."

"A Novena, for your information, only goes for nine days!" BeBe sniffed in her best superior way. Having even the slightest bit of knowledge about Latin affected people that way.

"Yeah, I know," Mitch sighed. "I'm just doing a little extra. I'd do a million days if it makes her life better."

"I'm surprised."

"What?"

"I didn't think you homosexuals knew any prayers."

"Oh, Aunt BeBe, us homosexuals are just full of surprises."

"I noticed. Upstairs."

"Maybe that was a surprise to you, but Mary's been out quite a while. But, I guess you haven't been around lately?"

"She could change."

"Could you change?"

Aunt BeBe snorted in disgust. "Absolutely not!"

"Then, why do you think Mary could change?"

"Because it would be the right thing to do."

373

"For whom?"

"For everyone concerned."

"It wouldn't be better for Mary."

"You don't know that."

"Yes, I do. I've talked to Mary. A lot, lately. Have you?"

"I'm not discussing this further. I'm going."

She stood to leave. "Aren't you going as well?"

"Not yet," Mitch said quietly.

"Why not?"

"God's not done talking to me yet."

If Aunt BeBe rolled her eyes, Mitch didn't see it. She kept her eyes on the crucifix for a moment and then closed them. Aunt BeBe padded out. She couldn't stomp. The rug was too thick.

"Dear Lord, if you wish for me to go around and around in circles and never get anywhere, could you just turn me into a windmill now and get it over with?" Mitch extended her arms and gave him or her a moment. Apparently, today wasn't the day for windmills. Mitch meandered upstairs. Things were better there, which would have been unbelievable a few months ago. Reb and Lisa were chatting amiably about polymers. A "ho-hum topic" unless it happened to make you a millionaire. It was the chatting amiably part that was unbelievable.

"So, the future is in plastics?" Reb was summing things up.

"Our future is in plastics," Mary said as she held hands with Lisa like a couple of teenagers. Ah, love. If Mitch felt a twinge, she chalked it up to hunger. She was starved.

"Where's BeBe?" Reb asked.

"Heading back to the mansion. What's for dinner?"

"I suppose the usual," Reb answered. "Is BeBe okay?"

"Define okay," Mitch replied.

"Never mind. We can talk later."

"What did you say was for dinner?"

"Are *you* okay?"

"I'm famished. Anybody want to go raid the candy bar machine?"

"Having a bit of a chocolate craving?" Lisa asked.

"Something like that," Mitch was ready to embark on a full-scale assault of the vending machine down the hall when dinner finally arrived. Reb was right, it was the usual. Mitch was so tired of the usual. She ate a few bites to stave off a possible fainting spell. Everyone else seemed enthralled with the fare. As they talked, Mitch absently counted her quarters. It would be enough for at least three candy bars. She lost track of the conversation that she really hadn't followed at all and closed her eyes. The next thing she knew, Rebecca's night nurse was checking her patient. It was midnight, she had slept through Mary and Lisa's departure and someone had covered her with a blanket. Mitch stood up and stretched. She went to the bathroom and then spent about thirty minutes watching Rebecca sleep. She ached for their old life back. Back when they could sleep together without nurses popping in and a thousand other problems. It would happen. Soon. Mitch kept her eyes on Rebecca until they could withstand no more of her beauty. Once they closed, Mitch was back asleep within seconds.

"Good morning!" Reb roused Mitch awake. It was six a.m., time for the usual breakfast. Mitch started fingering her quarters again.

"I guess I fell asleep."

"You snored up a storm."

"Tell me I didn't."

"Everyone was glad you were getting such good sleep."

"Oh, great!"

"Including me. You seemed a little out of sorts yesterday. Was it Lisa?"

"Yes," Mitch nodded.

"Or Aunt BeBe?" Rebecca finished the question.

"Yes."

Mitch was two for two, and it was getting easier, this prevaricating thing.

"Maybe you should take a day off," Reb said.

"Maybe we both should," Mitch answered back.

"I doubt that that's possible." Reb said as she ate. "You know how important my rehab schedule is."

"Now, that's what I like to hear," Chris announced her entrance into the room.

"I imagine so," Mitch remarked dryly, but there was an undercurrent between them, borne of a conspiracy rather than sarcasm. Even Reb sensed something. God, she was good.

"What's going on?"

"You have a little something different on your schedule today."

"Let me guess, weightlifting with my toes."

It was the only part of her body that she hadn't had worked over this week.

"Sorry, no. We have something more fun in mind," Chris smiled.

"Well, what?"

"Mitch gets to take you for a drive today."

"Oh really!" Reb brightened considerably. It had been days and days since she had been out for a drive. In fact, the accident was the last time she had been in a car, but that didn't seem to spook her at all.

376

"Well, I guess I'd better get ready." She transferred to her wheelchair and rolled toward the bathroom.

"We are leaving now, aren't we?" she asked over her shoulder.

"Just as soon as you're ready," Mitch assured her breezily, trying to mask her growing apprehension. This had sounded like *such* a good idea at the time. Chris, God bless her, noticed.

"Are you ready for this? It's a big step."

"She's ready. That's what matters most."

"I know you've planned well, but page me if you get in a jam."

"Okay."

"And one more very important thing," Chris looked somber.

"What?" Mitch asked, somewhat alarmed.

"Have fun," Chris broke into a mischievous smile.

Mitch exhaled and grinned. "Thanks!"

If Rebecca had expected a simple ride in a station wagon, she was favorably impressed with the vehicle that Mitch steered her toward. It was a fully equipped van, complete with bathroom facilities. They had enough provisions to survive forty days in the desert.

"Looks like you're ready for a couple of major traffic jams."

"Chris says this is just standard stuff," Mitch shrugged her shoulders, feigning nonchalance. Chris and Mitch had schemed for hours. Hopefully, Reb would think nothing more about it. They used the lift to raise Reb into the van and then secured her chair on the passenger side of the front area. Mitch took the wheel and ventured out into traffic like she had done this all before. Rebecca watched

out the window for a long while as Mitch drove her route.
It was quite a while before Rebecca wanted to talk. Talking
she had done with Mitch every day. Looking out the
window of a car, well, she hadn't done in a while.
"This is nice."
"Everyone needs a change of scenery once in a while."
"Where are we going?"
"This way," Mitch pointed down the highway.
"Are we going to be back in time for lunch?"
Maybe it was just Mitch's nervousness that made Rebecca
sound concerned.
"Chris packed us a picnic. She sure is helpful."
"She sure is. What did she pack?"
"I honestly don't know. Are you hungry? I could pull off
the road and rummage through the supplies."
"No, that's okay. I was just curious."
"Are you needing a break, otherwise?"
"I'm fine."
They traveled for miles in silence. Mitch hummed a tune
under her breath, tapping out the beat on the steering wheel.
The smooth rhythmic movement of the van lulled Rebecca
to sleep. Her head rested comfortably on the pillow that
Chris had the therapist design for this kind of travel. By
the time she awoke, they were past the state line. You
couldn't tell by the scenery unless you happened to see a
marker.
"How long was I asleep?"
"I don't know. I didn't wear a watch."
"I couldn't find mine this morning, either."
"How about that."
"I see," Rebecca began to shift in her chair again.
"You're ready for a break, I can tell."

"I'm ready for you to explain why we just passed a sign that said it's 140 miles to Santa Fe."

"Because it's not 150 miles to Santa Fe?"

"What are you up to and how much trouble are we in back at the rehab center?"

"Let's pull over and have that lunch break."

"This had better be good."

"It is."

They pulled off the road at Springer, New Mexico, where the map indicated a picnic spot. It looked pretty desolate, so they camped inside the van. Reb managed to navigate the van's bathroom facilities while Mitch set the picnic feast on a small built in table. It was all that healthy stuff that Chris was forever touting, but now, away from the rehab center, it tasted better.

"You still haven't told me what you're up to," Reb said after they were halfway through the main course of turkey sandwiches that had a bunch of red lettuce and some low-fat mayo on whole-wheat seedy bread.

"Chris put me in charge of your *recreational* therapy."

"She did not."

"Did, too."

"Who's idea was this, originally?"

"Okay, so I had a bright idea and I talked it over with Chris and she thought it was a great idea, mind you!"

"To kidnap me and take me to Santa Fe?"

"Kidnap is such a strong word."

"Abscond with?"

"Too impersonal. How about 'Take you under my wing'?"

"Sounds too maternal."

"And 'custody' sounds like a divorce settlement. How about 'accompanied'?"

379

"You're accompanying me to Santa Fe for…?"

"Recreational therapy."

"I see."

Somehow, she didn't sound thrilled.

"Are you worried about being away from the rehab center? It has been your home away from home for quite a while."

"I still have my official duties to perform."

Mitch knew what that meant, all that governing stuff.

"I've arranged for that."

"And my unique needs."

Mitch knew what that meant, as well.

"I've arranged for that."

"And all in secret?"

"If Chris hadn't helped, I guess I could have been considered---the lone arranger?"

"Oh, geez!" Reb had the good grace to groan. "I don't even want to hear one 'Hi Ho Silver' outa you!"

"Whatever you say, Tonto."

"Enough! Let's get back on the road."

Type A, she was, even on the highway.

A good seventy miles passed between words.

"I was wondering something," Mitch said. Finally.

"This ought to be good!"

"What do you mean?"

"You've given us an hour of lonely highway to discuss whatever has just popped into your mind."

"And it took me a whole hour to summon up the courage," Mitch admitted candidly.

"Well, let's hear it."

"Why did you pretend to have a headache the evening of the sex workshop?"

"I did have a headache."

"No, you didn't."

"I was getting a headache. Discussing my sex life with a bunch of strangers gives me a headache."

"You've done a lot of that? Discussing your sex life with strangers?"

"You should know. The first time you discussed our sex life with the press, you came down with a full-fledged migraine!"

Mitch nodded. Ah, yes. The pain, the sweet sleep, the teasing kiss. It was worth it.

"Okay, I'll buy that. Now, tell me why we can't talk about it just between us."

"I wasn't aware we weren't."

The double negatives were confusing to Mitch. She decided to be direct.

"I don't want to push you about it, but I do want you to know that when you're ready to discuss out future sex life, I'm ready...to discuss our future sex life."

The next sixty miles were filled with morgue-like silence. Something was up. Something major.

It was cocktail hour by the time they reached the Santa Fe villa. Mitch worked the lift, bringing Reb and her wheelchair down to the walkway level. It was bumpy at first, but smoothed out as she wheeled up to the door. Bella was already on the porch, waiting anxiously. Another wonderful surprise was there as well, Doozie. She barked a welcome.

"Hello, Bella," Reb was her usual cheerful self.

"Is good to see you again," Bella did her best to be formal while wanting to fuss over the governor's arrival.

"It's good to see you as well."

Doozie barked again and Reb gave her permission to jump up on her lap.

"How did you get Doozie down here?" Reb asked Mitch, obviously pleased with the surprise.

"She wanted to drive, but I insisted she fly."

"Don't tell me, her paws are tired."

"I don't know about hers, but mine are plum pooped."

Together, they entered the tranquil confines of the adobe house. Everything was the same as they had remembered it, except for the slight changes here and there to make the house more accessible for Reb. Of course, she checked out the bathroom first, a female-of-the-species thing. It had grip bars and a roll-in shower.

"Someone has been busy."

"Tim did some remodeling."

"So, he's gifted in many respects?"

The first time Rebecca and Tim came face to face, Tim was in his birthday suit. Needless to say, he left quite the impression.

"You're making me blush," Mitch kidded back, remembering the moment as well.

"Who, you? Blush?"

"Come see the studio."

Reb rolled as Mitch walked to the expansive room. It still contained the art supplies that Mitch had left behind, but there was also a great selection of exercise equipment similar to the machines available back home in rehab.

"You bought all this stuff?"

"I'm leasing with an option to buy."

"I'm impressed."

"Well, you didn't think I brought you all the way down here so you could go flabby, did you?"

"When do I start?"

"Tomorrow."

"Why not today?"

"Because your visiting nurse is due here any minute and we don't want to keep her waiting."

"Any minute, huh? You certainly are prepared."

"I had to make a hundred promises to Chris before she agreed to this. I wasn't about to leave anything to chance."

They watched each other for a heartbeat of silence. This room held memories. They had argued here, reconciled here, made love here. It was home field advantage for both of them, and they knew it. Still, things were awkward. Mitch had time to be patient.

The arrival of the nurse eased Rebecca into familiar territory. All the usual checks were performed, bed sores topping the list. It had been a long ride down, but there wasn't even a hint of a problem. As this was going on, Mitch was busy getting in the way in the kitchen. For once, Bella didn't seem to mind. She was preparing low-fat paella and it smelled a whole lot better than anything they served at the center. The table was set and candlelight toyed with shadow. Everyone had outdone themselves. When Bella had first heard of Rebecca's accident, she called until she got through to the Governor's staff. Mitch always knew she had the persistence of a bloodhound. After that message had trickled through, Mitch called her with updates. At some point, inspiration had guided Mitch to consider the wonderful possibilities of the villa as hideaway. It was all one level, perfect for the wheelchair and roomy enough for redecoration. Tim had been ready and willing, and very able with a hammer. His wife was equally employable as help to Bella. So when Mitch floated the idea to bring Reb down for some vacation, Field General Lugosi whipped the troops into shape.

"Everything is perfect, Bella."

"Is kay. Jus kay. Cheeken is never good like when I whas a youn girl. Nowday, it has no taste!"

"Smells divine."

"Jou go find the gubernor. Dinner she is ready."

"Yes, ma'am."

Who said Mitch couldn't follow orders. She located Rebecca having a conversation with her nurse. Still. It appeared serious, and Mitch hesitated. She was trapped between interrupting a private medical discussion and getting in trouble with Bella. Nobody was naked and Bella was waiting.

"Mind if I interrupt?"

"We're almost finished."

"Will you be staying for dinner?" Mitch directed the question toward the nurse and then cringed inwardly. It hadn't come out quite the way she intended. Reb came to the rescue.

"Yes, please stay for dinner."

"I'd love to, but I need to get home to my family."

"Can we send some dinner home with you?" Mitch asked, perhaps a bit eagerly. Anyone would think she wanted some quite time alone with Rebecca.

"No, thanks. I have something in the crock pot at home." With that, she left. Finally.

Mitch followed Rebecca to the dining room and sat opposite her. Bella had laid out the feast and then discreetly departed. As they dished up their plates, Mitch asked, "Do you like the nurse?"

"She's fine. Although she does seem to have your handprints on her back."

"Was I that bad?"

384

"You practically pushed her out the door!"

"I was hungry. It was a long drive down here."

"So, eat your dinner."

She did, happily.

"This is great," Mitch declared.

"Bella outdid herself."

"She called about a dozen times to check out menus. 'Can she eat this? Can she eat that?' She fusses over you, you know that, don't you?"

"I'm very lucky in that respect. I have people who fuss over me."

"Yes, you are. Yes, you do."

Mitch couldn't help but be agreeable. The truth made it easier to chat about inconsequential things through the remainder of the meal. Afterwards, Mitch cleaned up the dishes and put away the leftovers while Rebecca entertained Doozie. They were playing pitch and catch with a ball, a game they both enjoyed immensely. Mitch joined in after chores and then before long, Doozie required a nap. Mitch understood the feeling.

"You look ready for bed," Reb said noncommittally.

"It's been a long day."

"I can do most of the work to get myself to bed."

"You are making remarkable progress."

"So, you can go to bed anytime. I'll be in later."

"Okay. Wake me up if you need anything."

Mitch was barely settled in bed when Rebecca started her own bedtime process. She took a bit longer than normal, but managed to get in bed all by herself. She was quiet for a few moments, catching her breath after the exertion. Then, she said, "I know why you wanted to bring me here."

"Why?" Mitch asked drowsily.

"Because you wanted to be closer to me."

Mitch raised up on one elbow, "Honey, I couldn't be closer to you if I tried."

"What do you mean?"

"I carry you inside me every minute of every day. You never leave. You never go away. I pray you never do."

"I'm here, aren't I?"

"And I'm the luckiest woman on the planet."

"Goodnight."

"Night."

Chapter 22

"How's Albert doing?" Robbie asked over dinner.
"For someone who's just had a heart attack, quite well."
"That's good."
Trish, being the insightful soul that all writers, would-be and otherwise are, looked up from her plate and studied Robbie. They had been like the proverbial ships passing in the night, and not even the night was cooperating. Robbie had two patients that were demanding extra care. That translated into longer hours. The extra pay was nice, but that was never the reason that Robbie took on the extra work. It was her caring spirit that answered the call where her patients were concerned.
"What's on your mind?" Trish asked. It had been awfully quiet at the table.
"Nothing much," Robbie said with that unmistakable façade that never successfully hides a candid thought.
"Tell me anyway."
"Children don't fix a marriage."
Trish furrowed her brow. This topic was going to be interesting to discuss.
"I agree with you. Why would you bring that up now?"
"Because people make that mistake a lot."
"Is this a conversation about your childhood or our relationship?"
"My parents are still together."
"Having you was very important to them."
"You seem to think you know a lot about my parents."
Trish felt stuck. She wanted to back out of the conversation for two reasons. The first was to keep her promise to Rose. The second was just because Robbie had had a rough couple of days.

"I'm no expert on your family," Trish hoped that concession would be a wise conversational choice.

"Look, I'm sorry. I'm grouchy."

"It's okay," Trish smiled. "You can be grouchy. Everybody is entitled to be grouchy once in a while."

"You don't seem to ever be grouchy."

"My time will come. Are you worried about us?"

"I think I'm having a huge case of nerves. You make everything sound so easy. Tell my parents, live together, have kids, and it's all happily ever after."

"Which part makes you the most nervous?"

"Not very many people get the 'happily ever after' part."

"That may be true," Trish nodded, "but I can assure you of one thing."

"What?"

"Nobody ever gets the 'happily ever after' part unless they go for it."

"Can't win if you don't play?"

"Exactly."

This logic was the tipping point in favor of entering into the scary realm of partnership for Robbie.

"When do you want to tell my parents?"

"I'd like to do that in person."

"That would be very respectful."

"I think so, too. Then, what step do you want to take next?"

"You're going to think I'm very old fashioned."

"No, I won't."

"Promise?"

"Promise."

"I'd like to have a courtship. That would be wonderful."

"You mean, like dating…and stuff."

"Like dating. I told you I was old fashioned."

"Dating is good. Dinner, movies, long walks on the beach," Trish sighed audibly.

"You're ready for more than that, aren't you."

Robbie made the question sound more like a statement.

"No," Trish shook her head. "I'm fine with dating. Dating is fine. Whenever I try to rush into a relationship, it's a disaster. So, do me a favor?"

"What kind of favor?"

"Make me wait for you."

"I'll give it my best shot."

Mitch woke up to an empty bed. Well damn, that much hadn't changed. Even Doozie was gone. Putting one foot in front of the other, Mitch wandered into the bathroom. She debated spending a minimum or maximum amount of time primping and chose the former. After all, she was on vacation. And hungry. Bella had fixed something which smelled great, but Mitch wanted to check in with Reb, the early bird. She found her doing reps under the watchful eye of the therapist Chris had recommended. Not wanting to interrupt, Mitch served herself a plate of food and sat by herself to eat. Eventually, Doozie padded over and looked up with those sad beagle eyes as if to say," She's ignoring me, too."

"I know, girl," Mitch commiserated. "But she has to work hard to fight back."

Mitch fed Doozie a couple of bites of low fat quiche at they talked.

"Maybe when she gets done, she'll take us for a walk."

At the word "walk," Doozie fetched her leash. Great – two Type A exercisers.

389

"Are you feeding Doozie from the table?" the voice floated from the studio.

"No, Dear," Mitch lied and then gave a warning glance to Doozie. She whimpered, holding her leash limply in her mouth.

"Did you sleep well?" Reb rolled into the room, followed by the therapist.

"Like a stone. Doozie wants to take a walk."

"Probably needs to work off those table scraps you've been feeding her."

Mitch could have sworn she saw Doozie nod her head. Traitor!

"Have you met Greta?" Reb asked as she poured a glass of juice.

"No," Mitch stood and stretched out her hand. "Nice to meet you."

"Likewise."

"Care for some breakfast?"

"No, thanks. I've *already* eaten."

She made it sound like Mitch had slept in all hours of the day. Geez, it was only nine.

"Tomorrow! Same time!" Greta nodded toward Reb.

"Yes, thank you."

Greta turned and marched out like a Marine drill sergeant. Even Doozie seemed to salute.

"Good session?"

"She's a toughie. I know I'm going to be sore. Are you ready for that walk?"

"On one condition."

"Just one?"

"It must also be a talk."

"Okay. You're on."

With Doozie leading the way, they took a nice cool-down walk. When the terrain got bumpy, Mitch helped Reb over the ruts in the road. By the time they needed a breather, they had traveled about a mile. It might just as well have been a hundred, so isolated the area.

"You wanted to talk," reminded Reb.

"Actually, I wanted *you* to talk."

"About what?"

"About us. I want just a clue about why you are so afraid to approach the subject of sexual contact."

"You'll hate me," Reb looked away, pretending to study some far off rock formation.

"No, I won't," Mitch reassured her quickly, although Reb's words surprised her.

"You will be angry with me."

"Why?" Mitch couldn't keep from asking. Now, she was really curious.

"Because I've been listening to my sister and believing in foolishness."

"Aunt BeBe has been waxing philosophical again? What did she said to you?"

"She talked to me about how God punishes people."

Mitch knelt in front of Reb and took both her hands. They were facing each other now. No more geological studies by Rebecca of the surrounding land masses. They looked at each other, not a thing between them except the theories of Aunt BeBe.

"What does Aunt BeBe say about punishment?"

"Anyone who wants to desperately believe in an active, day-to-day God, believes in all sorts of signs and omens. They're always seeking a clue as to God's wonder, or God's approval, or God's disapproval."

"I've seen that," Mitch nodded. "If a tornado destroys a gay center, it's a sign from God that he disapproves. If the same tornado demolished a church one block away, it's a sign that God wanted the parishioners to have a new church building."

Reb nodded meekly, "Yeah, that's about the size of it."

"So, what is Aunt BeBe's insight, exactly?"

"She knows that God is punishing me for my relationship with you by taking away my ability to experience sexual fulfillment. She knows, because God tells her, you see, that if I go back to Jeff, I'll recover fully from all my injuries. I'll be able to walk again, and everything."

"I see."

"You're upset, I knew it."

"Well, I just didn't know you had a sister who had dialogues with God. I, myself, simply have monologues. Did God happen to tell BeBe who's going to win the Superbowl during any of their talks? I'd like to get a bet down early."

"I'm not going back to Jeff," Reb snapped, "so, you don't have to worry!"

"That will certainly ease his girlfriend's mind," Mitch ruminated out loud.

"He has a girlfriend?" Reb asked with only about a thousand times too much surprise in her voice.

"Sure. You didn't know?"

"He and I haven't discussed it."

"He's busy running your campaign. Hey! Maybe Aunt BeBe could engage God in a talk about your campaign. If we knew beforehand who was going to win, it sure would save us a lot of time and trouble."

"You shouldn't poke fun at her beliefs."

"Rebecca, think about it! If every man who had an affair lost his ability to have sexual arousal, do you know what would happen?"

Reb wanted so badly to answer with the droll, "Nothing," but instead said, "What?"

"The end of the world as we know it," Mitch did her best imitation of Orsen Wells.

"I think we'd better be heading back," Reb said suddenly.

"I guess so. I mean, if the end of the world is coming, I'd prefer to be indoors."

Reb struggled to roll away and then conceded the point that she needed help to get to level ground. Mitch helped without comment. She knew Reb had heard enough of her opinions for the moment. What Mitch would have characterized as blunt, Reb considered flippant. Well, at least it was a start. Mitch knew what she was up against. There was nothing quite like a visit from the straight and narrow side of the family to make people revisit childhood dogma.

The mile back passed quickly. They would be home long before lunch time. There would be no food to give them an excuse not to talk to each other. Reb spent her time on the phone, conducting Governor-type business. Mitch took a turn on the weight machine. Doozie took a nap. Bella stormed in about eleven thirty, apologizing half in Spanish and half in English for being late and then whilrwinded around the kitchen preparing lunch. Mitch was there to help and when Bella sensed her mood, she graciously allowed her to reach dishes and offer help.

"Jou two havin a fight?"

"Rehab is tough."

"Hi can imagine!"

Reb invited Bella to stay but she skittered away like
marbles on tile flooring. Once again, they faced each other.
"Did you get all of your phone calls made?"
"All but one."
"That's good!"
"I only had two to make."
"Batting 500."
"You always look on the bright side, don't you?"
"I do my best."

After a moment, Reb asked pointedly, "What do you
believe in?"
"You mean, God-wise? Like what we were talking about
this morning?" Mitch asked between bites of grilled
salmon.
"Yes."
"Well, I don't really know what I believe."
"You sure don't believe in Aunt BeBe's theory."
"I don't believe in a direct-action God, if that's what you
mean. I don't believe that God took time out of his or her
busy, busy day to damage your spine so that you can't feel
an orgasm because you and I have found such love and
fulfillment together."
"So, you don't believe in a punishing God. Do you believe
in a God at all?"
Mitch chewed thoughtfully, not answering right away. It
made Reb nervous, so she clarified, "It's just that we've
never talked about it. Much."
"You're right. We never have. What do you believe?"
"Oh no! I asked first."
"Okay. I guess that if I don't believe in a direct-action type
of God, then I must believe in an indirect-action kind of

God. How else could anyone ever make sense out of life? Things like the Holocaust for instance. Why would a direct-action God refuse to intervene in the Nazi death camps? Take the starving, tortured people in his hands and soothe them. If God wanted to intervene, it would have been a perfect opportunity. That's what I would have done with those kind of powers."

"How does the indirect-God theory work?"

"I think God is an empowering God. We are given strengths and challenged to use them wisely."

"And what about our weaknesses?"

"We are given the opportunity to turn our weaknesses into strengths."

"And what about right and wrong?"

"If our actions help to make the world a better place, that's right. If our actions are harmful or unjust, that's wrong."

"And so it all boils down to intent."

"For me, it does. I intended to make your life a wonderful, loving existence. If God didn't want that, he should have struck me dead and left you alone."

"If God struck you dead, I *would* be alone. Truly alone."

"And I don't believe that God or Aunt BeBe want that. Not really."

For eating only half of her lunch, Mitch felt full. Reb lost her appetite as well. Deep conversations tend to do that to people in love. It was just as well. Mitch glanced up at the clock and smiled. "It's almost time for your surprise!"

"My *surprise*?" Reb sounded skeptical.

"And it's probably a good thing that we ate a light lunch."

"Really?" Reb packed a lot into one word.

"Come on. We need to drive somewhere."

"Drive somewhere?"

"Yeah."

Reb resigned herself to the fact that she lived with the most maddening woman on the planet.

The building was suspiciously shaped like a rectangle. Weren't all buildings, therefore, suspicious by nature? No, the Sydney Opera House wouldn't qualify. Neither would the Pentagon. And if ever there was a building that aroused suspicion....

Anyway, what this building really looked suspiciously like was a swimming facility. A dead giveaway was the name on the front, Aqua Rehab Center. Three giant drops of blue water were painted decoratively over the doorway.

"I don't have my swimsuit," Reb said nervously.
"Me, neither. I think Chris called ahead and gave them your size."
"You and Chris cooked this up?"
"Your rehab team came up with the idea of swimming therapy."
"I can't use my legs. I'll drown."
"Don't worry," Mitch assured her. "They know what they're doing."

Together they entered the building and signed in. Almost immediately, three people descended on them, ready to begin the process. Rebecca was escorted to the changing area while Mitch was given a tour of the pool area. In order to avoid accidents, Rebecca would be placed in a state-of-the-art harness system. Today, the schedule would be light. Get in. Get a feel for the procedure. A couple of laps. Just another day at the pool. As the therapist worked with Reb, Mitch wandered around, looking through the locker rooms and generally familiarizing herself with the premises. It was very nice. And very big. It required a lot of wandering.

As Mitch got closer to the actual pool area, she heard the trouble before she actually saw it, and it was in the form of the unmistakable voice of Rebecca.
"I said, leave me the hell alone!"
Mitch walked up to the side of the pool where Reb had moored. The recreational therapist appeared young and slightly terrified. Reb could be overpowering at times.
"Let me handle this," Mitch mouthed to the poor girl.
"Be my guest," she muttered. "Just be sure she doesn't drown."
"I'll do my best," Mitch nodded.
The therapist swam away like she had escaped Alcatraz.
Mitch looked down. Reb was resting her head in her arms. She could be crying or angry or about a hundred other things. One thing was sure, Mitch wouldn't be able to tell from here. She crouched down and then, fully clothed, lowered herself into the water. Good thing she had her T-shirt tucked into her Jeans. Otherwise, it would've bubbled up. Reb noticed the change in the water and glanced over.
"You are a nut!"
"Yeah, I know. Now, I'm a soggy nut."
They bobbed together for a moment.
"I heard you were upset," Mitch breached the topic.
"I guess I *was* yelling."
"The poor dear is probably taking a Valium."
"She needs one. She's just a little too perky for me."
"I missed the beginning. What happened?"
"I can't swim."

"Really?"

"At least, not like I used to."

Now, Mitch got it. Finally. Sheesh. Took her long enough. "Come with me."

Mitch took gentle hold of Reb and guided her to an area of the pool that was specially designed as a resting spot. Mitch sat on a tile outcrop and drew Reb into a close embrace. They were both still submerged right up to their chins in water and the smell of chlorine permeated their senses. Mitch was able to hold Reb close. Closer than they had been in weeks.

"I promised Perky that I wouldn't let you drown."

"Good for you."

Mitch just smiled and snuggled closer. It took Reb a minute, but she finally relaxed into Mitch's arms. It was just them, and a few tons of water.

"If you want to cry or yell or talk or anything, I'm right here for you."

"You always are," Reb agreed as she began to cry. Softly. "I can't even get across the pool once! Hell, I used to do hundreds of laps."

"You did?"

"I was a champion."

"I remember something about that. You told me in Vegas."

"I did, didn't I. Those were the days."

"Those were those days and now these are these days."

"Is that supposed to be some sort of profound statement?" Mitch pulled back away just a little so she could meet Reb's eyes.

"There's this big part of me that wants so desperately to tell you that everything is going to be just the way it used to be. And then there's the pragmatic side that reminds me that things are never going to be the same. You may never be

398

able to swim a hundred laps again, but at least you're in the pool. Right?" Mitch's voice began to quiver with emotion. Pep talks weren't exactly her specialty.

Reb nodded and then, with a silly smile, reminded, "And you're in the pool, as well."

"Can't get anything past you." Mitch teased back.

Reb took Mitch's face in both hands and kissed her. She made it quick in order to monitor the effect. Mitch was affected and getting more so every second. More than just her voice quivered now. She kissed her again, following the pattern that she knew drove Mitch to distraction. She kissed and then pulled back until Mitch held her steady, needing more than kiss and run. They kissed deeply until Mitch needed to breathe. She rested her head on Reb's shoulder, which was quite comfortable in spite of all the muscling up she had recently accomplished.

"I'm so sorry," Reb whispered in her ear.

"You haven't anything to be sorry for."

"I've made you wait too long. Much too long."

"I would have waited a lifetime. Two, if I was reincarnated."

"Maybe you already have been? Reincarnated, that is."

"If that's true, I must have been a really, really good person in a previous life to be rewarded with your love."

"Geez, you are so romantic."

"It's easy to be with you. Come on, I'll race you home."

"You're all wet!"

"Can you think of a better reason to hurry?"

Albert was still camping out at Phoenix General. Trish had eased up on the interviews, knowing that he was putting on

a brave face, but she never missed a day's visit. She
brought him flowers, books and newspapers.

"You trying to spoil an old man?"

"Who me?"

"Yeah, you. Why aren't you asking me the usual
questions?"

"Oh, I thought I'd take it easy on you."

"Oh, phooey! I survived the Third Reich. You think you
are tougher than that?"

"Gosh, I hope not."

"So, let's get to work. I told you about living with the
dogs."

"You said you were forced to be a pet."

"I could bark just like them. At first they were dominant.
They were trained to be mean, you know, but they were
good to begin with. Which made them different from their
masters, who were born mean."

Trish nodded. She didn't need to write it all down again,
since it was a recap of previous conversation. If he had
forgotten that he had said it all before, she wasn't going to
embarrass him by stating the obvious.

"Which is how I managed to survive."

"How?"

"The dogs."

"How did the dogs help you to survive?"

"Two ways. I'll tell you the first and then I'll ask you to do
a favor for me before I tell you the second."

"Okay," Trish agreed without equivocation.

"They finally shared their food with me. It took a while,
but I finally found their good core. Have you ever eaten
dog biscuits, Ms. Weingarten?"

Trish hoped that eating dog food wasn't the favor he was
going to ask of her.

"Not to my knowledge."

"You think someone snuck some by you?"

"No, not really."

"Well, when you're starving, you'll eat anything. I know all about the controversy surrounding that issue."

"What controversy?"

"You know," he said with an air of conspiracy. "Cannibalism."

The word hung between them like the most taboo of subjects.

"You think we were all angels! All perfect, with halos of blinding light and harps of gold. It's a pretty picture."

"From everything you've told me, I know that it took a lot of compromise to survive."

"Compromise. A respectable word to describe humans eating the flesh of other humans. But who am I to judge. If it helped someone to survive, who am I to judge!"

Trish sat, quietly pondering the moral dilemma of survival.

"You taking a nap?" Albert asked.

"No. I'm just thinking about all the things you have said."

"You must do something."

"What?"

"Back in my room, at Cypress, there's an envelope. You must get it."

"Right now?"

"The sooner the better."

"Where is it?"

"You know those built-in dressers?"

"Yes, in the closet area."

"Right. There's a standard size envelope in the dresser. Bring it next time."

"Okay. I'll see you tomorrow."

"Good."

Mitch came three times. Okay, that was a bit of an exaggeration. Two and one-half would be more accurate. During the third time around, she got to giggling and finally dissolved into Reb's waiting arms. Reb offered the refuge of her shoulder and Mitch cuddled up.

"God, you're good," Mitch exhaled quietly.

"Haven't lost my touch, have I."

"Not one bit."

Usually, they weren't shy about debriefing each other about these issues, but after these concise comments, they were both quiet for a long time.

Mitch knew the unvarnished truth, Reb hadn't felt a thing below her belly button. To make up for this, Mitch had spent much more time fiddling with all those wonderful accouterments above her waist. She had to admit to herself that, overall, she had given short shrift to the exploration of these treasures in the past. Always ready to go right for the climax, Mitch wasn't exactly an expert in extended foreplay. Now that that was all that Reb could feel, Mitch adjusted to the new reality. She had found soft places to kiss that raised goose bumps, a stirring treat for Reb. This, combined with soft, sensual touching, provided Reb a fulfilling experience.

"You were great, too." Reb said, reading Mitch's mind.

"I studied."

"You studied?"

"Uh huh. There are books out there that address this issue."

"Well, you passed the test. I'm tingly all over. Well, almost."

"Do you miss…*it*?"

"When you don't feel anything, there's really not much to miss. But the rest of me is *so* glad you kidnapped me."

"Me, too. Do you need anything?"

"Dinner."

"Dinner it is, then. Let's go out."

"Okay. And then I do want to call that pool therapist and apologize."

"I'm sure she will appreciate that. I should probably apologize for contaminating the pool with my street clothes as well."

"But you looked so cute squishing your way down the hall."

"That turns you on, huh?"

"Squish, squish, squish."

"Come on. I'll buy you dinner and then we're coming right back here."

"You got yourself a deal, Squishy."

Trish walked tentatively into Albert's room at Cypress like she was some sort of burglar. This had sounded so innocent when Albert has asked the favor, but here and now, it felt sneaky. She checked over her shoulder twice, for what, she wasn't quite sure. She sidled up to the dresser and opened the top drawer. There were socks and handkerchiefs. Neat and tidy. No envelope. One down, three to go. The second drawer had more underwear and Trish closed it after the briefest of inspections. Maybe this was what was making her jumpy. Going through other people's underwear drawers gave her a case of the willies. Drawer number three held more promise. There were books and papers, which Trish riffled through carefully. If

403

there was an envelope here, it was hiding. Drawer four held only a watch, one shoe, an artist's paint brush and a box of tissue. Trish went back to the third drawer and did a more thorough search. About halfway through the process, she became tired of bending over and pulled over a low stool to sit on. She searched through the books for the elusive envelope and then paged through the paperwork. No luck, it was all standard nursing home literature. She closed the drawer and thought about Albert and how his mind worked. He survived the Holocaust. Only cautious, careful people managed to do that. Instinctively, Trish pulled out the top drawer again and from her low perch, she saw the corner of the envelope. It was taped to the bottom of the drawer, just like in all the old mystery movies.

"Oh, Albert, for goodness sake," Trish muttered as she carefully removed it from its hiding place. She had just tucked it away in her own portfolio when Robbie appeared. Trish jumped a mental mile.

"Hi, there. Somebody said that they saw you come in here."

"Oh…hi!" Trish stood up and closed the top drawer.

"Looking for something?"

Trish thought fast. If whatever was in the envelope was important enough for Albert to tape it to the bottom of a drawer, it was important to keep his secret, at least for now.

"Albert wanted some personal stuff, you know, underwear. So, I volunteered, but now it feels a little awkward. Could you pack up a few things for him?"

"Sure. Maybe a couple of changes?"

"Yeah, that would be good. It will give him a choice and make his hospital stay so much more tolerable."

"I think you are doing more good for him than any clothing ever could. Why don't I send his spare robe, pajamas and slippers as well!"

"He would love you forever."

"I'd be in line, right behind you."

"Not a bad place to be," Trish smiled and then stole a kiss. Robbie blushed for ten minutes.

Chapter 23

Mary and Lisa were becoming quite the travelers. After
Mitch had squired Reb to Santa Fe, Lisa and Mary had
returned home to California. With her mother out of town
and Aunt BeBe holed up at the mansion, there was nothing
else binding Mary to Colorado. And although Lisa made
the transition worthwhile, there were still adjustments to
make. After only two days of living in the lap of luxury,
Mary fairly hummed of restlessness. Lisa, tuned in as
usual, suggested a drive. They ended up at the Hotel Del
Coronado, only one of the most beautiful hotels in the
region. They checked in and took dinner in their room.
Lisa wanted to get a feel for Mary's state of mind.
"I will guarantee you see your mother any time you wish,"
Lisa took her best guess during the entrée of tenderloin
steak, lobster and champagne.
"I know. You are so good to me."
"Do you want to move back there? We could buy a place."
"No, let's not do that."
"Getting spoiled by California already?"
"Not so much that, as I just don't know where my Mom is
going to be in a few weeks."
"Oh yeah, the election. She's going to be in Washington!"
"You sound confident."
"She's in a Democratic district, right?"
"Right, but that's no guarantee."
"She'll win. Let's go swimming."
"We can't go swimming right now. Not after this dinner."
"Well, what do you suggest?"
Mary cupped Lisa's face in her hands. "Do you even need
to ask?"

"Why, Ms. Fairbanks! You certainly come up with some good ideas."

"I do, don't I."

The swim was put on hold, as was a stroll on the beach and a tour of the hotel grounds. Instead, Mary and Lisa relaxed in each other's arms and talked about dreams and hopes. This created, especially for Mary, the intimacy that she now realized had been lacking in her prior relationship. She could say anything.

"What are you thinking?"

"I'm glad my Mom took our visit so well."

"Your Aunt BeBe was another story."

"She always has been. Even when I was little, we were all terrified of her. You know that saying about people and religious beliefs."

"Tell me."

"People who want so badly to tell you their religious beliefs rarely want to hear your religious beliefs in turn. That's Aunt BeBe. She speaks her beliefs and then tolerates no debate."

"How does your mother put up with her?"

"Actually, they were a lot alike until Mitch came on the scene. How she transformed my Mother was nothing short of a miracle."

"Mitch has that capacity."

Mary nodded. Who better than Lisa to know the wonders of Mitch.

"I heard that."

"I didn't say anything."

"You didn't have to. I know what you're thinking," Lisa said.

"You do?"

"You're wondering if my former relationship with Mitch is going to be a major distraction for us."

"That's about it in a nutshell."

"I know I haven't been perfect."

"Perfection is neurotic."

"Nonetheless, I know I have my faults. I don't consider them to be character flaws and neither did Mitch. She has a rare gift for finding room for improvement in people without crowding them. If I hadn't fallen so deeply in love with you, I would still probably be chiding myself for letting Mitch get away."

"When did that happen?"

"Which time?" Lisa asked.

"What which time?"

"I'm confused. Ask your question again."

"When did you fall in love with me? So deeply."

"Oh, that! Why, the first moment I laid eyes on you."

"No!"

"Yes!"

"You fell in love with Mary the Maid?"

"Must have been your feather duster."

Mary began to turn a gorgeous shade of crimson.

"This is more fun than swimming."

"Unless you count the breaststroke," Lisa arched an eyebrow playfully.

"Oh, yes," Mary agreed as Lisa demonstrated. With her tongue.

Rebecca did much better in the pool after a day of rest and recreation, Mitch style. The perky therapist graciously accepted Reb's apology and was a bit more on the realistic side of advice.

"I didn't know you were a swimmer before the accident. No wonder you had such high expectations."

"I guess I thought being in the water would make all the difference."

"Apparently your girlfriend had the same idea," the girl smiled shyly.

Reb and Mitch were never really out of the public eye.

"Mitch has her own style, that's for sure."

"Well, whatever works. Just, well, next time, maybe she could at least take off her shoes."

"I'll mention it to her, but I don't think she'll be jumping in again anytime soon."

"She's welcome in anytime. Really. Perhaps we could loan her a suit?"

"I'll ask. Later."

Getting down to business, Reb attacked the pool with renewed patience. Not only was the exercise good for her arms, but it gave her a chance to move somewhat freely while putting weight on her legs. This was so important due to the loss of calcium that plagued wheelchair users. The nurses had discussed the issue of osteoporosis long ago, back when Mitch's head was still swimming with other more salient issues. And while this was an issue that most people associated with old age, the therapy had to begin now. The first two years were critical and so when Mitch had suggested this secretive getaway to Chris, she couldn't have been more receptive.

Reb accomplished about three times the work of her first visit and swam slowly over to the side of the pool where Mitch sat cross-legged.

"Hey, sailor."

"Hey, mermaid."

"They said they would provide you with a suit."

"Oh, I don't think so. You can still out swim me."

"I can still out do you in a whole lot of ways."

"Damn if that isn't true."

"Did I ever tell you that you are so good for my ego?"

"No, I don't think you've mentioned it. Not lately, anyway."

"Well, you are!"

"I know," Mitch just smiled.

The swimming therapist listened to this exchange with just a hint of a smile.

"You're finished for today, Governor."

"Really? I figured I was good for a couple more laps."

Reb directed this comment more to Mitch, but if Mitch had a silly comment, she kept it to herself. She just winked at Reb. There were, after all, tender ears present.

After the day at the pool, Mitch and Reb again collapsed into bed together. Mitch worked on self-control issues as she massaged Reb's back. Ever so slowly. It helped her relax those stubborn muscles. As Mitch worked on her shoulders, she leaned down and nuzzled the back of her neck. It didn't take long for Mitch to forget all about the massage.

"Ohhh, that feels good."

"I can tell you're getting relaxed."

"I can tell you're not."

"Don't worry about me."

"Our relationship has changed, that's for sure."

"In what ways?" Mitch wanted to hear more.

"Gone are the days when I could wrestle you down and take advantage of you."

"The way you're developing your upper body strength, it won't be long before you get the best of me."

"We both know that won't happen."

"Can we keep trying anyway?"

"I never realized how humbling a disability can be."

Mitch noticed Reb's muscles beginning to tense up. This was an emotional subject for her, and rightly so. Mitch stretched out next to Reb, ensuring that if and when she wanted to make eye contact, she could. Then, Mitch waited.

"When you were shot, I really didn't understand how deeply the damage affected you. I was absolutely no support during your rehab and haven't had the decency to offer any help."

Mitch searched for soothing words and couldn't think of much to say at first. Then, she spoke, "You were supportive. What little damage happened to my arm is nothing compared to what you're going through. I'd have to walk on my hands to even begin to equate the two injuries. You are facing more pain and more barriers than I ever had."

Reb stayed silent.

"Why would you ever think you weren't helpful?"

"I didn't jump fully clothed into a swimming pool."

"Thanks, I think?"

"You know what I love about you best?"

"What?"

"I love how you don't treat me like an invalid."

"You don't give me any other choice."

"Come here. I want to wrestle you down."

"Thank God!"

Mitch did as little as possible to help Reb in her quest. She had already demonstrated strength and endurance the last time they made love. So what if it was a touch on the awkward side. Anyone who knew the ins and outs of real life lovemaking knew that it was always full of awkward moments, unlike romance novels where everyone was a cross between a gymnast and a ballerina. Mitch thoroughly enjoyed Reb's romantic advances and then spent time exploring that little spot on her neck that gave her chills.

"Your body has so many wonderful places that I've neglected these many months."

"I'm glad you got around to them."

"Finally, huh."

"Finally."

Trish held the envelope up to the light. It was odd. She could tell that it contained documents. That logic was inescapable. What seemed strange was the thickness of the middle portion. It was like there was something in the envelope that was too short to stretch from side to side. She stuffed it in her jacket pocket as she entered the Phoenix General. Albert would be waiting. He was asleep. He was doing more and more of that lately, and it was good. Trish sat down in the high back chair standard in all hospitals and watched Albert breathe. It was comforting, watching him rest, knowing he was dreaming peacefully. She would have known otherwise. Before long, he was waking her up from her nap.

"Good morning, Ms. Weingarten."

Trish opened her eyes and smiled, a tad embarrassed.

"Good morning. I don't know why I fell asleep."

"Maybe because you were tired."

Trish nodded.

"So, do you have it?"

The question pulled Trish out of her haze.

"You mean, the envelope?"

"That's right! What else would I mean?"

"It took a while to find it. Why on earth did you hide it?"

"I knew a bright girl like you would know where to look."

If Trish chafed at being called "girl" she hid it well. He was seventy, after all. Every female under the age of fifty would be a girl to him.

"So, why the mystery?"

"First, about the dogs."

"Right. The second part of your story."

"The dogs saved my life."

"I know they shared your food with you."

"That's right. But soon, I was sent back to the main camp. The commandant's wife lost interest in her pet. It had everything to do with the end of the war. The Allies were coming from both sides and things were confused."

"So, you were in the camp with the other prisoners."

"So many new faces. The old ones were gone. Not very many people lived through years of interment. The other prisoners knew where I had been. They knew I hadn't starved lately. Some were hateful and stole my food or spilled my water. I wish I could say otherwise, with all my heart. I would beg on my knees to be able to testify that all prisoners were decent to each other. Some were. Many were not."

Trish sat quietly, offering no comment. She had to hear the bad with the good and Albert was not ready to gloss over the Holocaust.

"And then, things came apart. The Allies were descending and the Nazis went into full-fledged panic. Did you know that prior to the end of the war, some camps were completely demolished? They were razed to the ground,

413

planted over and camouflaged. If you go there today and dig, you would find bones. My camp was different. They kept it going and then they evacuated it at the last possible moment. I knew that the march would be deadly, so I hid. When they used the dogs to search for those like me, the dogs, they remembered me. We looked at each other. They knew me. They passed me by."

Albert stopped talking, lost in his fifty-year-old-plus recollections. He was still looking into the eyes of the dogs. They were still looking back.

"And then the camp was liberated. With me there. So many of those on the evacuation march died. I tried to find out. It was mayhem after the war. Some people spent years trying to put their lives back together."
"What did you do after the war?"
"I ended up here, didn't I?"
"Fifty years summed up?"
"I lived my life. Now, I'm dying. It happens all the time."
"You're not dying."
"We're all dying, Ms. Weingarten."
"Not today."
"You won't know that until tomorrow."
"So, before tomorrow, tell me about the envelope."
"You haven't opened it yet?"
"No!"
"You find an envelope taped to the bottom of a drawer and you resist the temptation to open it?"
"I'm not a snoop," Trish explained, trying not to think about holding the envelope up to the light.
"Do you know why Hitler lost the war?" Albert bounced to this topic. He had to be getting tired.

414

"Because the other side won?"

"And they say the younger generation has no sense of history."

"Tell me your perspective."

"Hitler and the Nazis lost the war because they allowed themselves to become preoccupied with things other than winning the war."

"What kinds of things?"

"I can name two offhand. The first was Hitler's obsession with the total and complete annihilation of the Jews. When his soldiers needed supplies, Hitler instead had the trains transporting Jews to their death. Does that sound like good wartime judgment to you?"

"No."

"Another thing that Hitler and his minions were obsessed with was making themselves rich. They spent so much time amassing personal fortunes for themselves that they were distracted from war strategy. They used the armed forces to transport great works of art and gold to their hideaways, so they could be rich. Imagine a soldier who spends more time packing art than packing a gun. Hatred and greed got in the way of Hitler's victory, and it was his own greed. His own hatred."

Trish understood a small part of this situation, having read occasional newspaper headlines now and then, but she wasn't totally convinced about Albert's theory. She felt that the war was won because of the valiant effort on the part of the United States and other countries. That had always been enough truth for her.

"When I die," Albert got to the point quickly, "then you open the envelope. It has my final instructions."

"Oh, I see," Trish said in a business-like manner, and then added, "Don't you have family? Someone else that should be entrusted with this?"

"You afraid I'm dying broke? You think you're getting stuck with the bills, aren't you!"

"Not at all. I can afford one helluva sendoff for you. I just want to make sure that I locate the people I need to."

"Everyone who needs to be found is already in this room. I wish you good luck with your story. Many writers starve. I hope your work is worth the sacrifice."

"Thank you," was all that Trish could think to say. Albert was too tired to continue their visit and was asleep before Trish left the room.

Chapter 24

September, for many the month of transition, brought several gradual changes as well to the lives of Mary and Lisa. Mary had moved into the California mansion. In retrospect, it was more of a transition for the hired help. They often found her cooking or cleaning or unloading groceries or gardening. It disconcerted them so much that Lisa, on more than one occasion, had served as buffer to all parties concerned.

"Madam, *she's* in the kitchen again!"
"She does like to cook."
"She's *rearranging* the spice cabinet."
"I see. Should we shoot her at dawn?"
"Madam, the *spice cabinet*."
"Okay, alright, I'll go talk to her."

Lisa wandered into the kitchen, catching Mary red handed. Literally. She had a bit of chili powder on her finger and was tasting it.
"Hi there, Gorgeous."
"Hiya. I thought you were working?" Mary quizzed as she continued undeterred to wreak havoc on the spice cabinet.
"I needed a break. Looks like you have a project underway."
"I hate old spices. A lot of these are expired or out of date."
"So, you're fixing the problem."
"The butler is complaining again, isn't he?"
"They are paid to do the work. When you do the work, they feel that they're not doing their job."
"Well, nobody's been taking care of these spices, now have they?"

Lisa had taken up residence on the counter. Good thing no one was watching. Sitting on the counter was a serious offense in this place.

"If you were bored, would you admit it?"

"Who could possibly be bored around here. I have so many people to get in the way of."

"Including me, I hope. I love how you get in my way."

"Oh, you do, do you?"

"I adore how you get in my way. If I pretended to be an out-of-date spice, would you show me a thing or two?"

"An out-of-date spice?"

"I could be the old sage."

Mary stopped working long enough to be amused. Lisa was making every attempt to broker peace in the household and the least Mary could do was cooperate. She situated herself next to Lisa on the counter.

"I know why I'm doing this," Mary admitted.

"The spice thing or everything?"

"Everything. I need to feel like I live here. I'm not going to make it around here if I can't rearrange things or change things. The world will continue to spin on its axis if I plant a few marigolds in the east garden. Won't it?"

"Won't what?" Lisa asked, distracted by the mere presence of Mary so close next to her.

"The earth. Keep spinning."

"Whenever you're this close to me, the room spins. Let the world take care of itself."

"It's just that this place is so much. So big."

"I bought it with you in mind, you know."

Mary studied Lisa. She was serious.

"You did?"

"I thought about it a long time. I knew that you lived in the mansion in Colorado, surrounded by servants. How could I offer anything less?"

"It wasn't always that way. I'm not like that. Honestly, you were thinking about me when you bought this place?"

"I've been planning for quite a while to have you in my life. I was just so glad that it was you who had to follow the bouncing orange basketball."

"What would you have done if it wasn't me?"

"The only possible next step. I would have come back to Colorado and wooed you proper."

"I think we ought to sit on the kitchen counter more often."

"Why?" Lisa watched Mary for insight.

"Because you are so romantic when you sit here."

"I could do a whole lot more than sit here!"

"Imagine how much trouble that would get us into!" Mary made it sound more like a dare than an admonition.

"Hey, it's our kitchen counter. We can do whatever we want up here," Lisa explained as she pulled Mary into a kiss.

Oh boy, the cook wasn't going to be happy about this.

October came like the proverbial thief in the night and stole someone very precious from Trish. Albert died in his sleep, after suffering a major stroke. When Trish opened the envelope, she found nothing whatsoever to do with burial plans or final wishes or anything amounting to bank statements or other sources of income. So, Albert did leave Trish with the expenses after all. To avoid a state burial, she popped for a nice casket and a service that few at Cypress attended. Even Robbie had to work. Maybe Albert was confused in his final days. Maybe he thought

419

that if you avoided making final arrangements, death would never come. October proved him wrong. What was in the envelope, however, did prove interesting, in a puzzling sort of way. Taped to a sheet of paper was a black and white picture of a picture. Along with this, there was a handwritten note.

"To whom it may concern. Whoever has custody of this picture has sole rights to the picture." Albert had signed the note with his full name, which was indecipherable as far as Trish was concerned. She stuck the envelope back into her pocket and later put it in her portfolio, for lack of a better place. This she carried back to Colorado with her at the end of the month. November was upon them.

Rebecca had dedicated the entire month of October to rehab. After Mitch had stolen her away for the delicious retreat in Santa Fe, they came back ready for more. More of everything, actually. Jeff had the campaign effort humming along at full speed and Reb actually had time and energy to make campaign appearances. She was trying to learn how to drive again, which was nothing but a blast as far as Mitch was concerned. She got to ride shotgun in the hand-i-van. It sported huge campaign signs on the sides and back, so everyone now knew that the Governor-hopeful-Senator had wheels. And she knew how to use them. Her rehabilitation had been nothing short of earth shattering as far as the hospital staff was concerned. Maybe everyone ought to go to Santa Fe for a dip in the pool?

Meanwhile, Aunt BeBe was her usual self. She had resigned herself to the fact that she knew full well what went on in Santa Fe, and that Rebecca and Jeff were never going to get back together, so she took her frustrations out on the crew that was supposedly remodeling the Governor's mansion. It had now turned into a race for the finish. Whose house would be ready first, Mitch's or BeBe's? In her heart of hearts, Mitch knew that for all the effort spent to remodel the mansion, it wasn't going to be necessary. Rebecca had to win the election. Hopefully, Washington D. C. would be ready. Of course, nothing was being done in vain. The mansion would be ready for any visitor from now on. Or any governor.

The first Tuesday in November was here before Mitch's stomach was ready. Maybe it was the thought of all those thousands of lobster puffs due to arrive for the party? Gee, if she had been nervous prior to the event, imagine how the lobsters felt? There had been quite the conversation concerning where to hold the party. Prior to the Santa Fe excursion, everyone figured that the rehab center was the foregone conclusion. Now that Reb had bounced back so quickly, other options had been discussed. Usually during a major election year, each political party would come to consensus on a place to celebrate. Hotels with grand ballrooms were preferred. Then, each candidate would rent a room and either celebrations or commiserations would occur, depending on the voters. This wasn't one of those years, however. Just your normal, average, run-of-the-mill, off-year election. Reb, in her usual decisive manner, stuck with the rehab center. They were the reason she was able to keep running for office after the accident. If the press wanted to talk to her, win or lose, they knew where to find her. Mary and Lisa came to town for the event. God, they looked gorgeous together. Being millionaires really agreed with the both of them, Mitch pondered as she fed Doozie a dog biscuit. It had taken quite the persuasion to get Trish to come to the party as well, and once she arrived, she stayed as far out of the limelight as she could. Albert's death was still weighing heavily on her, and she hadn't returned to Phoenix since the burial. Mitch tried three times to talk to her, but they were always interrupted. Well-wishers, staff, volunteers, press people and caterers were all pressing for a word. Deep conversations were not to be tonight.

When the preliminary results came in, it was too close to call. Rebecca was as cool as she could be, but Mitch was about ready to swallow her tongue. She hated this. She wasn't cut out to be in politics, even on the sidelines. Mitch took Doozie for a walk while everyone else headed for the cash bar. It was going to be a long night.

Trish caught up with Mitch on the second lap around the building.
"You shouldn't be alone out here in the dark."
"I'm not alone. I have Doozie, the Wonder Pup."
"Rebecca will win."
"It's a lot closer than it should be. People are deserting her in droves."
"The final count is all that matters."
"Seems like you and I are having a hard time being in the in-crowd tonight."
"Some nights you feel like talking. Other nights you don't."

"Rose and Max said they would stop by later," Mitch stated, wondering if that was good or bad news. Lately, no one knew what was going through Trish's mind.

"I think I'll head out. Maybe watch the returns at home."

"Okay."

"I'm gonna miss you when you go to Washington."

"You come out and visit. I'll come back and visit. We'll meet in the middle."

"Where would that be?"

"Oh, probably somewhere in Missouri."

"I've always wanted to see St. Louis."

"Oh yeah, me too."

"Stop by before you go east."

"Kiss me now just in case things get hectic."

Trish gave Mitch her usual friendly kiss. If the press was watching, perhaps leaning out of windows with telescopic lenses, well, what the hell.

This parting of the ways only added to Mitch's otherwise morose mood. Now, here she was, on lap three around the hospital, feeling more lost than found. Until Reb rolled up.

"Hey there, Governor Fairbanks," Mitch greeted.

"That's *Senator* Fairbanks to you!"

"No kidding?" Mitch was jumping on the inside.

"No kidding!"

"I'm so proud of you!" Mitch leaned down and held on to her like she was going to slip away forever.

"It wasn't a landslide by any means. I don't have a mandate."

"You have a victory. I knew you would do it."

"Is that why you've been doing laps around the building?"

"Hey, I'm just getting in shape for D.C. I heard you need to do a lot of walking."

423

"Honey, if I only know one thing, I know that we're ready for Washington."

Mitch nodded. "I hope they're ready for us."

www.ingramcontent.com/pod-product-compliance
Lightning Source LLC
Chambersburg PA
CBHW070350260626
47161CB00001B/86